Sir Walter Scott

Lyrics, dramas and miscellaneous pieces

Sir Walter Scott

Lyrics, dramas and miscellaneous pieces

ISBN/EAN: 9783744766166

Printed in Europe, USA, Canada, Australia, Japan

Cover: Foto ©Andreas Hilbeck / pixelio.de

More available books at **www.hansebooks.com**

POETICAL W

POCKET EDIT

VOL. VI

Roslin.

LYRICS, DRAMAS

AND

MISCELLANEOUS PIECES

By SIR WALTER SCOTT, Bart.

EDINBURGH

ADAM AND CHARLES BLACK

1875.

LYRICAL

AND

MISCELLANEOUS PIECES.

Juvenile Lines.

From Virgil.

1872.—Ætat. 11.

" Scott's Autobiography tells us that his translations in verse from Horace and Virgil were often approved by Dr. Adam, [Rector of the High School, Ediuburgh.]   One of these little pieces, written in a weak boyish scrawl, within pencilled marks still visible, had been carefully preserved by his mother; it was found folded up in a cover, inscribed by the old lady—'*My Walter's First Lines, 1782.*'"—LOCKHART, *Life of Scott,* vol. i. p. 129.

In awful ruins Ætna thunders nigh,
And sends in pitchy whirlwinds to the sky
Black clouds of smoke, which, still as they aspire,
From their dark sides there bursts the glowing fire;
At other times huge balls of fire are toss'd,
That lick the stars, and in the smoke are lost:
Sometimes the mount, with vast convulsions torn,
Emits huge rocks, which instantly are borne
With loud explosions to the starry skies,
The stones made liquid as the huge mass flies,
Then back again with greater weight recoils,
While Ætna thundering from the bottom boils.

On a Thunder Storm.

1783.— Ætat. 12.

"In Scott's Introduction to the Lay, he alludes to an original effusion of these 'schoolboy days,' prompted by a thunder-storm, which he says 'was much approved of, until a malevolent critic sprung up in the shape of an apothecary's blue-buskined wife,' &c. &c. These lines, and another short piece 'On the Setting Sun,' were lately found wrapped up in a cover, inscribed by Dr. Adam—'Walter Scott, July 1783.'"

Loud o'er my head though awful thunders roll,
And vivid lightnings flash from pole to pole,
Yet 'tis thy voice, my God, that bids them fly,
Thy arm directs those lightnings through the sky
Then let the good thy mighty name revere,
And harden'd sinners thy just vengeance fear.

On the Setting Sun.

1783.

Those evening clouds, that setting ray,
And beauteous tints, serve to display
    Their great Creator's praise ;
Then let the short-lived thing call'd man,
Whose life's comprised within a span,
    To him his homage raise.

We often praise the evening clouds,
    And tints so gay and bold,
But seldom think upon our God,
    Who tinged these clouds with gold![1]

[1] "It must, I think, be allowed that these lines, though of the class to which the poet himself modestly ascribes them, and not to be compared with the efforts of Pope, still less of Cowley at the same period, show, nevertheless, praiseworthy dexterity for a boy of twelve."—*Life of Scott*, vol. i. p. 131.

Fragments.

(1.) Bothwell Castle

1799.

THE following fragment of a ballad written at Bothwell Castle,
in the autumn of 1799, was first printed in the Life of Sir Walter
Scott, vol. ii. p. 28.

WHEN fruitful Clydesdale's apple-bowers
    Are mellowing in the noon;
When sighs round Pembroke's ruin'd towers
    The sultry breath of June;

When Clyde, despite his sheltering wood,
    Must leave his channel dry;
And vainly o'er the limpid flood
    The angler guides his fly;

If chance by Bothwell's lovely braes
    A wanderer thou hast been,
Or hid thee from the summer's blaze
    In Blantyre's bowers of green,

Full where the copsewood opens wild
    Thy pilgrim step hath staid,
Where Bothwell's towers, in ruin piled,
    O'erlook the verdant glade;

And many a tale of love and fear
    Hath mingled with the scene—
Of Bothwell's banks that bloom'd so dear,
    And Bothwell's bonny Jean.

O! If with rugged minstrel lays
  Unsated be thy ear,
And thou of deeds of other days
  Another tale wilt hear.—

Then all beneath the spreading beech,
  Flung careless on the lea,
The Gothic muse the tale shall teacn
  Of Bothwell's sisters three.

Wight Wallace stood on Deckmont head,
  He blew his bugle round,
Till the wild bull in Cadyow wood
  Has started at the sound.

St. George's cross, o'er Bothwell hung,
  Was waving far and wide,
And from the lofty turret flung
  Its crimson blaze on Clyde ;

And rising at the bugle blast
  That marked the Scottish foe,
Old England's yeomen muster'd fast,
  And bent the Norman bow.

Tall in the midst Sir Aylmer[1] rose,
  Proud Pembroke's Earl was he—
While"—— . . . .

(2.) 𝕿𝖍𝖊 𝕾𝖍𝖊𝖕𝖍𝖊𝖗𝖉'𝖘 𝕿𝖆𝖑𝖊.[2]

1799.

" ANOTHER imperfect ballad, in which he had meant to blend
together two legends familiar to every reader of Scottish history

---

[1] Sir Aylmer de Valence, Earl of Pembroke, Edward the First's Governor of Scotland, usually resided at Bothwell Castle, the ruins of which attest
the magnificence of the invader.—ED.

[2] *Life of Scott*, vol. ii. p. 31.

and romance, has been found in the same portfolio, and the
handwriting proves it to be of the same early date."—LOCKHART,
vol. ii. p. 30.

* * * * * *

AND ne'er but once, my son, he says,
　Was yon sad cavern trod,
In persecution's iron days,
　When the land was left by God.

From Bewlie bog, with slaughter red,
　A wanderer hither drew,
And oft he stopt and turn'd his head,
　As by fits the night-wind blew;

For trampling round by Cheviot edge
　Were heard the troopers keen,
And frequent from the Whitelaw ridge
　The death-shot flash'd between.

The moonbeams through the misty shower
　On yon dark cavern fell;
Through the cloudy night the snow gleam'd white,
　Which sunbeam ne'er could quell.

" Yon cavern dark is rough and rude,
　And cold its jaws of snow;
But more rough and rude are the men of blood,
　That hunt my life below!

" Yon spell-bound den, as the aged tell,
　Was hewn by demon's hands;
But I had lourd [1] melle with the fiends of hell,
　Than with Clavers and his band."

He heard the deep-mouth'd bloodhound bark,
　He heard the horses neigh,
He plunged him in the cavern dark,
　And downward sped his way.

[1] *Lourd;* *i. e.* liefer—rather.

Now faintly down the winding path
    Came the cry of the faulting hound,
And the mutter'd oath of baulked wrath
    Was lost in hollow sound.

He threw him on the flinted floor,
    And held his breath for fear;
He rose, and bitter cursed his foes,
    As the sounds died on his ear.

" O bare thine arm, thou battling Lord,
    For Scotland's wandering band;
Dash from the oppressor's grasp the sword,
    And sweep him from the land !

" Forget not thou thy people's groans
    From dark Dunnotter's tower,
Mix'd with the seafowl's shrilly moans,
    And ocean's bursting roar !

" O! in fell Clavers' hour of pride,
    Even in his mightiest day,
As bold he strides through conquest's tide,
    O stretch him on the clay !

" His widow and his little ones,
    O may their tower of trust
Remove its strong foundation stones,
    And crush them in the dust !"—

" Sweet prayers to me," a voice replied,
    " Thrice welcome, guest of mine !"
And glimmering on the cavern side,
    A light was seen to shine.

An aged man, in amice brown,
    Stood by the wanderer's side,
By powerful charm, a dead man's arm
    The torch's light supplied.

From each stiff finger, stretch'd upright,
　Arose a ghastly flame,
That waved not in the blast of night
　Which through the cavern came.

O! deadly blue was that taper's hue,
　That flamed the cavern o'er,
But more deadly blue was the ghastly hue
　Of his eyes who the taper bore.

He laid on his head a hand like lead,
　As heavy, pale, and cold—
" Vengeance be thine, thou guest of mine,
　If thy heart be firm and bold.

" But if faint thy heart, and caitiff fear
　Thy recreant sinews know,
The mountain erne thy heart shall tear,
　Thy nerves the hooded crow."

The wanderer raised him undismay'd :
　" My soul, by dangers steel'd,
Is stubborn as my border blade,
　Which never knew to yield.

" And if thy power can speed the hour
　Of vengeance on my foes,
Theirs be the fate, from bridge and gate,
　To feed the hooded crows."

The Brownie look'd him in the face,
　And his colour fled with speed—
I fear me," quoth he " uneath it will bo
　To match thy word and deed.

" In ancient days when English bands
　Sore ravaged Scotland fair,
The sword and shield of Scottish land
　Was valiant Halbert Kerr.

" A warlock loved the warrior well,
  Sir Michael Scott by name,
And he sought for his sake a spell to make,
  Should the Southern foemen tame.

" ' Look thou,' he said, ' from Cessford head,
  As the July sun sinks low,
And when glimmering white on Cheviot's height
  Thou shalt spy a wreath of snow,
The spell is complete which shall bring to thy feet
  The haughty Saxon foe.'

" For many a year wrought the wizard here,
  In Cheviot's bosom low,
Till the spell was complete, and in July's heat
  Appear'd December's snow ;
But Cessford's Halbert never came
  The wondrous cause to know.

" For years before in Bowden aisle
  The warrior's bones had lain,
And after short while, by female guile,
  Sir Michael Scott was slain.

" But me and my brethren in this cell
  His mighty charms retain,—
And he that can quell the powerful spell
  Shall o'er broad Scotland reign."

He led him through an iron door
  And up a winding stair,
And in wild amaze did the wanderer gaze
  On the sight which open'd there.

Through the gloomy night flash'd ruddy light,—
  A thousand torches glow ;
The cave rose high, like the vaulted sky,
  O'er stalls in double row.

In every stall of that endless hall
  Stood a steed in barbing bright ;

At the foot of each steed, all arm'd save the head,
  Lay stretch'd a stalwart knight.

In each mail'd hand was a naked brand:
  As they lay on the black bull's hide,
Each visage stern did upwards turn,
  With eyeballs fix'd and wide.

A launcegay strong, full twelve ells long,
  By every warrior hung;
At each pommel there, for battle yare,
  A Jedwood axe was slung.

The casque hung near each cavalier;
  The plumes waved mournfully
At every tread which the wanderer made
  Through the hall of gramarye.

The ruddy beam of the torches' gleam
  That glared the warriors on,
Reflected light from armour bright,
  In noontide splendour shone.

And onward seen in lustre sheen,
  Still lengthening on the sight,
Through the boundless hall stood steeds in stall,
  And by each lay a sable knight.

Still as the dead lay each horseman dread,
  And moved nor limb nor tongue;
Each steed stood stiff as an earthfast cliff,
  Nor hoof nor bridle rung.

No sounds through all the spacious hall
  The deadly still divide,
Save where echoes aloof from the vaulted roof
  To the wanderer's step replied.

At length before his wondering eyes,
  On an iron column borne,

Of antique shape, and giant size,
  Appear'd a sword and horn.

" Now choose thee here," quoth his leader,
  " Thy venturous fortune try ;
Thy woe and weal, thy boot and bale,
  In yon brand and bugle lie."

To the fatal brand he mounted his hand,
  But his soul did quiver and quail ;
The life-blood did start to his shuddering heart,
  And left him wan and pale.

The brand he forsook, and the horn he took
  To 'say a gentle sound ;
But so wild a blast from the bugle brast,
  That the Cheviot rock'd around.

From Forth to Tees, from seas to seas,
  The awful bugle rung ;
On Carlisle wall, and Berwick withal,
  To arms the warders sprung.

With clank and clang the cavern rang,
  The steeds did stamp and neigh ;
And loud was the yell as each warrior fell
  Sterte up with hoop and cry.

" Woe, woe," they cried, " thou caitiff coward,
  That ever thou wert born !
Why drew ye not the knightly sword
  Before ye blew the horn ! "

The morning on the mountain shone,
  And on the bloody ground
Hurl'd from the cave with shiver'd bone,
  The mangled wretch was found.

And still beneath the cavern dread,
  Among the glidders grey,

A shapeless stone with lichens spread,
Marks where the wanderer lay.[1]

*   *   *   *   *   *   *

(3.) 𝕮𝖍𝖊𝖛𝖎𝖔𝖙.

1799.

*   *   *   *   *   *   *

Go, sit old Cheviot's crest below,
And pensive mark the lingering snow
  In all his scaurs abide,
And slow dissolving from the hill
In many a sightless, soundless rill,
  Feed sparkling Bowmont's tide.

[1] " The reader may be interested by comparing with this ballad the author's prose version of part of its legend, as given in one of the last works of his pen. He says, in the *Letters on Demonology and Witchcraft*, 1830:— ' Thomas of Ercildowne, during his retirement, has been supposed, from time to time, to be levying forces to take the field in some crisis of his country's fate. The story has often been told of a daring horse-jockey having sold a black horse to a man of venerable and antique appearance, who appointed the remarkable hillock upon Eildon hills, called the Luckenhare, as the place where, at twelve o'clock at night, he should receive the price. He came, his money was paid in ancient coin, and he was invited by his customer to view his residence. The trader in horses followed his guide in the deepest astonishment through several long ranges of stalls, in each of which a horse stood motionless, while an armed warrior lay equally still at the charger's feet. 'All these men,' said the wizard in a whisper, ' will awaken at the battle of Sheriffmuir.' At the extremity of this extraordinary depot hung a sword and a horn, which the prophet pointed out to the horse-dealer as containing the means of dissolving the spell. The man in confusion took the horn, and attempted to wind it. The horses instantly started in their stalls, stamped and shook their bridles, the men arose and clashed their armour, and the mortal, terrified at the tumult he had excited, dropped the horn from his hand. A voice like that of a giant, louder even than the tumult around, pronounced these words:—

    ' Woe to the coward that ever he was born,
    That did not draw the sword before he blew the horn.'

A whirlwind expelled the horse-dealer from the cavern, the entrance to which he could never again find. A moral might be perhaps extracted from the legend, namely, that it is better to be armed against danger before bidding it defiance."

Fair shines the stream by bank and lea,
As wimpling to the eastern sea
  She seeks Till's sullen bed,
Indenting deep the fatal plain,
Where Scotland's noblest, brave in vain,
  Around their monarch bled.

And westward hills on hills you see,
Even as old Ocean's mightiest sea
  Heaves high her waves of foam,
Dark and snow-ridged from Cutsfeld's wold
To the proud foot of Cheviot roll'd,
  Earth's mountain billows come.

*   *   *   *   *   *   *

(4.) The Reiver's Wedding.

1802.

IN "The Reiver's Wedding," the Poet had evidently designed
to blend together two traditional stories concerning his own forefathers, the Scots of Harden, which are detailed in the first chapters of his *Life*.   The biographer adds:—" I know not for what
reason Lochwood, the ancient fortress of the Johnstones in Annandale, has been substituted for the real locality of his ancestor's drumhead Wedding Contract."—*Life*, vol. ii. p. 94.

O WILL ye hear a mirthful bourd?
  Or will ye hear of courtesie?
Or will ye hear how a gallant lord
  Was wedded to a gay ladye?

" Ca' out the kye," quo' the village herd,
  As he stood on the knowe,
" Ca' this ane's nine and that ane's ten,
  And bauld Lord William's cow."—

" Ah ! by my sooth," quoth William then,
  " And stands it that way now,
When knave and churl have nine and ten,
  That the Lord has but his cow ?

" I swear by the light of the Michaelmas moon,
  And the might of Mary high,
And by the edge of my braidsword brown,
  They shall soon say Harden's kye."

He took a bugle frae his side,
  With names carved o'er and o'er —
Full many a chief of meikle pride
  That Border bugle bore — [1]

He blew a note baith sharp and hie,
  Till rock and water rang around —
Three score of moss-troopers and three
  Have mounted at that bugle sound.

The Michaelmas moon had enter'd then,
  And ere she wan the full,
Ye might see by her light in Harden glen
  A bow o' kye and a bassen'd bull.

And loud and loud in Harden tower
  The quaigh gaed round wi' meikle glee ;
For the English beef was brought in bower,
  And the English ale flow'd merrilie.

And mony a guest from Teviotside
  And Yarrow's Braes was there ;
Was never a lord in Scotland wide
  That made more dainty fare.

They ate, they laugh'd, they sang and quaff'd,
  Till nought on board was seen,
When knight and squire were boune to dine,
  But a spur of silver sheen.

---

[1] This celebrated horn is still in the possession of the chief of the Harden family, Lord Polwarth.

Lord William has ta'en his berry brown steed —
  A sore shent man was he;
" Wait ye, my guests, a little speed—
  Weel feasted ye shall be."

He rode him down by Falsehope burn,
  His cousin dear to see,
With him to take a riding turn—
  Wat-draw-the-sword was he.

And when he came to Falsehope glen,
  Beneath the trysting tree,
On the smooth green was carved plain,[1]
  " To Lochwood bound are we."

" O if they be gane to dark Lochwood
  To drive the Warden's gear,
Betwixt our names, I ween, there's feud;
  I 'll go and have my share :

" For little reck I for Johnstone's feud,
  The Warden though he be."
So Lord William is away to dark Lochwood,
  With riders barely three.

The Warden's daughters in Lochwood sate,
  Were all both fair and gay,
All save the Lady Margaret,
  And she was wan and wae.

The sister, Jean, had a full fair skin,
  And Grace was bauld and braw;
But the leal-fast heart her breast within
  It weel was worth them a'.

---

[1] " At Linton, in Roxburghshire, there is a circle of stones surrounding a smooth plot of turf, called the *Tryst*, cr place of appointment, which tradition avers to have been the rendezvous of the neighbouring warriors. The name of the leader was cut in the turf, and the arrangement of the letters announced to his followers the course which he had taken."— *Introduction to the Minstrelsy*, p. 185.

Her father 's pranked her sisters twa
  With meikle joy and pride;
But Margaret maun seek Dundrennan's wa'—
  She ne'er can be a bride.

On spear and casque by gallants gent
  Her sisters' scarfs were borne,
But never at tilt or tournament
  Were Margaret's colours worn.

Her sisters rode to Thirlstane bower,
  But she was left at hame
To wander round the gloomy tower,
  And sigh young Harden's name.

" Of all the knights, the knights most fair,
  From Yarrow to the Tyne,"
Soft sigh'd the maid, " is Harden's heir,
  But ne'er can he be mine;

" Of all the maids, the foulest maid
  From Teviot to the Dee,
Ah!" sighing sad, that lady said,
  " Can ne'er young Harden's be."—

She looked up the briery glen,
  And up the mossy brae,
And she saw a score of her father's men
  Yclad in the Johnstone grey.

O fast and fast they downwards sped
  The moss and briers among,
And in the midst the troopers led
  A shackled knight alone.

*   *   *   *   *   *

Health to Lord Melville.[1]

1806.

AIR—*Carrickfergus.*

" THE impeachment of Lord Melville was among the first measures of the new (Whig) Government ; and personal affection and gratitude graced as well as heightened the zeal with which Scott watched the issue of this, in his eyes, vindictive proceeding ; but, though the ex-minister's ultimate acquittal was, as to all the charges involving his personal honour, complete, it must now be allowed that the investigation brought out many circumstances by no means creditable to his discretion ; and the rejoicings of his friends ought not, therefore, to have been scornfully jubilant. Such they were, however—at least in Edinburgh ; and Scott took his share in them by inditing a song, which was sung by James Ballantyne, and received with clamorous applauses, at a public dinner given in honour of the event, on the 27th of June 1806."—*Life,* vol. ii. p. 322.

SINCE here we are set in array round the table,
 Five hundred good fellows well met in a hall,
Come listen, brave boys, and I 'll sing as I 'm able,
 How innocence triumph'd, and pride got a fall.
   But push round the claret—
   Come, stewards, don't spare it—
With rapture you 'll drink to the toast that I give :
   Here, boys,
   Off with it merrily—
MELVILLE for ever, and long may he live !

What were the Whigs doing, when boldly pursuing,
 PITT banish'd Rebellion, gave Treason a string ?
Why, they swore on their honour, for ARTHUR O'CONNOR,
 And fought hard for DESPARD against country and king.

[1] Published on a broadside, and reprinted in the *Life of Scott,* 1837.

Well, then, we knew, boys,
PITT and MELVILLE were true boys,
And the tempest was raised by the friends of Reform.
Ah, woe!
Weep to his memory;
Low lies the Pilot that weather'd the storm!

And pray, don't you mind when the Blues first were raising,
And we scarcely could think the house safe o'er our heads!
When villains and coxcombs, French politics praising,
Drove peace from our tables and sleep from our beds?
Our hearts they grew bolder
When, musket on shoulder,
Stepp'd forth our old Statesman example to give.
Come, boys, never fear,
Drink the Blue Grenadier—
Here's to old HARRY, and long may he live!

They would turn us adrift; though rely, sir, upon it—
Our own faithful chronicles warrant us that
The free mountaineer and his bonny blue bonnet
Have oft gone as far as the regular's hat.
We laugh at their taunting,
For all we are wanting
Is licence our life for our country to give.
Off with it merrily,
Horse, foot, and artillery,
Each loyal Volunteer, long may he live!

'Tis not us alone, boys—the Army and Navy
Have each got a slap 'mid their politic pranks;
CORNWALLIS cashier'd, that watch'd winters to save ye,
And the Cape call'd a bauble, unworthy of thanks.
But vain is their taunt;
No soldier shall want
The thanks that his country to valour can give:
Come, boys,
Drink it off merrily,—
SIR DAVID and POPHAM, and long may they live!

And then our revenue—Lord knows how they view'd it,
 While each petty statesman talked lofty and big;
But the beer-tax was weak, as if Whitbread had brew'd it,
 And the pig-iron duty a shame to a pig.
    In vain is their vaunting;
    Too surely there's wanting
What judgment, experience, and steadiness give:
    Come, boys,
    Drink about merrily,—
Health to sage MELVILLE, and long may he live!

Our King, too—our Princess—I dare not say more, sir,—
 May Providence watch them with mercy and might!
While there's one Scottish hand that can wag a claymore, sir,
 They shall ne'er want a friend to stand up for their right.
    Be damn'd he that dare not,—
    For my part, I'll spare not
To beauty afflicted a tribute to give:
    Fill it up steadily,
    Drink it off readily—
Here's to the Princess, and long may she live!

And since we must not set Auld Reekie in glory,
 And make her brown visage as light as her heart;[1]
Till each man illumine his own upper story,
 Nor law-book nor lawyer shall force us to part.
    In GRENVILLE and SPENCER,
    And some few good men, sir,
High talents we honour, slight difference forgive;
    But the Brewer we'll hoax,
    Tallyho to the Fox,
And drink MELVILLE for ever, as long as we live!

[1] The Magistrates of Edinburgh had rejected an application for illumination of the town on the arrival of the news of Lord Melville's acquittal.

𝔏etter in 𝔙erse

ON THE VOYAGE WITH THE COMMISSIONERS OF
NORTHERN LIGHTS.

"Of the letters which Scott wrote to his friends during those happy six weeks, I have recovered only one, and it is, thanks to the leisure of the yacht, in verse. The strong and easy heroics of the first section prove, I think, that Mr. Canning did not err when he told him that if he chose he might emulate even Dryden's command of that noble measure; and the dancing anapæsts of the second, show that he could with equal facility have rivalled the gay graces of Cotton, Anstey, or Moore."—LOCKHART, *Life*, vol. iv. p. 372.

––––––––

TO HIS GRACE THE DUKE OF BUCCLEUCH,
&c. &c. &c.

Lighthouse Yacht in the Sound of Lerwick,
Zetland, 8th August 1814.

HEALTH to the chieftain from his clansman true!
From her true minstrel, health to fair Buccleuch!
Health from the isles, where dewy Morning weaves
Her chaplet with the tints that Twilight leaves;
Where late the sun scarce vanish'd from the sight,
And his bright pathway graced the short-lived night,
Though darker now as autumn's shades extend,
The north winds whistle and the mists ascend!
Health from the land where eddying whirlwinds toss
The storm-rock'd *cradle* of the Cape of Noss;
On outstretch'd cords the giddy engine slides,
His own strong arm the bold adventurer guides,
And he that lists such desperate feat to try,
May, like the sea-mew, skim 'twixt surf and sky,
And feel the mid-air gales around him blow,
And see the billows rage five hundred feet below.

Here, by each stormy peak and desert shore,
The hardy Islesman tugs the daring oar,

Practised alike his venturous course to keep
Through the white breakers or the pathless deep,
By ceaseless peril and by toil to gain
A wretched pittance from the niggard main.
And when the worn-out drudge old ocean leaves,
What comfort greets him, and what hut receives?
Lady! the worst your presence ere has cheer'd
(When want and sorrow fled as you appear'd)
Were to a Zetlander as the high dome
Of proud Drumlanrig to my humble home.
Here rise no groves, and here no gardens blow,
Here even the hardy heath scarce dares to grow;
But rocks on rocks, in mist and storm array'd,
Stretch far to sea their giant colonnade,
With many a cavern seam'd, the dreary haunt
Of the dun seal and swarthy cormorant.
Wild round their rifted brows, with frequent cry
As of lament, the gulls and gannets fly,
And from their sable base, with sullen sound,
In sheets of whitening foam the waves rebound.

Yet even these coasts a touch of envy gain
From those whose land has known oppression's chain;
For here the industrious Dutchman comes once more
To moor his fishing craft by Bressay's shore;
Greets every former mate and brother tar,
Marvels how Lerwick 'scaped the rage of war,
Tells many a tale of Gallic outrage done,
And ends by blessing God and Wellington.
Here too the Greenland tar, a fiercer guest,
Claims a brief hour of riot, not of rest;
Proves each wild frolic that in wine has birth,
And wakes the land with brawls and boisterous mirth.
A sadder sight, on yon poor vessel's prow
The captive Norseman sits in silent woe,
And eyes the flags of Britain as they flow.
Hard fate of war, which bade her terrors sway
His destined course, and seize so mean a prey;
A bark with planks so warp'd and seams so riven,
She scarce might face the gentlest airs of heaven:

Pensive he sits, and questions oft if none
Can list his speech, and understand his moan ;
In vain—no Islesman now can use the tongue
Of the bold Norse, from whom their lineage sprung.
Not thus of old the Norsemen hither came,
Won by the love of danger or of fame ;
On every storm-beat cape a shapeless tower
Tells of their wars, their conquests, and their power ;
For ne'er for Grecia's vales, nor Latian land,
Was fiercer strife than for this barren strand ;
A race severe—the isle and ocean lords,
Loved for its own delight the strife of swords ;
With scornful laugh the mortal pang defied,
And blest their gods that they in battle died.

Such were the sires of Zetland's simple race,
And still the eye may faint resemblance trace
In the blue eye, tall form, proportion fair,
The limbs athletic, and the long light hair—
(Such was the mien, as Scald and Minstrel sings,
Of fair-hair'd Harold, first of Norway's Kings ;)
But their high deeds to scale these crags confined,
Their only warfare is with waves and wind.

Why should I talk of Mousa's castled coast !
Why of the horrors of the Sumburgh Rost !
May not these bald disjointed lines suffice,
Penn'd while my comrades whirl the rattling dice—
While down the cabin skylight lessening shine
The rays, and eve is chased with mirth and wine !
Imagined, while down Mousa's desert bay
Our well-trimm'd vessel urged her nimble way,
While to the freshening breeze she lean'd her side,
And bade her bowsprit kiss the foamy tide ?

Such are the lays that Zetland Isles supply ;
Drench'd with the drizzly spray and dropping sky,
Weary and wet, a sea-sick Minstrel I.
W. SCOTT.

POSTSCRIPTUM.

Kirkwall, Orkney, Aug. 13, 1814

In respect that your Grace has commission'd a Kraken,
You will please be inform'd that they seldom are taken;
It is January two years, the Zetland folks say,
Since they saw the last Kraken in Scalloway bay;
He lay in the offing a fortnight or more,
But the devil a Zetlander put from the shore,
Though bold in the seas of the north to assail
The morse and the sea-horse, the grampus and whale.
If your Grace thinks I'm writing the thing that is not,
You may ask at a namesake of ours, Mr. Scott—
(He 's not from our clan, though his merits deserve it,
But springs, I 'm inform'd, from the Scotts of Scotstarvet;)
He question'd the folks who beheld it with eyes,
But they differ'd confoundedly as to its size.
For instance, the modest and diffident swore
That it seem'd like the keel of a ship, and no more—
Those of eyesight more clear, or of fancy more high,
Said it rose like an island 'twixt ocean and sky—
But all of the hulk had a steady opinion
That 'twas sure a *live* subject of Neptune's dominion—
And I think, my Lord Duke, your Grace hardly would
　　　wish,
To cumber your house, such a kettle of fish.
Had your order related to night-caps or hose,
Or mittens of worsted, there 's plenty of those.
Or would you be pleased but to fancy a whale?
And direct me to send it—by sea or by mail?
The season, I 'm told, is nigh over, but still
I could get you one fit for the lake at Bowhill.
Indeed, as to whales, there 's no need to be thrifty,
Since one day last fortnight two hundred and fifty,
Pursued by seven Orkneymen's boats and no more,
Betwixt Truffness and Luffness were drawn on the shore!

---

1 The Scotts of Scotstarvet, and other families of the name in Fife and
elsewhere, claim no kindred with the great clan of the Border,—and their
armorial bearings are different.

You'll ask if I saw this same wonderful sight:
I own that I did not, but easily might—
For this mighty shoal of leviathans lay
On our lee-beam a mile, in the loop of the bay,
And the islesmen of Sanda were all at the spoil,
And *flinching* (so term it) the blubber to boil:
(Ye spirits of lavender, drown the reflection
That awakes at the thoughts of this odorous dissection.)
To see this huge marvel full fain would we go,
But Wilson, the wind, and the current, said no.
We have now got to Kirkwall, and needs I must stare
When I think that in verse I have once call'd it *fair.*
'Tis a base little borough, both dirty and mean—
There is nothing to hear, and there's nought to be seen,
Save a church, where, of old times, a prelate harangued,
And a palace that's built by an earl that was hang'd.
But, farewell to Kirkwall—aboard we are going,
The anchor's a-peak, and the breezes are blowing;
Our commodore calls all his band to their places,
And 'tis time to release you—Good-night to your Graces!

Letter

**TO HIS GRACE THE DUKE OF BUCCLEUCH,
DRUMLANRIG CASTLE.**

Sanquhar, 2 o'clock, July 30, 1817.

FROM Ross, where the clouds on Benlomond are sleeping—
From Greenock, where Clyde to the Ocean is sweeping—
From Largs, where the Scotch gave the Northmen a drilling—
From Ardrossan, whose harbour cost many a shilling—
From Old Cumnock, where beds are as hard as a plank, sir—
From a chop and green pease, and a chicken in Sanquhar,
This eve, please the Fates, at Drumlanrig we anchor.

W. S.

[Sir Walter's companion on this excursion was captain, now
Sir Adam Ferguson.—See *Life,* vol. v. p. 234.]

To J. G. Lockhart, Esq.

ON THE COMPOSITION OF MAIDA'S EPITAPH.

1824.

> "Maidæ Marmorea dormis sub imagine Maida!
> Ad januam domini sit tibi terra levis."
> See *Life of Scott*, vol. vii. pp. 273-281.

'DEAR JOHN,—I some time ago wrote to inform his
Fat worship of *jaces*, misprinted for *dormis;*
But that several Southrons assured me the *januam*
Was a twitch to both ears of Ass Priscian's cranium.
You, perhaps, may observe that one Lionel Berguer,
In defence of our blunder appears a stout arguer:
But at length I have settled, I hope, all these clatters,
By a *rowt* in the papers—fine place for such matters.
I have, therefore, to make it for once my command, sir,
That my gudeson shall leave the whole thing in my hand, sir,
And by no means accomplish what James says you threaten,
Some banter in Blackwood to claim your dog-Latin.
I have various reasons of weight, on my word, sir,
For pronouncing a step of this sort were absurd, sir.—
Firstly, erudite sir, 'twas against your advising
I adopted the lines this monstrosity lies in;
For you modestly hinted my English translation
Would become better far such a dignified station.
Second—how, in God's name, would my bacon be saved,
By not having writ what I clearly engraved?
On the contrary, I, on the whole, think it better
To be whipped as the thief, than his lousy resetter.
Thirdly—don't you perceive that I don't care a boddle
Although fifty false metres were flung at my noddle,
For my back is as broad and as hard as Benlomon's,
And I treat as I please both the Greeks and the Romans,
Whereas the said heathens might rather look serious
At a kick on their drum from the scribe of Valerius.
And, fourthly and lastly—it is my good pleasure
To remain the sole source of that murderous measure.

So *stet pro ratione voluntas*—be tractile,
Invade not, I say, my own dear little dactyl;
If you do, you'll occasion a breach in our intercourse:
To-morrow will see me in town for the winter-course,
But not at your door, at the usual hour, sir,
My own pye-house daughter's good prog to devour, sir.
Ergo—peace!—on your duty, your squeamishness throttle,
And we'll soothe Priscian's spleen with a canny third bottle.
A fig for all dactyls, a fig for all spondees,
A fig for all dunces and dominie Grundys;
A fig for dry thrapples, south, north, east, and west, sir,
Speates and raxes[1] ere five for a famishing guest, sir;
And as Fatsman[2] and I have some topics for haver, he'll
Be invited, I hope, to meet me and Dame Peveril,
Upon whom, to say nothing of Oury and Anne, you a
Dog shall be deemed if you fasten your *Janua*.

"𝕎hen with 𝕡oetry 𝔻ealing."

June, 1825.

While Scott was engaged in writing the Life of Napoleon, Mr. Lockhart says—" The rapid accumulation of books and MSS. was at once flattering and alarming; and one of his notes to me, about the middle of June, had these rhymes by way of postscript:—

> When with Poetry dealing,
> Room enough in a shieling:

[1] There is an excellent story (but too long for quotation) in the *Memoire of the Somervilles* (vol. i. p. 240) about an old Lord of that family, who, when he wished preparations to be made for high feasting at his Castle of Cowthally, used to send on a billet inscribed with this laconic phrase—" *Speates and raxes*," i. e. *spits and ranges*. Upon one occasion, Lady Somerville (being newly married, and not yet skilled in her husband's hieroglyphics) read the mandates as *spears* and *jacks*, and sent forth 200 armed horsemen, whose appearance on the moors greatly alarmed Lord Somerville and his guest, who happened to be no less a person than King James III.—See *Scott's Miscellaneous Prose*, vol. xxii. p. 312.

[2] *Fatsman* was one of Mr. James Ballantyne's many *aliases*. Another (to which Constable mostly adhered) was Mr. " Basketfill"—an allusion to the celebrated printer Baskerville.

Neither cabin nor hovel
Too small for a novel:
Though my back I should rub
On Diogenes' tub,
How my fancy could prance
In a dance of romance!
But my house I must swap
With some Brobdignag chap,
Ere I grapple, God bless me! with Emperor Nap."

Life, vol. vii. p. 391.

Lines to Sir Cuthbert Sharp.

1827.

" Sir Cuthbert Sharp, who had been particularly kind and attentive to Scott when at Sunderland, happened, in writing to him on some matter of business, to say he hoped he had not forgotten his friends in that quarter. Sir Walter's answer to Sir Cuthbert (who had been introduced to him by his old and dear friend Mr. Surtees of Mainsforth) begins thus:—

Forget thee?   No! my worthy fere!
Forget blithe mirth and gallant cheer?
Death sooner stretch me on my bier!
> Forget thee? No.

Forget the universal shout[1]
When " canny Sunderland " spoke out—
A truth which knaves affect to doubt—
> Forget thee? No.

Forget you?   No—though now-a-day
I've heard your knowing people say,
Disown the debt you cannot pay,
You'll find it far the thriftiest way—
> But I?—O no.

---

[1] An allusion to the enthusiastic reception of the Duke of Wellington at Sunderland.—Ed.

Forget your kindness found for all room,
In what, though large, seem'd still a small room,
Forget my *Surtees* in a ball-room—
                    Forget you? No.

Forget your sprightly dumpty-diddles,
And beauty tripping to the fiddles,
Forget my lovely friends the *Liddells*—
                    Forget you? No.

" So much for oblivion, my dear Sir C.; and now, having dismounted from my Pegasus, who is rather spavined, I charge
a-foot, like an old dragoon as I am," &c. &c.—*Life of Scott*, vol
ix. p. 165.

———

The Death of Keeldar.

1828.

PERCY or Percival Rede of Trochend, in Redesdale, Northumberland, is celebrated in tradition as a huntsman, and a soldier.
He was, upon two occasions, singularly unfortunate; once, when
an arrow, which he had discharged at a deer, killed his celebrated dog Keeldar; and again, when, being on a hunting party,
he was betrayed into the hands of a clan called Crossar, by
whom he was murdered. Mr. Cooper's painting of the first of
these incidents, suggested the following stanzas.[1]

Up rose the sun, o'er moor and mead;
Up with the sun rose Percy Rede;
Brave Keeldar, from his couples freed,
    Career'd along the lea;

[1] These stanzas, accompanying an engraving from Mr. Cooper's subject
" The Death of Keeldar," appeared in *The Gem* of 1829, a literary journal
edited by Thomas Hood, Esq. In the acknowledgment to his contributors,
Mr. Hood says, " To Sir Walter Scott—not merely a literary feather in my
cap, but a whole plume of them—I owe, and with the hand of my heart
acknowledge, a deep obligation. A poem from his pen, is likely to confer
on the book that contains it, if not perpetuity, at least a very Old Mor-
tality."—*Preface*, p. 4. The original painting by Cooper, remains at Abbotsford.—ED.

The Palfrey sprung with sprightly bound,
As if to match the gamesome hound;
His horn the gallant huntsman wound:
    They were a jovial three !

Man, hound, or horse, of higher fame,
To wake the wild deer never came,
Since Alnwick's Earl pursued the game
    On Cheviot's rueful day;
Keeldar was matchless in his speed,
Than Tarras, ne'er was stancher steed,
A peerless archer, Percy Rede :
    And right dear friends were they.

The chase engross'd their joys and woes,
Together at the dawn they rose,
Together shared the noon's repose,
    By fountain or by stream;
And oft, when evening skies were red,
The heather was their common bed,
Where each, as wildering fancy led,
    Still hunted in his dream.

Now is the thrilling moment near,
Of sylvan hope and sylvan fear,
Yon thicket holds the harbour'd deer,
    The signs the hunters know;—
With eyes of flame, and quivering ears,
The brake sagacious Keeldar nears;
The restless palfrey paws and rears;
    The archer strings his bow.

The game's afoot!—Halloo! Halloo!
Hunter, and horse, and hound pursue;—
But woe the shaft that erring flew—
    That e'er it left the string !
And ill betide the faithless yew !
The stag bounds scathless o'er the dew,
And gallant Keeldar's life-blood true
    Has drench'd the grey-goose wing.

The noble hound—he dies, he dies,
Death, death has glazed his fixed eyes,
Stiff on the bloody heath he lies,
    Without a groan or quiver.
Now day may break and bugle sound,
And whoop and hallow ring around,
And o'er his couch the stag may bound,
    But Keeldar sleeps for ever.

Dilated nostrils, staring eyes,
Mark the poor palfrey's mute surprise,
He knows not that his comrade dies.
    Nor what is death—but still
His aspect hath expression drear
Of grief and wonder, mix'd with fear.
Like startled children when they hear
    Some mystic tale of ill.

But he that bent the fatal bow.
Can well the sum of evil know,
And o'er his favourite, bending low,
    In speechless grief recline ;
Can think he hears the senseless clay,
In unreproachful accents say,
The hand that took my life away,
    Dear master, was it thine !

" And if it be, the shaft be bless'd,
Which sure some erring aim address'd,
Since in your service prized, caress'd
    I in your service die ;
And you may have a fleeter hound,
To match the dun-deer's merry bound,
But by your couch will ne'er be found
    So true a guard as I."

And to his last stout Percy rued
The fatal chance ; for when he stood
'Gainst fearful odds in deadly feud,
    And fell amid the fray,

E'en with his dying voice he cried,
" Had Keeldar but been at my side,
Your treacherous ambush had been spied —
    I had not died to-day!"

Remembrance of the erring bow
Long since had join'd the tides which flow,
Conveying human bliss and woe
    Down dark oblivion's river;
But Art can Time's stern doom arrest,
And snatch his spoil from Lethe's breast,
And, in her Cooper's colours drest,
    The scene shall live for ever.

Lines on Fortune

1831.

" By the advice of Dr. Ebenezer Clarkson, Sir Walter con-
sulted a skilful mechanist, by name *Fortune*, about a contrivance
for the support of the lame limb, which had of late given him
much pain, as well as inconvenience. Mr. Fortune produced a
clever piece of handiwork, and Sir Walter felt at first great
relief from the use of it: insomuch that his spirits rose to quite
the old pitch, and his letter to me upon the occasion overflows
with merry applications of sundry maxims and verses about
Fortune. "*Fortes Fortuna adjuvat* "—he says—"never more
sing I

FORTUNE, my Foe, why dost thou frown on me?
And will my Fortune never better be?
Wilt thou, I say, for ever breed my pain?
And will thou ne'er return my joys again?[1]

---

[1] " I believe this is the only verse of the old song (often alluded to by
Shakspeare and his contemporaries) that has as yet been recovered."—
LOCKHART, *Life*, vol. x. p. 39.

No—let my ditty be henceforth—

Fortune, my Friend, how well thou favourest me!
A kinder Fortune man did never see!
Thou propp'st my thigh, thou ridd'st my knee of pain,
I 'll walk, I 'll mount—I 'll be a man again.—
Life, vol. x. p. 38.

The Violet.

1797.

It appears from the *Life of Scott,* vol. i. p. 333, that these lines,
first published in the *English Minstrelsy,* 1810, were written in
1797, on occasion of the Poet's disappointment in love.— Ed.

The violet in her green-wood bower,
    Where birchen boughs with hazels mingle,
May boast itself the fairest flower
    In glen, or copse, or forest dingle.

Though fair her gems of azure hue,
    Beneath the dew-drop's weight reclining;
I 've seen an eye of lovelier blue,
    More sweet through wat'ry lustre shining.

The summer sun that dew shall dry,
    Ere yet the day be past its morrow;
Nor longer in my false love's eye
    Remain'd the tear of parting sorrow.

To a Lady.

WITH FLOWERS FROM A ROMAN WALL.

1797.

Written in 1797, on an excursion from Gillsland, in Cumberland.
(See *Life*, vol. i. p. 365.)

TAKE these flowers, which, purple waving,
  On the ruin'd rampart grew,
Where, the sons of freedom braving,
  Rome's imperial standards flew.

Warriors from the breach of danger
  Pluck no longer laurels there;
They but yield the passing stranger
  Wild-flower wreathes for Beauty's hair.

The Bard's Incantation.

WRITTEN UNDER THE THREAT OF INVASION IN THE AUTUMN OF 1804.

THE forest of Glenmore is drear,
  It is all of black pine and the dark oak-tree;
And the midnight wind, to the mountain deer,
  Is whistling the forest lullaby:
The moon looks through the drifting storm,
But the troubled lake reflects not her form,
For the waves roll whitening to the land,
And dash against the shelvy strand.

There is a voice among the trees,
  That mingles with the groaning oak—
That mingles with the stormy breeze,
  And the lake-waves dashing against the rock;—

There is a voice within the wood,
The voice of the bard in fitful mood ;
His song was louder than the blast,
As the bard of Glenmore through the forest past.

" Wake ye from your sleep of death,
     Minstrels and bards of other days !
  For the midnight wind is on the heath,
     And the midnight meteors dimly blaze :
  The Spectre with his Bloody Hand,[1]
  Is wandering through the wild woodland ;
  The owl and the raven are mute for dread,
  And the time is meet to awake the dead !

" Souls of the mighty, wake and say,
     To what high strain your harps were strung,
  When Lochlin plow'd her billowy way,
     And on your shores her Norsemen flung ?
  Her Norsemen train'd to spoil and blood,
  Skill'd to prepare the Raven's food,
  All, by your harpings, doom'd to die
  On bloody Largs and Loncarty.[2]

" Mute are ye all ? No murmurs strange
     Upon the midnight breeze sail by ;
  Nor through the pines, with whistling change,
     Mimic the harp's wild harmony !
  Mute are ye now !—Ye ne'er were mute,
  When Murder with his bloody foot,
  And Rapine with his iron hand,
  Were hovering near yon mountain strand.

" O yet awake the strain to tell,
     By every deed in song enroll'd,
  By every chief who fought or fell,
     For Albion's weal in battle bold :—
  From Coilgach,[3] first who roll'd his car
  Through the deep ranks of Roman war,

---

[1] The forest of Glenmore is haunted by a spirit called Lhamdearg, or Red-Hand. [2] The Galgacus of Tacitus.

[3] Where the Norwegian invader of Scotland received two bloody defeats.

To him, of veteran memory dear,
Who victor died on Aboukir.

"By all their swords, by all their scars,
By all their names, a mighty spell!
By all their wounds, by all their wars,
Arise, the mighty strain to tell!
For fiercer than fierce Hengist's strain,
More impious than the heathen Dane,
More grasping than all-grasping Rome,
Gaull's ravening legions hither come!"

The wind is hush'd, and still the lake—
Strange murmurs fill my tinkling ears,
Bristles my hair, my sinews quake,
At the dread voice of other years—
"When targets clash'd, and bugles rung,
And blades round warriors' heads were flung,
The foremost of the band were we,
And hymn'd the joys of Liberty!"

———

Hellvellyn.

1805.

IN the spring of 1805, a young gentleman of talents, and of
a most amiable disposition, perished by losing his way on the
mountain Hellvellyn.   His remains were not discovered till three
months afterwards, when they were found guarded by a faithful
terrier-bitch, his constant attendant during frequent solitary ram-
bles through the wilds of Cumberland and Westmoreland.

I CLIMB'D the dark brow of the mighty Hellvellyn,
Lakes and mountains beneath me gleam'd misty and wide;
All was still, save by fits, when the eagle was yelling,
And starting around me the echoes replied.

On the right, Striden-edge round the Red-tarn was bending,
And Catchedicam its left verge was defending,
One huge nameless rock in the front was ascending,
    When I mark'd the sad spot where the wanderer had died.

Dark-green was that spot 'mid the brown mountain-heather,
    Where the Pilgrim of Nature lay stretch'd in decay,
Like the corpse of an outcast abandon'd to weather,
    Till the mountain-winds wasted the tenantless clay.
Nor yet quite deserted, though lonely extended,
For, faithful in death, his mute favourite attended,
The much-loved remains of her master defended,
    And chased the hill-fox and the raven away.

How long didst thou think that his silence was slumber?
    When the wind waved his garment, how oft didst thou start?
How many long days and long weeks didst thou number,
    Ere he faded before thee, the friend of thy heart?
And oh! was it meet, that—no requiem read o'er him—
No mother to weep, and no friend to deplore him,
And thou, little guardian, alone stretch'd before him—
    Unhonour'd the Pilgrim from life should depart?

When a Prince to the fate of the Peasant has yielded,
    The tapestry waves dark round the dim-lighted hall;
With scutcheons of silver the coffin is shielded,
    And pages stand mute by the canopied pall:
Through the courts, at deep midnight, the torches are gleaming;
In the proudly-arch'd chapel the banners are beaming,
Far adown the long aisle sacred music is streaming,
    Lamenting a Chief of the people should fall.

But meeter for thee, gentle lover of nature,
    To lay down thy head like the meek mountain-lamb,
When, wilder'd, he drops from some cliff huge in stature,
    And draws his last sob by the side of his dam.
And more stately thy couch by this desert lake lying,
Thy obsequies sung by the grey plover flying,
With one faithful friend but to witness thy dying,
    In the arms of Hellvellyn and Catchedicam.

The Dying Bard.[1]

1806.

AIR — Daffydz Gangwen.

THE Welsh tradition bears, that a Bard, on his deathbed, demanded his harp, and played the air to which these verses are
adapted; requesting that it might be performed at his funeral.

I.

DINAS EMLINN, lament; for the moment is nigh,
When mute in the woodlands thine echoes shall die:
No more by sweet Teivi Cadwallon shall rave,
And mix his wild notes with the wild dashing wave.

II.

In spring and in autumn, thy glories of shade
Unhonour'd shall flourish, unhonour'd shall fade;
For soon shall be lifeless the eye and the tongue,
That view'd them with rapture, with rapture that sung.

III.

Thy sons, Dinas Emlinn, may march in their pride,
And chase the proud Saxon from Prestatyn's side;
But where is the harp shall give life to their name?
And where is the bard shall give heroes their fame?

IV.

And oh, Dinas Emlinn! thy daughters so fair,
Who heave the white bosom, and wave the dark hair;
What tuneful enthusiast shall worship their eye,
When half of their charms with Cadwallon shall die?

V.

Then adieu, silver Teivi! I quit thy loved scene,
To join the dim choir of the bards who have been;

1 This and the following were written for Mr. George Thomson's *Welsh
Airs,* and are contained in his *Select Melodies,* vol. i.—ED.

With Lewarch, and Meilor, and Merlin the Old,
And sage Taliessin, high harping to hold.

VI.

And adieu, Dinas Emlinn! still green be thy shades,
Unconquer'd thy warriors, and matchless thy maids!
And thou, whose faint warblings my weakness can tell,
Farewell, my loved Harp! my last treasure, farewell!

The Norman Horse-Shoe.

1806.

AIR — *The War-Song of the Men of Glamorgan.*

THE Welsh, inhabiting a mountainous country, and possessing
only an inferior breed of horses, were usually unable to encounter
the shock of the Anglo-Norman cavalry. Occasionally, however,
they were successful in repelling the invaders; and the following
verses are supposed to celebrate a defeat of CLARE, Earl of Striguil and Pembroke, and of NEVILLE, Baron of Chepstow, Lords-
Marchers of Monmouthshire. Rymny is a stream which divides
the counties of Monmouth and Glamorgan: Caerphili, the scene
of the supposed battle, is a vale upon its banks, dignified by the
ruins of a very ancient castle.

I.

RED glows the forge in Striguil's bounds,
And hammers din, and anvil sounds,
And armourers, with iron toil,
Barb many a steed for battle's broil.
Foul fall the hand which bends the steel
Around the courser's thundering heel,
That e'er shall dint a sable wound
On fair Glamorgan's velvet ground!

II.

From Chepstow's towers, ere dawn of morn,
Was heard afar the bugle-horn;

And forth, in banded pomp and pride,
Stout Clare and fiery Neville ride.
They swore, their banners broad should gleam,
In crimson light, on Rymny's stream ;
They vow'd, Caerphili's sod should feel
The Norman charger's spurning heel.

III.

And sooth they swore : the sun arose,
And Rymny's wave with crimson glows ;
For Clare's red banner, floating wide,
Roll'd down the stream to Severn's tide !
And sooth they vow'd : the trampled green
Show'd where hot Neville's charge had been ;
In every sable hoof-tramp stood
A Norman horseman's curdling blood !

IV.

Old Chepstow's brides may curse the toil,
That arm'd stout Clare for Cambrian broil ;
Their orphans long the art may rue,
For Neville's war-horse forged the shoe.
No more the stamp of armed steed
Shall dint Glamorgan's velvet mead ;
Nor trace be there, in early spring,
Save of the Fairies' emerald ring.

The Maid of Toro.[1]

1806.

O, low shone the sun on the fair lake of Toro,
　　And weak were the whispers that waved the dark wood,
All as a fair maiden, bewilder'd in sorrow,
　　Sorely sigh'd to the breezes, and wept to the flood.

----

[1] This, and the three following, were first published in Haydn's Collection
of Scottish Airs, Edin. 1806.—Ed.

" O saints ! from the mansions of bliss lowly bending—
   Sweet Virgin ! who hearest the suppliant's cry,
Now grant my petition, in anguish ascending,
   My Henry restore, or let Eleanor die ! "

All distant and faint were the sounds of the battle;
   With the breezes they rise, with the breezes they fail,
Till the shout, and the groan, and the conflict's dread rattle,
   And the chase's wild clamour, came loading the gale.
Breathless she gazed on the woodlands so dreary;
   Slowly approaching, a warrior was seen ;
Life's ebbing tide mark'd his footsteps so weary,
   Cleft was his helmet, and woe was his mien.

" O save thee, fair maid, for our armies are flying !
   O save thee, fair maid, for thy guardian is low !
Deadly cold on yon heath thy brave Henry is lying,
   And fast through the woodland approaches the foe."
Scarce could he falter the tidings of sorrow,
   And scarce could she hear them, benumb'd with despair :
And when the sun sank on the sweet lake of Toro,
   For ever he set to the Brave and the Fair.

The Palmer.

1806.

" O open the door, some pity to show !
   Keen blows the northern wind !
The glen is white with the drifted snow,
   And the path is hard to find.

" No outlaw seeks your castle gate,
   From chasing the King's deer,
Though even an outlaw's wretched state
   Might claim compassion here.

"A weary Palmer, worn and weak,
    I wander for my sin ;
O open, for Our Lady's sake !
    A pilgrim's blessing win !

"I'll give you pardons from the Pope,
    And reliques from o'er the sea ;
Or if for these you will not ope,
    Yet open for charity.

"The hare is crouching in her form,
    The hart beside the hind ;
An aged man, amid the storm,
    No shelter can I find.

"Your hear the Ettrick's sullen roar,
    Dark, deep, and strong is he,
And I must ford the Ettrick o'er,
    Unless you pity me.

"The iron gate is bolted hard,
    At which I knock in vain ;
The owner's heart is closer barr'd,
    Who hears me thus complain.

"Farewell, farewell ! and Mary grant,
    When old and frail you be,
You never may the shelter want,
    That's now denied to me !"

The Ranger on his couch lay warm,
    And heard him plead in vain ;
But oft, amid December's storm,
    He'll hear that voice again :

For lo, when through the vapours dank
    Morn shone on Ettrick fair,
A corpse amid the alders rank,
    The Palmer welter'd there.

The Maid of Neidpath.

1806.

THERE is a tradition in Tweeddale, that, when Neidpath
Castle, near Peebles, was inhabtied by the Earls of March, a
mutual passion subsisted between a daughter of that noble family,
and a son of the Laird of Tushielaw, in Ettrick Forest.   As the
alliance was thought unsuitable by her parents, the young man
went abroad.   During his absence, the lady fell into a con-
sumption ; and at length, as the only means of saving her life,
her father consented that her lover should be recalled.   On the
day when he was expected to pass through Peebles, on the road
to Tushielaw, the young lady, though much exhausted, caused
herself to be carried to the balcony of a house in Peebles, belonging to the family, that she might see him as he rode past.
Her anxiety and eagerness gave such force to her organs, that
she is said to have distinguished his horse's footsteps at an in-
credible distance.   But Tushielaw, unprepared for the change
in her appearance, and not expecting to see her in that place,
rode on without recognising her, or even slackening his pace.
The lady was unable to support the shock ; and, after a short
struggle, died in the arms of her attendants.   There is an
incident similar to this traditional tale in Count Hamilton's
" Fleur d' Epine."

> O LOVERS' eyes are sharp to see,
>   And lovers' ears in hearing ;
> And love, in life's extremity,
>   Can lend an hour of cheering.
> Disease had been in Mary's bower,
>   And slow decay from mourning,
> Though now she sits on Neidpath's tower,
>   To watch her love's returning.
>
> All sunk and dim her eyes so bright,
>   Her form decay'd by pining,
> Till through her wasted hand, at night,
>   You saw the taper shining ;

By fits, a sultry hectic hue
  Across her cheek was flying;
By fits, so ashy pale she grew,
  Her maidens thought her dying.

Yet keenest powers to see and hear,
  Seem'd in her frame residing ;
Before the watch-dog prick'd his ear,
  She heard her lover's riding ;
Ere scarce a distant form was ken'd,
  She knew, and waved to greet him ;
And o'er the battlement did bend,
  As on the wing to meet him.

He came—he pass'd—an heedless gaze,
  As o'er some stranger glancing ;
Her welcome, spoke in faltering phrase,
  Lost in his courser's prancing—
The castle arch, whose hollow tone
  Returns each whisper spoken,
Could scarcely catch the feeble moan
  Which told her heart was broken.

Wandering Willie.

1806.

ALL joy was bereft me the day that you left me,
  And climb'd the tall vessel to sail yon wide sea ;
O weary betide it ! I wander'd beside it,
  And bann'd it for parting my Willie and me.

Far o'er the wave hast thou follow'd thy fortune,
  Oft fought the squadrons of France and of Spain ;
Ae kiss of welcome 's worth twenty at parting,
  Now I hae gotten my Willie again.

When the sky it was mirk, and the winds they were wailing,
  I sat on the beach wi' the tear in my ee,
And thought o' the bark where my Willie was sailing,
  And wish'd that the tempest could a' blaw on me.

Now that thy gallant ship rides at her mooring,
  Now that my wanderer's in safety at hame,
Music to me were the wildest winds' roaring,
  That e'er o'er Inchkeith drove the dark ocean faem.

When the lights they did blaze, and the guns they did rattle,
  And blithe was each heart for the great victory,
In secret I wept for the dangers of battle,
  And thy glory itself was scarce comfort to me.

But now shalt thou tell, while I eagerly listen,
  Of each bold adventure, and every brave scar ;
And trust me, I 'll smile, though my een they may glisten ;
  For sweet after danger's the tale of the war.

And oh ! how we doubt when there's distance 'tween lovers,
  When there's naething to speak to the heart thro' the ee ;
How often the kindest and warmest prove rovers,
  And the love of the faithfullest ebbs like the sea.

Till, at times—could I help it ?—I pined and I ponder'd,
  If love could change notes like the bird on the tree—
Now I 'll ne'er ask if thine eyes may hae wander'd ;
  Enough, thy leal heart has been constant to me.

Welcome, from sweeping o'er sea and through channel,
  Hardships and danger despising for fame,
Furnishing story for glory's bright annal,
  Welcome, my wanderer, to Jeanie and hame !

Enough, now thy story in annals of glory
  Has humbled the pride of France, Holland, and Spain ;
No more shalt thou grieve me, no more shalt thou leave me,
  I never will part with my Willie again.

Hunting Song.[1]

1808.

WAKEN, lords and ladies gay !
On the mountain dawns the day ;
All the jolly chase is here,
With hawk, and horse, and hunting spear !
Hounds are in their couples yelling,
Hawks are whistling, horns are knelling ;
Merrily, merrily, mingle they—
" Waken, lords and ladies gay !"

Waken, lords and ladies gay !
The mist has left the mountain grey,
Springlets in the dawn are steaming,
Diamonds on the brake are gleaming ;
And foresters have busy been,
To track the buck in thicket green ;
Now we come to chant our lay—
" Waken, lords and ladies gay !"

Waken, lords and ladies gay !
To the green-wood haste away ;
We can show you where he lies,
Fleet of foot, and tall of size ;
We can show the marks he made,
When 'gainst the oak his antlers fray'd ;
You shall see him brought to bay—
" Waken, lords and ladies gay !"

Louder, louder chant the lay,
Waken, lords and ladies gay !
Tell them, youth, and mirth, and glee,
Run a course as well as we ;

---

[1] First published in the continuance of Strutt's " Queenhoo-hall," 1808,
inserted in the Edinburgh Annual Register of the same year, and set to a
Welsh air in Thomson's *Select Melodies*, vol. iii., 1817.—ED.

Time, stern huntsman ! who can baulk,
Stanch as hound, and fleet as hawk !
Think of this, and rise with day,
Gentle lords and ladies gay !

The Resolve.[1]

IN IMITATION OF AN OLD ENGLISH POEM.

1808.

My wayward fate I needs must plain,
  Though bootless be the theme :
I loved, and was beloved again,
  Yet all was but a dream ;
For, as her love was quickly got,
  So it was quickly gone ;
No more I 'll bask in flame so hot,
  But coldly dwell alone.

Not maid more bright than maid was e'er
  My fancy shall beguile,
By flattering word, or feigned tear,
  By gesture, look, or smile :
No more I 'll call the shaft fair shot,
  Till it has fairly flown,
Nor scorch me at a flame so hot ;—
  I 'll rather freeze alone.

Each ambush'd Cupid I 'll defy,
  In cheek, or chin, or brow,
And deem the glance of woman's eye
  As weak as woman's vow :

[1] Published anonymously in the Edinburgh Annual Register of 1808. Writing to his brother Thomas, the author says, " The Resolve is mine ; and it is not—or, to be less enigmatical, it is an old fragment, which I coopered up into its present state with the purpose of quizzing certain judges of poetry, who have been extremely delighted, and declare that no living poet could write in the same exquisite taste."—*Life of Scott*, vol. iii. p. 330.

I 'll lightly hold the lady's heart,
 That is but lightly won ;
I 'll steel my breast to beauty's art,
 And learn to live alone.

The flaunting torch soon blazes out,
 The diamond's ray abides ;
The flame its glory hurls about,
 The gem its lustre hides :
Such gem I fondly deem'd was mine,
 And glow'd a diamond stone,
But, since each eye may see it shine,
 I 'll darkling dwell alone.

No waking dream shall tinge my thought
 With dyes so bright and vain,
No silken net, so slightly wrought,
 Shall tangle me again :
No more I 'll pay so dear for wit,
 I 'll live upon mine own ;
Nor shall wild passion trouble it,—
 I 'll rather dwell alone.

And thus I 'll hush my heart to rest,—
 " Thy loving labour 's lost ;
Thou shalt no more be wildly blest,
 To be so strangely crost ;
The widow'd turtles mateless die,
 The phœnix is but one ;
They seek no loves—no more will I—
 I 'll rather dwell alone."

𝔈𝔭𝔦𝔱𝔞𝔭𝔥,[1]

DESIGNED FOR A MONUMENT IN LICHFIELD CATHEDRAL, AT THE
BURIAL-PLACE OF THE FAMILY OF MISS SEWARD.

AMID these aisles, where once his precepts show'd
The Heavenward pathway which in life he trod,

This simple tablet marks a Father's bier,
And those he loved in life, in death are near ;
For him, for them, a Daughter bade it rise,
Memorial of domestic charities.
Still wouldst thou know why o'er the marble spread,
In female grace the willow drops her head ;
Why on her branches, silent and unstrung,
The minstrel harp is emblematic hung ;
What poet's voice is smother'd here in dust,
Till waked to join the chorus of the just,——
Lo ! one brief line an answer sad supplies,
Honour'd, beloved, and mourn'd, here SEWARD lies !
Her worth, her warmth of heart, let friendship say,—
Go seek her genius in her living lay.

𝔓rologue

TO MISS BAILLIE'S PLAY OF THE FAMILY LEGEND.[1]

1809.

'Tis sweet to hear expiring Summer's sigh,
Through forests tinged with russet, wail and die ;
'Tis, sweet and sad the latest notes to hear
Of distant music, dying on the ear ;
But far more sadly sweet, on foreign strand,
We list the legends of our native land,
Link'd as they come with every tender tie,
Memorials dear of youth and infancy.

Chief, thy wild tales, romantic Caledon,
Wake keen remembrance in each hardy son.
Whether on India's burning coasts he toil,
Or till Acadia's[2] winter-fetter'd soil,

Miss Baillie's *Family Legend* was produced with considerable success on the Edinburgh stage in the winter of 1809-10. This prologue was spoken on that occasion by the Author's friend, Mr. Daniel Terry.—ED.

[2] Acadia, or Nova Scotia.

He hears, with throbbing heart and moisten'd eyes,
And, as he hears, what dear illusions rise!
It opens on his soul his native dell,
The woods wild waving, and the water's swell;
Tradition's theme, the tower that threats the plain,
The mossy cairn that hides the hero slain;
The cot, beneath whose simple porch were told,
By grey-hair'd patriarch, the tales of old;
The infant group, that hush'd their sports the while,
And the dear maid who listen'd with a smile:
The wanderer, while the vision warms his brain,
Is denizen of Scotland once again.

Are such keen feelings to the crowd confined,
And sleep they in the Poet's gifted mind?
Oh no! For she, within whose mighty page
Each tyrant Passion shows his woe and rage,
Has felt the wizard influence they inspire,
And to your own traditions tuned her lyre.
Yourselves shall judge. Whoe'er has raised the sail
By Mull's dark coast, has heard this evening's tale:
The plaided boatman, resting on his oar,
Points to the fatal rock amid the roar
Of whitening waves, and tells whate'er to-night
Our humble stage shall offer to your sight;
Proudly preferr'd that first our efforts give
Scenes glowing from her pen to breathe and live:
More proudly yet, should Caledon approve
The filial token of a Daughter's love.

The Poacher.

WRITTEN IN IMITATION OF CRABBE, AND PUBLISHED IN THE
EDINBURGH ANNUAL REGISTER OF 1809.[1]

WELCOME, grave Stranger, to our green retreats,
Where health with exercise and freedom meets!

[1] See *Life of Scott*, vol. iii. p. 329.

Thrice welcome, Sage, whose philosophic plan
By nature's limits metes the rights of man;
Generous as he, who now for freedom bawls,
Now gives full value for true Indian shawls:
O'er court, o'er customhouse, his shoe who flings,
Now bilks excisemen, and now bullies kings.
Like his, I ween, thy comprehensive mind
Holds laws as mouse-traps baited for mankind;
Thine eye, applausive, each sly vermin sees,
That baulks the snare, yet battens on the cheese;
Thine ear has heard, with scorn instead of awe,
Our buckskinn'd justices expound the law,
Wire-draw the acts that fix for wires the pain,
And for the netted partridge noose the swain;
And thy vindictive arm would fain have broke
The last light fetter of the feudal yoke,
To give the denizens of wood and wild,
Nature's free race, to each her free-born child.
Hence hast thou mark'd, with grief, fair London's race,
Mock'd with the boon of one poor Easter chase,
And long'd to send them forth as free as when
Pour'd o'er Chantilly the Parisian train,
When musket, pistol, blunderbuss, combined,
And scarce the field-pieces were left behind!
A squadron's charge each leveret's heart dismay'd,
On every covey fired a bold brigade:
La Douce Humanité approved the sport,
For great the alarm indeed, yet small the hurt;
Shouts patriotic solemnized the day,
And Seine re-echo'd *Vive la Liberté!*
But mad *Citoyen*, meek *Monsieur* again,
With some few added links, resumes his chain.
Then, since such scenes to France no more are known,
Come, view with me a hero of thine own!
One, whose free actions vindicate the cause
Of silvan liberty o'er feudal laws.

Seek we yon glades, where the proud oak o'ertops
Wide-waving seas of birch and hazel copse,
Leaving between deserted isles of land,
Where stunted heath is patch'd with ruddy sand;

And lonely on the waste the yew is seen,
Or straggling hollies spread a brighter green.
Here, little worn, and winding dark and steep,
Our scarce-mark'd path descends yon dingle deep:
Follow—but heedful, cautious of a trip,—
In earthly mire philosophy may slip.
Step slow and wary o'er that swampy stream,
Till, guided by the charcoal's smothering steam,
We reach the frail yet barricaded door
Of hovel form'd for poorest of the poor;
No hearth the fire, no vent the smoke receives,
The walls are wattles, and the covering leaves;
For, if such hut, our forest statutes say,
Rise in the progress of one night and day,
(Though placed where still the Conqueror's hests o'erawe
And his son's stirrup shines the badge of law,)
The builder claims the unenviable boon,
To tenant dwelling,[1] framed as slight and soon
As wigwam wild, that shrouds the native frore
On the bleak coast of frost-barr'd Labrador.[2]

Approach, and through the unlatticed window peep—
Nay, shrink not back—the inmate is asleep;
Sunk 'mid yon sordid blankets, till the sun
Stoop to the west, the plunderer's toils are done.
Loaded and primed, and prompt for desperate hand,
Rifle and fowling-piece beside him stand;
While round the hut are in disorder laid
The tools and booty of his lawless trade;
For force or fraud, resistance or escape,
The crow, the saw, the bludgeon, and the crape.
His pilfer'd powder in yon nook he hoards,
And the filch'd lead the church's roof affords—
(Hence shall the Rector's congregation fret,
That while his sermon's dry his walls are wet.)

[1] Such is the law in the New Forest, Hampshire, tending greatly to increase the various settlements of thieves, smugglers, and deer-stealers, who infest it. In the forest courts the presiding judge wears as a badge of office an antique stirrup, said to have been that of William Rufus. See Mr. William Rose's spirited poem, entitled "The Red King."

[2] "To the bleak coast of *savage* Labrador."—FALCONER.

The fish-spear barb'd, the sweeping net, are there,
Doe-hides, and pheasant plumes, and skins of hare,
Cordage for toils, and wiring for the snare.
Barter'd for game from chase or warren won,
Yon cask holds moonlight,[1] run when moon was none ;
And late-snatch'd spoils lie stow'd in hutch apart,
To wait the associate higgler's evening cart.

Look on his pallet foul, and mark his rest :
What scenes perturb'd are acting in his breast !
His sable brow is wet and wrung with pain,
And his dilated nostril toils in vain ;
For short and scant the breath each effort draws,
And 'twixt each effort Nature claims a pause.
Beyond the loose and sable neckcloth stretch'd,
His sinewy throat seems by convulsion twitch'd,
While the tongue falters, as to utterance loath,
Sounds of dire import— watchword, threat, and oath.
Though, stupified by toil, and drugg'd with gin,
The body sleep, the restless guest within
Now plies on wood and wold his lawless trade,
Now in the fangs of justice wakes dismay'd.—

·' Was that wild start of terror and despair,
Those bursting eyeballs, and that wilder'd air,
Signs of compunction for a murder'd hare ?
Do the locks bristle and the eyebrows arch,
For grouse or partridge massacred in March ?"—

No, scoffer, no ! Attend, and mark with awe,
There is no wicket in the gate of law !
He, that would e'er so lightly set ajar
That awful portal, must undo each bar :
Tempting occasion, habit, passion, pride,
Will join to storm the breach, and force the barrier wide.

That ruffian, whom true men avoid and dread,
Whom bruisers, poachers, smugglers, call Black Ned,

1 A cant term for smuggled spirits.

Was Edward Mansell once ;—the lightest heart
That ever play'd on holiday his part !
The leader he in every Christmas game,
The harvest-feast grew blither when he came,
And liveliest on the chords the bow did glance,
When Edward named the tune and led the dance.
Kind was his heart, his passions quick and strong,
Hearty his laugh, and jovial was his song ;
And if he loved a gun, his father swore,
" 'Twas but a trick of youth would soon be o'er,
Himself had done the same some thirty years before."

But he whose humours spurn law's awful yoke,
Must herd with those by whom law's bonds are broke ;
The common dread of justice soon allies
The clown, who robs the warren or excise,
With sterner felons train'd to act more dread,
Even with the wretch by whom his fellow bled.
Then, as in plagues the foul contagions pass,
Leavening and festering the corrupted mass,—
Guilt leagues with guilt, while mutual motives draw,
Their hope impunity, their fear the law ;
Their foes, their friends, their rendezvous the same,
Till the revenue baulk'd, or pilfer'd game,
Flesh the young culprit, and example leads
To darker villany, and direr deeds.

Wild howl'd the wind the forest glades along,
And oft the owl renew'd her dismal song ;
Around the spot where erst he felt the wound,
Red William's spectre walk'd his midnight round.
When o'er the swamp he cast his blighting look,
From the green marshes of the stagnant brook
The bittern's sullen shout the sedges shook !
The waning moon, with storm-presaging gleam,
Now gave and now withheld her doubtful beam ;
The old Oak stoop'd his arms, then flung them high,
Bellowing and groaning to the troubled sky—
'Twas then, that, couch'd amid the brushwood sere,
In Malwood-walk young Mansell watch'd the deer :

The fattest buck received his deadly shot—.
The watchful keeper heard, and sought the spot.
Stout were their hearts, and stubborn was their strife,
O'erpower'd at length the Outlaw drew his knife.
Next morn a corpse was found upon the fell—
The rest his waking agony may tell !

———————

Song.

Oh, say not, my love, with that mortified air,
   That your spring-time of pleasure is flown,
Nor bid me to maids that are younger repair,
   For those raptures that still are thine own.

Though April his temples may wreathe with the vine,
   Its tendrils in infancy curl'd,
'Tis the ardour of August matures us the wine,
   Whose life-blood enlivens the world.

Though thy form, that was fashion'd as light as a fay's,
   Has assumed a proportion more round,
And thy glance, that was bright as a falcon's at gaze
   Looks soberly now on the ground,—

Enough, after absence to meet me again,
   Thy steps still with ecstasy move ;
Enough, that those dear sober glances retain
   For me the kind language of love.

———————

The Bold Dragoon;[1]

OR,

THE PLAIN OF BADAJOS

1812.

'T was a Maréchal of France, and he fain would honour gain,
And he long'd to take a passing glance at Portugal from Spain;
    With his flying guns this gallant gay,
    And boasted corps d'armée—
O he fear'd not our dragoons, with their long swords, boldly
    riding,
    Whack, fal de ral, &c.

To Campo Mayor come, he had quietly sat down,
Just a fricassee to pick, while his soldiers sack'd the town,
    When, 'T was peste! morbleu! mon General,
    Hear the English bugle-call!
And behold the light dragoons, with their long swords, boldly
    riding,
    Whack, fal de ral, &c.

Right about went horse and foot, artillery and all,
And, as the devil leaves a house, they tumbled through the
    wall;[2]
    They took no time to seek the door,
    But, best foot set before—
O they ran from our dragoons, with their long swords, boldly
    riding,
    Whack, fal de ral, &c.

[1] This song was written shortly after the battle of Badajos, (April 1812,) for a Yeomanry Cavalry dinner It was first printed in Mr. George Thomson's Collection of Select Melodies, and stands in vol. vi. of the last edition of that work.—Ed.

[2] In their hasty evacuation of Campo Mayor, the French pulled down a part of the rampart, and marched out over the glacis.

Those valiant men of France they had scarcely fled a mile,
When on their flank there sous'd at once the British rank
   and file;
  For Long, De Grey, and Otway, then
  Ne'er minded one to ten,
But came on like light dragoons, with their long swords,
  boldly riding,
  Whack, fal de ral, &c.

Three hundred British lads they made three thousand reel,
Their hearts were made of English Oak, their swords of
   Sheffield steel,
  Their horses were in Yorkshire bred,
  And Beresford them led;
So huzza for brave dragoons, with their long swords, boldly
  riding,
  Whack, fal de ral, &c.

Then here's a health to Wellington, to Beresford, to Long,
And a single word of Bonaparte before I close my song:
  The eagles that to fight he brings
  Should serve his men with wings,
When they meet the bold dragoons, with their long swords,
  boldly riding,
  Whack, fal de ral, &c.

On the Massacre of Glencoe.[1]

1814.

" In the beginning of the year 1692, an action of unexampled
barbarity disgraced the Government of King William III. in
Scotland. In the August preceding, a proclamation had been
issued, offering an indemnity to such insurgents as should take
the oaths to the King and Queen, on or before the last day of

----

December; and the chiefs of such tribes as had been in arms for James soon after took advantage of the proclamation. But Macdonald of Glencoe was prevented by accident, rather than by design, from tendering his submission within the limited time. In the end of December he went to Colonel Hill, who commanded the garrison in Fort-William, to take the oaths of allegiance to the Government ; and the latter having furnished him with a letter to Sir Colin Campbell, Sheriff of the county of Argyll, directed him to repair immediately to Inverary, to make his submission in a legal manner before that magistrate. But the way to Inverary lay through almost impassable mountains, the season was extremely rigorous, and the whole country was covered with a deep snow. So eager, however, was Macdonald to take the oaths before the limited time should expire, that though the road lay within half a mile of his own house, he stopped not to visit his family, and, after various obstructions, arrived at Inverary. The time had elapsed, and the Sheriff hesitated to receive his submission; but Macdonald prevailed by his importunities, and even tears, in inducing that functionary to administer to him the oath of allegiance, and to certify the cause of his delay. At this time Sir John Dalrymple, afterwards Earl of Stair, being in attendance upon William as Secretary of State for Scotland, took advantage of Macdonald's neglecting to take the oath within the time prescribed, and procured from the King a warrant of military execution against that chief and his whole clan. This was done at the instigation of the Earl of Breadalbane, whose lands the Glencoe men had plundered, and whose treachery to Government in negotiating with the Highland clans, Macdonald himself had exposed. The King was accordingly persuaded that Glencoe was the main obstacle to the pacification of the Highlands; and the fact of the unfortunate chief's submission having been concealed, the sanguinary orders for proceeding to military execution against his clan were in consequence obtained. The warrant was both signed and countersigned by the King's own hand, and the Secretary urged the officers who commanded in the Highlands to execute their orders with the utmost rigour. Campbell of Glenlyon, a captain in Argyle's regiment, and two subalterns, were ordered to repair to Glencoe on the 1st of February with an hundred and twenty men. Campbell, being uncle to young Macdonald's wife, was received by the father with all manner of friendship and hospitality. The men were lodged at free quarters in the houses of his tenants, and received the kindest entertainment. Till the 13th of the month the troops lived in the utmost harmony and familiarity with the people ; and on the very night of the massacre the officers passed the evening at cards in Macdonald's house. In the night, Lieutenant Lindsay, with a party of soldiers, called in a friendly manner at his door, and was instantly admitted. Macdonald, while in the act of rising to receive his guest, was shot dead through the back with two bullets. His wife had already dressed ; but she was stripped naked by the soldiers, who tore the rings off her fingers with their teeth. The slaughter now became general, and neither age nor infirmity was spared. Some women, in defending their children, were killed ; boys imploring mercy, were shot dead by officers on whose knees they hung. In one place nine persons, as they sat enjoying themselves at table, were butchered by the soldiers. In Inverriggon, Campbell's own quarters, nine men were first bound by the soldiers, and then shot at intervals, one by one. Nearly forty persons were massacred by the troops ; and several who fled to the mountains perished by famine and the inclemency of the season. Those who escaped owed their lives to a tempestuous night. Lieutenant-Colonel Hamilton, who had received the charge of the execution from Dalrymple, was on his march with four hundred men, to guard all the passes from the valley of Glencoe ; but he was obliged to stop by the severity of the weather, which proved the safety of the unfortunate clan. Next day he entered the valley, laid the houses in ashes, and carried away the cattle and spoil, which were divided among the officers and soldiers."— *Article* "BRITAIN ;" *Encyc. Britannica—New Edition.*—ED.

"O TELL me, Harper, wherefore flow
  Thy wayward notes of wail and woe, :
  Far down the desert of Glencoe,
    Where none may list their melody ?
  Say, harp'st thou to the mists that fly,
  Or to the dun-deer glancing by,
  Or to the eagle, that from high
    Screams chorus to thy minstrelsy ?"—

" No, not to these, for they have rest,—
  The mist-wreath has the mountain-crest,
  The stag his lair, the erne her nest,
    Abode of lone security.
But those for whom I pour the lay,
Not wild-wood deep, nor mountain grey,
Not this deep dell, that shrouds from day,
    Could screen from treach'rous cruelty.

" Their flag was furl'd, and mute their drum,
The very household dogs were dumb,
Unwont to bay at guests that come
    In guise of hospitality.
His blithest notes the piper plied,
Her gayest snood the maiden tied,
The dame her distaff flung aside,
    To tend her kindly housewifery.

" The hand that mingled in the meal,
At midnight drew the felon steel,
And gave the host's kind breast to feel
    -Meed for his hospitality !
The friendly hearth which warm'd that hand,
At midnight arm'd it with the brand,
That bade destruction's flames expand
    Their red and fearful blazonry.

" Then woman's shriek was heard in vain,
Nor infancy's unpited plain,
More than the warrior's groan, could gain
    Respite from ruthless butchery !
The winter wind that whistled shrill,
The snows that night that cloked the hill,
Though wild and pitiless, had still
    Far more than Southern clemency.

" Long have my harp's best notes been gone,
Few are its strings, and faint their tone,
They can but sound in desert lone
    Their grey-hair'd master's misery.

Were each grey hair a minstrel string,
Each chord should imprecations fling,
Till startled Scotland loud should ring,
  ' Revenge for blood and treachery !' "

ℱor a' that an' a' that.[1]

A NEW SONG TO AN OLD TUNE.

1814.

THOUGH right be aft put down by strength,
  As mony a day we saw that,
The true and leilfu' cause at length
  Shall bear the grie for a' that.
For a' that an' a' that,
  Guns, guillotines, and a' that,
The Fleur-de-lis, that lost her right,
  Is queen again for a' that !

We'll twine her in a friendly knot
  With England's Rose, and a' that;
The Shamrock shall not be forgot,
  For Wellington made braw that.
The Thistle, though her leaf be rude,
  Yet faith we'll no misca' that,
She shelter'd in her solitude
  The Fleur-de-lis, for a' that.

The Austrian Vine, the Prussian Pine
  (For Blucher's sake, hurra that,)
The Spanish Olive, too, shall join,
  And bloom in peace for a' that.
Stout Russia's Hemp, so surely twined
  Around our wreath we'll draw that,
And he that would the cord unbind,
  Shall have it for his gra-vat !

[1] Sung at the first meeting of the Pitt Club of Scotland ; and published in the Scots Magazine for July 1814. — ED.

Or, if to choke sae puir a sot,
   Your pity scorn to thraw that,
The Devil's elbow be his lot,
   Where he may sit and claw that.
In spite of slight, in spite of might,
   In spite of brags, an' a' that,
The lads that battled for the right,
   Have won the day, an' a' that!

There 's ae bit spot I had forgot,
   America they ca' that!
A coward plot her rats had got
   Their father's flag to gnaw that:
Now see it fly top-gallant high,
   Atlantic winds shall blaw that,
And Yankee loon, beware your croun,
   There 's kames in hand to claw that!

For on the land, or on the sea,
   Where'er the breezes blaw that,
The British Flag shall bear the grie,
   And win the day for a' that!

Song,

FOR THE ANNIVERSARY MEETING OF THE PITT CLUB OF SCOTLAND.

1814.

O! DREAD was the time, and more dreadful the omen,
   When the brave on Marengo lay slaughter'd in vain,
And beholding broad Europe bow'd down by her foemen,
   PITT closed in his anguish the map of her reign!
Not the fate of broad Europe could bend his brave spirit
   To take for his country the safety of shame;
O! then in her triumph remember his merit,
   And hallow the goblet that flows to his name.

Round the husbandman's head, while he traces the furrow,
   The mists of the winter may mingle with rain ;
He may plough it with labour, and sow it in sorrow,
   And sigh while he fears he has sow'd it in vain ;
He may die ere his children shall reap in their gladness,
   But the blithe harvest-home shall remember his claim ;
And their jubilee-shout shall be soften'd with sadness,
   While they hallow the goblet that flows to his name.

Though anxious and timeless his life was expended,
   In toils for our country preserved by his care,
Though he died ere one ray o'er the nations ascended,
   To light the long darkness of doubt and despair ;
The storms he endured in our Britain's December,
   The perils his wisdom foresaw and o'ercame,
In her glory's rich harvest shall Britain remember,
   And hallow the goblet that flows to his name.

Nor forget His grey head, who, all dark in affliction,
   Is deaf to the tale of our victories won,
And to sounds the most dear to paternal affection,
   The shout of his people applauding his Son ;
By his firmness unmoved in success and disaster,
   By his long reign of virtue, remember his claim !
With our tribute to Pitt join the praise of his Master,
   Though a tear stain the goblet that flows to his name.

Yet again fill the wine-cup, and change the sad measure,
   The rites of our grief and our gratitude paid,
To our Prince, to our Heroes, devote the bright treasure,
   The wisdom that plann'd, and the zeal that obey'd
Fill Wellington's cup till it beam like his glory,
   Forget not our own brave Dalhousie and Græme ;
A thousand years hence hearts shall bound at their story,
   And hallow the goblet that flows to their fame.

Pharos Loquitur.[1]

FAR in the bosom of the deep,
O'er these wild shelves my watch I keep;
A ruddy gem of changeful light,
Bound on the dusky brow of night,
The seaman bids my lustre hail,
And scorns to strike his timorous sail.

Lines,[2]

ADDRESSED TO RANALD MACDONALD, ESQ. OF STAFFA.[3]

1814.

STAFFA, sprung from high Macdonald,
Worthy branch of old Clan-Ranald!
Staffa! king of all kind fellows!
Well befall thy hills and valleys,
Lakes and inlets, deeps and shallows—
Cliffs of darkness, caves of wonder,
Echoing the Atlantic thunder;

[1] "On the 30th of July 1814, Mr. Hamilton,* Mr. Erskine,† and Mr. Duff,‡ Commissioners, along with Mr. (now Sir) Walter Scott, and the writer, visited the Lighthouse; the Commissioners being then on one of their voyages of Inspection, noticed in the Introduction. They breakfasted in the Library, when Sir Walter, at the entreaty of the party, upon inscribing his name in the Album, added these interesting lines."—*Stevenson's Account of the Bell-Rock Lighthouse.* 1824.—Scott's Diary of the Voyage is now published in the 4th volume of his *Life.*—ED.

[2] These lines were written in the Album kept at the Sound of Ulva Inn, in the month of August 1814.

[3] Afterwards Sir Reginald Macdonald Stewart Seton of Staffa, Allanton, and Touch, Baronet. He died 16th April 1838, in his 61st year. The reader will find a warm tribute to Staffa's character as a Highland landlord, in Scott's article on Sir John Carr's Caledonian Sketches, *Miscellaneous Prose Works,* vol. xix.—ED.

* The late Robert Hamilton, Esq., Advocate, long Sheriff-Depute of Lanarkshire, and afterwards one of the Principal Clerks of Session in Scotland—died in 1831.   † Afterwards Lord Kinneder.
‡ The late Adam Duff, Esq., Sheriff-Depute of the county of Edinburgh

Mountains which the grey mist covers,
Where the Chieftain spirit hovers,
Pausing while his pinions quiver,
Stretch'd to quit our land for ever !
Each kind influence reign above thee !
Warmer heart, 'twixt this and Jaffa
Beats not, than in breast of Staffa !

Farewell to Mackenzie,

HIGH CHIEF OF KINTAIL.

FROM THE GAELIC.

1815.—Æt. 44.

THE original verses are arranged to a beautiful Gaelic air, of
which the chorus is adapted to the double pull upon the oars of
a galley, and which is therefore distinct from the ordinary jor-
rams, or boat-songs.   They were composed by the Family Bard
upon the departure of the Earl of Seaforth, who was obliged to
take refuge in Spain, after an unsuccessful effort at insurrection
in favour of the Stuart family, in the year 1718.

FAREWELL to Mackenneth, great Earl of the North,
The Lord of Lochcarron, Glenshiel, and Seaforth ;
To the Chieftain this morning his course who began,
Launching forth on the billows his bark like a swan.
For a far foreign land he has hoisted his sail,
Farewell to Mackenzie, High Chief of Kintail !

O swift be the galley, and hardy her crew,
May her captain be skilful, her mariners true,
In danger undaunted, unwearied by toil,
Though the whirlwind should rise, and the ocean should boil ;
On the brave vessel's gunnel I drank his bonail,[1]
And farewell to Mackenzie, High Chief of Kintail !

[1] Bonail, or Bonallez, the old Scottish phrase for a feast at parting with a
friend.

Awake in thy chamber, thou sweet southland gale !
Like the sighs of his people, breathe soft on his sail ;
Be prolong'd as regret, that his vassals must know,
Be fair as their faith, and sincere as their woe :
Be so soft, and so fair, and so faithful, sweet gale,
Wafting onward Mackenzie, High Chief of Kintail !

Be his pilot experienced, and trusty, and wise,
To measure the seas and to study the skies :
May he hoist all his canvass from streamer to deck,
But O ! crowd it higher when wafting him back—
Till the cliffs of Skooroora, and Conan's glad vale,
Shall welcome Mackenzie, High Chief of Kintail !

IMITATION OF THE PRECEDING SONG.[1]

So sung the old Bard, in the grief of his heart,
When he saw his loved Lord from his people depart.
Now mute on thy mountains, O Albyn, are heard
Nor the voice of the song, nor the harp of the bard ;
Or its strings are but waked by the stern winter gale,
As they mourn for Mackenzie, last Chief of Kintail.

From the far Southland Border a Minstrel came forth,
And he waited the hour that some Bard of the north
His hand on the harp of the ancient should cast,
And bid its wild numbers mix high with the blast ;
But no bard was there left in the land of the Gael,
To lament for Mackenzie, last Chief of Kintail.

And shalt thou then sleep, did the Minstrel exclaim,
Like the son of the lowly, unnoticed by fame ?

[1] " These verses were written shortly after the death of Lord Seaforth, the last male representative of his illustrious house. He was a nobleman of extraordinary talents, who must have made for himself a lasting reputation, had not his political exertions been checked by the painful natural infirmities alluded to in the fourth stanza."—See *Life of Scott*, vol. v. pp. 18, 19.

No, son of Fitzgerald! in accents of woe,
The song thou hast loved, o'er thy coffin shall flow,
And teach thy wild mountains to join in the wail
That laments for Mackenzie, last Chief of Kintail.

In vain, the bright course of thy talents to wrong,
Fate deaden'd thine ear and imprison'd thy tongue;
For brighter o'er all her obstructions arose
The glow of the genius they could not oppose;
And who in the land of the Saxon or Gael,
Might match with Mackenzie, High Chief of Kintail?

Thy sons rose around thee in light and in love,
All a father could hope, all a friend could approve;
What 'vails it the tale of thy sorrows to tell?—
In the spring-time of youth and of promise they fell!
Of the line of Fitzgerald remains not a male,
To bear the proud name of the Chief of Kintail.

And thou, gentle Dame, who must bear, to thy grief,
For thy clan and thy country the cares of a Chief,
Whom brief rolling moons in six changes have left,
Of thy husband, and father, and brethren bereft,
To thine ear of affection, how sad is the hail,
That salutes thee the Heir of the line of Kintail![1]

***

War-Song of Lachlan,

HIGH CHIEF OF MACLEAN.

FROM THE GAELIC.

1815.

This song appears to be imperfect, or, at least, like many of
the early Gaelic poems, makes a rapid transition from one sub-

[1] The Honourable Lady Hood, daughter of the last Lord Seaforth, widow
of Admiral Sir Samuel Hood, now Mrs. Stewart Mackenzie of Seaforth and
Glasserton.—1833.—Ed.

ject to another; from the situation, namely, of one of the daughters of the clan, who opens the song by lamenting the absence of her lover, to an eulogium over the military glories of the Chieftain. The translator has endeavoured to imitate the abrupt style of the original.

A WEARY month has wander'd o'er,
Since last we parted on the shore;
Heaven! that I saw thee, Love, once more,
    Safe on that shore again!—
'T was valiant Lachlan gave the word—
Lachlan, of many a galley lord:
He call'd his kindred bands on board,
    And launch'd them on the main.

Clan-Gillian[1] is to ocean gone—
Clan-Gillian, fierce in foray known;
Rejoicing in the glory won
    In many a bloody broil:
For wide is heard the thundering fray,
The rout, the ruin, the dismay,
When from the twilight glens away
    Clan-Gillian drives the spoil.

Woe to the hills that shall rebound
Our banner'd bag-pipes' maddening sound;
Clan-Gillian's onset, echoing round,
    Shall shake their inmost cell.
Woe to the bark whose crew shall gaze
Where Lachlan's silken streamer plays!
The fools might face the lightning's blaze
    As wisely and as well!

[1] *i. e.* The clan of Maclean, literally the race of Gillian.

Song,

ON THE LIFTING OF THE BANNER OF THE HOUSE OF BUCCLEUCH,

AT A GREAT FOOT-BALL MATCH ON CARTERHAUGH.[1]

1815.

FROM the brown crest of Newark its summons extending,
   Our signal is waving in smoke and in flame;
And each forester blithe, from his mountain descending,
   Bounds light o'er the heather to join in the game.

CHORUS.

Then up with the Banner! let forest winds fan her!
   She has blazed over Ettrick eight ages and more;
In sport we'll attend her, in battle defend her,
   With heart and with hand, like our fathers before.

When the Southern invader spread waste and disorder,
   At the glance of her crescents he paused and withdrew,
For around them were marshall'd the pride of the Border,
   The Flowers of the Forest, the Bands of BUCCLEUCH.
       Then up with the Banner, &c.

A stripling's weak hand[2] to our revel has borne her,
   No mail-glove has grasp'd her, no spearmen surround;
But ere a bold foeman should scathe or should scorn her,
   A thousand true hearts would be cold on the ground.
       Then up with the Banner, &c.

We forget each contention of civil dissension,
   And hail, like our brethren, HOME, DOUGLAS, and CAR:
And ELLIOT and PRINGLE in pastime shall mingle,
   As welcome in peace as their fathers in war.
       Then up with the Banner, &c.

[1] This song appears with Music in Mr. G. Thomson's Collection, 1826.—
The foot-ball match on which it was written took place on December 5,
1815, and was also celebrated by the Ettrick Shepherd. See *Life of Scott*,
vol. v. pp. 112, 116-122. —ED.

[2] The bearer of the standard was the Author's eldest son. —ED.

Then strip, lads, and to it, though sharp be the weather,
  And if, by mischance, you should happen to fall,
There are worse things in life than a tumble on heather,
  And life is itself but a game at foot-ball.
     Then up with the Banner, &c.

And when it is over, we'll drink a blithe measure
  To each Laird and each Lady that witness'd our fun,
And to every blithe heart that took part in our pleasure,
  To the lads that have lost, and the lads that have won.
     Then up with the Banner, &c.

May the Forest still flourish, both Borough and Landward,
  From the hall of the Peer to the Herd's ingle-nook!
And huzza! my brave hearts, for BUCCLEUCH and his standard,
  For the King and the Country, the Clan and the Duke!

Then up with the Banner! let forest winds fan her!
She has blazed over Ettrick eight ages and more;
In sport we'll attend her, in battle defend her,
With heart and with hand, like our fathers before.

Lullaby of an Infant Chief.

AIR—" *Cadul gu lo.*" [1]

1815.

I.

O, HUSH thee, my babie!—thy sire was a knight,
Thy mother a lady, both lovely and bright;
The woods and the glens, from the towers which we see,
They all are belonging, dear babie, to thee.
    O ho ro, i ri ri, cadul gu lo,
    O ho ro, i ri ri, &c.

---

[1] " Sleep on till day." These words, adapted to a melody somewhat different from the original, are sung in my friend Mr. Terry's drama of "Guy Mannering." [The " Lullaby" was first printed in Mr. Terry's drama: it was afterwards set to music in Thomson's Collection. 1822.]

II.

O, fear not the bugle, though loudly it blows,
It calls but the warders that guard thy repose ;
Their bows would be bended, their blades would be red,
Ere the step of a foeman draws near to thy bed.
    O ho ro, i ri ri, &c.

III.

O, hush thee, my babie !—the time soon will come,
When thy sleep shall be broken by trumpet and drum ;
Then hush thee, my darling, take rest while you may,
For strife comes with manhood, and waking with day.
    O ho ro, i ri ri, &c.

The Return to Ulster.[1]

1816.

Once again,—but how changed since my wand'rings began,—
I have heard the deep voice of the Lagan and Bann,
And the pines of Clanbrassil resound to the roar
That wearies the echoes of fair Tullamore.
Alas ! my poor bosom, and why shouldst thou burn ?
With the scenes of my youth can its raptures return ?
Can I live the dear life of delusion again,
That flow'd when these echoes first mix'd with my strain ?

It was then that around me, though poor and unknown,
High spells of mysterious enchantment were thrown ;
The streams were of silver, of diamond the dew,
The land was an Eden, for fancy was new.
I had heard of our bards, and my soul was on fire
At the rush of their verse, and the sweep of their lyre :
To me 'twas not legend, nor tale to the ear,
But a vision of noontide, distinguish'd and clear.

Ultonia's old heroes awoke at the call,
And renew'd the wild pomp of the chase and the hall ;

---

[1] First published in Mr. G. Thomson's Collection of Irish Airs, 1816.—Ed.

And the standard of Fion flash'd fierce from on high,
Like a burst of the sun when the tempest is nigh.[1]
It seem'd that the harp of green Erin once more
Could renew all the glories she boasted of yore.—
Yet why at remembrance, fond heart, shouldst thou burn?
They were days of delusion, and cannot return.

But was she, too, a phantom, the Maid who stood by,
And listed my lay, while she turn'd from mine eye?
Was she, too, a vision, just glancing to view,
Then dispers'd in the sunbeam, or melted to dew?
Oh! would it had been so!—Oh! would that her eye
Had been but a star-glance that shot through the sky,
And her voice, that was moulded to melody's thrill,
Had been but a zephyr, that sigh'd and was still!

Oh! would it had been so!—not then this poor heart
Had learn'd the sad lesson, to love and to part;
To bear, unassisted, its burthen of care,
While I toil'd for the wealth I had no one to share.
Not then had I said, when life's summer was done,
And the hours of her autumn were fast speeding on,
" Take the fame and the riches ye brought in your train,
And restore me the dream of my spring-tide again."

Jock of Hazeldean.

Air—*A Border Melody.*

1816.

The first stanza of this Ballad is ancient. The others were written for Mr. Campbell's Albyn's Anthology.

I.
" Why weep ye by the tide, ladie?
Why weep ye by the tide?

----

[1] In ancient Irish poetry, the standard of Fion, or Fingal, is called the
Sun-burst, an epithet feebly rendered by the *Sun-beam* of Macpherson.

I'll wed ye to my youngest son,
   And ye sall be his bride :
And ye sall be his bride, ladie,
   Sae comely to be seen"—
But aye she loot the tears down fa'
   For Jock of Hazeldean.

II.

" Now let this wilfu' grief be done,
   And dry that cheek so pale ;
Young Frank is chief of Errington,
   And lord of Langley-dale ;
His step is first in peaceful ha',
   His sword in battle keen"—
But aye she loot the tears down fa'
   For Jock of Hazeldean.

III.

" A chain of gold ye sall not not lack,
   Nor braid to bind your hair ;
Nor mettled hound, nor managed hawk,
   Nor palfrey fresh and fair ;
And you, the foremost o' them a',
   Shall ride our forest queen"—
But aye she loot the tears down fa'
   For Jock of Hazeldean.

IV.

The kirk was deck'd at morning-tide,
   The tapers glimmer'd fair ;
The priest and bridegroom wait the bride,
   And dame and knight are there.
They sought her baith by bower and ha';
   The ladie was not seen !
She's o'er the Border, and awa'
   Wi' Jock of Hazeldean.

Pibroch of Donald Dhu.

Air—"*Piobair of Donuil Dhuidh.*"[1]

1816.

This is a very ancient pibroch belonging to Clan MacDonald, and supposed to refer to the expedition of Donald Balloch, who, in 1431, launched from the Isles with a considerable force, invaded Lochaber, and at Inverlochy defeated and put to flight the Earls of Mar and Caithness, though at the head of an army superior to his own. The words of the set, theme, or melody, to which the pipe variations are applied, run thus in Gaelic:—

Piobaireachd Dhonuil Dhuidh, piobaireachd Dhonuil;
Piobaireachd Dhonuil Dhuidh, piobaireachd Dhonuil;
Piobaireachd Dhonuil Dhuidh, piobaireachd Dhonuil:
Piob agus bratach air faiche Inverlochi.
The pipe-summons of Donald the Black,
The pipe-summons of Donald the Black,
The war-pipe and the pennon are on the gathering-place at Inverlochy.[2]

PIBROCH of Donuil Dhu,
  Pibroch of Donuil,
Wake thy wild voice anew,
  Summon Clan-Conuil.
Come away, come away,
  Hark to the summons!
Come in your war array,
  Gentles and commons.

Come from deep glen, and
  From mountain so rocky,
The war-pipe and pennon
  Are at Inverlocky.
Come every hill-plaid, and
  True heart that wears one,
Come every steel blade, and
  Strong hand that bears one.

1 "The pibroch of Donald the Black." This song was writen for Campbell's Albyn's Anthology, 1816. It may also be seen, set to music, in Thomson's Collection, 1830.— Ed.

2 Compare this with the gathering-song in the third Canto of the *Lady of the Lake.*— Ed.

Leave untended the herd,
    The flock without shelter;
Leave the corpse uninterr'd,
    The bride at the altar;
Leave the deer, leave the steer,
    Leave nets and barges:
Come with your fighting gear,
    Broadswords and targes.

Come as the winds come, when
    Forests are rended;
Come as the waves come, when
    Navies are stranded:
Faster come, faster come,
    Faster and faster,
Chief, vassal, page and groom,
    Tenant and master.

Fast they come, fast they come;
    See how they gather!
Wide waves the eagle plume,
    Blended with heather.
Cast your plaids, draw your blades,
    Forward each man set!
Pibroch of Donuil Dhu,
    Knell for the onset!

Nora's Vow.

Air—" *Cha teid mis a chaoidh.*[1]

WRITTEN FOR ALBYN'S ANTHOLOGY.[2]

1816.

IN the original Gaelic, the Lady makes protestations that she
will not go with the Red Earl's son, until the swan should build

[1] " I will never go with him."
[2] See also Mr. Thomson's Scottish Collection, 1822.—ED.

in the cliff, and the eagle in the lake—until one mountain should change places with another, and so forth. It is but fair to add, that there is no authority for supposing that she altered her mind—except the vehemence of her protestation.

I.

HEAR what Highland Nora said,—
" The Earlie's son I will not wed,
Should all the race of nature die,
And none be left but he and I.
For all the gold, for all the gear,
And all the lands both far and near,
That ever valour lost or won,
I would not wed the Earlie's son."

II.

" A maiden's vows," old Callum spoke,
" Are lightly made and lightly broke ;
The heather on the mountain's height
Begins to bloom in purple light ;
The frost-wind soon shall sweep away
That lustre deep from glen and brae ;
Yet Nora, ere its bloom be gone,
May blithely wed the Earlie's son."—

III.

" The swan," she said, " the lake's clear breast
May barter for the eagle's nest ;
The Awe's fierce stream may backward turn,
Ben-Cruaichan fall, and crush Kilchurn ;
Our kilted clans, when blood is high,
Before their foes may turn and fly ;
But I, were all these marvels done,
Would never wed the Earlie's son."

IV.

Still in the water-lily's shade
Her wonted nest the wild-swan made ;
Ben-Cruaichan stands as fast as ever,
Still downward foams the Awe's fierce river ;

To shun the clash of foeman's steel,
No Highland brogue has turn'd the heel ;
But Nora's heart is lost and won,
—She 's wedded to the Earlie's son :

𝕸𝖆𝖈𝖌𝖗𝖊𝖌𝖔𝖗'𝖘 𝕲𝖆𝖙𝖍𝖊𝖗𝖎𝖓𝖌.

AIR—" *Thain' a Grigalach.*" [1]

WRITTEN FOR ALBYN'S ANTHOLOGY.

1816.

THESE verses are adapted to a very wild, yet lively gathering-
tune, used by the MacGregors.   The severe treatment of this
Clan, their outlawry, and the proscription of their very name,
are alluded to in the ballad. [2]

THE moon 's on the lake, and the mist 's on the brae,
And the clan has a name that is nameless by day ;
  Then gather, gather, gather Grigalach !
  Gather, gather, gather, &c.

Our signal for fight, that from monarchs we drew,
Must be heard but by night in our vengeful haloo !
  Then haloo, Grigalach ! haloo, Grigalach !
  Haloo, haloo, haloo, Grigalach, &c.

Glen Orchy's proud mountains, Coalchuirn and her towers,
Glenstrae and Glenlyon no longer are ours ;
  We 're landless, landless, landless, Grigalach !
  Landless, landless, landless, &c.

But doom'd and devoted by vassal and lord,
MacGregor has still both his heart and his sword !
  Then courage, courage, courage, Grigalach !
  Courage, courage, courage, &c.

[1] " The MacGregor is come."
[2] For the history of the clan, see Introduction to *Rob Roy, Waverley
Novels.* vol. iv.—ED.

If they rob us of name, and pursue us with beagles,
Give their roofs to the flame, and their flesh to the eagles!
    Then vengeance, vengeance, vengeance, Grigalach!
    Vengeance, vengeance, vengeance, &c.

While there's leaves in the forest, and foam on the river,
MacGregor, despite them, shall flourish for ever!
    Come then, Grigalach, come then, Grigalach,
    Come then, come then, come then, &c.

Through the depths of Loch Katrine the steed shall career,
O'er the peak of Ben-Lomond the galley shall steer,
And the rocks of Craig-Royston [1] like icicles melt,
Ere our wrongs be forgot, or our vengeance unfelt!
    Then gather, gather, gather, Grigalach!
    Gather, gather, gather, &c.

Verses,

COMPOSED FOR THE OCCASION, ADAPTED TO HAYDN'S AIR,

" God Save the Emperor Francis,"

**AND SUNG BY A SELECT BAND AFTER THE DINNER GIVEN BY
THE LORD PROVOST OF EDINBURGH TO THE**

GRAND-DUKE NICHOLAS OF RUSSIA, AND HIS SUITE,

19th DECEMBER 1816.

God protect brave ALEXANDER,
Heaven defend the noble Czar,
Mighty Russia's high Commander,
First in Europe's banded war!

[1] "Rob Roy MacGregor's own designation was of Innersnaid; but he appears to have acquired a right of *some kind or other to the property or possession* of Craig-Royston, a domain of rock and forest, lying on the east side of Loch Lomond, where that beautiful lake stretches into the dusky mountains of Glenfalloch."—*Introduction to Rob Roy, Waverley Novels*, vol. iv. p. 14.

For the realms he did deliver
From the tyrant overthrown,
Thou, of every good the Giver,
Grant him long to bless his own!
Bless him, 'mid his land's disaster,
For her rights who battled brave,
Of the land of foemen master,
Bless him who their wrongs forgave!

O'er his just resentment victor,
Victor over Europe's foes,
Late and long supreme director,
Grant in peace his reign may close!
Hail! then, hail! illustrious stranger!
Welcome to our mountain strand!
Mutual interests, hopes, and danger,
Link us with thy native land.
Freemen's force, or false beguiling,
Shall that union ne'er divide,
Hand in hand while peace is smiling,
And in battle side by side.[1]

The Search after Happiness;[2]

OR,

THE QUEST OF SULTAUN SOLIMAUN.

1817.

I.

O for a glance of that gay Muse's eye,
That lighten'd on Bandello's laughing tale,

[1] Mr., afterwards Sir William Arbuthnot, the Lord Provost of Edinburgh, who had the honour to entertain the Grand-Duke, now Emperor of Russia, was a personal friend of Sir Walter Scott's; and these *Verses*, with their heading, are now given from the newspapers of 1816.—ED. [1834.]

[2] First published in " The Sale Room, No. V." February 1, 1817.—ED.

And twinkled with a lustre shrewd and sly,
When Giam Battista bade her vision hail !—[1]
Yet fear not, ladies, the *naïve* detail
Given by the natives of that land canorous ;
Italian license loves to leap the pale,
We Britons have the fear of shame before us,
And, if not wise in mirth, at least must be decorous.

II.

In the far eastern clime, no great while since,
Lived Sultaun Solimaun, a mighty prince,
Whose eyes, as oft as they perform'd their round,
Beheld all others fix'd upon the ground ;
Whose ears received the same unvaried phrase,
"Sultaun ! thy vassal hears, and he obeys !"
All have their tastes—this may the fancy strike
Of such grave folks as pomp and grandeur like :
For me, I love the honest heart and warm
Of Monarch who can amble round his farm,
Or, when the toil of state no more annoys,
In chimney-corner seek domestic joys—
I love a Prince will bid the bottle pass,
Exchanging with his subjects glance and glass ;
In fitting time, can, gayest of the gay,
Keep up the jest, and mingle in the lay—
Such Monarchs best our free-born humours suit,
But Despots must be stately, stern, and mute.

III.

This Solimaun, Serendib had in sway—
And where is Serendib ? may some critic say.—
Good lack, mine honest friend, consult the chart,
Scare not my Pegasus before I start !
If Rennell has it not, you'll find, mayhap,
The isle laid down in Captain Sindbad's map,—
Famed mariner ! whose merciless narrations
Drove every friend and kinsman out of patience,

---

[1] The hint of the following tale is taken from *La Camiscia Magica,*
a Novel of Giam Battista Casti.

Till, fain to find a guest who thought them shorter,
He deign'd to tell them over to a porter—[1]
The last edition see, by Long. and Co.,
Rees, Hurst, and Orme, our fathers in the Row.

IV.

Serendib found,—deem not my tale a fiction,—
This Sultaun, whether lacking contradiction—
(A sort of stimulant which hath its uses,
To raise the spirits and reform the juices,
—Sovereign specific for all sort of cures
In my wife's practice, and perhaps in yours,)
The Sultaun lacking this same wholesome bitter,
Or cordial smooth, for Prince's palate fitter—
Or if some Mollah had hag-rid his dreams
With Degial, Ginnistan, and such wild themes
Belonging to the Mollah's subtle craft,
I wot not—but the Sultaun never laugh'd,
Scarce ate or drank, and took a melancholy
That scorn'd all remedy—profane or holy;
In his long list of melancholies, mad,
Or mazed, or dumb, hath Burton none so bad.[2]

V.

Physicians soon arrived, sage, ware, and tried,
    As e'er scrawl'd jargon in a darken'd room;
With heedful glance the Sultaun's tongue they eyed,
Peep'd in his bath, and God knows where beside,
    And then in solemn accent spoke their doom,
" His Majesty is very far from well."
Then each to work with his specific fell:
The Hakim Ibrahim *instanter* brought
His unguent Mahazzim al Zerdukkaut,
While Roompot, a practitioner more wily,
Relied on his Munaskif al fillfily.[3]
More and yet more in deep array appear,
And some the front assail, and some the rear;

[1] See the Arabian Nights' Entertainments.
[2] See Burton's Anatomy of Melancholy.
[3] For these hard words see D'Herbelot, or the learned editor of the
Recipes of Avicenna.

Their remedies to reinforce and vary,
Came surgeon eke, and eke apothecary ;
Till the tired Monarch, though of words grown chary,
Yet dropt, to recompense their fruitless labour,
Some hint about a bowstring or a sabre.
There lack'd, I promise you, no longer speeches
To rid the palace of those learned leeches.

VI.

Then was the council call'd ;—by their advice,
(They deem'd the matter ticklish all, and nice,
   And sought to shift it off from their own shoulders.)
Tartars and couriers in all speed were sent,
To call a sort of Eastern Parliament
   Of feudatory chieftains and freeholders—
Such have the Persians at this very day,
My gallant Malcolm calls them *couroultai;*—[1]
I 'm not prepared to show in this slight song
That to Serendib the same forms belong,—
E'en let the learn'd go search, and tell me if I 'm wrong

VII.

The Omrahs,[2] each with hand on scymitar,
Gave, like Sempronius, still their voice for war—
" The sabre of the Sultaun in its sheath
Too long has slept, nor own'd the work of death ;
Let the Tambourgi bid his signal rattle,
Bang the loud gong, and raise the shout of battle !
This dreary cloud that dims our Sovereign's day,
Shall from his kindled bosom flit away,
When the bold Lootie wheels his courser round,
And the arm'd elephant shall shake the ground.
Each noble pants to own the glorious summons—
And for the charges—Lo ! your faithful Commons !"
The Riots who attended in their places
   (Serendib language calls a farmer Riot)
Look'd ruefully in one another's faces,
   From this oration auguring much disquiet,

[1] See Sir John Malcolm's admirable History of Persia.   [2] Nobility

Double assessment, forage, and free quarters;
And fearing these as China-men the Tartars,
Or as the whisker'd vermin fear the mousers,
Each fumbled in the pocket of his trousers.

VIII.

And next came forth the reverend Convocation,
　　Bald heads, white beards, and many a turban green;
Imaum and Mollah there of every station,
　　Santon, Fakir, and Calendar were seen.
Their votes were various;—some advised a Mosque
　　With fitting revenues should be erected,
With seemly gardens and with gay Kiosque,
　　To recreate a band of priests selected;
Others opined that through the realms a dole
　　Be made to holy men, whoso prayers might profit
The Sultaun's weal in body and in soul.
　　But their long-headed chief, the Sheik Ul-Sofit,
More closely touch'd the point:—" Thy studious mood,"
Quoth he, " O Prince! hath thicken'd all thy blood,
And dull'd thy brain with labour beyond measure;
Wherefore relax a space, and take thy pleasure,
And toy with beauty, or tell o'er thy treasure;
From all the cares of state, my Liege, enlarge thee,
And leave the burden to thy faithful clergy."

IX.

These counsels sage availed not a whit,
　　And so the patient (as is not uncommon
Where grave physicians lose their time and wit)
　　Resolved to take advice of an old woman;
His mother she, a dame who once was beauteous,
And still was called so by each subject duteous.
Now, whether Fatima was witch in earnest,
　　Or only made believe, I cannot say—
But she profess'd to cure disease the sternest,
　　By dint of magic amulet or lay;
And, when all other skill in vain was shown,
She deem'd it fitting time to use her own.

X.

" *Sympathia magica* hath wonders done,"
(Thus did old Fatima bespeak her son,)
" It works upon the fibres and the pores,
And thus, insensibly, our health restores,
And it must help us here.—Thou must endure
The ill, my son, or travel for the cure.
Search land and sea, and get, where'er you can,
The inmost vesture of a happy man,
I mean his SHIRT, my son; which, taken warm
And fresh from off his back, shall chase your harm,
Bid every current of your veins rejoice,
And your dull heart leap light as shepherd-boy's."
Such was the counsel from his mother came;—
I know not if she had some under-game,
As Doctors have, who bid their patients roam
And live abroad, when sure to die at home;
Or if she thought, that, somehow or another,
Queen-Regent sounded better than Queen-Mother;
But, says the Chronicle (who will go look it,).
That such was her advice—the Sultaun took it

XI.

All are on board—the Sultaun and his train,
In gilded galley prompt to plough the main.
    The old Rais[1] was the first who questioned, "Whither?"
They paused—"Arabia," thought the pensive Prince,
" Was call'd The Happy many ages since—
    For Nokba, Rais."—And they came safely thither.
But not in Araby, with all her balm,
Not where Judea weeps beneath her palm,
Not in rich Egypt, not in Nubian waste,
Could there the step of happiness be traced.
One Copt alone profess'd to have seen her smile,
When Bruce his goblet fill'd at infant Nile:
She bless'd the dauntless traveller as he quaff'd,
But vanish'd from him with the ended draught.

---

    [1] Master of the vessel.

· XII.

" Enough of turbans," said the weary King;
" These dolimans of ours are not the thing:
Try we the Giaours; these men of coat and cap, I
Incline to think some of them must be happy;
At least, they have as fair a cause as any can,
They drink good wine, and keep no Ramazan.
Then northward, ho!"—The vessel cuts the sea,
And fair Italia lies upon her lee.—·
But fair Italia, she who once unfurl'd
Her eagle banners o'er a conquer'd world,
Long from her throne of domination tumbled,
Lay, by her quondam vassals sorely humbled;
The Pope himself look'd pensive, pale, and lean,
And was not half the man he once had been.
" While these the priest, and those the noble fleeces,
Our poor old boot,"[1] they said, " is torn to pieces.
Its tops[2] the vengeful claws of Austria feel,
And the Great Devil is rending toe and heel.[3]
If happiness you seek, to tell you truly,
We think she dwells with one Giovanni Bulli;
A tramontane, a heretic,—the buck,
Poffaredio! still has all the luck;
By land or ocean never strikes his flag—
And then—a perfect walking money-bag."
Off set our Prince to seek John Bull's abode,
But first took France—it lay upon the road.

XIII.

Monsieur Baboon, after much late commotion,
Was agitated like a settling ocean,
Quite out of sorts, and could not tell what ail'd him,
Only the glory of his house had fail'd him;
Besides, some tumours on his noddle biding,
Gave indication of a recent hiding.[4]

[1] The well-known resemblance of Italy in the map.

[2] Florence, Venice, &c.

[3] The Calabrias, infested by bands of assassins. One of the leaders was called Fra Diavolo, i. e. Brother Devil.

[4] Or drubbing; so called in the Slang Dictionary.

Our Prince, though Sultauns of such things are heedless,
Thought it a thing indelicate and needless
  To ask, if at that moment he was happy.
And Monsieur, seeing that he was *comme il faut*, a
Loud voice mustered up, for " *Vive le Roi!* "
  Then whisper'd, " Ave you any news of Nappy?"
The Sultaun answer'd him with a cross question,—
  "'Pray, can you tell me aught of one John Bull,
  That dwells somewhere beyond your herring-pool?"
The query seem'd of difficult digestion,
The party shrugg'd, and grinn'd, and took his snuff,
And found his whole good-breeding scarce enough.

XIV.

Twitching his visage into as many puckers
As damsels wont to put into their tuckers,
(Ere liberal Fashion damn'd both lace and lawn,
And bade the veil of modesty be drawn,)
Replied the Frenchman, after a brief pause,
" Jean Bool!—I vas not know him—Yes, I vas—
I vas remember dat, von year or two,
I saw him at von place call'd Vaterloo—
Ma foi! il s'est tres joliment battu,
Dat is for Englishman,—m'entendez-vous?
But den he had with him one damn son gun,
Rogue I no like—dey call him Vellington."
Monsieur's politeness could not hide his fret,
So Solimaun took leave, and cross'd the strait.

XV.

John Bull was in his very worst of moods,
Raving of sterile farms and unsold goods;
His sugar-loaves and bales about he threw,
And on his counter beat the devil's tattoo.
His wars were ended, and the victory won,
But then, 'twas reckoning-day with honest John;
And authors vouch, 'twas still this Worthy's way,
" Never to grumble till he came to pay;
And then he always thinks, his temper's such,
The work too little, and the pay to much."[1]

---

[1] See the *True-Born Englishman*, by Daniel De Foe.

Yet, grumbler as he is, so kind and hearty,
That when his mortal foe was on the floor,
And past the power to harm his quiet more,
    Poor John had wellnigh wept for Bonaparte !
Such was the wight whom Solimaun salam'd,—
" And who are you," John answer'd, " and be d—d ?"

XVI.

" A stranger, come to see the happiest man,—
So, signior, all avouch,—in Frangistan."—[1]
" Happy ?—my tenants breaking on my hand ;
Unstock'd my pastures, and untill'd my land ;
Sugar and rum a drug, and mice and moths
The sole consumers of my good broadcloths—
Happy ?—why, cursed war and racking tax
Have left us scarcely raiment to our backs."
" In that case, signior, I may take my leave ;
I came to ask a favour—but I grieve"——
" Favour ?" said John, and eyed the Sultaun hard.
" It 's my belief you come to break the yard !—
But, stay ; you look like some poor foreign sinner,—
Take that to buy yourself a shirt and dinner."—
With that he chuck'd a guinea at his head ;
But, with due dignity, the Sultaun said,
" Permit me, sir, your bounty to decline ;
A *shirt* indeed I seek, but none of thine.
Signior, I kiss your hands, so fare you well."—
" Kiss and be d—d," quoth John, " and go to hell !"

XVII.

Next door to John there dwelt his sister Peg,
Once a wild lass as ever shook a leg
When the blithe bagpipe blew—but, soberer now,
She *doucely* span her flax and milk'd her cow.
And whereas erst she was a needy slattern,
Nor now of wealth or cleanliness a pattern,
Yet once a-month her house was partly swept,
And once a-week a plenteous board she kept.

1 Europe.

And whereas, eke, the vixen used her claws
  And teeth, of yore, on slender provocation,
Sho now was grown amenable to laws,
  A quiet soul as any in the nation;
The sole remembrance of her warlike joys
Was in old songs she sang to please her boys.
John Bull, whom, in their years of early strife,
She wont to lead a cat-and-doggish life,
Now found the woman, as he said, a neighbour
Who look'd to the main chance, declined no labour,
Loved a long grace, and spoke a northern jargon,
And was d—d close in making of a bargain.

XVIII.

The Sultaun enter'd, and he made his leg,
And with decorum curtsy'd sister Peg;
(She loved a book, and knew a thing or two,
And guess'd at once with whom she had to do.")
She bade him "Sit into the fire," and took
Her dram, her cake, her kebbuck from the nook;
Ask'd him "about the news from Eastern parts,
And of her absent bairns, puir Highland hearts!
If peace brought down the price of tea and pepper.
And if the *nitmugs* were grown *ony* cheaper;—
Were there nae *speerings* of our Mungo Park—
Ye'll be the gentleman that wants the sark?
If ye wad buy a web o' auld wife's spinnin',
I'll warrant ye it's a weel-wearing linen."

XIX.

Then up got Peg, and round the house 'gan scuttle
  In search of goods her customer to nail,
Until the Sultaun strain'd his princely throttle,
  And hollo'd—" Ma'am, that is not what I ail.
Pray, are you happy, ma'am, in this snug glen?"—
"Happy?" said Peg; " what for d'ye want to ken?
Besides, just think upon this by-gane year,
  Grain wadna pay the yoking of the pleugh."—
" What say you to the present?"—" Meal's sae dear,
  To mak' their *brose* my bairns have scarce aneugh."—

"The devil take the shirt," said Solimaun,
" I think my quest will end as it began.—
Farewell, ma'am ; nay, no ceremony, I beg"———
" Ye'll no be for the linen then ?" said Peg,

XX.

Now for the land of verdant Erin
The Sultaun's royal bark is steering,
The Emerald Isle, where honest Paddy dwells,
The cousin of John Bull, as story tells.
For a long space had John, with words of thunder,
Hard looks, and harder knocks, kept Paddy under,
Till the poor lad, like boy that's flogg'd unduly,
Had gotten somewhat restive and unruly.
Hard was his lot and lodging, you'll allow,
A wigwam that would hardly serve a sow ;
His landlord, and of middle-men two brace,
Had screw'd his rent up to the starving-place ;
His garment was a top-coat, and an old one,
His meal was a potato, and a cold one ;
But still for fun or frolic, and all that,
In the round world was not the match of Pat.

XXI.

The Sultaun saw him on a holiday,
Which is with Paddy still a jolly day :
When mass is ended, and his load of sins
Confess'd, and Mother Church hath from her binns
Dealt forth a bonus of imputed merit,
Then is Pat's time for fancy, whim, and spirit !
To jest, to sing, to caper fair and free,
And dance as light as leaf upon the tree.
" By Mahomet !" said Sultaun Solimaun,
" That ragged fellow is our very man !
Rush in and seize him—do not do him hurt,
But, will he nill he, let me have his *shirt*."—

XXII.

Shilela their plan was wellnigh after baulking,
(Much less provocation will set it a-walking,)

But the odds that foil'd Hercules foil'd Paddy Whack :
They seized, and they floor'd, and they stripp'd him—Alack !
Up-bubboo ! Paddy had not —— a shirt to his back ! ! !
And the King, disappointed, with sorrow and shame,
Went back to Serendib as sad as he came.

Mr. Kemble's Farewell Address.[1]

ON TAKING LEAVE OF THE EDINBURGH STAGE,

1817.

As the worn war-horse, at the trumpet's sound,
Erects his mane, and neighs, and paws the ground—
Disdains the ease his generous lord assigns,
And longs to rush on the embattled lines,
So I, your plaudits ringing on mine ear,
Can scarce sustain to think our parting near ;
To think my scenic hour for ever past,
And that these valued plaudits are my last.

[1] These lines first appeared, April 5, 1817, in a weekly sheet, called the
"Sale Room," conducted and published by Messrs, Ballantyne and Co. at
Edinburgh. In a note prefixed, Mr. James Ballantyne says—"The character
fixed upon, with happy propriety, for Kemble's closing scene, was Macbeth,
in which he took his final leave of Scotland on the evening of Saturday, the
29th March 1817. He had laboured under a severe cold for a few days before, but on this memorable night the physical annoyance yielded to the
energy of his mind.—' He was,' he said in the green-room, immediately
before the curtain rose, ' determined to leave behind him the most perfect
specimen of his art which he had ever shown,' and his success was complete.
At the moment of the tyrant's death, the curtain fell by the universal
acclamation of the audience. The applauses were vehement and prolonged ;
they ceased—were resumed—rose again—were reiterated—and again were
hushed. In a few minutes the curtain ascended, and Mr. Kemble came
forward in the dress of Macbeth, (the audience by a consentaneous move-
ment rising to receive him,) to deliver his farewell." . . . . . . " Mr.
Kemble delivered these lines with exquisite beauty, and with an effect that
was evidenced by the tears and sobs of many of the audience. His own
emotions were very conspicuous. When his farewell was closed, he lingered
long on the stage, as if unable to retire. The house again stood up, and
cheered him with the waving of hats, and long shouts of applause. At
length, he finally retired, and, in so far as regards Scotland, the curtain
dropped upon his professional life for ever."—ED.

Why should we part, while still some powers remain,
That in your service strive not yet in vain?
Cannot high zeal the strength of youth supply,
And sense of duty fire the fading eye;
And all the wrongs of age remain subdued
Beneath the burning glow of gratitude?
Ah no!—the taper, wearing to its close,
Oft for a space in fitful lustre glows;
But all too soon the transient gleam is past—
It cannot be renew'd, and will not last;
Even duty, zeal, and gratitude, can wage
But short-lived conflict with the frosts of age.
Yes! it were poor, remembering what I was,
To live a pensioner on your applause,
To drain the dregs of your endurance dry,
And take, as alms, the praise I once could buy;
Till every sneering youth around inquires,
" Is this the man who once could please our sires?"
And scorn assumes compassion's doubtful mien,
To warn me off from the encumber'd scene.
This must'not be;—and higher duties crave
Some space between the theatre and the grave,
That, like the Roman in the Capitol,
I may adjust my mantle ere I fall:
My life's brief act in public service flown,
The last, the closing scene, must be my own.

Here, then, adieu! while yet some well-graced parts
May fix an ancient favourite in your hearts,
Not quite to be forgotten, even when
You look on better actors, younger men:
And if your bosoms own this kindly debt
Of old remembrance, how shall mine forget—
O, how forget!—how oft I hither came
In anxious hope, how oft return'd with fame!
How oft around your circle this weak hand
Has waved immortal Shakspeare's magic wand,
Till the full burst of inspiration came,
And I have felt, and you have fann'd the flame!
By mem'ry treasured, while her reign endures,
Those hours must live—and all their charms are yours.

O favour'd Land! renown'd for arts and arms,
For manly talent, and for female charms,
Could this full bosom prompt the sinking line,
What fervent benedictions now were thine!
But my last part is play'd, my knell is rung,
When e'en your praise falls faltering from my tongue;
And all that you can hear, or I can tell,
Is—Friends and Patrons, hail! and FARE YOU WELL!

Lines,[1]

WRITTEN FOR MISS SMITH,

1817.

WHEN the lone pilgrim views afar
The shrine that is his guiding star,
With awe his footsteps print the road
Which the loved saint of yore has trod.
As near he draws, and yet more near,
His dim eye sparkles with a tear;
The Gothic fane's unwonted show,
The choral hymn, the tapers' glow,
Oppress his soul; while they delight
And chasten rapture with affright.
No longer dare he think his toil
Can merit aught his patron's smile;
Too light appears the distant way,
The chilly eve, the sultry day—

---

[1] These lines were first printed in "The Forget-Me-Not, for 1834." They were written for recitation by the distinguished actress, Miss Smith, now Mrs. Bartley, on the night of her benefit at the Edinburgh Theatre, in 1817, but reached her too late for her purpose. In a letter which inclosed them, the poet intimated that they were written on the morning of the day on which they were sent—that he thought the idea better than the execution, and forwarded them with the hope of their adding perhaps "a little salt to the bill."—ED.

All these endured no favour claim,
But murmuring forth the sainted name,
He lays his little offering down,
And only deprecates a frown.

We, too, who ply the Thespian art,
Oft feel such bodings of the heart,
And, when our utmost powers are strain'd,
Dare hardly hope your favour gain'd.
She, who from sister climes has sought
The ancient land where Wallace fought —
Land long renown'd for arms and arts,
And conquering eyes and dauntless hearts,— [1]
She, as the flutterings *here* avow,
Feels all the pilgrim's terrors *now;*
Yet sure on Caledonian plain
The stranger never sued in vain.
'T is yours the hospitable task
To give the applause she dare not ask;
And they who bid the pilgrim speed,
The pilgrim's blessing be their meed.

The Sun upon the Weirdlaw Hill.

1817.

["Scott's enjoyment of his new territories was, however, interrupted by various returns of his cramp, and the depression of spirit which always attended, in his case, the use of opium, the only medicine that seemed to have power over the disease. It was while struggling with such languor, on one lovely evening of this autumn, that he composed the following beautiful verses. They mark the very spot of their birth,—namely, the then naked

[1] " O favour'd land! renown'd for arts and arms,
For manly talent, and for female charms."
Lines written for Mr. J. Kemble. — ED.

height overhanging the northern side of the Cauldshiels Loch, from which Melrose Abbey to the eastward, and the hills of Ettrick and Yarrow to the west, are now visible over a wide range of rich woodland,—all the work of the poet's hand."—*Life*, vol. v. p. 237.]

AIR—" Rimhin aluin 'stu mo run."

The air composed by the Editor of Albyn's Anthology.[1]   The words written for Mr. George Thomson's Scottish Melodies, [1822.]

THE sun upon the Weirdlaw Hill,
    In Ettrick's vale, is sinking sweet;
The westland wind is hush and still,
    The lake lies sleeping at my feet.
Yet not the landscape to mine eye
    Bears those bright hues that once it bore,
Though evening, with her richest dye,
    Flames o'er the hills of Ettrick's shore.

With listless look along the plain,
    I see Tweed's silver current glide,
And coldly mark the holy fane
    Of Melrose rise in ruin'd pride.
The quiet lake, the balmy air,
    The hill, the stream, the tower, the tree,—
Are they still such as once they were?
    Or is the dreary change in me?

Alas! the warp'd and broken board,
    How can it bear the painter's dye!
The harp of strain'd and tuneless chord,
    How to the minstrel's skill reply!
To aching eyes each landscape lowers,
    To feverish pulse each gale blows chill;
And Araby's or Eden's bowers
    Were barren as this moorland hill.

[1] " Nathaniel Gow told me that he got the air from an old gentleman, a Mr. Dalrymple of Orangefield (he thinks,) who had it from a friend in the Western Isles, as an old Highland air."—GEORGE THOMSON.

The Monks of Bangor's March.

AIR—" Ymdaith Mionge."

WRITTEN FOR MR. GEORGE THOMSON'S WELSH MELODIES,

1817.

ETHELFRID or OLFRID, King of Northumberland, having be-
sieged Chester in 613, and BROCKMAEL, a British Prince, advancing to relieve it, the religious of the neighbouring Monastery
of Bangor marched in procession, to pray for the success of their
countrymen.　But the British being totally defeated, the heathen
victor put the monks to the sword, and destroyed their Monastery.　The tune to which these verses are adapted is called the
Monks' March, and is supposed to have been played at their
ill-omened procession.

WHEN the heathen trumpet's clang
Round beleaguer'd Chester rang,
Veiled nun and friar grey
March'd from Bangor's fair Abbaye;
High their holy anthem sounds,
Cestria's vale the hymn rebounds,
Floating down the silvan Dee,
　　　　　　O miserere, Domine!

On the long procession goes,
Glory round their crosses glows,
And the Virgin-mother mild
In their peaceful banner smiled;
Who could think such saintly band
Doom'd to feel unhallow'd hand!
Such was the Divine decree,
　　　　　　O miserere, Domine!

Bands that masses only sung,
Hands that censers only swung,
Met the northern bow and bill,
Heard the war-cry wild and shrill:

Woe to Brocknael's feeble hand,
Woe to Olfrid's bloody brand,
Woe to Saxon cruelty,
          O miserere, Domine!

Weltering amid warriors slain,
Spurn'd by steeds with bloody mane,
Slaughter'd down by heathen blade,
Bangor's peaceful monks are laid:
Word of parting rest unspoke,
Mass unsung, and bread unbroke;
For their souls for charity,
          Sing, O miserere, Domine!

Bangor! o'er the murder wail!
Long thy ruins told the tale,
Shatter'd towers and broken arch
Long recall'd the woeful march:[1]
On thy shrine no tapers burn,
Never shall thy priests return;
The pilgrim sighs, and sings for thee,
          O miserere, Domine.

Epilogue to the Appeal.[2]

SPOKEN BY MRS. HENRY SIDDONS,

FEB. 16, 1818.

A CAT of yore (or else old Æsop lied)
Was changed into a fair and blooming bride,

---

[1] William of Malmsbury says, that in his time the extent of the ruins of the monastery bore ample witness to the desolation occasioned by the massacre;—"tot semiruti parietes ecclesiarum, tot anfractus porticum, tanta turba ruderum quantum vix alibi cernas."

[2] "The Appeal," a Tragedy, by John Galt, the celebrated author of the ' Annals of the Parish," and other Novels, was played for four nights at this time in Edinburgh.—ED.

But spied a mouse upon her marriage-day,
Forgot her spouse, and seized upon her prey ;
Even thus my bridegroom lawyer, as you saw,
Threw off poor me, and pounced upon papa.
His neck from Hymen's mystic knot made loose,
He twisted round my sire's the literal noose.
Such are the fruits of our dramatic labour
Since the New Jail became our next-door neighbour. [1]

Yes, times *are* changed ; for, in your fathers' age,
The lawyers were the patrons of the stage ;
However high advanced by future fate,
There stands the bench *(points to the Pit)* that first
        received their weight.
The future legal sage, 't was ours to see,
Doom though unwigg'd, and plead without a fee.

But now, astounding each poor mimic elf,
Instead of lawyers comes the law herself ;
Tremendous neighbour on our right she dwells,
Builds high her towers, and excavates her cells ;
While on the left she agitates the town,
With the tempestuous question, Up or down ? [2]
'Twixt Scylla and Charybdis thus stand we,
Law's final end, and law's uncertainty.
But soft ! who lives at Rome the Pope must flatter,
And jails and lawsuits are no jesting matter.
Then — just farewell !   We wait with serious awe
Till your applause or censure gives the law.
Trusting our humble efforts may assure ye,
We hold you Court and Counsel, Judge and Jury.

[1] It is necessary to mention, that the allusions in this piece are all local, and addressed only to the Edinburgh audience. The new prisons of the city, on the Calton Hill, are not far from the theatre.

[2] At this time the public of Edinburgh was was much agitated by a lawsuit betwixt the Magistrates and many of the Inhabitants of the City, concerning a range of new buildings on the western side of the North Bridge, which the latter insisted should be removed as a deformity. — Ed.

Mackrimmon's Lament.[1]

1818.

Air—"*Cha till mi tuille.*"[2]

Mackrimmon, hereditary piper to the Laird of Macleod, is said to have composed this Lament when the Clan was about to depart upon a distant and dangerous expedition. The Minstrel was impressed with a belief, which the event verified, that he was to be slain in the approaching feud; and hence the Gaelic words—"*Cha till mi tuille; ged thillis Macleod, cha till Mackrimmon,*"—"I shall never return; although Macleod returns, yet Mackrimmon shall never return!" The piece is but too well known, from its being the strain with which the emigrants from the West Highlands and Isles usually take leave of their native shore.

Macleod's wizard flag from the grey castle sallies,
The rowers are seated, unmoor'd are the galleys;
Gleam war-axe and broadsword, clang target and quiver,
As Mackrimmon sings, "Farewell to Dunvegan for ever!
Farewell to each cliff, on which breakers are foaming;
Farewell, each dark glen, in which red-deer are roaming;
Farewell, lonely Skye, to lake, mountain, and river;
Macleod may return, but Mackrimmon shall never!

"Farewell the bright clouds that on Quillan are sleeping;
Farewell the bright eyes in the Dun that are weeping;
To each minstrel delusion, farewell!—and for ever—
Mackrimmon departs, to return to you never!
The *Banshee's* wild voice sings the death-dirge before me,[3]
The pall of the dead for a mantle hangs o'er me;
But my heart shall not flag, and my nerves shall not shiver,
Though devoted I go—to return again never!

"Too oft shall the notes of Mackrimmon's bewailing
Be heard when the Gael on their exile are sailing;

[1] Written for Albyn's Anthology.　　　　[2] "We return no more."
[3] See a note on *Banshee*, Lady of the Lake, vol. iii.

Dear land ! to the shores, whence unwilling we sever,
Return—return—return shall we never !
 Cha till, cha till, cha till, sin tullie !
 Cha till, cha till, cha till, sin tullie,
 Cha till, cha till, cha till, sin tullie,
 Gea thilis Macleod, cha till Mackrimmon !"

Donald Caird's Come Again.[1]

AIR—" *Malcolm Caird's come again.*"[2]

1818.

CHORUS.

DONALD CAIRD 's *come again!*
Donald Caird's come again!
Tell the news in brugh and glen,
Donald Caird's come again!

Donald Caird can lilt and sing,
Blithely dance the Hieland fling,
Drink till the gudeman be blind,
Fleech till the gudewife be kind ;
Hoop a leglin, clout a pan,
Or crack a pow wi' ony man ;
Tell the news in brugh and glen,
Donald Caird 's come again.

Donald Caird's come again!
Donald Caird's come again!
Tell the news in brugh and glen,
Donald Caird's come again!

1 Written for Albyn's Anthology. vol. ii., 1818, and set to music in Mr
Thomson's Collection, in 1822.
  2 Caird signifies Tinker.

Donald Caird can wire a maukin,
Kens the wiles o' dun-deer staukin',
Leisters kipper, makes a shift
To shoot a muir-fowl in the drift;
Water-bailiffs, rangers, keepers,
He can wauk when they are sleepers;
Not for bountith or reward
Dare ye mell wi' Donald Caird.

> *Donald Caird's come again!*
> *Donald Caird's come again!*
> *Gar the bagpipes hum amain,*
> *Donald Caird's come again!*

Donald Caird can drink a gill
Fast as hostler-wife can fill;
Ilka ane that sells gude liquor
Kens how Donald bends a bicker;
When he's fou he's stout and saucy,
Keeps the cantle o' the causey;
Hieland chief and Lawland laird
Maun gie room to Donald Caird!

> *Donald Caird's come again!*
> *Donald Caird's come again!*
> *Tell the news in brugh and glen,*
> *Donald Caird's come again!*

Steek the aumrie, lock the kist,
Else some gear may weel be miss't;
Donald Caird finds orra things
Where Allan Gregor fand the tings;
Dunts of kebbuck, taits o' woo,
Whiles a hen, and whiles a sow,
Webs or duds frae hedge or yard—
'Ware the wuddie, Donald Caird!

> *Donald Caird's come again!*
> *Donald Caird's come again!*
> *Dinna let the Shirra ken*
> *Donald Caird's come again.*

On Donald Caird the doom was stern ---
Craig to tether, legs to airn ;
But Donald Caird, wi' mickle study,
Caught the gift to cheat the wuddie ;
Rings of airn, and bolts of steel,
Fell like ice frae hand and heel !
Watch the sheep in fauld and glen —
Donald Caird's come again !

Donald Caird's come again!
Donald Caird's come again!
Dinna let the Justice ken
Donald Caird's come again.[1]

Epitaph on Mrs. Erskine.[2]

1819.

PLAIN, as her native dignity of mind,
Arise the tomb of her we have resign'd ;
Unflaw'd and stainless be the marble scroll,
Emblem of lovely form and candid soul. —
But, oh ! what symbol may avail, to tell
The kindness, wit, and sense, we loved so well !
What sculpture show the broken ties of life,
Here buried with the parent, friend, and wife !
Or on the tablet stamp each title dear,
By which thine urn, EUPHEMIA, claims the tear !
Yet taught, by thy meek sufferance, to assume
Patience in anguish, hope beyond the tomb,
Resign'd though sad, this votive verse shall flow,
And brief, alas ! as thy brief span below.

[1] Mr. D. Thomson, of Galashiels, produced a parody on this song at an annual dinner of the manufacturers there, which Sir Walter Scott usually attended, and the Poet was highly amused with a sly allusion to his two-fold character of Sheriff of Selkirkshire, and *author-suspect* of "Rob Roy," in the chorus—   "*Think ye, does the Shirra ken*
      Rob M'Gregor's come again ? "—ED.

[2] Mrs. Euphemia Robison, wife of William Erskine, Esq. (afterwards Lord Kinnedder,) died September 1819, and was buried at Saline, in the county of Fife, where these lines are inscribed on the tombstone.—ED.

On Ettrick Forest's Mountains Dun.[1]

1822.

On Ettrick Forest's mountains dun,
'Tis blithe to hear the sportsman's gun,
And seek the heath-frequenting brood
Far through the noonday solitude;
By many a cairn and trenched mound,
Where chiefs of yore sleep lone and sound,
And springs, where grey-hair'd shepherds tell,
That still the fairies love to dwell.

Along the silver streams of Tweed,
'Tis blithe the mimic fly to lead,
When to the hook the salmon springs,
And the line whistles through the rings ;
The boiling eddy see him try,
Then dashing from the current high,
Till watchful eye and cautious hand
Have led his wasted strength to land.

'Tis blithe along the midnight tide,
With stalwart arm the boat to guide;
On high the dazzling blaze to rear,
And heedful plunge the barbed spear;
Rock, wood, and scaur, emerging bright,
Fling on the stream their ruddy light,
And from the bank our band appears
Like Genii, arm'd with fiery spears.[2]

'Tis blithe at eve to tell the tale,
How we succeed, and how we fail,

---

[1] Written after a week's shooting and fishing, in which the poet had been engaged with some friends. The reader may see these verses set to music in Mr. Thomson's Scottish Melodies for 1822. — ED.

[2] See the famous salmon-spearing scene in *Guy Mannering.* — *Waverley Novels*, vol. iii. p. 259-63. — ED.

Whether at Alywn's[1] lordly meal,
Or lowlier board of Ashestiel;[4]
While the gay tapers cheerly shine,
Bickers the fire, and flows the wine—
Days free from thought, and nights from care,
My blessing on the Forest fair!

Farewell to the Muse [3]

1822.

ENCHANTRESS, farewell, who so oft has decoy'd me,
    At the close of the evening through woodlands to roam,
Where the forester, lated, with wonder espied me
    Explore the wild scenes he was quitting for home.
Farewell! and take with thee thy numbers wild speaking
    The language alternate of rapture and woe:
Oh! none but some lover, whose heart-strings are breaking,
    The pang that I feel at our parting can know.

Each joy thou couldst double,—and when there came sorrow,
    Or pale disappointment, to darken my way,
What voice was like thine, that could sing of to-morrow,
    Till forgot in the strain was the grief of to-day!
But when friends drop around us in life's weary waning,
    The grief, Queen of Numbers, thou canst not assuage;
Nor the gradual estrangement of those yet remaining,
    The languor of pain, and the chillness of age.

'Twas thou that once taught me, in accents bewailing,
    To sing how a warrior lay stretch'd on the plain,

---

[1] *Alwyn*, the seat of the Lord Somerville; now, alas! untenanted, by the lamented death of that kind and hospitable nobleman, the author's nearest neighbour and intimate friend. Lord S. died in February 1819.—ED.

[2] *Ashestiel*, the poet's residence at that time.—ED.

[3] Written, during illness, for Mr. Thomson's Scottish Collection, and first published in 1822, united to an air composed by George Kinloch of Kinloch, Esq.—ED.

And a maiden hung o'er him with aid unavailing,
  And held to his lips the cold goblet in vain :
As vain thy enchantments, O Queen of wild Numbers,
  To a bard when the reign of his fancy is o'er,
And the quick pulse of feeling in apathy slumbers—
  Farewell, then, Enchantress! I meet thee no more!

The Maid of Isla.

Air—" *The Maid of Isla.*"

WRITTEN FOR MR. GEORGE THOMSON'S SCOTTISH MELODIES.

1822.

Oh, Maid of Isla, from the cliff,
  That looks on troubled wave and sky,
Dost thou not see yon little skiff
  Contend with ocean gallantly?
Now beating 'gainst the breeze and surge,
  And steep'd her leeward deck in foam,
Why does she war unequal urge?—
  Oh, Isla's maid, she seeks her home!

Oh, Isla's maid, yon sea-bird mark;
  Her white wing gleams through mist and spray
Against the storm-cloud, lowering dark,
  As to the rock she wheels away;—
Where clouds are dark, and billows rave,
  Why to the shelter should she come
Of cliff, exposed to wind and wave?—
  Oh, maid of Isla, 'tis her home!

As breeze and tide to yonder skiff,
  Thou 'rt adverse to the suit I bring,
And cold as is yon wintry cliff,
  Where sea-birds close their wearied wing.

> Yet cold as rock, unkind as wave,
>   Still, Isla's maid, to thee I come;
> For in thy love, or in his grave,
>   Must Allan Vourich find his home!

Carle, now the King's come.[1]

BEING NEW WORDS TO AN AULD SPRING.

1822.

THE news has flown frae mouth to mouth,
The North for ance has bang'd the South;
The deil a Scotsman's die o' drouth,
         Carle, now the King's come!

CHORUS.
Carle, now the King's come!
Carle, now the King's come!
Thou shalt dance, and I will sing,
         Carle, now the King's come!

Auld England held him lang and fast;
And Ireland had a joyfu' cast;
But Scotland's turn is come at last—
         Carle, now the King's come!

Auld Reekie, in her rokelay grey,
Thought never to have seen the day;
He's been a weary time away—
         But, Carle, now the King's come!

She's skirling frae the Castle-hill;
The Carline's voice is grown sae shrill,
Ye'll hear her at the Canon-mill—
         Carle, now the King's come!

[1] This imitation of an old Jacobite ditty was written on the appearance,
in the Frith of Forth, of the fleet which conveyed his Majesty King George
the Fourth to Scotland, in August 1822; and was published as a broadside.
—ED.

" Up, bairns !" she cries, " baith grit and sma',
    And busk ye for the weapon-shaw !
    Stand by me, and we 'll bang them a'—
            Carle, now the King 's come !

" Come from Newbattle's ancient spires,
    Bauld Lothian, with your knights and squires,
    And match the mettle of your sires —
            Carle, now the King 's come !

" You 're welcome hame, my Montagu !
    Bring in your hand the young Buccleuch ;
    I 'm missing some that I may rue —
            Carle, now the King 's come ![1]

" Come, Haddington, the kind and gay,
    You 've graced my causeway mony a day ;
    I 'll weep the cause if you should stay—
            Carle, now the King 's come ![2]

" Come, premier Duke,[3] and carry doun
    Frae yonder craig[4] his ancient croun ;
    It 's had a lang sleep and a soun'—
            But, Carle, now the King 's come !

" Come, Athole, from the hill and wood,
    Bring down your clansmen like a clud ;
    Come, Morton, show the Douglas' blood,—[5]
            Carle, now the King 's come !

" Come, Tweeddale, true as sword to sheath ;
    Come, Hopetoun, fear'd on fields of death ;

[1] Lord Montagu, uncle and guardian to the young Duke of Buccleuch, placed his Grace's residence of Dalkeith at his Majesty's disposal during his visit to Scotland. — ED.

[2] Charles, the tenth Earl of Haddington, died in 1828.

[3] The Duke of Hamilton, as Earl of Angus, carried the ancient royal crown of Scotland on horseback, in King George's procession, from Holyrood to the Castle. — ED.   [4] The Castle.

[5] MS.—" Come, Athole, from your hills and woods,
            Bring down your Hielandmen in cluds,
            With bannet, brogue, and tartan duds."

Come, Clerk,[1] and give your bugle breath ;
  Carle, now the King's come !

" Come, Wemyss, who modest merit aids ;
Come, Rosebery, from Dalmeny shades ;
Breadalbane, bring your belted plaids ;
  Carle, now the King's come !

" Come, stately Niddrie, auld and true,
Girt with the sword that Minden knew ;
We have o'er few such lairds as you—
  Carle, now the King's come !

" King Arthur's grown a common crier,
He's heard in Fife and far Cantire,—
' Fie, lads, behold my crest of fire !'[2]
  Carle, now the King's come !

" Saint Abb roars out, ' I see him pass,
Between Tantallon and the Bass !'
Calton, get your keeking-glass—
  Carle, now the King's come !"

The Carline stopp'd ; and, sure I am,
For very glee had ta'en a dwam,
But Oman[3] help'd her to dram—
  Cogie, now the King's come !

  Cogie, now the King's come !
  Cogie, now the King's come !

[1] Sir George Clerk of Pennycuik, Bart. The Baron of Pennycuik is bound by his tenure, whenever the King comes to Edinburgh, to receive him at the Harestone (in which the standard of James IV. was erected when his army encamped on the Boroughmuir, before his fatal expedition to England), now built into the park-wall at the end of Tipperlin Lone, near the Borough-muir-head ; and, standing thereon, to give three blasts on a horn.—ED.

[2] MS.—" Brave Arthur Seat's a story higher ;
  Saint Abbe is shouting to Kintire,—
  ' You Lion, light up a crest of fire.'"
As seen from the west, the ridge of Arthur's Seat bears a marked resemblance to a lion couchant.—ED.

[3] Mr. Oman, landlord of the Waterloo Hotel.

I 'se be fou' and ye 's be toom,[1]
Cogie, now the King 's come!

CARLE, NOW THE KING'S COME.

PART SECOND.

A HAWICK gill of mountain dew
Heised up Auld Reekie's heart, I trow;
It minded her of Waterloo—
          Carle, now the King 's come!

Again I heard her summons swell,
For, sic a dirdum and a yell,
It drown'd Saint Giles's jowing bell—
          Carle, now the King 's come!

" My trusty Provost, tried and tight,
Stand forward for the Good Town's right,
There 's waur than you been made a knight—[2]
          Carle, now the King 's come!

" My reverend Clergy, look ye say
The best of thanksgivings ye ha'e,
And warstle for a sunny day—
          Carle, now the King 's come!

" My Doctors, look that you agree,
Cure a' the town without a fee;
My Lawyers, dinna pike a plea—
          Carle, now the King 's come!

" Come forth, each sturdy Burgher's bairn,
That dints on wood, or clanks on airn,

---

[1] Empty.
[2] The Lord Provost had the agreeable surprise to hear his health proposed, at the civic banquet given to George IV. in the Parliament-ꝰ as " Sir William Arbuthnot, Bart."—ED.

That fires the o'en, or winds the pirn —
    Carle, now the King 's come !

" Come forward with the Blanket Blue ;[1]
Your sires were loyal men and true,
As Scotland's foemen oft might rue —
    Carle, now the King 's come !

" Scots downa loup, and rin, and rave —
We 're steady folks, and something grave ;
We 'll keep the causeway firm and brave —
    Carle, now the King 's come !

" Sir Thomas,[2] thunder from your rock,[3]
Till Pentland dinnles wi' the shock,
And lace wi' fire my snood o' smoke —
    Carle, now the King 's come !

" Melville, bring out your bands of blue,
A' Louden lads, baith stout and true,
With Elcho, Hope, and Cockburn, too —[4]
    Carle, now the King 's come !

[1] The Blue Blanket is the standard of the Incorporated Trades of Edinburgh, and is kept by their Convener, " at whose appearance therewith," observes Maitland, " 'tis said, that not only the artificers of Edinburgh are obliged to repair to it, but all the artificers or craftsmen within Scotland are bound to follow it, and fight under the Convener of Edinburgh as aforesaid." According to an old tradition, this standard was used in the Holy Wars by a body of crusading citizens of Edinburgh, and was the first that was planted on the walls of Jerusalem, when that city was stormed by the Christian army under the famous Godfrey. But the real history of it seems to be this:—James III., a prince who had virtues which the rude age in which he lived could not appreciate, having been detained for nine months in the Castle of Edinburgh by his factious nobles, was relieved by the citizens of Edinburgh, who assaulted the castle and took it by surprise; on which occasion James presented the citizens with this banner, " with a power to display the same in defence of their king, country, and their own rights."—*Note to this stanza in the "Account of the King's Visit,"* &c. 8vo. 1822.

[2] Sir Thomas Bradford, then Commander of the Forces in Scotland.

[3] Edinburgh Castle.

[4] Lord Melville was Colonel of the Mid-Lothian Yeomanry Cavalry: Sir Sir John Hope of Pinkie, Bart., Major; and Robert Cockburn, Esq., and Lord Elcho, were Captains in the same corps, to which Sir Walter Scott had formerly belonged. — ED

" And you, who on yon bluidy braes
　　Compell'd the vanquish'd Despot's praise,
　　Rank out—rank out—my gallant Greys—[1]
　　　　Carle, now the King 's come !

" Cock o' the North, my Huntly bra',
　　Where are you with the Forty-twa ?[2]
　　Ah ! wae 's my heart that ye 're awa'—
　　　　Carle, now the King 's Come !

" But yonder come my canty Celts,
　　With durk and pistols at their belts :
　　Thank God, we 've still some plaids and kilts---
　　　　Carle, now the King 's come!

" Lord, how the pibrochs groan and yell !
　　Macdonnell 's [3] ta'en the field himsell ;
　　Macleod comes branking o'er the fell—
　　　　Carle, now the King 's come !

" Bend up your bow, each Archer spark,
　　For you 're to guard him, light and dark ;
　　Faith, lads, for ance ye 've hit the mark—
　　　　Carle, now the King 's come !

" Young Errol,[4] take the sword of state,
　　The sceptre, Panie-Morarchate ;[5]

[1] The Scots Greys, headed by their gallant Colonel, General Sir James Stewart of Coltness, Bart., were on duty at Edinburgh during the King's visit. Bonaparte's exclamation at Waterloo is well known: " Ces beaux chevaux gris, comme ils travaillent !"—ED.

[2] Marquis of Huntly, who since became the last Duke of Gordon, was Colonel of the 42d Regiment, and died in 1836.

[3] Colonel Ronaldson Macdonell of Glengarry—who died in January 1828.

[4] The Earl of Errol is hereditary Lord High-Constable of Scotland.

[5] In more correct Gaelic orthography, *Banamhorar-Chat*, or the Great Lady, (literally *Female Lord of the Chatte*), the Celtic title of the Countess of Sutherland. "Evin unto this day, the countrey of Sutherland is yet called Cattey, the inhabitants Catteigh, and the Earl of Sutherland Mor-weir Cattey, in old Scottish or Irish ; which language the inhabitants of this countrey doe still use."—GORDON's *Genealogical History of the Earls of Sutherland*, p. 18. It was determined by his Majesty, that the right of

Knight Mareschal,[6] see ye clear the gate —
    Carle, now the King's come !

" Kind cummer, Leith, ye've been mis-set,
  But dinna be upon the fret —
  Ye'se hae the hansel of him yet,
    Carle, now the King's come !

" My daughters, come with een sae blue,
  Your garlands weave, your blossoms strew ;
  He ne'er saw fairer flowers than you —
    Carle, now the King's come !

" What shall we do for the propine ?——
  We used to offer something fine,
  But ne'er a groat's in pouch of mine —
    Carle, now the King's come !

" Deil care — for that I'se never start,
  We'll welcome him with Highland heart ;
  Whate'er we have he's get a part —
    Carle, now the King's come !

" I'll show him mason-work this day —
  Nane of your bricks of Babel clay,
  But towers shall stand till Time's away —
    Carle, now the King's come !

" I'll show him wit, I'll show him lair,
  And gallant lads and lasses fair,
  And what wad kind heart wish for mair ? —
    Carle, now the King's come !

---

carrying the sceptre lay with this noble family ; and Lord Francis Leveson
Gower, (now Egerton,) second son of the Countess (afterwards Duchess) of
Sutherland, was permitted to act as deputy for his mother in that honour-
able office. After obtaining his Majesty's permission to depart for Dunrobin
Castle, his place was supplied by the Honourable John M. Stuart, second
son of the Earl of Moray. — ED.

6 The Author's friend and relation, the late Sir Alexander Keith, of Dun-
ottar and Ravelstone. — ED.

"Step out, Sir John,[1] of projects rife,
Come win the thanks of an auld wife,
And bring him health and length of life—
        Carle, now the King's come!"

The Bannatyne Club.[2]

1823.

I.

ASSIST me, ye friends of Old Books and Old Wine,
To sing in the praises of sage Bannatyne,
Who left such a treasure of old Scottish lore
As enables each age to print one volume more.
        One volume more, my friends, one volume more,
        We'll ransack old Banny for one volume more.

II.

And first, Allan Ramsay, was eager to glean
From Bannatyne's *Hortus* his bright Evergreen;
Two light little volumes (intended for four)
Still leave us the task to print one volume more.
        One volume more, &c.

III.

His ways were not ours, for he cared not a pin
How much he left out, or how much he put in;
The truth of the reading he thought was a bore,
So this accurate age calls for one volume more.
        One volume more, &c.

---

[1] MS.—"Rise up, Sir John, of projects rife,
        And wuss him health and length of life,
        And win the thanks of an auld wife."
The Right Honourable Sir John Sinclair, Bart., author of "The Code of
Health and Longevity," &c. &c.,—the well-known patron and projector of
national and patriotic plans and improvements innumerable, died 21st December 1835, in his eighty-second year.—ED.

[2] Sir Walter Scott was the first President of the Club, and wrote these
verses for the anniversary dinner of March 1823.—See *Life*, vol. vii. p. 137.

IV.

Correct and sagacious, then came my Lord Hailes,
And weigh'd every letter in critical scales,
But left out some brief words, which the prudish abhor,
And castrated Banny in one volume more.
>One volume more, my friends, one volume more:
>We'll restore Banny's manhood in one volume more.

V.

John Pinkerton next,—and I'm truly concern'd
I can't call that worthy so candid as learn'd;
He rail'd at the plaid, and blasphemed the claymore,
And set Scots by the ears in his one volume more.
>One volume more, my friends, one volume more,
>Celt and Goth shall be pleased with one volume more.

VI.

As bitter as gall, and as sharp as a razor,
And feeding on herbs as a Nebuchadnezzar;[1]
His diet too acid, his temper too sour,
Little Ritson came out with his two volumes more,[2]
>But one volume, my friends, one volume more,
>We'll dine on roast-beef, and print one volume more.

VII.

The stout Gothic yeditur, next on the roll,[3]
With his beard like a brush and as black as a coal;
And honest Greysteel[4] that was true to the core,
Lent their hearts and their hands each to one volume more.
>One volume more, &c.

[1] In accordance with his own regimen, Mr. Ritson published a volume entitled, "An Essay on Abstinence from Animal Food as a Moral Duty, 1802."

[2] See an account of the Metrical Antiquarian Researches of Pinkerton, Ritson, and Herd, &c. in the Introductory Remarks on Popular Poetry, in Vol. VI., *post.*

[3] James Sibbald, editor of Scottish Poetry, &c. "The Yeditur" was the name given him by the late Lord Eldin, then Mr. John Clerk, advocate. The description of him here is very accurate.

[4] David Herd, editor of Songs and Historical Ballads, 2 vols. He was called Greysteel by his intimates, from having been long in unsuccessful quest of the romance of that name.—Ed.

VIII.

Since by these single champions what wonders were done,
What may not be achieved by our thirty and one?
Law, Gospel, and Commerce, we count in our corps,
And the Trade and the Press join for one volume more.
         One volume more, &c.

IX.

Ancient libels and contraband books, I assure ye,
We'll print as secure from Exchequer or Jury;
Then hear your Committee and let them count o'er
The Chiels they intend in their three volumes more.
         Three volumes more, &c.

X.

They'll produce you King Jamie, the sapient and Sext,
And the Rob of Dumblane and her Bishops come next;
One tome miscellaneous they'll add to your store,
Resolving next year to print four volumes more.
         Four volumes more, my friends, four volumes more;
         Pay down your subscriptions for four volumes more.

This Club was instituted in the year 1822, for the publication or reprint of rare and curious works connected with the history and antiquities of Scotland. It consisted, at first, of a very few members,—gradually extended to one hundred, at which number it has now made a final pause. They assume the name of the Bannatyne Club from George Bannatyne, of whom little is known beyond that prodigious effort which produced his present honours, and is, perhaps, one of the most singular instances of its kind which the literature of any country exhibits. His labours as an amanuensis were undertaken during the time of pestilence, in 1568. The dread of infection had induced him to retire into solitude, and under such circumstances he had the energy to form and execute the plan of saving the literature of the whole nation; and, undisturbed by the general mourning for the dead, and general fears of the living, to devote himself to the task of collecting and recording the triumphs of human genius in the poetry of his age and country;—thus, amid the wreck of all that was mortal, employing himself in preserving the lays by which immortality is at once given to others, and obtained for the writer himself. He informs us of some of the numerous difficulties he had to contend with in this self-imposed task. The volume containing his labours, deposited in the Library of the Faculty of Advocates at Edinburgh, is no less than eight hundred pages in length, and very neatly and closely written, containing nearly all the ancient poetry of Scotland now known to exist.

This Caledonian association, which boasts several names of distinction, both from rank and talent, has assumed rather a broader foundation than the parent society, the Roxburghe Club in London, which, in its plan, being restricted to the reprinting of single tracts, each executed at the expense of an individual member, it follows as almost a necessary consequence, that no volume of considerable size has emanated from it, and its range has been thus far limited in point of utility. The Bannatyne, holding the same system with respect to the ordinary species of club reprints, levies, moreover, a fund among its members of about £500 a-year, expressly to be applied for the editing and printing of works of acknowledged importance, and likely to be attended with expense beyond the reasonable bounds of an individual's contribution. In this way either a member of the Club, or a competent person under its patronage, superintends a particular volume, or set of volumes. Upon these occasions, a very moderate number of copies are thrown off for general sale; and those belonging to the Club are only distinguished from the others by being printed on the paper, and ornamented with the decorations peculiar to the Society. In this way several useful and eminently valuable works have recently been given to the public for the first time, or at least with a degree of accuracy and authenticity which they had never before attained.—*Abridged from the Quarterly Review—*Art. *Pitcairn's Ancient Criminal Trials. February* 1831.

Lines,

ADDRESSED TO MONSIEUR ALEXANDRE,[1] THE CELBRATED VENTRILOQUIST.

1824.

Of yore, in old England, it was not thought good
To carry two visages under one hood;
What should folk say to *you?* who have faces such plenty,
That from under one hood, you last night show'd us twenty!

[1] " *When Monsieur Alexandre, the celebrated ventriloquist, was in Scotland, in 1824, he paid a visit to Abbotsford, where he entertained his distinguished host, and the other visiters, with his unrivalled imitations. Next morning, when he was about to depart, Sir Walter felt a good deal embarrassed as to the sort of acknowledgment he should offer; but at length, resolving that it would probably be most agreeable to the young foreigner to be paid in professional coin, if in any, he stepped aside for a few minutes, and, on returning, presented him with this epigram. The reader need hardly be reminded that Sir Walter Scott held the office of Sheriff of the county of Selkirk.*"—Scotch newspaper, 1830

Stand forth, arch deceiver, and tell us in truth,
Are you handsome or ugly, in age or in youth?
Man, woman, or child—a dog or a mouse?
Or are you, at once, each live thing in the house?
Each live thing, did I ask?—each dead implement, too,
A work-shop in your person,—saw, chisel, and screw!
Above all, are you one individual? I know
You must be at least Alexandre and Co.
But I think you're a troop—an assemblage—a mob,
And that I, as the Sheriff, should take up the job;
And instead of rehearsing your wonders in verse,
Must read you the Riot-Act, and bid you disperse.

ABBOTSFORD, *23d April.*[1]

Epilogue

TO THE DRAMA FOUNDED ON " ST. RONAN'S WELL."

1824.

" AFTER the play, the following humorous address (ascribed
to an eminent literary character) was spoken with infinite effect
by Mr. Mackay in the character of MEG DODS."—*Edinburgh
Weekly Journal, 9th June* 1824.

Enter MEG DODS, *encircled by a crowd of unruly boys,
whom a Town's Officer is driving off.*

THAT's right, friend—drive the gaitlings back,
And lend yon muckle ane a whack;
Your Embro' bairns are grown a pack
    Sae proud and saucy,
They scarce will let an auld wife walk
    Upon your causey.

[1] The lines, with this date, appeared in the Edinburgh Annual Register
of 1824.

I 've seen the day they would been scaur'd
Wi' the Tolbooth, or wi' the Guard,
Or maybe wud hae some regard
        For Jamie Laing—[1]
The Water-hole [2] was right well wared
        On sic a gang.

But whar 's the gude Tolbooth [3] gane now?
Whar 's the auld Claught, [4] wi' red and blue?
Whar 's Jamie Laing? and whar 's John Doo? [5]
        And whar 's the Weigh-house? [6]
Deil hae 't I see but what is new,
        Except the Playhouse.

Yoursells are changed frae head to heel:
There 's some that gar the causeway reel
With clashing hufe and rattling wheel,
        And horses canterin',
Wha's fathers daunder'd hame as weel
        Wi' lass and lantern.

Mysell being in the public line,
I look for howfs I kenn'd lang syne,
Whar gentles used to drink gude wine,
        And eat cheap dinners;
But deil a soul gangs there to dine,
        Of saunts or sinners!

---

[1] James Laing was one of the Depute-Clerks of the city of Edinburgh, and in his official connexion with the Police and the Council-Chamber, his name was a constant terror to evil doers. He died in February 1806.

[2] The Watch-hole.

[3] The Tolbooth of Edinburgh, The Heart of Mid-Lothian, was pulled down in 1817.

[4] The ancient Town Guard. The reduced remnant of this body of police was finally disbanded in 1817.

[5] John Doo, or Dhu—a terrific-looking and high-spirited member of the Town Guard, and of whom there is a print by Kay, etched in 1784.

[6] The Weigh-House, situated at the head of the West Bow, Lawnmarket, and which had long been looked upon as an encumbrance to the street, was demolished in order to make way for the royal procession to the Castle, which took place on the 22d of August 1822.—ED.

Fortune's [1] and Hunter's [2] gane, alas!
And Bayle's [3] is lost in empty space;
And now, if folk would splice a brace,
    Or crack a bottle,
They gang to a new-fangled place
    They ca' a Hottle.

The deevil hottle them for Meg!
They are sae greedy and sae gleg,
That if ye're served but wi' an egg,
    (And that's puir pickin',)
In comes a chiel, and makes a leg,
    And charges chicken!

" And wha may ye be," gin ye speer,
" That brings your auld-warld clavers here!"
Troth, if there's onybody near
    That kens the roads,
I'll haud ye Burgundy to beer,
    He kens Meg Dods.

I came a piece frae west o' Currie;
And, since I see you're in a hurry,
Your patience I'll nae langer worry,
    But be sae crouse
As speak a word for ane Will Murray, [4]
    That keeps this house.

Plays are auld-fashion'd things, in truth,
And ye've seen wonders mair uncouth;

1 Fortune's Tavern—a house on the west side of the Old Stamp-Office Close, High Street, and which was, in the early part of the last century, the mansion of the Earl of Eglintoun.—The Lord High Commissioner to the General Assembly of the day held his levees and dinners in this tavern.

2 Hunter's—another once much-frequented tavern, in Writer's Court, Royal Exchange.

3 Bayle's Tavern and Coffeehouse, originally on the North Bridge, east side, afterwards in Shakspeare Square, but removed to admit of the opening of Waterloo Place. Such was the dignified character of this house, that the waiter always appeared in full dress, and nobody was admitted who had not a white neckcloth—then considered an indispensable insignium of a gentleman.

4 Mr. William Murray became Manager of the Edinburgh Theatre in 1815. —ED.

Yet actors shouldna suffer drouth,
   Or want of dramock,
Although they speak but wi' their mouth,
   Not with their stamock.

But ye take care of a' folk's pantry;
And surely to hae stooden sentry
Ower this big house, (that's far frae rent-free,)
   For a lone sister,
Is claim as gude's to be a ventri—
   How 'st ca'd—loquister.

Weel, sirs, gude-e'en, and have a care
The bairns mak fun o' Meg nae mair;
For gin they do, she tells you fair,
   And without failzie,
As sure as ever ye sit there,
   She'll tell the Bailie.

Epilogue.[1]

1824.

THE sages—for authority, pray look
Seneca's morals, or the copy-book—
The sages, to disparage woman's power,
Say, beauty is a fair but fading flower;—
I cannot tell—I've small philosophy—
Yet, if it fades, it does not surely die,
But, like the violet, when decay'd in bloom,
Survives through many a year in rich perfume.
Witness our theme to-night;—two ages gone,
A third wanes fast, since Mary fill'd the throne.

[1] "I recovered the above with some difficulty. I believe it was never spoken, but written for some play, afterwards withdrawn, in which Mrs. H. Siddons was to have spoken it in the character of Queen Mary."—*Extract from a Letter of Sir Walter Scott to Mr. Constable, 22d October 1824.*

Brief was her bloom, with scarce one sunny day,
 Twixt Pinkie's field and fatal Fotheringay:
But when, while Scottish hearts and blood you boast,
Shall sympathy with Mary's woes be lost?
O'er Mary's mem'ry the learn'd quarrel,
By Mary's grave the poet plants his laurel,
Time's echo, old tradition, makes her name
The constant burden of his fault'ring theme;
In each old hall his grey-hair'd heralds tell
Of Mary's picture, and of Mary's cell,
And show—my fingers tingle at the thought—
The loads of tapestry which that poor Queen wrought,
In vain did fate bestow a double dower
Of ev'ry ill that waits on rank and pow'r,
Of ev'ry ill on beauty that attends—
False ministers, false lovers, and false friends.
Spite of three wedlocks, so completely curst,
They rose in ill, from bad to worse, and worst,
In spite of errors—I dare not say more,
For Duncan Targe lays hand on his claymore.
In spite of all, however humours vary,
There is a talisman in that word Mary,
That unto Scottish bosoms all and some
Is found the genuine *open sesamum!*
In history, ballad, poetry, or novel,
It charms alike the castle and the hovel;
Even you—forgive me—who, demure and shy,
Gorge not each bait, nor stir at every fly,
Must rise to this, else in her ancient reign
The Rose of Scotland has survived in vain.

The Foray.[1]

SET TO MUSIC BY JOHN WHITEFIELD, MUS. DOC. CAM.

1830.

THE last of our steers on the board has been spread,
And the last flask of wine in our goblet is red;

1 Set to music in Mr. Thomson's Scottish Collection, 1830.

Up! up, my brave kinsmen! belt swords, and begone!—
There are dangers to dare, and there's spoil to be won.

The eyes, that so lately mix'd glances with ours,
For a space must be dim, as they gaze from the towers,
And strive to distinguish through tempest and gloom,
The prance of the steed, and the toss of the plume.

The rain is descending; the wind rises loud;
And the moon her red beacon has veil'd with a cloud;
'Tis the better, my mates! for the warder's dull eye
Shall in confidence slumber, nor dream we are nigh.

Our steeds are impatient! I hear my blithe Grey!
There is life in his hoof-clang, and hope in his neigh;
Like the flash of a meteor, the glance of his mane
Shall marshal your march through the darkness and rain.

The drawbridge has dropp'd, the bugle has blown;
One pledge is to quaff yet—then mount and begone!—
To their honour and peace, that shall rest with the slain!
To their health and their glee, that see Teviot again!

Inscription

FOR THE MONUMENT OF THE REV. GEORGE SCOTT. [1]

1830.

To youth, to age, alike, this tablet pale
Tells the brief moral of its tragic tale.
Art thou a parent?—Reverence this bier—
The parents' fondest hopes lie buried here.

[1] This young gentleman, a son of the author's friend and relation, Hugh Scott of Harden, Esq. (now Lord Polwarth,) became Rector of Kentisbeare, in Devonshire, in 1828, and died there the 9th June 1830. This epitaph appears on his tomb in the chancel there.—ED.

Art thou a youth, prepared on life to start,
With opening talents and a generous heart,
Fair hopes and flattering prospects all thine own ? --
Lo ! here their end—a monumental stone !
But let submission tame each sorrowing thought,
Heaven crown'd its champion ere the fight was fought

Saint Cloud.

[*Paris, 5th September,* 1815.]

Soft spread the southern summer night
   Her veil of darksome blue ;
Ten thousand stars combined to light
   The terrace of Saint Cloud.

The evening breezes gently sigh'd,
   Like breath of lover true,
Bewailing the deserted pride
   And wreck of sweet Saint Cloud.

The drum's deep roar was heard afar,
   The bugle wildly blew
Good-night to Hulan and Hussar,
   That garrison Saint Cloud.

The startled Naiads from the shade
   With broken urns withdrew,
And silenced was that proud cascade,
   The glory of Saint Cloud.

We sate upon its steps of stone,
   Nor could its silence [1] rue,
When waked, to music of our own,
   The echoes of Saint Cloud.

      ·   1 MS.—"Absence."

Slow Seine might hear each lovely note
   Fall light as summer dew,
While through the moonless[1] air they float,
   Prolong'd from fair Saint Cloud.

And sure a melody more sweet
   His waters never knew,
Though music's self was wont to meet
   With Princes at Saint Cloud.

Nor then, with more delighted ear,
   The circle round her drew,
Than ours, when gather'd round to hear
   Our songstress[2] at Saint Cloud.

Few happy hours poor mortals pass,—
   Then give those hours their due,
And rank among the foremost class
   Our evenings at Saint Cloud.

The Dance of Death.[3]

1815.

I.

Night and morning[4] were at meeting
   Over Waterloo;
Cocks had sung their earliest greeting;
   Faint and low they crew,
For no paly beam yet shone
On the heights of Mount Saint John;
Tempest-clouds prolong'd the sway
Of timeless darkness over day;

[1] MS.—"Midnight."   [4] MS.—"Dawn and darkness."

[2] These lines were written after an evening spent at Saint Cloud with the
late Lady Alvanley and her daughters, one of whom was the songstress
alluded to in the text.—Ed.

[3] Originally published in 1815, in the Edinburgh Annual Register, vol. v.

Whirlwind, thunder-clap, and shower,
Mark'd it a predestined hour.
Broad and frequent through the night
Flash'd the sheets of levin-light;
Muskets, glancing lightnings back,
Show'd the dreary bivouac
    Where the soldier lay,
Chill and stiff, and drench'd with rain,
Wishing dawn of morn again,
    Though death should come with day.

II.

'Tis at such a tide and hour,
Wizard, witch, and fiend have power,
And ghastly forms through mist and shower
    Gleam on the gifted ken;
And then the affrighted prophet's ear
Drinks whispers strange of fate and fear
Presaging death and ruin near
    Among the sons of men;—
Apart from Albyn's war-array,
'Twas then grey Allan sleepless lay—
Grey Allan, who, for many a day,
    Had follow'd, stout and stern,
Where, through battle's rout and reel,
Storm of shot and hedge of steel,
Led the grandson of Lochiel,
    Valiant Fassiefern.
Through steel and shot he leads no more,
Low laid 'mid friends' and foemen's gore—
But long his native lake's wild shore,
And Sunart rough, and high Ardgower
    And Morven long shall tell,
And proud Bennevis hear with awe,
How, upon bloody Quatre-Bras,
Brave Cameron heard the wild hurra
    Of conquest as he fell?[1]

<hr>

[1] See Note, *ante,* p. 290.

III.

'Lone on the outskirts of the host,
The weary sentinel held post,
And heard, through darkness far aloof,
The frequent clang[1] of courser's hoof,
Where held the cloak'd patrol their course.
And spurr'd 'gainst storm the swerving horse;
But there are sounds in Allan's ear,
Patrol nor sentinel may hear,
And sights before his eye aghast,
Invisible to them have pass'd,
    When down the destined plain,
'Twixt Britain and the bands of France,
Wild as marsh-borne meteor's glance,
Strange phantoms wheel'd a revel dance,
    And doom'd the future slain.—
Such forms were seen, such sounds were heard,
When Scotland's James his march prepared
    For Flodden's fatal plain;[2]
Such, when he drew his ruthless sword,
As Choosers of the Slain, adored
    The yet unchristen'd Dane.
An indistinct and phantom band,
They wheel'd their ring-dance hand in hand,
    With gestures wild and dread;
The Seer, who watch'd them ride the storm,
Saw through their faint and shadowy form
    The lightning's flash more red;
And still their ghastly roundelay
Was of the coming battle-fray,
    And of the destined dead.

IV.

Song

    " Wheel the wild dance
    While lightnings glance,
      And thunders rattle loud,

---

[1] MS.—" Oft came the clang," &c.

[2] See *ante*, Marmion, canto v., stanzas 24, 25, 26, and Appendix, Note 4 A.

And call the brave
To bloody grave,
   To sleep without a shroud.
Our airy feet,
So light and fleet,
   They do not bend the rye
That sinks its head when whirlwinds rave,
And swells again in eddying wave,
   As each wild gust blows by;
But still the corn,
At dawn of morn,
   Our fatal steps that bore,
At eve lies waste,
A trampled paste
   Of blackening mud and gore.

V.

" Wheel the wild dance
While lightnings glance,
   And thunders rattle loud,
And call the brave
To bloody grave,
   To sleep without a shroud.

Wheel the wild dance!
Brave sons of France,
   For you our ring makes room
Make space full wide
For martial pride,
   For banner, spear, and plume.
Approach, draw near,
Proud cuirassier!
   Room for the men of steel!
Through crest and plate
The broadsword's weight
   Both head and heart shall feel

VI.

" Wheel the wild dance
While lightnings glance,
   And thunders rattle loud,

And call the brave
To bloody grave,
  To sleep without a shroud.

Sons of the spear!
You feel us near
  In many a ghastly dream;
With fancy's eye
Our forms you spy,
  And hear our fatal scream.
With clearer sight
Ere falls the night,
  Just when to weal or woe
Your disembodied souls take flight
On trembling wing—each startled sprite
  Our choir of death shall know.

VII.

" Wheel the wild dance
While lightnings glance,
  And thunders rattle loud,
And call the brave
To bloody grave,
  To sleep without a shroud.

Burst, ye clouds, in tempest showers,
Redder rain shall soon be ours—
  See the east grows wan—
Yield we place to sterner game,
Ere deadlier bolts and direr flame
Shall the welkin's thunders shame;
Elemental rage is tame
  To the wrath of man."

VIII.

At morn, grey Allan's mates with awe
Heard of the vision'd sights he saw,
  The legend heard him say;
But the Seer's gifted eye was dim,
Deafen'd his ear, and stark his limb,
  Ere closed that bloody day—

He sleeps far from his Highland heath,—
But often of the Dance of Death
His comrades tell the tale,
On picquet-post, when ebbs the night,
And waning watch-fires glow less bright,
And dawn is glimmering pale.

Romance of Dunois.[1]

FROM THE FRENCH.

1815.

The original of this little Romance makes part of a manuscript collection of French Songs, probably compiled by some young officer, which was found on the field of Waterloo, so much stained with clay and with blood, as sufficiently to indicate the fate of its late owner. The Song is popular in France, and is rather a good specimen of the style of composition to which it belongs. The translation is strictly literal.[2]

IT was Dunois, the young and brave, was bound for Palestine,
But first he made his orisons before St. Mary's shrine :
" And grant, immortal Queen of Heaven," was still the Soldier's
        prayer,
" That I may prove the bravest knight, and love the fairest fair."

His oath of honour on the shrine he graved it with his sword,
And follow'd to the Holy Land the banner of his Lord ;
Where, faithful to his noble vow, his war-cry fill'd the air—
" Be honour'd aye the bravest knight, beloved the fairest fair."

----

[1] This ballad appeared in 1815, in Paul's Letters, and in the Edinburgh Annual Register. It has since been set to music by G. F. Graham, Esq., in Mr. Thomson's Select Melodies, &c.

[2] The original romance,—
        " Partant pour la Syrie,
        Le jeune et brave Dunois," &c.
was written, and set to music also, by Hortense Beauharnois, Duchesse de St. Leu, Ex-Queen of Holland.—ED.

They owed the conquest to his arm, and then his Liege-Lord said,
" The heart that has for honour beat by bliss must be repaid ;—
My daughter Isabel and thou shall be a wedded pair,
For thou art bravest of the brave, she fairest of the fair."

And then they bound the holy knot before Saint Mary's shrine,
That makes a paradise on earth, if hearts and hands combine ;
And every lord and lady bright, that were in chapel there,
Cried, " Honour'd be the bravest knight, beloved the fairest fair !"

The Troubadour.[1]

FROM THE SAME COLLECTION.

1815.

GLOWING with love, on fire for fame,
  A Troubadour that hated sorrow,
Beneath his Lady's window came,
  And thus he sung his last good-morrow:
" My arm it is my country's right,
  My heart is in my true-love's bower ;
Gaily for love and fame to fight,
  Befits the gallant Troubadour."

And while he march'd with helm on head
  And harp in hand, the descant rung,
As, faithful to his favourite maid,
  The minstrel-burden still he sung :
" My arm it is my country's right,
  My heart is in my lady's bower ;
Resolved for love and fame to fight,
  I come, a gallant Troubadour."

[1] The original of this ballad also was written and composed by the
Duchesse de St. Leu. The translation has been set to music by Mr. Thomson. See his Collection of Scottish Songs, 1826.

Even when the battle-roar was deep,
  With dauntless heart he hew'd his way
'Mid splintering lance and falchion-sweep
  And still was heard his warrior-lay:
" My life it is my country's right,
  My heart is in my lady's bower ;
For love to die, for fame to fight,
  Becomes the valiant Troubadour.

Alas ! upon the bloody field
  He fell beneath the foeman's glaive,
But still reclining on his shield,
  Expiring sung the exulting stave :—
" My life it is my country's right,
  My heart is in my lady's bower ;
For love and fame to fall in fight
  Becomes the valiant Troubadour."

𝔉rom t𝔥e 𝔉renc𝔥.[1]

1815.

It chanced that Cupid on a season,
  By Fancy urged, resolved to wed,
But could not settle whether Reason
  Or Folly should partake his bed.

What does he then?—Upon my life
  'T was bad example for a deity—
He takes me Reason for a wife,
  And Folly for his hours of gaiety.

[1] This trifle also is from the French Collection, found at Waterloo. See
Paul's Letters.

Though thus he dealt in petty treason,
  He loved them both in equal measure;
Fidelity was born of Reason,
  And folly brought to bed of Pleasure..

BALLADS,

TRANSLATED, OR IMITATED,

from the German, &c.

BALLADS,

TRANSLATED, OR IMITATED,

From the German, &c.

William and Helen.

[1796.[1]]

IMITATED FROM THE "LENORE" OF BÜRGER.

THE Author had resolved to omit the following version of a well-known Poem, in any collection which he might make of his poetical trifles. But the publishers having pleaded for its admission, the Author has consented, though not unaware of the disadvantage at which this youthful essay (for it was written in 1795) must appear with those which have been executed by much more able hands, in particular that of Mr. Taylor of Norwich, and that of Mr. Spencer.

The following Translation was written long before the Author saw any other, and originated in the following circumstances :— A lady of high rank in the literary world read this romantic tale as translated by Mr. Taylor, in the house of the celebrated Pro

---

[1] THE CHASE and WILLIAM AND HELEN; two Ballads, from the German of Gottfried Augustus Bürger. Edinburgh: Printed by Mundell and Son Royal Bank Close, for Manners and Miller, Parliament Square; and sold by T. Cadell, jun., and W. Davies, in the Strand, London. 1796. 4to.—See "Essay on Imitations of the Ancient Ballad," *post*, vol. vi., and *Life of Scott*, vol. i. chapters 7 and 8.

fessor Dugald Stewart of Edinburgh. The Author was not present, nor indeed in Edinburgh at the time ; but a gentleman who had the pleasure of hearing the ballad, afterwards told him the story, and repeated the remarkable chorus—

> "Tramp! tramp! across the land they spede,
>   Splash! splash! across the sea ;
> Hurrah! The dead can ride apace!
>   Dost fear to ride with me?"

In attempting a translation, then intended only to circulate among friends, the present Author did not hesitate to make use of this impressive stanza ; for which freedom he has since obtained the forgiveness of the ingenious gentleman to whom it properly belongs.

WILLIAM AND HELEN.

I.

From heavy dreams fair Helen rose,
  And eyed the dawning red ;
" Alas, my love, thou tarriest long !
  O art thou false or dead ?"—

II.

With gallant Fred'rick's princely power
  He sought the bold Crusade ;
But not a word from Judah's wars
  Told Helen how he sped.

III.

With Paynim and with Saracen
  At length a truce was made,
And every knight return'd to dry
  The tears his love had shed.

IV.

Our gallant host was homeward bound
  With many a song of joy ;
Green waved the laurel in each plume,
  The badge of victory.

V.

And old and young, and sire and son,
　To meet them crowd the way,
With shouts, and mirth, and melody,
　The debt of love to pay.

VI.

Full many a maid her true-love met,
　And sobb'd in his embrace, —
And flutt'ring joy in tears and smiles
　Array'd full many a face.

VII.

Nor joy nor smile for Helen sad;
　She sought the host in vain;
For none could tell her William's fate,
　If faithless, or if slain.

VIII.

The martial band is past and gone;
　She rends her raven hair,
And in distraction's bitter mood
　She weeps with wild despair.

IX.

" O rise, my child!" her mother said,
　" Nor sorrow thus in vain;
A perjured lover's fleeting heart
　No tears recall again."—

X.

" O mother, what is gone, is gone,
　What's lost, for ever lorn:
Death, death alone can comfort me;
　O had I ne'er been born!

XI.

" O break, my heart!—O break at once!
　Drink my life-blood, Despair!
No joy remains on earth for me,
　For me in heaven no share."—

XII.

" O enter not in judgment, Lord ! "
   The pious mother prays ;
" Impute not guilt to thy frail child !
   She knows not what she says.

XIII.

" O say thy pater noster, child !
   O turn to God and grace !
His will, that turn'd thy bliss to bale,
   Can change thy bale to bliss."—

XIV.

" O mother, mother, what is bliss ?
   O mother, what is bale ?
My William's love was heaven on earth,
   Without it, earth is hell.

XV.

" Why should I pray to ruthless Heaven,
   Since my lov'd William 's slain ?
I only pray'd for William's sake,
   And all my prayers were vain."—

XVI.

" O take the sacrament, my child,
   And check these tears that flow ;
By resignation's humble prayer,
   O hallow'd be thy woe !"—

XVII.

" No sacrament can quench this fire,
   Or slake this scorching pain ;
No sacrament can bid the dead
   Arise and live again.

XVIII.

" O break, my heart !—O break at once !
   Be thou my god, Despair !
Heaven's heaviest blow has fallen on me,
   And vain each fruitless prayer."—

XIX.

" O enter not in judgment, Lord,
  With thy frail child of clay !
She knows not what her tongue has spoke ;
  Impute it not, I pray !

XX.

" Forbear, my child, this desperate woe,
  And turn to God and grace ;
Well can devotion's heavenly glow
  Convert thy bale to bliss."—

XXI.

" O mother, mother, what is bliss ?
  O mother, what is bale ?
Without my William, what were heaven !
  Or with him, what were hell ?"—

XXII.

Wild she arraigns the eternal doom,
  Upbraids each sacred power,
Till spent, she sought her silent room,
  All in the lonely tower.

XXIII.

She beat her breast, she wrung her hands,
  Till sun and day were o'er,
And through the glimmering lattice shone
  The twinkling of the star.

XXIV.

Then, crash ! the heavy drawbridge fell
  That o'er the moat was hung ;
And, clatter ! clatter ! on its boards
  The hoof of courser rung.

XXV.

The clank of echoing steel was heard
  As off the rider bounded ;
And slowly on the winding stair
  A heavy footstep sounded.

XXVI.

And hark! and hark! a knock—Tap! tap!
  A rustling stifled noise;—
Door-latch and tinkling staples ring;—
  At length a whispering voice:—

XXVII.

" Awake, awake! arise, my love!
  How, Helen, dost thou fare?
Wak'st thou, or sleep'st? laugh'st thou, or weep'st!
  Hast thought on me, my fair?"—

XXVIII.

" My love! my love!—so late by night!—
  I waked, I wept for thee:
Much have I borne since dawn of morn;
  Where, William, couldst thou be?

XXIX.

" We saddle late—from Hungary
  I rode since darkness fell;
And to its bourne we both return
  Before the matin-bell."—

XXX.

" O rest this night within my arms,
  And warm thee in their fold!
Chill howls through hawthorn bush the wind:—
  My love is deadly cold."—

XXXI.

" Let the wind howl through hawthorn bush!
  This night we must away;
The steed is wight, the spur is bright;
  I cannot stay till day.

XXXII.

" Busk, busk, and boune! Thou mount'st behind
  Upon my black barb steed:
O'er stock and stile, a hundred miles,
  We haste to bridal bed."—

XXXIII.

" To-night—to-night a hundred miles!
  O dearest William, stay!
The bell strikes twelve—dark, dismal hour!
  O wait, my love, till day!"—

XXXIV.

" Look here, look here—the moon shines clear —
  Full fast I ween we ride;
Mount and away! for ere the day
  We reach our bridal bed.

XXXV.

" The black barb snorts, the bridle rings;
  Haste, busk, and boune, and seat thee!
The feast is made, the chamber spread,
  The bridal guests await thee."—

XXXVI.

Strong love prevail'd: She busks, she bounes,
  She mounts the barb behind,
And round her darling William's waist
  Her lily arms she twined.

XXXVII.

And hurry! hurry! off they rode,
  As fast as fast might be;
Spurn'd from the courser's thundering heels
  The flashing pebbles flee.

XXXVIII.

And on the right, and on the left,
  Ere they could snatch a view,
Fast, fast each mountain, mead, and plain,
  And cot, and castle, flew.

XXXIX.

" Sit fast—dost fear?—The moon shines clear—
  Fleet goes my barb—keep hold!
Fear'st thou?"—" O no!" she faintly said;
  " But why so stern and cold?

XL.

" What yonder rings? what yonder sings?
    Why shrieks the owlet grey?"—
" 'Tis death-bells' clang, 'tis funeral song,
    The body to the clay.

XLI.

" With song and clang, at morrow's dawn,
    Ye may inter the dead:
To night I ride, with my young bride,
    To deck our bridal bed.

XLII.

" Come with thy choir, thou coffin'd guest,
    To swell our nuptial song!
Come, priest, to bless our marriage feast!
    Come all, come all along!"—

XLIII.

Ceased clang and song; down sunk the bier;
    The shrouded corpse arose:
And, hurry! hurry! all the train
    The thundering steed pursues.

XLIV.

And, forward! forward! on they go;
    High snorts the straining steed;
Thick pants the rider's labouring breath,
    As headlong on they speed.

XLV.

" O William, why this savage haste?
    And where thy bridal bed?"—
" 'Tis distant far, low, damp, and chill,
    And narrow, trustless maid."—

XLVI.

" No room for me?"—" Enough for both;—
    Speed, speed, my barb, thy course!"—
O'er thundering bridge, through boiling surge,
    He drove the furious horse.

XLVII.

Tramp! tramp! along the land they rode,
  Splash! splash! along the sea;
The scourge is wight, the spur is bright,
  The flashing pebbles flee.

XLVIII.

Fled past on right and left how fast
  Each forest, grove, and bower!
On right and left fled past how fast
  Each city, town, and tower!

XLIX.

" Dost fear? dost fear? The moon shines clear,
  Dost fear to ride with me?—
Hurrah! hurrah! the dead can ride!"—
  " O William, let them be!—

L.

" See there! see there! What yonder swings
  And creaks 'mid whistling rain?"—
" Gibbet and steel, th' accursed wheel—
  A murderer in his chain.—

LI.

" Hollo! thou felon, follow here:
  To bridal bed we ride;
And thou shalt prance a fetter dance
  Before me and my bride."—

LII.

And hurry! hurry! clash, clash, clash!
  The wasted form descends;
And fleet as wind through hazel bush
  The wild career attends.

LIII.

Tramp! tramp! along the land they rode,
  Splash! splash! along the sea,
The scourge is red, the spur drops blood,
  The flashing pebbles flee.

LIV.

How fled what moonshine faintly show'd!
　How fled what darkness hid!
How fled the earth beneath their feet,
　The heaven above their head!

LV.

" Dost fear? dost fear? The moon shines clear,
　And well the dead can ride;
Does faithful Helen fear for them?"—
　" O leave in peace the dead!"—

LVI.

" Barb! Barb! methinks I hear the cock;
　The sand will soon be run:
Barb! Barb! I smell the morning air;
　The race is wellnigh done."—

LVII.

Tramp! tramp! along the land they rode,
　Splash! splash! along the sea;
The scourge is red, the spur drops blood,
　The flashing pebbles flee.

LVIII.

" Hurrah! hurrah! well ride the dead!
　The bride, the bride is come!
And soon we reach the bridal bed,
　For, Helen, here's my home!"—

LIX.

Reluctant on its rusty hinge
　Revolved an iron door,
And by the pale moon's setting beam
　Were seen a church and tower.

LX.

With many a shriek and cry whiz round
　The birds of midnight, scared;
And rustling like autumnal leaves
　Unhallow'd ghosts were heard.

LXI.

O'er many a tomb and tombstone pale
  He spurr'd the fiery horse,
Till sudden at an open grave
  He check'd the wondrous course.

LXII.

The falling gauntlet quits the rein,
  Down drops the casque of steel,
The cuirass leaves his shrinking side,
  The spur his gory heel.

LXIII.

The eyes desert the naked skull,
  The mould'ring flesh the bone,
Till Helen's lily arms entwine
  A ghastly skeleton.

LXIV.

The furious barb snorts fire and foam,
  And, with a fearful bound,
Dissolves at once in empty air,
  And leaves her on the ground.

LXV.

Half seen by fits, by fits half heard,
  Pale spectres flit along,
Wheel round the maid in dismal dance,
  And howl the funeral song:—

LXVI.

" E'en when the heart 's with anguish cleft,
  Revere the doom of Heaven;—
Her soul is from her body reft—
  Her spirit be forgiven!"

The Wild Huntsman.

THIS is a translation, or rather an imitation of the *Wilde Jägre*, of the German poet Bürger. The tradition upon which it is founded. bears, that formerly a Wildgrave, or a keeper of a royal forest, named Falkenburg, was so much addicted to the pleasures of the chase, and otherwise so extremely profligate and cruel, that he not only followed this unhallowed amusement on the Sabbath, and other days consecrated to religous duty, but accompanied it with the most unheard-of oppression upon the poor peasants who were under his vassalage. When this second Nimrod died, the people adopted a superstition, founded probably on the many various uncouth sounds heard in the depth of a German forest, during the silence of the night. · They conceived they still heard the cry of the Wildgrave's hounds; and the well-known cheer of the deceased hunter, the sounds of his horses' feet, and the rustling of the branches before the game, the pack, and the sportsmen, are also distinctly discriminated; but the phantoms are rarely, if ever, visible. Once, as a benighted *Chasseur* heard this infernal chase pass by him, at the sound of the halloo, with which the Spectre Huntsman cheered his hounds, he could not refrain from crying —" *Glück zu Falkenburg!*" [Good sport to ye, Falkenburg!] " Dost thou wish me good sport?" answered a hoarse voice;— " thou shalt share the game;" and there was thrown at him what seemed to be a huge piece of foul carrion. The daring *Chasseur* lost two of his best horses soon after, and never perfectly recovered the personal effects of this ghostly greeting. This tale, though told with some variations, is universally believed all over Germany.

The French had a similar tradition concerning an aërial hunter, who infested the forest of Fountainbleau. He was sometimes visible: when he appeared as a huntsman, surrounded with dogs, a tall grisly figure. Some account of him may be found in " Sully's Memoirs," who says he was called *Le Grand Veneur*. At one time he chose to hunt so near the palace, that the attendants, and, if I mistake not, Sully himself, came out into the court, supposing it was the sound of the king returning from the chase. This phantom is elsewhere called Saint Hubert.

The superstition seems to have been very general, as appears from the following fine poetical description of this phantom chase, as it was heard in the wilds of Ross-shire.

> " Ere since of old, the haughty thanes of Ross,—
> So to the simple swain tradition tells,—
> Were wont with clans, and ready vassals throng'd,
> To wake the bounding stag, or guilty wolf,
> There oft is heard, at midnight, or at noon,
> Beginning faint, but rising still more loud,
> And nearer, voice of hunters, and of hounds,
> And horns, hoarse winded, blowing far and keen :—
> Forthwith the hubbub multiplies; the gale
> Labours with wilder shrieks, and rifer din
> Of hot pursuit; the broken cry of deer
> Mangled by throttling dogs; the shouts of men,
> And hoofs, thick beating on the hollow hill.
> Sudden the grazing heifer in the vale
> Starts at the noise, and both the herdsman's ears
> Tingle with inward dread. Aghast, he eyes
> The mountain's height, and all the ridges round,
> Yet not one trace of living wight discerns,
> Nor knows, o'erawed, and trembling as he stands,
> To what, or whom, he owes his idle fear,
> To ghost, to witch, to fairy, or to fiend ;
> But wonders, and no end of wondering finds."
>
> *Albania*—reprinted in *Scottish De-*
> *scriptive Poems,* pp. 167, 168.

A posthumous miracle of Father Lesley, a Scottish capuchin, related to his being buried on a hill haunted by these unearthly cries of hounds and huntsmen. After his sainted relics had been deposited there, the noise was never heard more. The reader will find this, and other miracles, recorded in the life of Father Bonaventura, which is written in the choicest Italian.

THE WILD HUNTSMAN.

[1796.[1]]

The Wildgrave winds his bugle-horn,
    To horse, to horse !—halloo, halloo !
His fiery courser snuffs the morn,
    And thronging serfs their lord pursue.

[1] Published (1796) with William and Helen, and entitled " The Chase."

The eager pack, from couples freed,
  Dash through the bush, the brier, the brake;
While answering hound, and horn, and steed,
  The mountain echoes startling wake.

The beams of God's own hallow'd day
  Had painted yonder spire with gold,
And, calling sinful man to pray,
  Loud, long, and deep the bell had toll'd:

But still the Wildgrave onward rides;
  Halloo, halloo! and, hark again!
When, spurring from opposing sides,
  Two Stranger Horsemen join the train.

Who was each Stranger, left and right,
  Well may I guess, but dare not tell;
The right-hand steed was silver white,
  The left, the swarthy hue of hell.

The right-hand Horseman, young and fair,
  His smile was like the morn of May;
The left, from eye of tawny glare,
  Shot midnight lightning's lurid ray.

He waved his huntsman's cap on high,
  Cried—"Welcome, welcome, noble lord!
What sport can earth, or sea, or sky,
  To match the princely chase, afford?"—

"Cease thy loud bugle's changing knell,"
  Cried the fair youth, with silver voice;
"And for devotion's choral swell,
  Exchange the rude unhallow'd noise.

"To-day, the ill-omen'd chase forbear,
  Yon bell yet summons to the fane;
To-day the Warning Spirit hear,
  To-morrow thou mayst mourn in vain."

"Away, and sweep the glades along!"
    The Sable Hunter hoarse replies;
"To muttering monks leave matin-song,
    And bells, and books, and mysteries."

The Wildgrave spurr'd his ardent steed,
    And, launching forward with a bound,
"Who, for thy drowsy priestlike rede,
    Would leave the jovial horn and hound?

"Hence, if our manly sport offend!
    With pious fools go chant and pray:—
Well thou hast spoke, my dark-brow'd friend,
    Halloo, halloo! and, hark away!"

The Wildgrave spurr'd his courser light,
    O'er moss and moor, o'er holt and hill,
And on the left and on the right,
    Each Stranger Horseman follow'd still.

Up springs, from yonder tangled thorn,
    A stag more white than mountain snow;
And louder rung the Wildgrave's horn,
    "Hark forward, forward! holloa, ho!"

A heedless wretch has crossed the way;
    He gasps the thundering hoofs below;—
But, live who can, or die who may,
    Still, "Forward, forward!" on they go.

See, where yon simple fences meet,
    A field with Autumn's blessings crown'd;
See, prostrate at the Wildgrave's feet,
    A husbandman with toil embrown'd:—

"O mercy, mercy, noble lord!
    Spare the poor's pittance," was his cry,
"Earn'd by the sweat these brows have pour'd,
    In scorching hour of fierce July."—

Earnest the right-hand Stranger pleads,
  The left still cheering to the prey ;
The impetuous Earl no warning heeds,
  But furious holds the onward way.

" Away, thou hound ! so basely born,
  Or dread the scourge's echoing blow ! "—
Then loudly rung his bugle-horn,
  " Hark forward, forward ! holla, ho ! "

So said, so done :—A single bound
  Clears the poor labourer's humble pale
Wild follows man, and horse, and hound
  Like dark December's stormy gale .

And man and horse, and hound and horn,
  Destructive sweep the field along ;
While, joying o'er the wasted corn,
  Fell Famine marks the maddening throng

Again uproused, the timorous prey
  Scours moss and moor, and holt and hill ;
Hard run, he feels his strength decay,
  And trusts for life his simple skill.

Too dangerous solitude appear'd ;
  He seeks the shelter of the crowd ;
Amid the flock's domestic herd
  His harmless head he hopes to shroud.

O'er moss and moor, and holt and hill,
  His track the steady blood-hounds trace ;
O'er moss and moor, unwearied still,
  The furious Earl pursues the chase.

Full lowly did the herdsman fall ;—
  " O spare, thou noble Baron, spare
These herds, a widow's little all—
  These flocks, an orphan's fleecy care ! "—

Earnest the right-hand Stranger pleads,
   The left still cheering to the prey;
The Earl nor prayer nor pity heeds,
   But furious keeps the onward way.

"Unmanner'd dog! To stop my sport
   Vain were thy cant and beggar whine,
Though human spirits, of thy sort,
   Were tenants of these carrion kine!"—

Again he winds his bugle-horn,
   "Hark forward, forward! holla, ho!"—
And through the herd, in ruthless scorn,
   He cheers his furious hounds to go.

In heaps the throttled victims fall;
   Down sinks their mangled herdsman near;
The murderous cries the stag appal,—
   Again he starts, new-nerved by fear.

With blood besmear'd, and white with foam,
   While big the tears of anguish pour,
He seeks, amid the forest's gloom,
   The humble hermit's hallow'd bower.

But man and horse, and horn and hound,
   Fast rattling on his traces go;
The sacred chapel rung around
   With "Hark away! and, holla, ho!"

All mild, amid the rout profane,
   The holy hermit pour'd his prayer:—
"Forbear with blood God's house to stain;
   Revere his altar, and forbear!

"The meanest brute has rights to plead,
   Which, wrong'd by cruelty, or pride,
Draw vengeance on the ruthless head;—
   Be warn'd at length, and turn aside."

Still the Fair Horseman anxious pleads;
  The Black, wild whooping, points the prey:—
Alas! the Earl no warning heeds,
  But frantic keeps the forward way.

" Holy or not, or right or wrong,
  Thy altar, and its rites, I spurn;
Not sainted martyrs' sacred song,
  Not God himself, shall make me turn !"

He spurs his horse, he winds his horn,
  " Hark forward, forward ! holla, ho !"—
But off, on whirlwind's pinions borne,
  The stag, the hut, the hermit, go.

And horse and man, and horn and hound,
  And clamour of the chase, was gone;
For hoofs, and howls, and bugle-sound,
  A deadly silence reign'd alone.

Wild gazed the affrighted Earl around:
  He strove in vain to wake his horn,
In vain to call; for not a sound
  Could from his anxious lips be borne.

He listens for his trusty hounds;
  No distant baying reach'd his ears:
His courser, rooted to the ground,
  The quickening spur unmindful bears.

Still dark and darker frown the shades,
  Dark as the darkness of the grave;
And not a sound the still invades,
  Save what a distant torrent gave.

High o'er the sinner's humbled head
  At length the solemn silence broke;
And, from a cloud of swarthy red,
  The awful voice of thunder spoke:—

" Oppressor of creation fair !
  Apostate Spirits' harden'd tool !
Scorner of God ! scourge of the poor !
  The measure of thy cup is full.

" Be chased for ever through the wood ;
  For ever roam the affrighted wild ;
And let thy fate instruct the proud,
  God's meanest creature is his child."

'Twas hush'd :—One flash, of sombre glare,
  With yellow tinged the forests brown ;
Uprose the Wildgrave's bristling hair,
  And horror chill'd each nerve and bone.

Cold pour'd the sweat in freezing rill ;
  A rising wind began to sing ;
And louder, louder, louder still,
  Brought storm and tempest on its wing.

Earth heard the call ;—her entrails rend ;
  From yawning rifts, with many a yell,
Mix'd with sulphureous flames, ascend
  The misbegotten dogs of hell.

What ghastly Huntsman next arose,
  Well may I guess, but dare not tell ;
His eye like midnight lightning glows,
  His steed the swarthy hue of hell.

The Wildgrave flies o'er bush and thorn,
  With many a shriek of helpless woe ;
Behind him hound, and horse, and horn,
  And " Hark away ! and holla, ho ! "

With wild despair's reverted eye,
  Close, close behind, he marks the throng,
With bloody fangs and eager cry ;
  In frantic fear he scours along.—

Still, still shall last the dreadful chase,
　　Till time itself shall have an end ;
By day, they scour earth's cavern'd space,
　　At midnight's witching hour, ascend.

This is the horn, and hound, and horse,
　　That oft the lated peasant hears ;
Appall'd, he signs the frequent cross,
　　When the wild din invades his ears.

The wakeful priest oft drops a tear
　　For human pride, for human woe,
When, at his midnight mass, he hears
　　The infernal cry of " Hoila, ho ! "

The Fire=King.

" The blessings of the evil Genii, which are curses, were upon him."
Eastern Tale.

[1801.]

This Ballad was written at the request of Mr. Lewis, *to be inserted in his* "Tales of Wonder." [1]　*It is the third in a series of four ballads, on the subject of Elementary Spirits. The story is, however, partly historical; for it is recorded, that, during the struggles of the Latin kingdom of Jerusalem, a Knight-Templar, called Saint-Alban, deserted to the Saracens, and defeated the Christians in many combats, till he was finally routed and slain, in a conflict with King Baldwin, under the walls of Jerusalem.*

Bold knights and fair dames, to my harp give an ear,
Of love, and of war, and of wonder to hear ;
And you haply may sigh, in the midst of your glee,
At the tale of Count Albert, and fair Rosalie.

[1] Published in 1801.

O see you that castle, so strong and so high!
And see you that lady, the tear in her eye?
And see you that palmer, from Palestine's land,
The shell on his hat, and the staff in his hand?—

" Now palmer, grey palmer, O tell unto me,
What news bring you home from the Holy Countrie!
And how goes the warfare by Galilee's strand?
And how fare our nobles, the flower of the land?"—

" O well goes the warfare by Galilee's wave,
For Gilead, and Nablous, and Ramah we have;
And well fare our nobles by Mount Lebanon,
For the Heathen have lost, and the Christians have won."

A fair chain of gold 'mid her ringlets there hung;
O'er the palmer's grey locks the fair chain has she fluug:
" O palmer, grey palmer, this chain be thy fee,
For the news thou hast brought from the Holy Countrie.

" And, palmer, good palmer, by Galilee's wave,
O saw ye Count Albert, the gentle and brave!
When the Crescent went back, and the Red-cross rush'd on,
O saw ye him foremost on Mount Lebanon?"—

' O lady, fair lady, the tree green it grows;
O lady, fair lady, the stream pure it flows;
Your castle stands strong, and your hopes soar on high ;
But, lady, fair lady, all blossoms to die.

" The green boughs they wither, the thunderbolt falls,
It leaves of your castle but levin-scorch'd walls ;
The pure stream runs muddy ; the gay hope is gone ;
Count Albert is prisoner on Mount Lebanon."

O she's ta'en a horse, should be fleet at her speed ;
And she's ta'en a sword, should be sharp at her need ;
And she has ta'en shipping for Palestine's land,
To ransom Count Albert from Soldanrie's hand.

Small thought had Count Albert on fair Rosalie,
Small thought on his faith, or his knighthood, had he;
A heathenish damsel his light heart had won—
The Soldan's fair daughter of Mount Lebanon.

" O Christian, brave Christian, my love wouldst thou be,
Three things must thou do ere I hearken to thee:
Our laws and our worship on thee shalt thou take;
And this thou shalt first do for Zulema's sake.

" And, next, in the cavern, where burns evermore
The mystical flame which the Curdmans adore,
Alone, and in silence, three nights shalt thou wake;
And this thou shalt next do for Zulema's sake.

" And, last, thou shalt aid us with counsel and hand,
To drive the Frank robber from Palestine's land;
For my lord and my love then Count Albert I'll take,
When all this is accomplish'd for Zulema's sake."

He has thrown by his helmet, and cross-handled sword,
Renouncing his knighthood, denying his Lord;
He has ta'en the green caftan, and turban put on,
For the love of the maiden of fair Lebanon.

And in the dread cavern, deep deep under ground,
Which fifty steel gates and steel portals surround,
He has watch'd until daybreak, but sight saw he none,
Save the flame burning bright on its altar of stone.

Amazed was the Princess, the Soldan amazed,
Sore murmur'd the priests as on Albert they gazed;
They search'd all his garments, and, under his weeds,
They found, and took from him, his rosary beads.

Again in the cavern, deep deep under ground,
He watch'd the lone night, while the winds whistled round;
Far off was their murmur, it came not more nigh,
The flame burn'd unmoved, and nought else did he spy

Loud murmur'd the priests, and amazed was the King,
While many dark spells of their witchcraft they sing;
They search'd Albert's body, and, lo! on his breast
Was the sign of the Cross, by his father impress'd.

The priests they erase it with care and with pain,
And the recreant return'd to the cavern again;
But, as he descended, a whisper there fell:
It was his good angel, who bade him farewell!

High bristled his hair, his heart flutter'd and beat,
And he turn'd him five steps, half resolved to retreat;
But his heart it was harden'd, his purpose was gone,
When he thought of the Maiden of fair Lebanon.

Scarce pass'd he the archway, the threshold scarce trode,
When the winds from the four points of heaven were abroad;
They made each steel portal to rattle and ring,
And, borne on the blast, came the dread Fire-King.

Full sore rock'd the cavern whene'er he drew nigh,
The fire on the altar blazed bickering and high;
In volcanic explosions the mountains proclaim
The dreadful approach of the Monarch of Flame.

Unmeasured in height, undistinguish'd in form,
His breath it was lightning, his voice it was storm;
I ween the stout heart of Count Albert was tame,
When he saw in his terrors the Monarch of Flame.

In his hand a broad falchion blue-glimmer'd through smoke,
And Mount Lebanon shook as the monarch he spoke:
" With this brand shalt thou conquer, thus long, and no more,
Till thou bend to the Cross, and the Virgin adore."

The cloud-shrouded Arm gives the weapon; and see!
The recreant receives the charm'd gift on his knee:
The thunders growl distant, and faint gleam the fires,
As, borne on the whirlwind, the phantom retires.

Count Albert has arm'd him the Paynim among,
Though his heart it was false, yet his arm it was strong;
And the Red-cross wax'd faiut, and the Crescent came on,
From the day he commanded on-mount Lebanon.

From Lebanon's forests to Galilee's wave,
The sands of Samaar drank the blood of the brave;
Till the Knights of the Temple, and Knights of Saint John
With Salem's King Baldwin, against him came on.

The war-cymbals clatter'd, the trumpets replied,
The lances were couch'd, and they closed on each side;
And horsemen and horses Count Albert o'erthrew,
Till he pierced the thick tumult King Baldwin unto.

Against the charm'd blade which Count Albert did wield,
The fence had been vain of the King's Red-cross shield;
But a Page thrust him forward the monarch before,
And cleft the proud turban the renegade wore.

So fell was the dint, that Count Albert stoop'd low
Before the cross'd shield, to his steel saddlebow;
And scarce had he bent to the Red-cross his head,—
"*Bonne Grace, Notre Dame!*" he unwittingly said.

Sore sigh'd the charm'd sword, for its virtue was o'er,
It sprung from his grasp, and was never seen more;
But true men have said, that the lightning's red wing
Did waft back the brand to the dread Fire-King.

He clench'd his set teeth, and his gauntleted hand;
He stretch'd, with one buffet, that Page on the strand;
As back from the stripling the broken casque roll'd,
You might see the blue eyes, and the ringlets of gold.

Short time had Count Albert in horror to stare
On those death-swimming eyeballs, and blood-clotted hair
For down came the Templars, like Cedron in flood,
And dyed their long lances in Saracen blood.

The Saracens, Curdmans, and Ishmaelites yield
To the scallop, the saltier, and crossleted shield;
And the eagles were gorged with the infidel dead,
From Bethsaida's fountains to Naphthali's head.

The battle is over on Bethsaida's plain.—
Oh, who is yon Paynim lies stretch'd 'mid the slain!
And who is yon Page lying cold at his knee?—
Oh, who but Count Albert and fair Rosalie!

The Lady was buried in Salem's bless'd bound;
The Count he was left to the vulture and hound:
Her soul to high mercy Our Lady did bring;
His went on the blast to the dread Fire-King.

Yet many a minstrel, in harping, can tell,
How the Red-cross it conquer'd, the Crescent it fell:
And lords and gay ladies have sigh'd, 'mid their glee,
At the tale of Count Albert and fair Rosalie.

Frederick and Alice.

[1801.]

*This Tale is imitated, rather than translated, from a fragment
introduced in Goethe's "Claudina von Villa Bella," where it is
sung by a member of a gang of banditti, to engage the attention
of the family, while his companions break into the castle. It
owes any little merit it may possess to my friend* MR. LEWIS,
*to whom it was sent in an extremely rude state; and who, af-
ter some material improvements, published it in his "Tales of
Wonder."*

FREDERICK leaves the land of France,
    Homeward hastes his steps to measure,
Careless casts the parting glance
    On the scene of former pleasure.

Joying in his prancing steed,
  Keen to prove his untried blade,
Hope's gay dreams the soldier lead
  Over mountain, moor, and glade.

Helpless, ruin'd, left forlorn,
  Lovely Alice wept alone;
Mourn'd o'er love's fond contract torn,
  Hope, and peace, and honour flown.

Mark her breast's convulsive throbs!
  See, the tear of anguish flows!—
Mingling soon with bursting sobs,
  Loud the laugh of frenzy rose.

Wild she cursed, and wild she pray'd;
  Seven long days and nights are o'er;
Death in pity brought his aid,
  As the village bell struck four.

Far from her, and far from France,
  Faithless Frederick onward rides;
Marking, blithe, the morning's glance
  Mantling o'er the mountain's sides.

Heard ye not the boding sound,
  As the tongue of yonder tower,
Slowly, to the hills around,
  Told the fourth, the fated hour?

Starts the steed, and snuffs the air,
  Yet no cause of dread appears;
Bristles high the rider's hair,
  Struck with strange mysterious fears.

Desperate, as his terrors rise,
  In the steed the spur he hides;
From himself in vain he flies;
  Anxious, restless, on he rides.

Seven long days, and seven long nights,
  Wild he wander'd, woe the while !
Ceaseless care, and causeless fright,
  Urge his footsteps many a mile.

Dark the seventh sad night descends ;
  Rivers swell, and rain-streams pour :
While the deafening thunder lends
  All the terrors of its roar.

Weary, wet, and spent with toil,
  Where his head shall Frederick hide !
Where, but in yon ruin'd aisle,
  By the lightning's flash descried.

To the portal, dank and low,
  Fast his steed the wanderer bound :
Down a ruin'd staircase slow,
  Next his darkling way he wound.

Long drear vaults before him lie !
  Glimmering lights are seen to glide !—
" Blessed Mary, hear my cry !
  Deign a sinner's steps to guide !"

Often lost their quivering beam,
  Still the lights move slow before,
Till they rest their ghastly gleam
  Right against an iron door.

Thundering voices from within,
  Mix'd with peals of laughter, rose ;
As they fell, a solemn strain
  Lent its wild and wondrous close !

Midst the din, he seem'd to hear
  Voice of friends, by death removed ;
Well he knew that solemn air,
  'Twas the lay that Alice loved.—

Hark ! for now a solemn knell
   Four times on the still night broke ;
Four times, at its deaden'd swell,,
   Echoes from the ruins spoke.

As the lengthen'd clangours die,
   Slowly opes the iron door !
Straight a banquet met his eye,
   But a funeral's form it wore !

Coffins for the seats extend ;
   All with black the board was spread ;
Girt by parent, brother, friend,
   Long since number'd with the dead !

Alice, in her grave-clothes bound,
   Ghastly smiling, points a seat ;
All arose, with thundering sound—
   All the expected stranger greet.

High their meagre arms they wave,
   Wild their notes of welcome swell ;—
" Welcome, traitor, to the grave !
   Perjured, bid the light farewell !"

The Battle of Sempach.

[1818.]

These verses are a literal translation of an ancient Swiss
Ballad upon the battle of Sempach, fought 9th July 1386, being
the victory by which the Swiss Cantons established their independence ; the author, Albert Tchudi, denominated the Souter,
from his profession of a shoemaker. He was a citizen of
Lucerne, esteemed highly among his countrymen, both for his
powers as a *Meister-Singer*, or minstrel, and his courage as a

soldier; so that he might share the praise conferred by Collins on Æschylus, that—

> "——Not alone he nursed the poet's flame,
> But reach'd from Virtue's hand the patriot steel."

The circumstance of their being written by a poet returning from the well-fought field he describes, and in which his country's fortune was secured, may confer on Tchudi's verses an interest which they are not entitled to claim from their poetical merit. But ballad poetry, the more literally it is translated, the more it loses its simplicity, without acquiring either grace or strength; and, therefore, some of the faults of the verses must be imputed to the translator's feeling it a duty to keep as closely as possible to his original. The various puns, rude attempts at pleasantry, and disproportioned episodes, must be set down to Tchudi's account, or to the taste of his age.

The military antiquary will derive some amusement from the minute particulars which the martial poet has recorded. The mode in which the Austrian men-at-arms received the charge of the Swiss, was by forming a phalanx, which they defended with their long lances. The gallant Winkelreid, who sacrificed his own life by rushing among the spears, clasping in his arms as many as he could grasp, and thus opening a gap in those iron battalions, is celebrated in Swiss history. When fairly mingled together, the unwieldy length of their weapons, and cumbrous weight of their defensive armour, rendered the Austrian men-at-arms a very unequal match for the light-armed mountaineers. The victories obtained by the Swiss over the German chivalry, hitherto deemed as formidable on foot as on horseback, led to important changes in the art of war. The poet describes the Austrian knights and squires as cutting the peaks from their boots ere they could act upon foot, in allusion to an inconvenient piece of foppery, often mentioned in the middle ages. Leopold III., Archduke of Austria, called " The handsome man-at-arms," was slain in the Battle of Sempach, with the flower of his chivalry.

THE BATTLE OF SEMPACH.[1]

'Twas when among our linden-trees
 The bees had housed in swarms,
(And grey-hair'd peasants say that these
 Betoken foreign arms,)

Then look'd we down to Willisow,
 The land was all in flame;
We knew the Archduke Leopold
 With all his army came.

The Austrian nobles made their vow,
 So hot their heart and bold—
"On Switzer carles we'll trample now,
 And slay both young and old."

With clarion loud, and banner proud,
 From Zurich on the lake,
In martial pomp and fair array,
 Their onward march they make.

" Now list, ye lowland nobles all—
 Ye seek the mountain strand,
Nor wot ye what shall be your lot
 In such a dangerous land.

" I rede ye, shrive ye of your sins,
 Before ye farther go;
A skirmish in Helvetian hills
 May send your souls to woe."—

" But where now shall we find a priest
 Our shrift that he may hear?"—

<hr>

1 This translation first appeared in Blackwood's Edinburgh Magazine for
February 1818.—E.

" The Switzer priest[1] has ta'en the field,
   He deals a penance drear.

" Right heavily upon your head
   He 'll lay his hand of steel;
And with his trusty partisan
   Your absolution deal."—

'Twas on a Monday morning then,
   The corn was steep'd in dew,
And merry maids had sickles ta'en,
   When the host to Sempach drew.

The stalwart men of fair Lucerne
   Together have they join'd;
The pith and core of manhood stern,
   Was none cast looks behind.

It was the Lord of Hare-castle,
   And to the Duke he said,
" Yon little band of brethren true
   Will meet us undismay'd."—

" O Hare-castle,[2] thou heart of hare!"
   Fierce Oxenstern replied. —
" Shalt see then how the game will fare,"
   The taunted knight replied.

There was lacing then of helmets bright,
   And closing ranks amain;
The peaks they hew'd from their boot-points
   Might wellnigh load a wain.[3]

---

[1] All the Swiss clergy who were able to bear arms fought in this patriotic war.

[2] In the original, *Haasenstein*, or *Hare-stone*.

[3] This seems to allude to the preposterous fashion, during the middle ages, of wearing boots with the points or peaks turned upwards, and so long, that in some cases they were fastened to the knees of the wearer with small chains. When they alighted to fight upon foot, it would seem that the Aus-

And thus they to each other said,
  " Yon handful down to hew
Will be no boastful tale to tell,
  The peasants are so few."—

The gallant Swiss Confederates there
  They pray'd to God aloud,
And he display'd his rainbow fair
  Against a swarthy cloud.

Then heart and pulse throbb'd more and more
  With courage firm and high,
And down the good Confederates bore
  On the Austrian chivalry.

The Austrian Lion[1] 'gan to growl,
  And toss his main and tail ;
And ball, and shaft, and crossbow bolt,
  Went whistling forth like hail.

Lance, pike, and halbert, mingled there,
  The game was nothing sweet ;
The boughs of many a stately tree
  Lay shiver'd at their feet.

The Austrian men-at-arms stood fast,
  So close their spears they laid ;
It chafed the gallant Winkelreid,
  Who to his comrades said—

" I have a virtuous wife at home,
  A wife and infant son ;
I leave them to my country's care,—
  This field shall soon be won.

" These nobles lay their spears right thick,
  And keep full firm array,

---

trian gentlemen found it necessary to cut off these peaks, that they might
move with the necessary activity.

    [1] A pun on the Archduke's name, Leopold.

Yet shall my charge their order break,
  And make my brethren way."

He rush'd against the Austrian band,
  In desperate career,
And with his body, breast, and hand,
  Bore down each hostile spear.

Four lances splinter'd on his crest,
  Six shiver'd in his side;
Still on the serried files he press'd—
  He broke their ranks, and died.

This patriot's self-devoted deed
  First tamed the Lion's mood,
And the four forest cantons freed
  From thraldom by his blood.

Right where his charge had made a lane,
  His valiant comrades burst,
With sword, and axe, and partisan,
  And hack, and stab, and thrust.

The daunted Lion 'gan to whine,
  And granted ground amain,
The Mountain Bull[1] he bent his brows,
  And gored his sides again.

Then lost was banner, spear, and shield,
  At Sempach in the flight,
The cloister vaults at Konig's-field
  Hold many an Austrian knight.

It was the Archduke Leopold,
  So lordly would he ride,
But he came against the Switzer churls,
  And they slew him in his pride.

[1] A pun on the Urus, or wild-bull, which gives name to the Canton of Uri.

The heifer said unto the bull—
  " And shall I not complain ?
There came a foreign nobleman
  To milk me on the plain.

" One thrust of thine outrageous horr
  Has gall'd the knight so sore,
That to the churchyard he is borne
  To range our glens no more."

·An Austrian noble left the stour,
  And fast the flight 'gan take ;
And he arrived in luckless hour
  At Sempach on the lake.

He and his squire a fisher call'd,
  (His name was Hans Von Rot,)
" For love, or meed, or charity,
  Receive us in thy boat !"

Their anxious call the fisher heard,
  And, glad the meed to win,
His shallop to the shore he steer'd,
  And took the flyers in.

And while against the tide and wind
  Hans stoutly row'd his way,
The noble to his follower sign'd
  He should the boatman slay.

The fisher's back was to them turn'd,
  The squire his dagger drew,
Hans saw his shadow in the lake,
  The boat he overthrew.

He 'whelm'd the boat, and as they strove,
  He stunn'd them with his oar—
" Now, drink ye deep, my gentle sirs,
  You'll ne'er stab boatman more.

" Two gilded fishes in the lake
　This morning have I caught,
Their silver scales may much avail,
　Their carrion flesh is naught. "

It was a messenger of woe
　Has sought the Austrian land :
" Ah ! gracious lady, evil news !
　My lord lies on the strand.

" At Sempach, on the battle-field,
　His bloody corpse lies there."—
" Ah, gracious God !" the lady cried,
　" What tidings of despair !"

Now would you know the minstrel wight
　Who sings of strife so stern,
Albert the Souter is he hight,
　A burgher of Lucerne.

A merry man was he, I wot,
　The night he made the lay,
Returning from the bloody spot,
　Where God had judged the day.

Ths Noble Moringer.

AN ANCIENT BALLAD.

TRANSLATED FROM THE GERMAN.

[1819.[1]]

THE original of these verses occurs in a collection of German popular songs, entitled, *Sammlung Deutschen Volkslieder*, Berlin, 1807, published by Messrs. Busching and Von Der Hagen, both, and more especially the last, distinguished for their accquaintance with the ancient popular poetry and legendary history of Germany.

In the German Editor's notice of the ballad, it is stated to have been extracted from a manuscript Chronicle of Nicolaus Thomann, chaplain to Saint Leonard in Weisenhorn, which bears the date 1533; and the song is stated by the author to have been generally sung in the neighbourhood at that early period. Thomann, as quoted by the German Editor, seems faithfully to have believed the event he narrates. He quotes tombstones and obituaries to prove the existence of the personages of the ballad, and discovers that there actually died, on the 11th May 1349, a Lady Von Neuffen, Countess of Marstetten, who was, by birth, of the house of Moringer. This lady he supposes to have been Moringer's daughter, mentioned in the ballad. He quotes the same authority for the death of Berckhold Von Neuffen, in the same year. The editors, on the whole, seem to embrace the opinion of Professor Smith of Ulm, who, from the language of the ballad, ascribes its date to the 15th century.

The legend itself turns on an incident not peculiar to Germany, and which, perhaps, was not unlikely to happen in more instances than one, when Crusaders abode long in the Holy Land, and their disconsolate dames received no tidings of their fate. A story, very similar in circumstances, but without the miraculous

---

[1] The translation of the Noble Moringer appeared originally in the Edinburgh Annual Register for 1816, *(published in* 1819.) It was composed during Sir Walter Scott's severe and alarming illness of April 1819, and dictated, in the intervals of exquisite pain, to his daughter Sophia, and his friend William Laidlaw. — ED. See *Life of Scott*, vol. vi. p. 71.

machinery of Saint Thomas, is told of one of the ancient Lords
of Haigh-hall in Lancashire, the patrimonial inheritance of the
late Countess of Balcarras; and the particulars are represented
on stained glass upon a window in that ancient manor-house.[1]

THE NOBLE MORINGER.

I.

O, WILL you hear a knightly tale of old Bohemian day?
It was the noble Moringer in wedlock bed he lay;
He halsed and kiss'd his dearest dame, that was as sweet as May,
And said, " Now, lady of my heart, attend the words I say.

II.

'Tis I have vow'd a pilgrimage unto a distant shrine,
And I must seek Saint Thomas-land, and leave the land that's
     mine;
Here shalt thou dwell the while in state, so thou wilt pledge thy
     fay,
That thou for my return wilt wait seven twelvemonths and a day."

III.

Then out and spoke that Lady bright, sore troubled in her cheer,
" Now tell me true, thou noble knight, what order takest thou here;
And who shall lead thy vassal band, and hold thy lordly sway,
And be thy lady's guardian true when thou art far away?"

IV.

Out spoke the noble Moringer, " Of that have thou no care,
There's many a valiant gentleman of me holds living fair;
The trustiest shall rule my land, my vassals and my state,
And be a guardian tried and true to thee, my lovely mate.

V.

" As Christian man, I needs must keep the vow which I have
     plight,
When I am far in foreign land, remember thy true knight;

[1] See Introduction to *The Betrothed*, Waverley Novels, vol. xxxvii.

And cease, my dearest dame, to grieve, for vain were sorrow now,
But grant thy Moringer his leave, since God hath heard his vow."

VI.

It was the noble Moringer from bed he made him boune,
And met him there his Chamberlain, with ewer and with gown:
He flung the mantle on his back, 't was furr'd with miniver,
He dipp'd his hand in water cold, and bathed his forehead fair.

VII.

" Now hear," he said, " Sir Chamberlain, true vassal art thou mine,
And such the trust that I repose in that proved worth of thine,
For seven years shalt thou rule my towers, and lead my vassal
    train,
And pledge thee for my Lady's faith till I return again."

VIII.

The Chamberlain was blunt and true, and sturdily said he,
" Abide, my lord, and rule your own, and take this rede from me ;
That woman's faith 's a brittle trust — Seven twelvemonths, didst
    thou say ?
I 'll pledge me for no lady's truth beyond the seventh fair day."

IX.

The noble Baron turn'd him round, his heart was full of care,
His gallant Esquire stood him nigh, he was Marstetten's heir,
To whom he spoke right anxiously, " Thou trusty squire to me,
Wilt thou receive this weighty trust when I am o'er the sea ?

X.

" To watch and ward my castle strong, and to protect my land,
And to the hunting or the host to lead my vassal band ;
And pledge thee for my Lady's faith till seven long years are gone,
And guard her as Our Lady dear was guarded by Saint John !"

XI.

Marstetten's heir was kind and true, but fiery, hot, and young,
And readily he answer made with too presumptuous tongue :
" My noble lord, cast care away, and on your journey wend,
And trust this charge to me until your pilgrimage have end.

XII.

" Rely upon my plighted faith, which shall be truly tried,
To guard your lands, and ward your towers, and with your vas-
      sals ride ;
And for your lovely Lady's faith, so virtuous and so dear,
I 'll gage my head it knows no change, be absent thirty year."

XIII.

The noble Moringer took cheer when thus he heard him speak,
And doubt forsook his troubled brow, and sorrow left his cheek ;
A long adieu he bids to all—hoists topsails, and away,
And wanders in Saint Thomas-land seven twelve-months and a
      day.

XIV.

It was the noble Moringer within an orchard slept,
When on the Baron's slumbering sense a boding vision crept ;
And whisper'd in his ear a voice, " 'Tis time, Sir Knight to wake,
Thy lady and thy heritage another master take ;

XV.

" Thy tower another banner knows, thy steeds another rein,
And stoop them to another's will thy gallant vassal train ;
And she, the Lady of thy love, so faithful once and fair,
This night within thy father's hall she weds Marstetten's heir."

XVI.

It is the noble Moringer starts up and tears his beard,
" O would that I had ne'er been born !—what tidings have I
      heard !—
To lose my lordship and my lands the less would be my care,
But, God ! that e'er a squire untrue should wed my Lady fair.

XVII.

" O good Saint Thomas, hear," he pray'd ; " my patron Saint art
      thou,
A traitor robs me of my land, even while I pay my vow !
My wife he brings to infamy, that was so pure of name,
And I am far in foreign land, and must endure the shame."

XVIII.

It was the good Saint Thomas, then, who heard his pilgrim's
        prayer,
And sent a sleep so deep and dead that it o'erpower'd his care;
He waked in fair Bohemian land, outstretch'd beside a rill,
High on the right a castle stood, low on the left a mill.

XIX.

The Moringer he started up as one from spell unbound,
And dizzy with surprise and joy gazed wildly all around;
"I know my fathers' ancient towers—the mill, the stream I
        know;—
Now blessed be my patron Saint, who cheer'd his pilgrim's woe!"

XX.

He leant upon his pilgrim staff, and to the mill he drew,
So alter'd was his goodly form that none their master knew;
The Baron to the miller said, "Good friend, for charity,
Tell a poor palmer in your land what tidings may there be?"

XXI.

The miller answered him again, "He knew of little news,
Save that the Lady of the land did a new bridegroom choose;
Her husband died in distant land, such is the constant word,
His death sits heavy on our souls, he was a worthy Lord.

XXII.

"Of him I held the little mill which wins me living free,
God rest the Baron in his grave, he still was kind to me!
And when Saint Martin's tide comes round, and millers take
        their toll,
The priest that prays for Moringer shall have both cope and
        stole."

XXIII.

It was the noble Moringer to climb the hill began,
And stood before the bolted gate a woe and weary man;
"Now help me, every saint in heaven that can compassion take,
To gain the entrance of my hall this woful match to break."

XXIV.

His very knock it sounded sad, his call was sad and slow,
For heart and head, and voice and hand, were heavy all with
     woe ;
And to the warder thus he spoke : " Friend, to thy Lady say,
A pilgrim from Saint Thomas-land craves harbour for a day.

XXV.

" I 've wander'd many a weary step, my strength is wellnigh done
And if she turn me from her gate I 'll see no morrow's sun ;
I pray, for sweet Thomas' sake, a pilgrim's bed and dole,
And for the sake of Moringer's, her once-loved husband's soul."

XXVI.

It was the stalwart warder then he came his dame before,—
" A pilgrim, worn and travel-toil'd, stands at the castle-door ;
And prays, for sweet Saint Thomas' sake, for harbour and for
     dole,
And for the sake of Moringer, thy noble husband's soul."

XXVII.

The Lady's gentle heart was moved ;—" Do up the gate," she
     said,
" And bid the wanderer welcome be to banquet and to bed ;
And since he names my husband's name, so that he lists to stay,
These towers shall be his harbourage a twelvemonth and a day."

XXVIII.

It was the stalwart warder then undid the portal broad,
It was the noble Moringer that o'er the threshold strode ;
" And have thou thanks, kind heaven," he said, " though from a
     man of sin,
That the true lord stands here once more his castle-gate within."

XXIX.

Then up the halls paced Moringer, his step was sad and slow ;
It sat full heavy on his heart, none seem'd their Lord to know ;
He sat him on a lowly bench, oppress'd with woe and wrong,
Short space he sat, but ne'er to him seem'd little space so long.

XXX.

Now spent was day, and feasting o'er, and come was evening hour,
The time was nigh when new-made brides retire to nuptial bower;
" Our castle's wont," a brides-man said, " hath been both firm
     and long, ·
No guest to harbour in our halls till he shall chant a song."

XXXI.

Then spoke the youthful bridegroom there as he sat by the bride,
" My merry minstrel folk," quoth he, " lay shalm and harp aside;
Our pilgrim guest must sing a lay, the castle's rule to hold,
And well his guerdon will I pay with garment and with gold."—

XXXII.

" Chill flows the lay of frozen age,"— 'twas thus the pilgrim
     sung,—
" Nor golden meed nor garment gay, unlocks his heavy tongue;
Once did I sit, thou bridegroom gay, at board as rich as thine,
And by my side as fair a bride with all her charms was mine.

XXXIII.

" But time traced furrows on my face, and I grew silver-hair'd,
For locks of brown, and cheeks of youth, she left this brow and
     beard;
Once rich, but now a palmer poor, I tread life's latest stage, ·
And mingle with your bridal mirth the lay of frozen age."

XXXIV.

It was the noble Lady there this woful lay that hears,
And for the aged pilgrim's grief her eye was dimm'd with tears;
She bade her gallant cupbearer a golden beaker take,
And bear it to the palmer poor, to quaff it for her sake.

XXXV.

It was the noble Moringer that dropp'd amid the wine
A bridal ring of burning gold so costly and so fine:
Now listen, gentles, to my song, it tells you but the sooth,
'Twas with that very ring of gold he pledged his bridal truth.

XXXVI.

Then to the cupbearer he said, " Do me one kindly deed,
And should my better days return, full rich shall be thy meed;
Bear back the golden cup again to yonder bride so gay,
And crave her of her courtesy to pledge the palmer grey."

XXXVII.

The cupbearer was courtly bred, nor was the boon denied,
The golden cup he took again, and bore it to the bride;
" Lady," he said, " your reverend guest sends this, and bids me
     pray,
That, in thy noble courtesy, thou pledge the palmer grey."

XXXVIII.

The ring hath caught the Lady's eye, she views it close and near,
Then might you hear her shriek aloud, " The Moringer is here !"
Then might you see her start from seat, while tears in torrents fell,
But whether 'twas for joy or woe, the ladies best can tell.

XXXIX.

But loud she utter'd thanks to Heaven, and every saintly power,
That had return'd the Moringer before the midnight hour;
And loud she utter'd vow on vow, that never was there bride,
That had like her preserved her troth, or been so sorely tried.

XL.

" Yes, here I claim the praise," she said, " to constant matrons
     due,
Who keeps the troth that they have plight, so stedfastly and true;
For count the term howe'er you will, so that you count aright,
Seven twelve-months and a day are out when bells toll twelve
     to-night."

XLI.

It was Marstetten then rose up, his falchion there he drew,
He kneel'd before the Moringer, and down his weapon threw;
" My oath and knightly faith are broke," these were the words
     he said,
" Then take, my liege, thy vassal's sword, and take thy vassal's
     head."

XLII.

The noble Moringer he smiled, and then aloud did say,
" He gathers wisdom that hath roam'd seven twelve-months and
     a day;
My daughter now hath fifteen years, fame speaks her sweet and
     fair,
I give her for the bride you lose, and name her for my heir.

XLIII.

"The young bridegroom hath youthful bride, the old bridegroom
     the old,
Whose faith was kept till term and tide so punctually were told;
But blessings on the warder kind that oped my castle gate,
For had I come at morrow tide, I came a day too late."

The Erl-King.[1]

FROM THE GERMAN OF GOETHE.

*(The Erl-King is a goblin that haunts the Black Forest in Thurin-
gia.—To be read by a candle particularly long in the snuff.)*

O, WHO rides by night thro' the woodland so wild?
It is the fond father embracing his child;
And close the boy nestles within his loved arm,
To hold himself fast, and to keep himself warm.

" O father, see yonder! see yonder!" he says.—
" My boy, upon what dost thou fearfully gaze?"—
" O, 'tis the Erl-King with his crown and his shroud."—
" No, my son, it is but a dark wreath of the cloud."

---

[1] 1797.—"*To Miss Christian Rutherford.*—I send a goblin story. You see
I have not altogether lost the faculty of rhyming. I assure you there is no
small impudence in attempting a version of that ballad, as it has been translated by *Lewis.* . . . W. S."—*Life,* vol. i. p. 378.

(The Erl-King speaks.)
" O come and go with me, thou loveliest child;
By many a gay sport shall thy time be beguiled;
My mother keeps for thee full many a fair toy,
And many a fine flower shall she pluck for my boy."

" O, father, my father, and did you not hear
The Erl-King whispers so low in my ear?"—
" Be still, my heart's darling—my child, be at ease;
It was but the wild blast as it sung thro' the trees."—

Erl-King.

" O wilt thou go with me, thou loveliest boy?
My daughter shall tend thee with care and with joy;
She shall bear thee so lightly thro' wet and thro' wild,
And press thee, and kiss thee, and sing to my child."—

" O father, my father, and saw you not plain,
The Erl-King's pale daughter glide past thro' the rain?"—
" O yes, my loved treasure, I knew it full soon;
It was the grey willow that danced to the moon."—

Erl-King.

" O come and go with me, no longer delay,
Or else, silly child, I will drag thee away."—
" O father! O father! now, now keep your hold,
The Erl-King has seized me—his grasp is so cold!"

Sore trembled the father; he spurr'd thro' the wild,
Clasping close to his bosom his shuddering child;
He reaches his dwelling in doubt and in dread,
But, clasp'd to his bosom, the infant was *dead!*"

DRAMATIC PIECES.

Dramatic Pieces.

HALIDON HILL;[1]

A DRAMATIC SKETCH FROM SCOTTISH HISTORY.

PREFACE.

THOUGH the Public seldom feel much interest in such communications, (nor is there any reason why they should,) the Author takes the liberty of stating, that these scenes were commenced with the purpose of contributing to a miscellany projected by a much esteemed friend.[2] But instead of being confined to a scene or two, as intended, the work gradually swelled to the size of an independent publication. It is designed to illustrate military antiquities, and the manners of chivalry. The drama (if it can be termed one) is, in no particular, either designed or calculated for the stage.[3]

[1] Published by Constable & Co., June 1822, in 8vo. 6s.

[2] The author alludes to a collection of small pieces in verse, edited, for a charitable purpose, by Mrs. Joanna Baillie. — See *Life of Scott*, vol. vii. pp. 7, 18, 169-70.—ED.

[3] In the first edition, the text added, " In case any attempt shall be made to produce it in action, (as has happened in similar cases,) the author takes the present opportunity to intimate, that it shall be at the peril of those who make such an experiment." Adverting to this passage, the *New Edinburgh Review* (July, 1822) said — "We, nevertheless, do not believe that any thing more essentially dramatic, in so far as it goes, more capable of stage effect, has appeared in England since the days of her greatest genius; and giving Sir Walter, therefore, full credit for his coyness on the present occasion, we ardently hope that he is but trying his strength in the most arduous of all literary enterprises, and that, ere long, he will demonstrate his right to the highest honours of the tragic muse." The *British Critic*, for October 1822, says, on the same head —" Though we may not accede to the author's declaration, that it is ' *in no particular* calculated for the stage,' we must not lead our readers to look for any thing amounting to a regular drama. It would, we think, form an underplot of very great interest, in an historical play of customary length; and although its incidents and personages are mixed up, in these scenes, with an event of real history, there is nothing in either to prevent their being interwoven in the plot of any drama of which the action should lie in the confines of England and Scotland, at any of the very numerous periods of Border warfare. The whole interest, indeed, of the story, is

The subject is to be found in Scottish history ; but not to over-
load so slight a publication with antiquarian research, or quota-
tions from obscure chronicles, may be sufficiently illustrated by
the following passage from *Pinkerton's History of Scotland*, vol.
i. p. 72 :—

" The Governor (anno 1402) dispatched a considerable force under Murdac, his eldest son : the Earls of Angus and Moray also
joined Douglas, who entered England with an army of ten thousand
men, carrying terror and devastation to the walls of Newcastle.

" Henry IV. was now engaged in the Welsh war against Owen
Glendour ; but the Earl of Northumberland, and his son, the
Hotspur Percy, with the Earl of March, collected a numerous
array, and awaited the return of the Scots, impeded with spoil,
near Millfield, in the north part of Northumberland.   Douglas
had reached Wooler, in his return ; and, perceiving the enemy,
seized a strong post between the two armies, called Homildon-hill.
In this method he rivalled his predecessor at the Battle of Otter-
burn, but not with like success.   The English advanced to the
assault, and Henry Percy was about to lead them up the hill,
when March caught his bridle, and advised him to advance no
farther, but to pour the dreadful shower of English arrows into
the enemy.   This advice was followed by the usual fortune ; for
in all ages the bow was the English instrument of victory ; and
though the Scots, and perhaps the French, were superior in the
use of the spear, yet this weapon was useless after the distant
bow had decided the combat.   Robert the Great, sensible of this
at the battle of Bannockburn, ordered a prepared detachment
of cavalry to rush among the English archers at the commence-
ment, totally to disperse them, and stop the deadly effusion.   But
Douglas now used no such precaution ; and the consequence was,
that his people, drawn up on the face of the hill, presented one
general mark to the enemy, none of whose arrows descended in
vain.   The Scots fell without fight, and unrevenged, till a spirited
knight, Swinton, exclaimed aloud, ' O my brave countrymen !
what fascination has seized you to-day, that you stand like deer
to be shot, instead of indulging your ancient courage, and meeting
your enemies hand to hand?   Let those who will, descend with
me, that we may gain victory, or life, or fall like men.'[1]   This

---

engrossed by two characters, imagined, as it appears to us, with great force
and probability, and contrasted with considerable skill and effect."—ED.

[1] " Miles magnanimus dominus Johannes Swinton, tanquam voce horrida
præconis exclamavit, dicens, O commilitones inclyti ! quis vos hodie fasci-
navit non indulgere solitæ probitati, quod nec dextris conseritis, nec ut viri
corda erigitis, ad invadendum æmulos, qui vos, tanquam damulos vel hin-
nulos imparcatos, sagittarum jaculis perdere festinant.   Descendant mecum
qui velint, et in nomine Domini hostes penetrabimus, ut vel sic vita potia-
mur, vel saltem ut milites cum honore occumbamus," &c. — *Fordun, Scoti-
Chronicon*, vol. ii. p. 434.—ED.

being heard by Adam Gordon, between whom and Swinton there remained an ancient deadly feud, attended with the mutual slaughter of many followers, he instantly fell on his knees before Swinton, begged his pardon, and desired to be dubbed a knight by him whom he must now regard as the wisest and the boldest of that order in Britain. The ceremony performed, Swinton and Gordon descended the hill, accompanied only by one hundred men; and a desperate valour led the whole body to death. Had a similar spirit been shown by the Scottish army, it is probable that the event of the day would have been different. Douglas, who was certainly deficient in the most important qualities of a general, seeing his army begin to disperse, at length attempted to descend the hill; but the English archers, retiring a little, sent a flight of arrows so sharp and strong, that no armour could withstand; and the Scottish leader himself, whose panoply was of remarkable temper, fell under five wounds, though not mortal. The English men-of-arms, knights, or squires, did not strike one blow, but remained spectators of the rout, which was now complete. Great numbers of the Scots were slain, and near five hundred perished in the river Tweed upon their flight. Among the illustrative captives was Douglas, whose chief wound deprived him of an eye; Murdac, son of Albany; the Earls of Moray and Angus; and about twenty-four gentlemen of eminent rank and power. The chief slain were, Swinton, Gordon, Livingston of Calendar, Ramsay of Dalhousie, Walter Sinclair, Roger Gordon, Walter Scott, and others. Such was the issue of the unfortunate battle of Homildon."

It may be proper to observe, that the scene of action has, in the following pages, been transferred from Homildon to Halidon Hill. For this there was an obvious reason;—for who would again venture to introduce upon the scene the celebrated Hotspur, who commanded the English at the former battle? There are, however, several coincidences which may reconcile even the severer antiquary to the substitution of Halidon Hill for Homildon. A Scottish army was defeated by the English on both occasions, and under nearly the same circumstances of address on the part of the victors, and mismanagement on that of the vanquished, for the English long-bow decided the day in both cases. In both cases, also, a Gordon was left on the field of battle; and at Halidon, as at Homildon, the Scots were commanded by an ill-fated representative of the great house of Douglas. He of Homildon was surnamed *Tineman*, i. e. *Loseman*, from his repeated defeats and miscarriages; and, with all the personal valour of his race, seems to have enjoyed so small a portion of their sagacity, as to be unable to learn military experience from reiterated calamity. I am far, however, from intimating, that the traits of imbecility and envy attributed to the Regent in the following sketch, are to be historically ascribed either to the elder Douglas of Halidon Hill, or to him called *Tineman*, who seems to have enjoyed the respect of his countrymen, notwithstanding that, like the celebrated Anne de Montmorency, he was either defeated, or wounded, or made prisoner, in every battle which he fought. The Regent of the sketch is a character purely imaginary.

The tradition of the Swinton family, which still survives in a lineal descent, and to which the author has the honour to be related, avers, that the Swinton who fell at Homildon in the manner related in the preceding extract, had slain Gordon's father; which seems sufficient ground for adopting that circumstance into the following dramatic sketch, though it is rendered improbable by other authorities.

If any reader will take the trouble of looking at Froissart, Fordun, or other historians of the period, he will find, that the character of the Lord of Swinton, for strength, courage, and conduct, is by no means exaggerated.

W. S.

ABBOTSFORD, 1822.

DRAMATIS PERSONÆ.

SCOTTISH.

THE REGENT OF SCOTLAND.

GORDON,
SWINTON,
LENNOX,
SUTHERLAND,
ROSS,
MAXWELL,
JOHNSTONE,
LINDESAY,
} *Scottish Chiefs and Nobles.*

ADAM DE VIPONT, *a Knight Templar.*
THE PRIOR OF MAISON-DIEU.
REYNALD, *Swinton's Squire.*
HOB HATTELEY, *a Border Moss-Trooper.*
Heralds.

ENGLISH.

KING EDWARD III.
CHANDOS,
PERCY,
RIBAUMONT,
} *English and Norman Nobles*

THE ABBOT OF WALTHAMSTOW.

Halidon Hill.

ACT. I.—SCENE I.

The northern side of the eminence of Halidon.   The back Scene
represents the summit of the ascent, occupied by the Rear-guard
of the Scottish army.   Bodies of armed men appear as advancing
from different points, to join the main body.

Enter De Vipont *and the* Prior of Maison-Dieu.

Vip. No farther, Father—here I need no guidance—
I have already brought your peaceful step
Too near the verge of battle.
        Pri. Fain would I see you join some Baron's banner,
Before I say farewell.   The honour'd sword
That fought so well in Syria, should not wave
Amid the ignoble crowd.
        Vip. Each spot is noble in a pitched field,
So that a man has room to fight and fall on 't.
But I shall find out friends.   'T is scarce twelve years
Since I left Scotland for the wars of Palestine,
And then the flower of all the Scottish nobles
Were known to me ; and I, in my degree,
Not all unknown to them.
        Pri. Alas ! there have been changes since that time !
The Royal Bruce, with Randolph, Douglas, Grahame,
Then shook in field the banners which now moulder
Over their graves i' the chancel.
        Vip. And thence comes it,
That while I look'd on many a well-known crest
And blazon'd shield,[1] as hitherward we came,
The faces of the Barons who displayed them
Were all unknown to me.   Brave youths they seem'd ;
Yet, surely, fitter to adorn the tilt-yard,
Than to be leaders of a war.   Their followers,
Young like themselves, seem like themselves unpractised —
Look at their battle-rank.
        Pri. I cannot gaze on 't with undazzled eye,
So thick the rays dart back from shield and helmet,
And sword and battle-axe, and spear and pennon.
Sure 'tis a gallant show ! The Bruce himself

---

[1] MS.—"I've look'd on many a well-known pennon
        Playing the air," &c.

Hath often conquer'd at the head of fewer
And worse appointed followers.

Vip. Ay, but 't was Bruce that led them.   Reverend Father,
'T is not the falchion's weight decides a combat;
It is the strong and skilful hand that wields it.
Ill fate, that we should lack the noble King,
And all his champions now! Time call'd them not,
For when I parted hence for Palestine,
The brows of most were free from grizzled hair.

Pri. Too true, alas! But well you know, in Scotland
Few hairs are silver'd underneath the helmet;
'T is cowls like mine which hide them.   'Mongst the laity,
War 's the rash reaper, who thrusts in his sickle
Before the grain is white.   In threescore years
And ten, which I have seen, I have outlived
Wellnigh two generations of our nobles.
The race which holds[1] yon summit is the third.

Vip. Thou mayst outlive them also.
Pri.   Heaven forfend!
My prayer shall be, that Heaven will close my eyes,
Before they look upon the wrath to come.

Vip. Retire, retire, good Father!— Pray for Scotland—
Think not on me.   Here comes an ancient friend,
Brother in arms, with whom to-day I 'll join me.
Back to your choir, assemble all your brotherhood,
And weary Heaven with prayers for victory.[2]

Pri. Heaven's blessing rest with thee,
Champion of Heaven, and of thy suffering country!
                    [*Exit* Prior.   Vipont *draws a little aside, and
                    lets down the beaver of his helmet.*

Enter Swinton, *followed by* Reynald *and others, to whom he
                    speaks as he enters.*

Swi. Halt here, and plant my pennon, till the Regent
Assign our band its station in the host.

Rey. That must be by the Standard.   We have had
That right since good Saint David's reign at least.
Fain would I see the Marcher would dispute it.

Swi. Peace, Reynald! Where the general plants the soldier,
There is his place of honour, and there only
His valour can win worship.   Thou 'rt of those
Who would have war's deep art bear the wild semblance
Of some disorder'd hunting, where, pell-mell,
Each trusting to the swiftness of his horse,
Gallants press on to see the quarry fall.

1 MS. — " The youths who hold," &c., " are."
2 MS. — ——— " with prayers for Scotland's weal."

Yon steel-clad Southrons, Reynald, are no deer;
And England's Edward is no stag at bay.

    Vip. (*advancing.*) There needed not, to blazon forth the Swinton,
His ancient burgonet, the sable Boar
Chain'd to the gnarl'd oak,[1]—nor his proud step,
Nor giant stature, nor the ponderous mace,
Which only he, of Scotland's realm, can wield:
His discipline and wisdom mark the leader,
As doth his frame the champion. Hail, brave Swinton!

    Swi. Brave Templar, thanks! Such your cross'd shoulder
       speaks you;
But the closed visor, which conceals your features,
Forbids more knowledge. Umfraville, perhaps—

    Vip. (*unclosing his helmet.*) No; one less worthy of our sacred
       Order.
Yet, unless Syrian suns have scorch'd my features
Swart as my sable visor, Alan Swinton
Will welcome Simon Vipont.

    Swi. (*embracing him.*) As the blithe reaper
Welcomes a practised mate, when the ripe harvest
Lies deep before him, and the sun is high!
Thou 'lt follow yon old pennon, wilt thou not?
'Tis tatter'd since thou saw'st it, and the Boar-heads
Look as if brought from off some Christmas board,
Where knives had notch'd them deeply.

    Vip. Have with them, ne'ertheless. The Stuart's Chequer,
The Bloody Heart of Douglas, Ross's Lymphads,
Sutherland's Wild-cats, nor the Royal Lion,
Rampant in golden treasure, wins me from them.
We 'll back the Boar-heads bravely. I see round them
A chosen band of lances—some well known to me.
Where 's the main body of thy followers?

    Swi. Symon de Vipont, thou dost see them all
That Swinton's bugle-horn can call to battle,
However loud it rings. There 's not a boy
Left in my halls, whose arm has strength enough
To bear a sword — there 's not a man behind,
However old, who moves without a staff.
Striplings and greybeards, every one is here;
And here all should be — Scotland needs them all;
And more and better men, were each a Hercules,
And yonder handful centuplied.

    Vip. A thousand followers — such, with friends and kinsmen,

---

[1] "The armorial bearings of the ancient family of Swinton are *sable*, a cheveron, *or*, between three boars' heads erased, *argent.* Crest—a boar chained to a tree, and above, on an escroll, *J'espère.* Supporters—two boars standing on a compartment, whereon are the words, *Je Pense.*"— *Douglas's Baronage*, p. 132.

Allies and vassals, thou wert wont to lead —
A thousand followers shrunk to sixty lances
In twelve years' space ? — And thy brave sons, Sir Alan ?
Alas ! I fear to ask.

    Swi. All slain, De Vipont.   In my empty home
A puny babe lisps to a widow'd mother,
Where is my grandsire ? wherefore do you weep ?"
But for that prattler, Lyulph's house is heirless.
I 'm an old oak, from which the foresters
Have hew'd four goodly boughs, and left beside me
Only a sapling, which the fawn may crush
As he springs over it.

    Vip. All slain ? — alas !

    Swi. Ay, all, De Vipont.   And their attributes,
John with the Long Spear — Archibald with the Axe —
Richard the Ready — and my youngest darling,
My fair-hair'd William — do but now survive
In measures which the grey-hair'd minstrels sing,
When they make maidens weep.

    Vip. These wars with England, they have rooted out
The flowers of Christendom.   Knights who might win
The sepulchre of Christ from the rude heathen,
Fall in unholy warfare !

    Swi. Unholy warfare ! ay, well hast thou named it ;
But not with England — would, her cloth-yard shafts
Had bored their cuirasses ! Their lives had been
Lost like their grandsire's, in the bold defence
Of their dear country[1] — but in private feud
With the proud Gordon, fell my Long-spear'd John,
He with the Axe, and he men call'd the Ready,
Ay, and my Fair-hair'd Will — the Gordon's wrath
Devour'd my gallant issue.

    Vip. Since thou dost weep, their death is unavenged ?

    Swi. Templar, what think'st thou me ? — See yonder rock,
From which the fountain gushes — is it less
Compact of adamant, though waters flow from it ?
Firm hearts have moister eyes. — They *are* avenged ;
I wept not till they were — till the proud Gordon
Had with his life-blood dyed my father's sword,
In guerdon that he thinn'd my father's lineage,
And then I wept my sons ; and, as the Gordon
Lay at my feet, there was a tear for him,
Which mingled with the rest.   We had been friends,
Had shared the banquet and the chase together,
Fought side by side, — and our first cause of strife,
Woe to the pride of both, was but a light one !

    [1] MS. — "Of the dear land that nursed them — but in feud."

Vip. You are at feud, then, with the mighty Gordon!
Swi. At deadly feud.   Here in this Border-land,
Where the sire's quarrels descend upon the son,
As due a part of his inheritance,
As the strong castle and the ancient blazon,
Where private Vengeance holds the scales of justice,
Weighing each drop of blood as scrupulously
As Jews or Lombards balance silver pence,
Not in this land, 'twixt Solway and Saint Abb's,
Rages a bitterer feud than mine and theirs,
The Swinton and the Gordon.
Vip. You, with some threescore lances — and the Gordon
Leading a thousand followers.
Swi. You rate him far too low.   Since you sought Palestine,
He hath had grants of baronies and lordships
In the far-distant North.   A thousand horse
His southern friends and vassals always number'd.
Add Badenoch kerne, and horse from Dee and Spey,
He'll count a thousand more.— And now, De Vipont,
If the Boar-heads seem in your eyes less worthy
For lack of followers — seek yonder standard —
The bounding Stag, with a brave host around it;
There the young Gordon makes his earliest field,
And pants to win his spurs.   His father's friend,
As well as mine, thou wert— go, join his pennon,
And grace him with thy presence.
Vip. When you were friends, I was the friend of both,
And now I can be enemy to neither;
But my poor person, though but slight the aid,
Joins on this field the banner of the two
Which hath the smallest following.
Swi. Spoke like the generous Knight who gave up all,
Leading and lordship, in a heathen land
To fight, a Christian soldier!   Yet, in earnest,
I pray, De Vipont, you would join the Gordon
In this high battle.   'Tis a noble youth,—
So fame doth vouch him,— amorous, quick, and valiant;
Takes knighthood, too, this day, and well may use
His spurs too rashly[1] in the wish to win them.
A friend like thee beside him in the fight,
Were worth a hundred spears, to rein his valour
And temper it with prudence:— 'tis the aged eagle
Teaches his brood to gaze upon the sun,
With eye undazzled.
Vip. Alas! brave Swinton! wouldst thou train the hunter
That soon must bring thee to the bay!   Your custom,

1 MS.—"Sharply."

Your most unchristian, savage, fiend-like custom,
Binds Gordon to avenge his father's death.
Swi. Why, be it so! I look for nothing else:
My part was acted when I slew his father,
Avenging my four sons—Young Gordon's sword,
If it should find my heart, can ne'er inflict there
A pang so poignant as his father's did.
But I would perish by a noble hand,
And such will his be if he bear him nobly,
Nobly and wisely on this field of Halidon.

Enter a PURSUIVANT.

Pur. Sir Knights, to council!—'tis the Regent's order,
That knights and men of leading meet him instantly
Before the royal standard. Edward's army
Is seen from the hill-summit.
Swi. Say to the Regent, we obey his orders.

[Exit PURSUIVANT.

[*To* REYNALD.] Hold thou my casque, and furl my pennon up
Close to the staff. I will not show my crest,
Nor standard, till the common foe shall challenge them.
I 'll wake no civil strife, nor tempt the Gordon
With aught that 's like defiance.
Vip. Will he not know your features?
Swi. He never saw me. In the distant North,
Against his will, 'tis said, his friends detain'd him
During his nurture—caring not, belike,
To trust a pledge so precious near the Boar-tusks.
It was a natural but needless caution:
I wage no war with children, for I think
Too deeply on mine own.
Vip. I have thought on it, and will see the Gordon
As we go hence [1] to council. I do bear
A cross, which binds me to be Christian priest,
As well as Christian champion.[2] God may grant,
That I, at once his father's friend and yours,
May make some peace betwixt you.[3]
Swi. When that your priestly zeal, and knightly valour,
Shall force the grave to render up the dead.

[Exeunt severally.

---

[1] MS.—"As we do pass," &c.
[2] MS.—"The cross I wear appoints me Christian priest,
    As well as Christian warrior," &c.
[3] In the MS., the scene terminates with this line.

SCENE II.

*The summit of Halidon Hill, before the Regent's Tent. The
Royal Standard of Scotland is seen in the back-ground, with
the Pennons and Banners of the principal Nobles around it.*

Council of Scottish Nobles and Chiefs. SUTHERLAND, ROSS, LEN-
NOX, MAXWELL, and other Nobles of the highest rank, are close
to the REGENT's person, and in the act of keen debate. VIPONT
with GORDON and others, remain grouped at some distance on
the right hand of the stage. On the left, standing also apart,
is SWINTON, alone and bare-headed. The Nobles are dressed in
Highland or Lowland habits, as historical costume requires.
Trumpets, Heralds, &c. are in attendance.*

LEN. Nay, Lordlings, put no shame upon my counsels.
I did but say, if we retired a little,
We should have fairer field and better vantage.
I've seen King Robert—ay, The Bruce himself—
Retreat six leagues in length, and think no shame on't.
   REG. Ay, but King Edward sent a haughty message,
Defying us to battle on this field,
This very hill of Halidon; if we leave it
Unfought withal, it squares not with our honour.
   SWI. (*apart.*) A perilous honour, that allows the enemy,
And such an enemy as this same Edward,
To choose our field of battle! He knows how
To make our Scottish pride betray its master
Into the pitfall.
   [*During this speech, the debate among the Nobles is continued.*]
   SUTH. (*aloud.*) We will not back one furlong—not one yard,
No, nor one inch; where'er we find the foe,
Or where the foe finds us, there will we fight him.
Retreat will dull the spirit of our followers,
Who now stand prompt for battle.
   ROSS. My Lords, methinks great Morarchat[1] has doubts,
That, if his Northern clans once turn the seam
Of their check'd hose behind, it will be hard
To halt and rally them.
   SUTH. Say'st thou, MacDonnell?—Add another falsehood,
And name when Morarchat was coward or traitor?
Thine island race, as chronicles can tell,
Were oft affianced to the Southron cause;
Loving the weight and temper of their gold,
More than the weight and temper of their steel.

---

[1] Morarchate is the ancient Gaelic designation of the Earls of Sutherland.
See *ante* vol. ii. page 394, *note.* — ED.

Reg. Peace, my Lords, ho!

Ross. (*throwing down his Glove.*) MacDonnell will not peace!
      There lies my pledge,
Proud Morarchat, to witness thee a liar.

Max. Brought I all Nithsdale from the Western Border,
Left I my towers exposed to foraying England,
And thieving Annandale, to see such misrule?

John. Who speaks of Annandale? Dare Maxwell slander
The gentle House of Lochwood?[1]

Reg. Peace, Lordlings, once again. We represent
The Majesty of Scotland—in our presence
Brawling is treason.

Suth. Were it in presence of the King himself,
What should prevent my saying——

Enter Lindesay.

Lin. You must determine quickly. Scarce a mile
Parts our vanguard from Edward's. On the plain
Bright gleams of armour flash through clouds of dust,
Like stars through frost-mist—steeds neigh, and weapons clash—
And arrows soon will whistle—the worst sound
That waits on English war.—You must determine.

Reg. We are determined. We will spare proud Edward
Half of the ground that parts us.—Onward, Lords!
Saint Andrew strike for Scotland! We will lead
The middle ward ourselves, the Royal Standard
Display'd beside us; and beneath its shadow
Shall the young gallants, whom we knight this day,
Fight for their golden spurs.—Lennox, thou 'rt wise,
And wilt obey command—lead thou the rear.

Len. The rear!—why I the rear? The van were fitter
For him who fought abreast with Robert Bruce.

Swi. (*apart.*) Discretion hath forsaken Lennox too!
The wisdom he was forty years in gathering
Has left him in an instant. 'T is contagious
Even to witness frenzy.

Suth. The Regent hath determined well. The rear
Suits him the best who counsell'd our retreat.

Len. Proud Northern Thane, the van were soon the rear,
Were thy disorder'd followers planted there.

Suth. Then, for that very word, I make a vow,
By my broad Earldom, and my father's soul,
That, if I have not leading of the van,
I will not fight to-day!

Ross. Morarchat! thou the leading of the van!
Not whilst MacDonnell lives.

---

[1] Lochwood Castle was the ancient seat of the Johnstones, Lords of Annandale.

Swi. (*apart.*) Nay, then, a stone would speak.
[*Addresses the* Regent.] May't please your Grace,
And you, great Lords, to hear an old man's counsel,
That hath seen fights enow. These open bickerings
Dishearten all our host. If that your Grace,
With these great Earls and Lords, must needs debate,
Let the closed tent conceal your disagreement;
Else 'twill be said, ill fares it with the flock,
If shepherds wrangle when the wolf is nigh.
　Reg. The old Knight counsels well. Let every Lord
Or Chief, who leads five hundred men or more,
Follow to council—others are excluded—
We'll have no vulgar censurers of our conduct—
　　　　　　　　　　　　[*Looking at* Swinton.
Young Gordon, your high rank and numerous following
Give you a seat with us, though yet unknighted.
　Gordon. I pray you, pardon me. My youth's unfit
To sit in council, when that Knight's grey hairs
And wisdom wait without.
　Reg. Do as you will; we deign not bid you twice.
　　[*The* Regent, Ross, Sutherland, Lennox, Maxwell, *&c.*
　　　enter the Tent. The rest remain grouped about the Stage.
　Gor. (*observing* Swi.) That helmetless old Knight, his giant
　　stature,
His awful accents of rebuke and wisdom,
Have caught my fancy strangely. He doth seem
Like to some vision'd form which I have dream'd of,
But never saw with waking eyes till now.
I will accost him.
　Vip.　　　　　　Pray you, do not so;
Anon I'll give you reason why you should not.
There's other work in hand ——
　Gor. I will but ask his name. There's in his presence
Something that works upon me like a spell,
Or like the feeling made my childish ear
Dote upon tales of superstitious dread,
Attracting while they chill'd my heart with fear.
Now, born the Gordon, I do feel right well
I'm bound to fear nought earthly—and I fear nought.
I'll know who this man is ——　　　　[*Accosts* Swinton.
Sir Knight, I pray you, of your gentle courtesy,
To tell your honour'd name. I am ashamed,
Being unknown in arms, to say that mine
Is Adam Gordon.
　Swinton (*shows emotion, but instantly subdues it.*)
It is a name that soundeth in my ear
Like to a death-knell—ay, and like the call

Of the shrill trumpet to the mortal lists;
Yet 'tis a name which ne'er hath been dishonour'd,
And never will, I trust—most surely never
By such a youth as thou.
   Gor. There's a mysterious courtesy in this,
And yet it yields no answer to my question.
I trust you hold the Gordon not unworthy
To know the name he asks?
   Swi. Worthy of all that openness and honour
May show to friend or foe—but, for my name,
Vipont will show it you; and, if it sound
Harsh in your ear,[1] remember that it knells there
But at your own request. This day, at least,
Though seldom wont to keep it in concealment,
As there's no cause I should, *you* had not heard it.
   Gor. This strange——
   Vip.   The mystery is needful. Follow me.
                  [*They retire behind the side scene.*
   Swi. (*looking after them.*) 'Tis a brave youth. How blush'd
      his noble cheek,
While youthful modesty, and the embarrassment
Of curiosity, combined with wonder,
And half suspicion of some slight intended,
All mingled in the flush!—but soon 'twill deepen
Into revenge's glow. How slow is Vipont!—
I wait the issue, as I 've seen spectators
Suspend the motion even of the eyelids,
When the slow gunner, with his lighted match,
Approach'd the charged cannon, in the act
To waken its dread slumbers.—Now 'tis out;
He draws his sword, and rushes towards me,
Who will nor seek nor shun him.

        Enter Gordon, *withheld by* Vipont.

   Vip. Hold, for the sake of Heaven! O, for the sake
Of your dear country, hold!—Has Swinton slain your father,
And must you, therefore, be yourself a parricide,
And stand recorded as the selfish traitor,
Who, in her hour of need, his country's cause
Deserts, that he may wreak a private wrong?
Look to yon banner—that is Scotland's standard;
Look to the Regent—he is Scotland's general;
Look to the English—they are Scotland's foemen!
Bethink thee, then, thou art a son of Scotland,
And think on nought beside.[2]

      [1] " A name unmusical to Volscian ears,
         And harsh in sound to thine."—*Coriolanus.*
   [2] In the MS., the five last lines of Vipont's speech are interpolated.

Gor. He hath come here to brave me!—Off! unhand me!—
Thou canst not be my father's ancient friend,
That stand'st 'twixt me and him who slew my father.
    Vip. You know not Swinton.   Scarce one passing thought
Of his high mind was with you ; now, his soul
Is fixed on this day's battle.   You might slay him
At unawares before he saw your blade drawn.—
Stand still and watch him close.[1]

Enter Maxwell *from the tent.*

    Swi. How go our councils, Maxwell, may I ask?
    Max. As wild, as if the very wind and sea
With every breeze and every billow battled
For their precedence.[2]
    Swi. Most sure they are possess'd! Some evil spirit,
To mock their valour, robs them of discretion.
Fie, fie, upon't!—O that Dunfermline's tomb
Could render up The Bruce! that Spain's red shore
Could give us back the good Lord James of Douglas!
Or that fierce Randolph, with his voice of terror,
Were here, to awe these brawlers to submission!
    Vip. (*to* Gor.) Thou hast perused him at more leisure now.
    Gor. I see the giant form which all men speak of,
The stately port—but not the sullen eye,
Not the bloodthirsty look, that should belong
To him that made me orphan.   I shall need
To name my father twice, ere I can strike
At such grey hairs, and face of such command ;
Yet my hand clenches on my falchion hilt,
In token he shall die.
    Vip. Need I again remind you, that the place
Permits not private quarrel?
    Gor. I 'm calm.   I will not seek—nay I will shun it—
And yet methinks that such debate 's the fashion.
You 've heard how taunts, reproaches, and the lie,
The lie itself, have flown from mouth to mouth ;
As if a band of peasants were disputing
About a foot-ball match, rather than Chiefs
Were ordering a battle.   I am young,
And lack experience : tell me, brave De Vipont,
Is such the fashion of your wars in Palestine?

---

[1] MS.—" You must not here—not where the Royal Standard
        Awaits the attack of Scotland's enemies,
        Against the common foe—wage private quarrel.
        He braves you not—his thought is on the event
        Of this day's field.   Stand still, and watch him closer."
    [2] " Mad as the sea and wind, when both contend
        Which is the mightier."—*Hamlet.*

Vip. Such it at times hath been ; and then the Cross
Hath sunk before the Crescent.   Heaven's cause
Won us not victory where wisdom was not.—
Behold yon English host come slowly on,
With equal front, rank marshall'd upon rank,
As if one spirit ruled one moving body ;
The leaders, in their places, each prepared
To charge, support, and rally, as the fortune
Of changeful battle needs : then look on ours,
Broken, disjointed, as the tumbling surges
Which the winds wake at random.   Look on both,
And dread the issue—Yet there might be succour.
  Gor. We're fearfully o'ermatch'd in discipline ;
So even my inexperienced eye can judge.
What succour save in Heaven ?
  Vip. Heaven acts by human means.   The artist's skill
Supplies in war, as in mechanic crafts,
Deficiency of tools.   There's courage, wisdom,
And skill enough, live in one leader here.
As, flung into the balance, might avail
To counterpoise the odds 'twixt that ruled host
And our wild multitude.—I must not name him
  Gor. I guess, but dare not ask.—What band is yonder,
Arranged so closely as the English discipline
Had marshall'd their best files ?
  Vip. Know'st thou not the pennon ?
One day, perhaps, thou 'lt see it all too closely ;—
It is Sir Alan Swinton's.
  Gor. These, then, are his—the relics of his power,
Yet worth an host of ordinary men. —
And I must slay my country's sagest leader,
And crush by numbers that determined handful,
When most my country needs their practised aid,
Or men will say, " There goes degenerate Gordon !
His father's blood is on the Swinton's sword,
And his is in his scabbard !"   [*Muses.*
  Vip. (*apart.*) High blood and mettle, mixed with early wisdom
Sparkle in this brave youth.   If he survive
This evil-omen'd day, I pawn my word,
That, in the ruin which I now forbode,
Scotland has treasure left. — How close he eyes
Each look and step of Swinton ! Is it hate,
Or is it admiration, or are both
Commingled strangely in that steady gaze ?
    [Swinton *and* Maxwell *return from the bottom of the stage*
  Max. The storm is laid at length amongst these counsellors ;
See, they come forth.

Swi.   And it is more than time;
For I can mark the vanguard archery
Handling their quivers — bending up their bows.

Enter the REGENT *and Scottish Lords.*

Reg. Thus shall it be, then, since we may no better;
And, since no Lord will yield one jot of way
To this high urgency, or give the vanguard
Up to another's guidance, we will abide them
Even on this bent; and as our troops are rank'd,
So shall they meet the foe.   Chief, nor Thane,
Nor Noble, can complain of the precedence
Which chance has thus assign'd him.
    Swi. (*apart.*) O, sage discipline,
That leaves to chance the marshalling of a battle!
    Gor. Move him to speech, De Vipont.
    Vip.   Move *him!* — Move whom?
    Gor. Even him, whom, but brief space since,
My hand did burn to put to utter silence.
    Vip. I 'll move it to him. — Swinton, speak to them;
They lack thy counsel sorely.
    Swi. Had I the thousand spears which once I led,
I had not thus been silent.   But men's wisdom
Is rated by their means.   From the poor leader
Of sixty lances, who seeks words of weight?
    Gor. (*steps forward.*) Swinton, there 's that of wisdom on thy
          brow,
And valour in thine eye, and that of peril
In this most urgent hour, that bids me say, —
Bids me, thy mortal foe, say, — Swinton, speak,
For King and Country's sake!
    Swi. Nay, if that voice commands me, speak I will;
It sounds as if the dead lays charge on me.
    Reg. (*to* Lennox, *with whom he has been consulting.*)
'T is better than you think.   This broad hill-side
Affords fair compass for our power's display,
Rank above rank rising in seemly tiers;
So that the rearward stands as fair and open ——
    Swi. As e'er stood mark before an English archer.
    Reg. Who dares to say so? — who is 't dare impeach
Our rule of discipline?
    Swi. A poor Knight of these Marches, good my Lord;
Alan of Swinton, who hath kept a house here,
He and his ancestry, since the old days
Of Malcolm, called the Maiden.
    Reg. You have brought here, even to this pitched field,
In which the Royal Banner is display'd,

I think some sixty spears, Sir Knight of Swinton;
Our musters name no more.

Swi. I brought each man I had; and Chief, or Earl,
Thane, Duke, or dignitary, brings no more:
And with them brought I what may here be useful—
An aged eye; which, what in England, Scotland,
Spain, France, and Flanders, hath seen fifty battles,
And ta'en some judgment of them; a stark hand too,
Which plays as with a straw with this same mace,—
Which if a young arm here can wield more lightly,
I never more will offer word of counsel.

Len. Hear him, my Lord; it is the noble Swinton—
He hath had high experience.

Max.   He is noted
The wisest warrior 'twixt the Tweed and Solway,—
I do beseech you hear him.

John. Ay, hear the Swinton—hear stout old Sir Alan;
Maxwell and Johnstone both agree for once.

Reg. Where's your impatience now?
Late you were all for battle, would not hear
Ourself pronounce a word—and now you gaze
On yon old warrior, in his antique armour,
As if he were arisen from the dead,
To bring us Bruce's counsel for the battle.

Swi. 'Tis a proud word to speak; but he who fought
Long under Robert Bruce, may something guess,
Without communication with the dead,
At what he would have counsell'd.—Bruce had bidden ye
Review your battle-order, marshall'd broadly
Here on the bare hill-side, and bidden you mark
Yon clouds of Southern archers, bearing down
To the green meadow-lands which stretch beneath—
The Bruce had warn'd you, not a shaft to-day
But shall find mark within a Scottish bosom,
If thus our field be order'd. The callow boys,
Who draw but four-foot bows, shall gall our front,
While on our mainward, and upon the rear,
The cloth-yard shafts shall fall like death's own darts,
And, though blind men discharge them, find a mark.
Thus shall we die the death of slaughter'd deer,
Which, driven into the toils, are shot at ease
By boys and women, while they toss.aloft,
All idly and in vain, their branchy horns,
As we shall shake our unavailing spears.

Reg. Tush, tell not me! If their shot fall like hail,
Our men have Milan coats to bear it out.

Swi. Never did armourer temper steel on stithy

That made sure fence against an English arrow ;
A cobweb gossamer were guard as good [1]
Against a wasp-sting.
   REG. Who fears a wasp-sting?
   SWI.   I, my Lord, fear none ;
Yet should a wise man brush the insect off,
Or he may smart for it.
   REG. We 'll keep the hill; it is the vantage-ground
When the main battle joins.
   SWI. It ne'er will join, while their light archery
Can foil our spearmen and our barbed horse.
To hope Plantagenet would seek close combat
When he can conquer riskless, is to deem
Sagacious Edward simpler than a babe
In battle knowledge. Keep the hill, my Lord,
With the main body, if it is your pleasure ;
But let a body of your chosen horse
Make execution on yon waspish archers.
I 've done such work before, and love it well ;
If 't is your pleasure to give me the leading,
The dames of Sherwood, Inglewood, and Weardale,
Shall sit in widowhood, and long for venison,
And long in vain. Whoe'er remembers Bannockburn,—
And when shall Scotsman, till the last loud trumpet,
Forget that stirring word !—knows *that* great battle
Even thus was fought and won.
   LEN. This is the shortest road to bandy blows ;
For when the bills step forth and bows go back,
Then is the moment that our hardy spearmen,
With their strong bodies, and their stubborn hearts,
And limbs well knit by mountain exercise,
At the close tug shall foil the short-breath'd Southron.
   SWI. I do not say the field will thus be won ;
The English host is numerous, brave, and loyal ;
Their Monarch most accomplish'd in war's art,
Skill'd, resolute, and wary——
   REG. And if your scheme secure not victory, [2]
What does it promise us?

<hr>

[1] MS. ——"Guard as thick."

[2] "The generous abandonment of private dissension, on the part of Gordon, which the historian has described as a momentary impulse, is depicted by the dramatist with great skill and knowledge of human feeling, as the result of many powerful and conflicting emotions. He has, we think, been very successful in his attempt to express the hesitating, and sometimes retrograde movements of a young and ardent mind, in its transition from the first glow of indignation against his hereditary foeman, the mortal antagonist of his father, to the no less warm and generous devotion of feeling which is inspired in it by the contemplation of that foeman's valour and virtues."—*British Critic.*

Swi.   This much at least,—
Darkling we shall not die : the peasant's shaft,
Loosen'd perchance without an aim or purpose,
Shall not drink up the life-blood we derive
From those famed ancestors, who made their breasts
This frontier's barrier for a thousand years.
We 'll meet these Southron bravely hand to hand,
And eye to eye, and weapon against weapon ;
Each man who falls shall see the foe who strikes him.
While our good blades are faithful to the hilts,
And our good hands to these good blades are faithful,
Blow shall meet blow, and none fall unavenged—
We shall not bleed alone.
Reg.   And this is all
Your wisdom hath devised ?
Swi. Not all ; for I would pray you, noble Lords,
(If one, among the guilty guiltiest, might,)
For this one day to charm to ten hours' rest
The never-dying worm of deadly feud,
That gnaws our vexed hearts—think no one foe
Save Edward and his host :—days will remain,[1]
Ay, days by far too many will remain,
To avenge old feuds or struggles for precedence ;—
Let this one day be Scotland's.—For myself,
If there is any here may claim from me
(As well may chance) a debt of blood and hatred,
My life is his to-morrow unresisting,
So he to-day will let me do the best
That my old arm may achieve for the dear country
That 's mother to us both.
                    [Gordon *shows much emotion during this and the*
                        preceding speech of Swinton.
Reg. It is a dream—a vision !—if one troop
Rush down upon the archers, all will follow,
And order is destroy'd—we 'll keep the battle-rank
Our fathers wont to do.   No more on 't.—Ho!
Where be those youths seek knighthood from our sword ?
Her. Here are the Gordon, Somerville, and Hay,
And Hepburn, with a score of gallants more
Reg. Gordon, stand forth.
Gor.   I pray your Grace, forgive me.
Reg. How ! seek you not for knighthood ?
Gor.   I do thirst for 't—
But, pardon me—'t is from another sword.

1 MS.—" For this one day to chase our country's curse
        From your vex'd bosoms, and think no one enemy
        But those in yonder army—days enow,
        Ay, days," &c.

Reg. It is your Sovereign's—seek you for a worthier!
Gor. Who would drink purely, seeks the secret fountain,
How small soever—not the general stream,
Though it be deep and wide. My Lord, I seek
The boon of knighthood from the honour'd weapon
Of the best knight, and of the sagest leader,
That ever graced a ring of chivalry.
—Therefore, I beg the boon on bended knee,
Even from Sir Alan Swinton.   [*Kneels.*
   Reg. Degenerate boy! abject at once and insolent!—
See, Lords, he kneels to him that slew his father!
   Gor. (*starting up.*) Shame be on him, who speaks such shame-
      ful word!
Shame be on him, whose tongue would sow dissension,
When most the time demands that native Scotsmen
Forget each private wrong!
   Swi. (*interrupting him.*) Youth, since you crave me
To be your sire in chivalry, I remind you
War has it duties, Office has its reverence;
Who governs in the Sovereign's name is Sovereign;—
Crave the Lord Regent's pardon.
   Gor. You task me justly, and I crave his pardon—
                [*Bows to the* Regent.
His and these noble Lords'; and pray them all
Bear witness to my words.—Ye noble presence,
Here I remit unto the Knight of Swinton
All bitter memory of my father's slaughter,
All thoughts of malice, hatred, and revenge;
By no base fear or composition moved,
But by the thought, that in our country's battle
All hearts should be as one. I do forgive him
As freely as I pray to be forgiven,
And once more kneel to him to sue for knighthood.
   Swi. (*affected, and drawing his sword.*)
Alas! brave youth, 'tis I should kneel to you,
And, tendering thee the hilt of the fell sword
That made thee fatherless, bid thee use the point
After thine own discretion. For thy boon—
Trumpets, be ready—In the Holiest name,
And in Our Lady's and Saint Andrew's name,
        [*Touching his shoulder with his sword.*
I dub thee Knight!—Arise, Sir Adam Gordon!
Be faithful, brave, and O, be fortunate,
Should this ill hour permit!
        [*The trumpets sound;—the Heralds cry
         "Largesse!" and the Attendants shout
         "A Gordon! A Gordon!"*

Rng. Beggars and flatterers! Peace, peace, I say!
We 'll to the Standard; knights shall there be made
Who will with better reason crave your clamour.
    Len. What of Swinton's counsel?
Here 's Maxwell and myself think it worth noting.
    Reg. (*with concentrated indignation.*)
Let the best knight, and let the sagest leader,—
So Gordon quotes the man who slew his father,—
With his old pedigree and heavy mace,
Essay the adventure if it pleases him,
With his fair threescore horse. As for ourselves,
We will not peril aught upon the measure.
    Gor. Lord Regent, you mistake; for if Sir Alan
Shall venture such attack, each man who calls
The Gordon chief, and hopes or fears from him
Or good or evil, follows Swinton's banner
In this achievement.
    Reg. Why, God ha' mercy! This is of a piece.
Let young and old e'en follow their own counsel,
Since none will list to mine.
    Ross. The Border cockerel fain would be on horseback;
'T is safe to be prepared for fight or flight:
And this comes of it to give Northern lands
To the false Norman blood.
    Gor. Hearken, proud Chief of Isles! Within my stalls
I have two hundred horse; two hundred riders
Mount guard upon my castle, who would tread
Into the dust a thousand of your Redshanks,
Nor count it a day's service.
    Swi.   Hear I this
From thee, young man, and on the day of battle?
And to the brave MacDonnell?
    Gor. 'T was he that urged me; but I am rebuked.
    Reg. He crouches like a leash-hound to his master![1]
    Swi. Each hound must do so, that would head the deer—
'T is mongrel curs that snatch at mate or master.
    Reg. Too much of this. Sirs, to the Royal Standard!
I bid you, in the name of good King David,
Sound trumpets—sound for Scotland and King David!
               [*The* Regent *and the rest go off, and the Scene closes.*
                 Manent Gordon, Swinton, *and* Vipont, *with* Rey-
                 nald *and followers.* Lennox *follows the* Regent;
                 but returns and addresses Swinton.
    Len. O, were my western horsemen but come up,
I would take part with you!
    Swi.   Better that you remain.

---

[1] In the MS., this speech and the next are interpolated.

They lack discretion ; such grey head as yours
May best supply that want.
Lennox, mine ancient friend, and honour'd lord,
Farewell, I think, for ever !

LEN. Farewell, brave friend !—and farewell, noble Gordon,
Whose sun will be eclipsed even as it rises !—
The Regent will not aid you.

SWI. We will so bear us, that as soon the blood-hound
Shall halt, and take no part, what time his comrade
Is grappling with the deer, as he stand still,
And see us overmatch'd.

LEN. Alas ! thou dost not know how mean his pride is,
How strong his envy.

SWI. Then we will die, and leave the shame with him.
[*Exit* LENNOX.

VIP. (*to* GORDON.) What ails thee, noble youth ?—what means
      this pause ?
Thou dost not rue thy generosity ?

GOR. I have been hurried on by strong impulse,
Like to a bark that scuds before the storm,
Till driven upon some strange and distant coast,
Which never pilot dream'd of.— Have I not forgiven ?
And am I not still fatherless ?

SWI.   Gordon, no ;
For while we live, I am a father to thee.

GOR. Thou, Swinton ?—no !—that cannot, cannot be.

SWI. Then change the phrase, and say, that while we live,
Gordon shall be my son. If thou art fatherless,
Am I not childless too ? Bethink thee, Gordon,
Our death-feud was not like the household fire
Which the poor peasant hides among its embers,
To smoulder on, and wait a time for waking.
Ours was the conflagration of the forest,
Which, in its fury, spares nor sprout nor stem,
Hoar oak nor sapling—not to be extinguish'd,
Till Heaven, in mercy, sends down all her waters ;
But, once subdued, its flame is quench'd for ever ;
And spring shall hide the track of devastation[1]
With foliage and with flowers.— Give me thy hand.

GOR. My hand and heart !—and freely now !—to fight !

VIP. How will you act ? [*to* SWINTON.] The Gordon's band
      and thine
Are in the rearward left, I think, in scorn—
Ill post for them who wish to charge the foremost !

SWI. We 'll turn that scorn to vantage, and descend

---

[1] MS.—" But, once extinguish'd, it is quench'd for ever,
        And spring shall hide the blackness of its ashes."

Sideloug the hill—some winding path there must be—
O, for a well-skill'd guide!
　　　　　　　　　　[HOB HATTELY *starts up from a Thicket.*
　HOB. So here he stands.—An ancient friend, Sir Alan.
Hob Hattely, or, if you like it better,
Hob of the Heron Plume, here stands your guide,
　SWI. An ancient friend?—a most notorious knave,
Whose throat I've destined to the dodder'd oak
Before my castle, these ten months and more.
Was it not you who drove from Simprim-mains,
And Swinton-quarter, sixty head of cattle?
　HOB. What then, if now I lead your sixty lances
Upon the English flank, where they'll find spoil
Is worth six hundred beeves?
　SWI. Why, thou canst do it, knave.　I would not trust thee
With one poor bullock; yet would risk my life,
And all my followers, on thine honest guidance.
　HOB.　There is a dingle, and a most discreet one,
(I've trod each step by star-light,) that sweeps round
The rearward of this hill, and opens secretly
Upon the archers' flank.—Will not that serve
Your present turn, Sir Alan?
　SWI.　　　　　　　　　　　Bravely, bravely!
　GOR. Mount, Sirs, and cry my slogan,
Let all who love the Gordon follow me!
　SWI. Ay, let all follow—but in silence follow.
Scare not the hare that's couchant on her form—
The cushat from her nest—brush not, if possible,
The dew-drop from the spray—
Let no one whisper, until I cry " Havoc!"
Then shout as loud's ye will.—On, on, brave Hob!
On, thou false thief, but yet most faithful Scotsman!　　[*Exeunt*

ACT II.—SCENE I.

*A rising Ground immediately in front of the Position of the
　English Main Body.* PERCY, CHANDOS, RIBAUMONT, *and other
　English and Norman Nobles, are grouped on the Stage.*

　PER. The Scots still keep the hill—the sun grows high.
Would that the charge would sound!
　CHA. Thou scent'st the slaughter, Percy.—Who comes here?
　　　　　　　　　　[*Enter the* ABBOT OF WALTHAMSTOW.
Now, by my life, the holy priest of Walthamstow,

Like to a lamb among a herd of wolves!
See, he 's about to bleat.
  AB. The King, methinks, delays the onset long.
  CHA. Your general, Father, like your rat-catcher,
Pauses to bait his traps, and set his snares.
  AB. The metaphor is decent.
  CHA.   Reverend sir,
I will uphold it just. Our good King Edward
Will presently come to this battle-field,
And speak to you of the last tilting match,
Or of some feat he did a twenty years since,
But not a word of the day's work before him :
Even as the artist, sir, whose name offends you,
Sits prosing o'er his can, until the trap fall,
Announcing that the vermin are secured,
And then 'tis up, and on them.
  PER. Chandos, you give your tongue too bold a license
  CHA. Percy, I am a necessary evil;—
King Edward would not want me, if he could,
And could not, if he would. I know my value.
My heavy hand excuses my light tongue.
So men wear weighty swords in their defence,
Although they may offend the tender shin,
When the steel-boot is doff'd.
  AB.   My Lord of Chandos,
This is but idle speech on brink of battle,
When Christain men should think upon their sins ;
For as the tree falls, so the trunk must lie,
Be it for good or evil. Lord, bethink thee,
Thou hast withheld from our most reverend house,
The tithes of Everingham and Settleton ;
Wilt thou make satisfaction to the Church
Before her thunders strike thee? I do warn thee
In most paternal sort.
  CHA. I thank you, Father, filially.
Though but a truant son of Holy Church,
I would not choose to undergo her censures,
When Scottish blades are waving at my throat.
I 'll make fair composition.
  AB. No composition ; I 'll have all, or none.
  CHA. None, then—'tis soonest spoke. I 'll take my chance,
And trust my sinful soul to Heaven's mercy,
Rather than risk my worldly goods with thee—
My hour may not be come.
  AB. Impious—impenitent—
  PER.   Hush! the King—the King!

Enter KING EDWARD, *attended by* BALIOL *and others.*

KING (*apart to* CHA.) Hark hither, Chandos!—Have the York-
    shire archers
Yet join'd the vanguard?
CHA.   They are marching thither.
K. ED. Bid them make haste, for shame—send a quick rider.
The loitering knaves! were it to steal my venison,
Their steps were light enough.—How now, Sir Abbot!
Say, is your Reverence come to study with us
The princely art of war?
AB. I've had a lecture from my Lord of Chandos,
In which he term'd you Grace a rat-catcher.
K. ED. Chandos, how's this?
CHA. O, I will prove it, sir!—These skipping Scots
Have changed a dozen times 'twixt Bruce and Baliol,
Quitting each House when it began to totter;
They 're fierce and cunning, treacherous, too, as rats,
And we, as such, will smoke them in their fastnesses.
K. ED. These rats have seen your back, my Lord of Chandos,
And noble Percy's too.
PER. Ay; but the mass which now lies weltering
On yon hill side, like a Leviathan
That's stranded on the shallows, then had soul in 't,
Order and discipline, and power of action.
Now 't is a headless corpse, which only shows,
By wild convulsions, that some life remains in 't.
K. ED. True, they had once a head; and 't was a wise,
Although a rebel head.
AB. (*bowing to the* KING.) Would he were here! we should
    find one to match him.
K. ED. There 's something in that wish which wakes an echo
Within my bosom. Yet it is as well,
Or better, that The Bruce is in his grave.
We have enough of powerful foes on earth,—
No need to summon them from other worlds.
PER. Your Grace ne'er met The Bruce?
K. ED. Never himself; but in my earliest field,
I did encounter with his famous captains,
Douglas and Randolph. Faith! they press'd me hard.
AB. My Liege, if I might urge you with a question.
Will the Scots fight to-day?
K. ED. (*sharply.*) Go look your breviary.
CHA. (*apart.*) The Abbot has it—Edward will not answer
On that nice point. We must observe his humour.—
                     [*Addresses the* KING.
Your first campaign, my Liege?—That was in Weardale,

When Douglas gave our camp yon midnight ruffle,
And turn'd men's beds to biers?
   K. ED. Ay, by Saint Edward!—I escaped right nearly.
I was a soldier then for holidays,
And slept not in mine armour: my safe rest
Was startled by the cry of "Douglas! Douglas!"
And by my couch, a grisly chamberlain,
Stood Alan Swinton, with his bloody mace.
It was a churchman saved me—my stout chaplain,
Heaven quit his spirit! caught a weapon up,
And grappled with the gaint.—How now, Louis?

Enter an Officer, who whispers the KING.

   K. ED. Say to him,—thus—and thus——　　[*Whispers.*
   AB. That Swinton's dead. A monk of ours reported,
Bound homeward from St. Ninian's pilgrimage,
The Lord of Gordon slew him.
   PER. Father, and if your house stood on our borders,
You might have cause to know that Swinton lives,
And is on horseback yet.
   CHA. 　　　　　　　　He slew the Gordon,
That's all the difference—a very trifle.
   AB. Trifling to those who wage a war more noble
Than with the arm of flesh.
   CHA. (*apart.*) The Abbot's vex'd, I'll rub the sore for him.—
(*Aloud.*) I have seen priests that used that arm of flesh,
And used it sturdily.—Most reverend Father,
What say you to the chaplain's deed of arms
In the King's tent at Weardale?
   AB. It was most sinful, being against the canon
Prohibiting all churchmen to bear weapons;
And as he fell in that unseemly guise,
Perchance his soul may rue it.
   K. ED. (*overhearing the last words.*) Who may rue?
And what is to be rued?
   CHA. (*apart.*) I'll match his Reverence for the tithes of Eve-
     ringham.
—The Abbot says, my Liege, the deed was sinful,
By which your chaplain, wielding secular weapons,
Secured your Grace's life and liberty,
And that he suffers for 't in purgatory.
   K. ED. (*to the* ABBOT.) Say'st thou my chaplain is in purga-
     tory?
   AB. It is the canon speaks it, good my Liege.
   K. ED. In purgatory! thou shalt pray him out on 't,
Or I will make thee wish thyself beside him.

AB. My Lord, perchance his soul is past the aid
Of all the Church may do — there is a place
From which there 's no redemption.

K. ED. And if I thought my faithful chaplain there,
Thou shouldst there join him, priest!—Go, watch, fast, pray,
And let me have such prayers as will storm Heaven—
None of your maim'd and mutter'd hunting masses.

AB. (*apart to* CHA.) For God's sake take him off.

CHA. Wilt thou compound, then,
The tithes of Everingham?

K. ED. I tell thee, if thou bear'st the keys of Heaven,
Abbot, thou shalt not turn a bolt with them
'Gainst any well-deserving English subject.

AB. (*to* CHA.) We will compound, and grant thee, too, a share
I' the next indulgence.   Thou dost need it much,
And greatly 't will avail thee.

CHA. Enough — we 're friends, and when occasion serves,
I will strike in.——   [*Looks as if towards the Scottish Army.*

K. ED. Answer, proud Abbot; is my chaplain's soul,
If thou know'st aught on 't, in the evil place?

CHA. My Liege, the Yorkshire men have gain'd the meadow
I see the pennon green of merry Sherwood.

K. ED. Then give the signal instant! We have lost
But too much time already.

AB. My Liege, your holy chaplain's blessed soul—

K. ED. To hell with it and thee! Is this a time
To speak of monks and chaplains?
     [*Flourish of Trumpets, answered by a distant sound of Bugles*
See, Chandos, Percy—Ha! Saint George! Saint Edward!
See it descending now, the fatal hail shower,
The storm of England's wrath — sure, swift, resistless,
Which no mail-coat can brook.— Brave English hearts!
How close they shoot together!—as one eye
Had aim'd five thousand shafts — as if one hand
Had loosed five thousand bowstrings!

PER.   The thick volley
Darkens the air, and hides the sun from us.

K. ED. It falls on those shall see the sun no more.
The winged, the resistless plague [1] is with them.
How their vex'd host is reeling to and fro,
Like the chafed whale with fifty lances in him,
They do not see, and cannot shun the wound.
The storm is viewless, as death's sable wing,
Unerring as his scythe.

PER. Horses and riders are going down together.

---

[1] MS. — "The viewless, the resistless plague," &c.

'T is almost pity to see nobles fall,
And by a peasant's arrow.
    Bal.   I could weep **them**,
Although they are my rebels.
    Cha. (*aside to* Per.) His conquerors, he means, who cast him
        out
From his usurped kingdom.—(*Aloud.*) 'T is the worst of it,
That knights can claim small honour in the field
Which archers win, unaided by our lances.
    K. Ed. The battle is not ended.   (*Looks towards the field.*)
Not ended?—scarce begun! What horse are these,
Rush from the thicket underneath the hill?
    Per. They're Hainaulters, the followers of Queen Isabel.
    K. Ed. (*hastily.*) Hainaulters!—thou art blind—wear Hain-
        aulters
Saint Andrew's silver cross?—or would they charge
Full on our archers, and make havoc of them?—
Bruce is alive again—ho, rescue! rescue!—
Who was 't surveyed the ground?
    Riba. Most royal Liege——.
    K. Ed. A rose hath fallen from thy chaplet,[1] Ribaumont.
    Riba. I'll win it back, or lay my head beside it.   [*Exit.*
    K. Ed. Saint George! Saint Edward!—Gentlemen, to horse,
And to the rescue!—Percy, lead the bill-men;
Chandos, do thou bring up the men-at-arms.—
If yonder numerous host should now bear down
Bold as their vanguard, (*to the Abbot,*) thou mayst pray for us,
We may need good men's prayers.—To the rescue!
Lords, to the rescue! ha, Saint George! Saint Edward![2]
                                [*Excunt.*

[1] The well-known expression by which Robert Bruce censured the negligence of Randolph, for permitting an English body of cavalry to pass his flank on the day preceding the battle of Bannockburn.

[2] " In the second act, after the English nobles have amused themselves in some trifling conversation with the Abbot of Walthamstow, Edward is introduced; and his proud courageous temper and short manner are very admirably delineated; though, if our historical recollections do not fail us, it is more completely the picture of Longshanks than of the Third Edward. . . . . We conceive it to be extremely probable that Sir Walter Scott had resolved to commemorate some of the events in the life of Wallace, and had already sketched that hero, and a Templar, and Edward the First, when his eye glanced over the description of Homildon Hill, in Pinkerton's History of Scotland; that, being pleased with the characters of of Swinton and Gordon, he transferred his Wallace to Swinton; and that, for the sake of retaining his portrait of Edward, as there happened to be a Gordon and a Douglas at the battle of Halidoun in the time of Edward the Third, and there was so much similarity in the circumstances of the contest, he preserved his Edward as Edward the Third, retaining also his old Knight Templar, in defiance of the anachronism."—*Monthly Review*, July 1822.

SCENE II.

A part of the field of battle betwixt the two Main Armies. Tumults behind the scenes; alarums, and cries of " Gordon, a Gordon," " Swinton," &c.

Enter, as victorious over the English vanguard,
VIPONT, REYNALD, *and others.*

VIP. 'T is sweet to hear these war-cries sound together,—
Gordon and Swinton.

REY. 'T is passing pleasant, yet 't is strange withal.
Faith, when at first I heard the Gordon's slogan
Sounded so near me, I had nigh struck down
The knave who cried it.[1]

Enter SWINTON *and* GORDON.

SWI. Pitch down my pennon in yon holly bush.

GOR. Mine in the thorn beside it; let them wave,
As fought this morn their masters, side by side.

SWI. Let the men rally, and restore their ranks
Here in this vantage-ground — disorder'd chase
Leads to disorder'd flight; we have done our part,
And if we 're succour'd now, Plantagenet
Must turn his bridle southward.—
Reynald, spur to the Regent with the basnet
Of stout De Grey, the leader of their vanguard;
Say, that in battle-front the Gordon slew him,
And by that token bid him send us succour.

GOR. And tell him, that when Selby's headlong charge
Had wellnigh borne me down, Sir Alan smote him.
I cannot send his helmet, never nutshell
Went to so many shivers. — Harkye, grooms!
                              [*To those behind the scenes*
Why do you let my noble steed stand stiffening
After so hot a course?

SWI. Ay, breathe your horses, they 'll have work anon,
For Edward's men-at-arms will soon be on us,
The flower of England, Gascony, and Flanders;
But with swift succour we will bide them bravely. —
De Vipont, thou look'st sad?[2]

VIP. It is because I hold a Templar's sword
Wet to the crossed hilt with Christian blood.

---

[1] The MS. adds —" such was my surprise."

[2] " While thus enjoying a breathing time, Swinton observes the thoughtful countenance of De Vipont. See what follows. Were ever England and Englishmen more nobly, more beautifully, more justly characterized, than by the latter, or was patriotic feeling ever better sustained than by the former and his brave companion in arms? "—*New Edinburgh Review.*

Swi. The blood of English archers — what can gild
A Scottish blade more bravely?
Vip. Even therefore grieve I for those gallant yeomen,
England's peculiar and appropriate sons,
Known in no other land.   Each boasts his hearth
And field as free as the best lord his barony,
Owing subjection to no human vassalage,
Save to their King and law.   Hence are they resolute,
Leading the van on every day of battle, ·
As men who know the blessings they defend.
Hence are they frank and generous in peace,
As men who have their portion in its plenty.
No other kingdom shows such worth and happiness
Veil'd in such low estate — therefore I mourn them.
Swi. I'll keep my sorrow for our native Scots,
Who, spite of hardship, poverty, oppression,
Still follow to the field their Chieftain's banner,
And die in the defence on't.
Gor. And if I live and see my halls again,
They shall have portion in the good they fight for.
Each hardy follower shall have his field,
His household hearth and sod-built home, as free
As ever Southron had.   They shall be happy! —
And my Elizabeth shall smile to see it! —[1]
I have betray'd myself.
Swi.　　　　　　　　　Do not believe it. —
Vipont, do thou look out from yonder height,
And see what motion in the Scottish host,
And in King Edward's. —　　　　　　　　[*Exit* Vipont.
　　　　　　　　　Now will I counsel thee:
The Templar's ear is for no tale of love,
Being wedded to his Order.   But I tell thee,
The brave young knight that hath no lady-love
Is like a lamp unlighted; his brave deeds,
And its rich painting, do seem then most glorious,
When the pure ray gleams through them. —
Hath thy Elizabeth no other name?[2]
Gor. Must I then speak of her to you, Sir Alan?
The thought of thee, and of thy matchless strength,
Hath conjured phantoms up amongst her dreams.
The name of Swinton hath been spell sufficient

[1] "There wanted but a little of the tender passion to make this youth every way a hero of romance. But the poem has no ladies. How admirably is this defect supplied! In his enthusiastic anticipation of prosperity, he allows a name to escape him." — *New Edinburgh Review.*

[2] "Amid the confusion and din of the battle, the reader is unexpectedly greeted with a dialogue, which breathes indeed the soft sounds of the lute in the clang of trumpets." — *Monthly Review.*

To chase the rich blood from her lovely cheek,
And wouldst thou now know hers?
 Swi.   I would, nay must
Thy father in the paths of chivalry,
Should know the load-star thou dost rule thy course by.
 Gor. Nay, then, her name is—hark——[*Whispers.*
 Swi. I know it well, that ancient northern house.
 Gor. O, thou shalt see its fairest grace and honour
In my Elizabeth. And if music touch thee——
 Swi. It did, before disasters had untuned me.
 Gor. O, her notes
Shall hush each sad remembrance to oblivion,
Or melt them to such gentleness of feeling,
That grief shall have its sweetness. Who but she
Knows the wild harpings of our native land?
Whether they lull the shepherd on his hill,
Or wake the knight to battle; rouse to merriment,
Or soothe to sadness; she can touch each mood.
Princes and statesmen, chiefs renown'd in arms,
And grey-hair'd bards, contend which shall the first
And choicest homage render to the enchantress.
 Swi. You speak her talent bravely.
 Gor.   Though you smile,
I do not speak it half. Her gift creative,
New measures adds to every air she wakes;
Varying and gracing it with liquid sweetness,
Like the wild modulation of the lark;
Now leaving, now returning to the strain!
To listen to her, is to seem to wander
In some enchanted labyrinth of romance,
Whence nothing but the lovely fairy's will,
Who wove the spell, can extricate the wanderer.
Methinks I hear her now!—
 Swi.   Bless'd privilege
Of youth! There's scarce three minutes to decide
'Twixt death and life, 'twixt triumph and defeat,
Yet all his thoughts are in his lady's bower,
List'ning her harping!——
          [*Enter* Vipont.
     Where are thine, De Vipont?
 Vip. On death—on judgment—on eternity!
For time is over with us.
 Swi. There moves not, then, one pennon to our aid,
Of all that flutter yonder!
 Vip. From the main English host come rushing forward
Pennons enow—ay, and their Royal Standard.
But ours stand rooted, as for crows to roost on.

Swi. (*to himself.*) I'll rescue him at least.—Young Lord of
　　Gordon,
Spur to the Regent—show the instant need——
　　Gor. I penetrate thy purpose ; but I go not.
　　Swi. Not at my bidding?—I, thy sire in chivalry—
Thy leader in the battle?—I command thee.
　　Gor. No, thou wilt not command me seek my safety,—
For such is thy kind meaning—at the expense
Of the last hope which Heaven reserves for Scotland.
While I abide, no follower of mine
Will turn his rein for life ; but were I gone,
What power can stay them? and, our band dispersed,
What swords shall for an instant stem yon host,
And save the latest chance for victory?
　　Vip. The noble youth speaks truth ; and were he gone,
There will not twenty spears be left with us.
　　Gor. No, bravely as we have begun the field,
So let us fight it out.　The Regent's eyes,
More certain than a thousand messages,
Shall see us stand, the barrier of his host
Against yon bursting storm.　If not for honour,
If not for warlike rule, for shame at least,
He must bear down to aid us.
　　Swi.　　　　　　　　　　Must it be so?
And am I forced to yield the sad consent,
Devoting thy young life?[1]　O, Gordon ! Gordon !
I do it as the patriarch doom'd his issue—
I at my country's, he at Heaven's command ;
But I seek vainly some atoning sacrifice,[2]
Rather than such a victim !—(*Trumpets.*)　Hark, they come !
That music sounds not like thy lady's lute.
　　Gor. Yet shall my lady's name mix with it gaily.—
Mount, vassals, couch your lances, and cry, " Gordon !
Gordon for Scotland and Elizabeth !"
　　　　　　　　　　　　　[*Exeunt.　Loud Alarums.*

SCENE III.

Another part of the Field of Battle, adjacent to the former Scene.

*Alarums.　**Enter** Swinton, **followed by** Hob Hattely.*

　　Swi. Stand to it yet !　The man who flies to-day,
May bastards warm them at his household hearth !

　　　　[1] MS.—" And am I doomed to yield the sad consent
　　　　　　　That thus devotes thy life ?"
　　　　[2] MS.—" O, could there be some lesser sacrifice !

Hob. That ne'er shall be my curse.   My Magdalen
Is trusty as my broadsword.
    Swi.   Ha, thou knave,
Art thou dismounted too?
    Hob.   I know, Sir Alan,
You want no homeward guide; so threw my reins
Upon my palfrey's neck, and let him loose.
Within an hour he stands before my gate;
And Magdalen will need no other token
To bid the Melrose Monks say masses for me.
    Swi. Thou art resolved to cheat the halter, then?
    Hob.   It is my purpose,
Having lived a thief, to die a brave man's death;
And never had I a more glorious chance for't.
    Swi. Here lies the way to it, knave.—Make in, make in.
And aid young Gordon!
            [*Exeunt. Loud and long Alarums. After which the back.*
              Scene rises and discovers Swinton *on the ground,* Gor-
              Don *supporting him; both much wounded.*
    Swi. All are cut down—the reapers have pass'd o'er us,
And hie to distant harvest.—My toil's over;
There lies my sickle. (*Dropping his sword.*) Hand of mine again
Shall never, never wield it![1]
    Gor. O valiant leader, is thy light extinguish'd!
That only beacon-flame which promised safety
In this day's deadly wrack!
    Swi. My lamp hath long been dim! But thine, young Gordon,
Just kindled, to be quench'd so suddenly,
Ere Scotland saw its splendour!——
    Gor. Five thousand horse hung idly on yon hill,
Saw us o'erpower'd, and no one stirr'd to aid us!
    Swi. It was the Regent's envy.—Out!—alas!
Why blame I him?—It was our civil discord,
Our selfish vanity, our jealous hatred,
Which framed this day of dole for our poor country.—
Had thy brave father held yon leading staff,
As well his rank and valour might have claim'd it,
We had not fall'n unaided.—How, O how
Is he to answer it, whose deed prevented——
    Gor. Alas! alas! the author of the death-feud,
He has his reckoning too! for had your sons
And num'rous vassals lived, we had lack'd no aid.
    Swi. May God assoil the dead, and him who follows!
We've drank the poison'd beverage which we brew'd:
Have sown the wind, and reap'd the tenfold whirlwind!—

   [1] This speech of Swinton's is interpolated on the blank page of the manuscript.

But thou, brave youth, whose nobleness of heart
Pour'd oil upon the wounds our hate inflicted—
Thou, who hast done no wrong, need'st no forgiveness,—
Why shouldst thou share our punishment!
   Gor. All need forgiveness—[*Distant alarum.*]—Hark, in yon-
      der shout
Did the main battles counter!
   Swi. Look on the field, brave Gordon, if thou canst,
And tell me how the day goes.—But I guess,
Too surely do I guess——
   Gor. All's lost! all's lost!—Of the main Scottish host,
Some wildly fly, and some rush wildly forward;
And some there are who seem to turn their spears
Against their countrymen.
   Swi. Rashness, and cowardice, and secret treason,
Combine to ruin us; and our hot valour,
Devoid of discipline, is madmen's strength,
More fatal unto friends than enemies!
I 'm glad that these dim eyes shall see no more on 't.—
Let thy hands close them, Gordon—I will dream
My fair-hair'd William renders me that office!   [*Dies.*
   Gor. And, Swinton, I will think I do that duty
To my dead father.

Enter De Vipont.

   Vip. Fly, fly, brave youth!— A handful of thy followers,
The scatter'd gleaning of this desperate day,
Still hover yonder to essay thy rescue.—
O linger not!—I 'll be your guide to them.
   Gor. Look there, and bid me fly!—The oak has fall'n;
And the young ivy bush, which learn'd to climb
By its support, must needs partake its fall.
   Vip. Swinton? Alas! the best, the bravest, strongest,
And sagest of our Scottish chivalry!
Forgive one moment, if, to save the living,
My tongue should wrong the dead.—Gordon, bethink thee,
Thou dost but stay to perish with the corpse[1]
Of him who slew thy father.
   Gor. Ay, but he was my sire in chivalry;—
He taught my youth to soar above the promptings
Of mean and selfish vengeance; gave my youth
A name that shall not die even on this death-spot.
Records shall tell this field had not been lost,
Had all men fought like Swinton and like Gordon.   [*Trumpets.*
Save thee, De Vipont.—Hark! the Southron trumpets.
   Vip. Nay, without thee I stir not.

---

  [1] MS.—"Thou hast small cause to tarry with the corpse."

Enter EDWARD, CHANDOS, PERCY, BALIOL, &c.

GOR. Ay, they come on — the Tyrant and the Traitor,
Workman and tool, Plantagenet and Baliol.—
O for a moment's strength in this poor arm,
To do one glorious deed! [*He rushes on the English, but is made
prisoner with* VIPONT.

K. ED. Disarm them—harm them not; though it was they
Made havoc on the archers of our vanguard,
They and that bulky champion.   Where is he ?
CHAN. Here lies the giant!   Say his name, young Knight ?
GOR. Let it suffice, he was a man this morning.[1]
CHA. I question'd thee in sport.   I do not need
Thy information, youth.   Who that has fought
Through all these Scottish wars, but knows his crest,
The sable boar chain'd to the leafy oak,
And that huge mace, still seen where war was wildest!
KING ED. 'T is Alan Swinton!
Grim chamberlain, who in my tent at Weardale,
Stood by my startled couch[2] with torch and mace,
When the Black Douglas' war-cry waked my camp.
GOR. (*sinking down.*) If thus thou know'st him,
Thou wilt respect his corpse.[3]
K. ED. As belted Knight and crowned King, I will.
GOR. And let mine
Sleep at his side, in token that our death
Ended the feud of Swinton and of Gordon.
K. ED. It is the Gordon!—Is there aught beside
Edward can do to honour bravery,
Even in an enemy ?

[1] In his narrative of events on the day after the battle of Sheriffmuir, Sir
Walter Scott says—"Amongst the gentlemen who fell on this occasion, were
several on both sides, alike eminent for birth and character. The body of
the gallant young Earl of Strathmore was found on the field, watched by a
faithful old domestic, who being asked the name of the person whose body
he waited upon with so much care, made this striking reply,—'He was a
man yesterday.'"—*Tales of a Grandfather.*
[2] MS.—"Stood arm'd beside my couch," &c.
[3] "The character of Swinton is obviously a favourite with the author, to
which circumstance we are probably indebted for the strong relief in which
it is given, and the perfect verisimilitude which belongs to it.   The stately
commanding figure of the veteran warrior, whom, by the illusion of his art,
the author has placed in veritable presentment before us ;—his venerable
age, superior prowess, and intuitive decision ;— the broils in which he had
engaged, the misfortunes he had suffered, and the intrepid fortitude with
which he sustained them,—together with that rigorous control of temper,
not to be shaken even by unmerited contumely and insult ;—these qualities, grouped and embodied in one and the same character, render it morally
impossible that we should not at once sympathize and admire.   The in-
herent force of his character is finely illustrated in the effect produced upon
Lord Gordon by the first appearance of the man 'who had made him fatherless.'"—*Edinburgh Magazine,* July 1822.

Gor. Nothing but this:
Let not base Baliol, with his touch or look,
Profane my corpse or Swinton's.   I 've some breath still,
Enough to say — Scotland — Elizabeth !
   Cha. Baliol, I would not brook such dying looks,
To buy the crown you aim at.
   K. Ed. (*to* Vip.) Vipont, thy crossed shield shows ill in warfare
Against a Christian king.
   Vip. That Christian King is warring upon Scotland.
I was a Scotsman ere I was a Templar,[1]
Sworn to my country ere I knew my Order.
   K. Ed. I will but know thee as a Christian champion,
And set thee free unransom'd.

Enter Abbot of Walthamstow.

   Ab. Heaven grant your Majesty
Many such glorious days as this has been !
   K. Ed. It is a day of much and high advantage ;
Glorious it might have been, had all our foes
Fought like these two brave champions. — Strike the drums,
Sound trumpets, and pursue the fugitives,
Till the Tweed's eddies whelm them.   Berwick's render'd —
These wars, I trust, will soon find lasting close.[2]

----

[1] A Venetian General, observing his soldiers testified some unwillingness
to fight against those of the Pope, whom they regarded as father of the
Church, addressed them in terms of similar encouragement, — "Fight on !
we were Venetians before we were Christians."

----

[2] "It is generally the case that much expectation ends in disappointment. The free delineation of character in some of the recent Scottish
Novels, and the admirable conversations interspersed throughout them,
raised hopes that, when a regular drama should be attempted by the person
who was considered as their author, the success would be eminent. Its
announcement, too, in a solemn and formal manner, did not diminish the
interest of the public. The drama, however, which was expected, turns out
to be in fact, and not only in name, merely a dramatic sketch, which is
entirely deficient in plot, and contains but three characters, Swinton, Gordon, and Edward, in whom any interest is endeavoured to be excited. With
some exceptions, the dialogue also is flat and coarse ; and for all these defects,
one or two vigorous descriptions of battle scenes will scarcely make sufficient atonement, except in the eyes of very enthusiastic friends."—*Monthly
Review.*

" Halidon Hill, we understand, unlike the earlier poems of its author, has
not been received into the ranks of popular favour. Such rumours, of
course, have no effect on our critical judgment ; but we cannot forbear saying, that, thinking as we do very highly of the spirit and taste with which
an interesting tale is here sketched in natural and energetic verse, we are
yet far from feeling surprised that the approbation, which it is our pleasing
duty to bestow, should not have been anticipated by the ordinary readers of
the work before us. It bears, in truth, no great resemblance to the narra-

tive poems from which Sir Walter Scott derived his first and high reputation, and by which, *for the present,* his genius must be characterised. It is
wholly free from many of their most obvious faults — their carelessness,
their irregularity, and their inequality both of conception and of execution ;
but it wants likewise no inconsiderable portion of their beauties — it has less
'pomp and circumstance,' less picturesque description, romantic association,
and chivalrous glitter, less sentiment and reflection, less perhaps of all their
striking charms, with the single exception of that one redeeming and suf-
ficing quality, which forms, in our view,—the highest recommendation of *all*
the author's works of imagination, their unaffected and unflagging vigour.
This perhaps, after all, is only saying, that we have before us a dramatic
poem, instead of a metrical tale of romance, and that the author has had too
much taste and discretion to bedizen his scenes with inappropriate and en-
cumbering ornament.   There is, however, a class of readers of poetry, and a
pretty large class, too, who have no relish for a work, however naturally and
strongly the characters and incidents may be conceived and sustained —
however appropriate and manly may be the imagery and diction — from
which they cannot select any isolated passages to store in their memories
or their commonplace books, to whisper into a lady's ear, or transcribe into
a lady's album.   With this tea-table and watering-place school of critics,
'Halidon Hill' must expect no favour; it has no rant — no mysticism — and
worst offence of all, no affectation."—*British Critic,* October 1822.

END OF HALIDON HILL.

MacDuff's Cross.

INTRODUCTION.

THESE few scenes had the honour to be included in a Miscellany, published in the year 1823, by Mrs. Joanna Baillie, and are here reprinted, to unite them with the trifles of the same kind which owe their birth to the author. The singular history of the Cross and Law of Clan MacDuff is given, at length enough to satisfy the keenest antiquary, in *The Ministrelsy of the Scottish Border*.[1] It is here only necessary to state, that the Cross was a place of refuge to any person related to MacDuff, within the ninth degree, who, having committed homicide in sudden quarrel, should reach this place, prove his descent from the Thane of Fife, and pay a certain penalty.

The shaft of the Cross was destroyed at the Reformation. The huge block of stone which served for its pedestal is still in existence near the town of Newburgh, on a kind of pass which commands the county of Fife to the southward, and to the north the windings of the magnificent Tay and fertile country of Angusshire. The Cross bore an inscription, which is transmitted to us in an unintelligible form by Sir Robert Sibbald.

ABBOTSFORD, *January* 1830.

TO

MRS. JOANNA BAILLIE,

AUTHORESS OF

"THE PLAYS ON THE PASSIONS."

PRELUDE.

NAY, smile not, Lady, when I speak of witchcraft,
And say that still there lurks amongst our glens
Some touch of strange enchantment.—Mark that fragment,
I mean that rough-hewn block of massive stone,
Placed on the summit of this mountain pass,

[1] Vol. iv. p. 266, in Appendix to Lord Soulis, "Law of Clan MacDuff."

Commanding prospect wide o'er field and fell,
And peopled village and extended moorland,
And the wide ocean and majestic Tay,
To the far distant Grampians.—Do not deem it
A loosen'd portion of the neighbouring rock,
Detach'd by storm and thunder,—'twas the pedestal
On which, in ancient times, a Cross was rear'd,
Carved o'er with words which foil'd philologists;
And the events it did commemorate
Were dark, remote, and undistinguishable,
As were the mystic characters it bore.
But, mark,—a wizard, born on Avon's bank,
Tuned but his harp to this wild northern theme,
And, lo! the scene is hallow'd.   None shall pass,
Now, or in after days, beside that stone,
But he shall have strange visions; thoughts and words,
That shake, or rouse, or thrill the human heart,
Shall rush upon his memory when he hears
The spirit-stirring name of this rude symbol:—
Oblivious ages, at that simple spell,
Shall render back their terrors with their woes,
Alas! and with their crimes—and the proud phantoms
Shall move with step familiar to his eye,
And accents which, once heard, the ear forgets not,
Though ne'er again to list them.   Siddons, thine,
Thou matchless Siddons! thrill upon our ear;
And on our eye thy lofty Brother's form
Rises as Scotland's monarch.—But, to thee,
Joanna, why to thee speak of such visions?
Thine own wild wand can raise them.

Yet since thou wilt an idle tale of mine,
Take one which scarcely is of worth enough
To give or to withhold.—Our time creeps on,
Fancy grows colder as the silvery hair
Tells the advancing winter of our life.
But if it be of worth enough to please,
That worth it owes to her who set the task;
If otherwise, the fault rests with the author.

DRAMATIS PERSONÆ.

NINIAN, WALDHAVE,	}	*Monks of Lindores.*
LINDESAY, MAURICE BERKELEY,	}	*Scottish Barons.*

ﯼﺎc﮳u﯁﮳'s ﯀﮳ross.

SCENE. — *The summit of a Rocky Pass near to Newburgh, about
two miles from the ancient Abbey of Lindores, in Fife. In the
centre is MacDuff's Cross, an antique Monument; and, at a
small distance, on one side, a Chapel with a lamp burning.*

Enter, as having ascended the Pass, NINIAN *and* WALDHAVE,
Monks of Lindores. NINIAN *crosses himself, and seems to
recite his devotions.* WALDHAVE *stands gazing on the prospect, as if in deep contemplation.*

NIN. Here stands the Cross, good brother, consecrated
By the bold Thane unto his patron saint
Magridius, once a brother of our house.
Canst thou not spare an ave or a creed?
Or hath the steep ascent exhausted you?
You trode it stoutly, though 'twas rough and toilsome.
    WAL. I have trode a rougher.
    NIN.   On the Highland hills—
Scarcely within our sea-girt province here,
Unless upon the Lomonds or Bennarty.
    WAL. I spoke not of the literal path, good father,
But of the road of life which I have travell'd,
Ere I assumed this habit; it was bounded,
Hedged in, and limited by earthly prospects,
As ours beneath was closed by dell and thicket.
Here we see wide and far, and the broad sky,
With wide horizon, opens full around,
While earthly objects dwindle.   Brother Ninian,
Fain would I hope that mental elevation
Could raise me equally o'er worldly thoughts,
And place me nearer heaven.
    NIN. 'Tis good morality.—But yet forget not,
That though we look on heaven from this high eminence,
Yet doth the Prince of all the airy space,
Arch-foe of man, possess the realms between.
    WAL. Most true, good brother; and men may be farther
From the bright heaven they aim at, even because
They deem themselves secure on 't.
    NIN. (*after a pause.*)   You do gaze—
Strangers are wont to do so—on the prospect.
Yon is the Tay roll'd down from Highland hills,
That rests his waves, after so rude a race,
In the fair plains of Gowrie—further westward,
Proud Stirling rises—yonder to the east,

Dundee, the gift of God, and fair Montrose,
And still more northward lie the ancient towers——
  Wal. Of Edzell.
  Nin.   How? know you the towers of Edzell?
  Wal. I 've heard of them.
  Nin.   Then have you heard a tale,
Which when he tells, the peasant shakes his head,
And shuns the mouldering and deserted walls.
  Wal. Why, and by whom, deserted?
  Nin.   Long the tale——
Enough to say that the last Lord of Edzell,
Bold Louis Lindesay, had a wife, and found——
  Wal. Enough is said, indeed—since a weak woman,
Ay, and a tempting fiend, lost Paradise,
When man was innocent.
  Nin.   They fell at strife,
Men say, on slight occasion: that fierce Lindesay
Did bend his sword against De Berkeley's breast,
And that the lady threw herself between:
That then De Berkeley dealt the Baron's death-wound
Enough, that from that time De Berkeley bore
A spear in foreign wars.   But, it is said,
He hath return'd of late; and, therefore, brother,
The Prior hath ordain'd our vigil here,
To watch the privilege of the sanctuary,
And rights of Clan MacDuff.
  Wal.   What rights are these?
  Nin. Most true; you are but newly come from Rome
And do not know our ancient usages.
Know then, when fell Macbeth beneath the arm
Of the predestined knight, unborn of woman,
Three boons the victor ask'd, and thrice did Malcolm,
Stooping the sceptre by the Thane restored,
Assent to his request.   And hence the rule,
That first when Scotland's King assumes the crown,
MacDuff's descendant rings his brow with it:
And hence, when Scotland's King calls forth his host,
MacDuff's descendant leads the van in battle:
And last, in guerdon of the crown restored,
Red with the blood of the usurping tyrant,
The right was granted in succeeding time,
That if a kinsman of the Thane of Fife
Commit a slaughter on a sudden impulse,
And fly for refuge to this Cross MacDuff,
For the Thane's sake he shall find sanctuary;
For here must the avenger's step be staid,
And here the panting homicide find safety.

Wal. And here a brother of your order watches,
To see the custom of the place observed?
    Nin. Even so;—such is our convent's holy right,
Since Saint Magridius—blessed be his memory!—
Did by a vision warn the Abbot Eadmir.
And chief we watch, when there is bickering
Among the neighbouring nobles, now most likely
From this return of Berkeley from abroad,
Having the Lindesay's blood upon his hand.
Wal. The Lindesay, then, was loved among his friends?
Nin. Honour'd and fear'd he was—but little loved;
For even his bounty bore a show of sternness;
And when his passions waked, he was a Sathan
Of wrath and injury.
    Wal. How now, Sir Priest! (*fiercely.*)—Forgive me—
        (*recollecting himself*)—I was dreaming
Of an old baron, who did bear about him
Some touch of your Lord Reynold.
    Nin. Lindesay's name, my brother,
Indeed was Reynold;—and methinks, moreover,
That, as you spoke even now, he would have spoken.
I brought him a petition from our convent:
He granted straight, but in such tone and manner,
By my good saint! I thought myself scarce safe
Till Tay roll'd broad between us.   I must now
Unto the chapel—meanwhile the watch is thine;
And, at thy word, the hurrying fugitive,
Should such arrive, must here find sanctuary;
And, at thy word, the fiery-paced avenger
Must stop his bloody course—e'en as swoln Jordan
Controll'd his waves, soon as they touch'd the feet
Of those who bore the ark.
    Wal.   Is this my charge?
    Nin. Even so; and I am near, should chance require me.
At midnight I relieve you on your watch,
When we may taste together some refreshment:
I have cared for it; and for a flask of wine—
There is no sin, so that we drink it not
Until the midnight hour, when lauds have toll'd.
Farewell a while, and peaceful watch be with you!
                        [*Exit towards the Chapel.*
    Wal. It is not with me, and alas! alas!
I know not where to seek it.   This monk's mind
Is with his cloister match'd, nor lacks more room.
Its petty duties, formal ritual,
Its humble pleasures and its paltry troubles,
Fill up his round of life; even as some reptiles,
They say, are moulded to the very shape,

And all the angles of the rocky crevice,
In which they live and die.   But for myself,
Retired in passion to the narrow cell,
Couching my tired limbs in its recesses,
So ill-adapted am I to its limits,
That every attitude is agony.——
How now! what brings him back?——[*Re-enter* NINIAN.

NIN. Look to your watch, my brother— horsemen come;
I heard their tread when kneeling in the chapel.

WAL. (*looking to a distance.*) My thoughts have wrapt me
      more than thy devotion,
Else had I heard the tread of distant horses
Farther than thou couldst hear the sacring bell;
But now in truth they come : — flight and pursuit
Are sights I 've been long strange to.

NIN. See how they gallop down the opposing hill!
Yon grey steed bounding down the headlong path,
As on the level meadow; while the black,
Urged by the rider with his naked sword,
Stoops on his prey, as I have seen the falcon
Dashing upon the heron.—Thou dost frown
And clench thy hand, as if it grasp'd a weapon!

WAL. 'T is but for shame to see a man fly thus
While only one pursues him.   Coward, turn! —
Turn thee, I say! thou art as stout as he,
And well may'st match thy single sword with his —
Shame, that a man should rein a steed like thee,
Yet fear to turn his front against a foe ! —
I am ashamed to look on them.

NIN. Yet look again ; they quit their horses now,
Unfit for the rough path : the fugitive
Keeps the advantage still.—They strain towards us.

WAL. I 'll not believe that ever the bold Thane
Rear'd up his Cross to be a sanctuary
To the base coward who shunn'd an equal combat.—
How 's this ?— that look, that mien—mine eyes grow dizzy !

NIN. He comes ! — thou art a novice on this watch, —
Brother, I 'll take the word and speak to him.
Pluck down thy cowl: know, that we spiritual champions
Have honour to maintain, and must not seem
To quail before the laity.
        [WALDHAVE *lets down his cowl, and steps back.*

Enter MAURICE BERKELEY.

NIN. Who art thou, stranger ? speak thy name and purpose.
BER. I claim the privilege of Clan Macduff.
My name is Maurice Berkeley, and my lineage
Allies me nearly with the Thane of Fife.

Nin. Give us to know the cause of sanctuary ?
Ber.　　　　　　　　　　　　Let him show it,
Against whose violence I claim the privilege.

Enter Lindesay, *with his sword drawn.　He rushes at*
Berkeley ; Ninian *interposes.*

Nin. Peace, in the name of Saint Magridius !
Peace, in our Prior's name, and in the name
Of that dear symbol, which did purchase peace
And good-will towards man ! I do command thee
To sheathe thy sword, and stir no contest here.
　Lin. One charm I'll try first,
To lure the craven from the enchanted circle
Which he hath harbour'd in.—Here you, De Berkeley,
This is my brother's sword—the hand it arms
Is weapon'd to avenge a brother's death :—
If thou hast heart to step a furlong off,
And change three blows,—even for so short a space
As these good men may say an ave-marie,—
So, Heaven be good to me ! I will forgive thee
Thy deed and all its consequences.
　Ber. Were not my right hand fetter'd by the thought
That slaying thee were but a double guilt
In which to steep my soul, no bridegroom ever
Stepp'd forth to trip a measure with his bride
More joyfully than I, young man, would rush
To meet thy challenge.
　Lin. He quails, and shuns to look upon my weapon
Yet boasts himself a Berkeley !
　Ber. Lindesay, and if there were no deeper cause
For shunning thee than terror of thy weapon,
That rock-hewn Cross as soon should start and stir,
Because a shepherd-boy blew horn beneath it,
As I for brag of thine.
　Nin. I charge you both, and in the name of Heaven,
Breathe no defiance on this sacred spot,
Where Christian men must bear them peacefully,
On pain of the Church thunders.　Calmly tell
Your cause of difference ; and, Lord Lindesay, thou
Be first to speak them.
　Lin. Ask the blue welkin—ask the silver Tay,
The northern Grampians—all things know my wrongs ;
But ask not me to tell them, while the villain,
Who wrought them, stands and listens with a smile.
　Nin. It is said—
Since you refer us thus to general fame—
That Berkeley slew thy brother, the Lord Louis,
In his own halls at Edzell——

Lin. Ay, in his halls—
In his own halls, good father, that's the word.
In his own halls he slew him, while the wine
Pass'd on the board between!   The gallant Thane
Who wreak'd Macbeth's inhospitable murder,
Rear'd not yon Cross to sanction deeds like these.

Ber. Thou say'st I came a guest!— I came a victim
A destined victim, train'd on to the doom
His frantic jealousy prepared for me.
He fix'd a quarrel on me, and we fought.
Can I forget the form that came between us,
And perish'd by his sword?   'Twas then I fought
For vengeance,—until then I guarded life,
But then I sought to take it, and prevail'd.

Lin. Wretch! thou didst first dishonour to thy victim,
And then didst slay him!

Ber. There is a busy fiend tugs at my heart,
But I will struggle with it!—Youthful knight,
My heart is sick of war, my hand of slaughter;
I come not to my lordships, or my land,
But just to seek a spot in some cold cloister,
Which I may kneel on living, and, when dead,
Which may suffice to cover me.
Forgive me that I caused your brother's death;
And I forgive thee the injurious terms
With which thou taxest me.

Lin. Take worse and blacker— Murderer! adulterer!
Art thou not moved yet?

Ber.   Do not press me further.
The hunted stag, even when he seeks the thicket,
Compell'd to stand at bay, grows dangerous!
Most true thy brother perish'd by my hand,
And if you term it murder— I must bear it.
Thus far my patience can; but if thou brand
The purity of yonder martyr'd saint,
Whom then my sword but poorly did avenge,
With one injurious word, come to the valley,
And I will show thee how it shall be answer'd!

Nin. This heat, Lord Berkeley, doth but ill accord
With thy late pious patience.

Ber. Father, forgive, and let me stand excused
To Heaven and thee, if patience brooks no more.
I loved this lady—fondly, truly loved—
Loved her, and was beloved, ere yet her father
Conferr'd her on another.   While she lived,
Each thought of her was to my soul as hallow'd
As those I send to Heaven; and on her grave,
Her bloody, early grave, while this poor hand
Can hold a sword, shall no one cast a scorn.

Lin. Follow me.   Thou shalt hear me call the adulteress
By her right name.— I 'm glad there 's yet a spur
Can rouse thy sluggard mettle.
  Ber. Make then obeisance to the blessed Cross,
For it shall be on earth thy last devotion. [*They are going off.*
  Wal. (*rushing forward..*) Madmen, stand !—
Stay but one second—answer but one question.—
There, Maurice Berkeley, can'st thou look upon
That blessed sign, and swear thou'st spoken truth ?
  Ber. I swear by Heaven,
And by the memory of that murder'd innocent,
Each seeming charge against her was as false
As our bless'd Lady 's spotless !—Hear, each saint !
Hear me, thou holy rood !—hear me from heaven,
Thou martyr'd excellence !—hear me from penal fire,
(For sure not yet thy guilt is expiated !)
Stern ghost of her destroyer !———
  Wal. (*throws back his cowl.*) He hears ! he hears ! Thy spell
        hath raised the dead.
  Lin. My brother ! and alive !—
  Wal. Alive,—but yet, my Richard, dead to thee,
No tie of kindred binds me to the world ;
All were renounced, when, with reviving life,
Came the desire to seek the sacred cloister.
Alas, in vain ! for to that last retreat,
Like to a pack of bloodhounds in full chase,
My passion and my wrongs have follow'd me,
Wrath and remorse—and, to fill up the cry,
Thou hast brought vengeance hither.
  Lin.   I but sought
To do the act and duty of a brother.
  Wal. I ceased to be so when I left the world ;
But if he can forgive as I forgive,
God sends me here a brother in mine enemy,
To pray for me and with me.   If thou canst,
De Berkeley, give thine hand.—
  Ber. (*gives his hand.*)   It is the will
Of Heaven, made manifest in thy preservation,
To inhibit farther bloodshed ; for De Berkeley,
The votary Maurice lays the title down.
Go to his halls, Lord Richard, where a maiden,
Kin to his blood, and daughter in affection,
Heirs his broad lands ;—If thou canst love her, Lindesay,
Woo her, and be successful.

END OF MACDUFF'S CROSS.

The Doom of Devorgoil.

PREFACE.

THE first of these dramatic pieces[1] was long since written, for the purpose of obliging the late Mr. Terry, then Manager of the Adelphi Theatre, for whom the Author had a particular regard. The manner in which the mimic goblins of Devorgoil are intermixed with the supernatural machinery, was found to be objectionable, and the production had other faults, which rendered it unfit for representation.[2] I have called the piece a Melo-drama, for want of a better name ; but, as I learn from the unquestionable authority of Mr. Colman's Random Records, that one species of the drama is termed an *extravaganza*, I am sorry I was not sooner aware of a more appropriate name than that which I had selected for Devorgoil.

The Author's Publishers thought it desirable, that the scenes, long condemned to oblivion, should be united to similar attempts of the same kind ; and as he felt indifferent on the subject, they are printed in the same volume with Halidon Hill and MacDuff's Cross, and thrown off in a separate form, for the convenience of those who possess former editions of the Author's Poetical Works.

The general story of the Doom of Devorgoil is founded on an old Scottish tradition, the scene of which lies in Galloway. The crime supposed to have occasioned the misfortunes of this devoted house, is similar to that of a Lord Herries of Hoddam Castle, who is the principal personage of Mr. Charles Kirkpatrick Sharpe's interesting ballad, in the Minstrelsy of the Scottish Border, vol. iv. p. 307. In remorse for his crime, he built the singular monument called the tower of Repentance. In many cases the Scottish superstitions allude to the fairies, or those who,

---

[1] " The Doom of Devorgoil," and " Auchindrane," were published together in an octavo volume, in the spring of 1830. For the origin and progress of the first, see *Life of Scott*, vol. v. pp. 197-204, 285-6.—ED.

[2] Mr. Daniel Terry, the comedian, distinguished for a very peculiar style of humour on the stage, and moreover, by personal accomplishments of various sorts not generally shared by members of his profession, was, during many years, on terms of intimacy with Sir Walter Scott. He died 22d June 1829.—ED.

for sins of a milder description, are permitted to wander with the
" rout that never rest," as they were termed by Dr. Leyden.
They imitate human labour and human amusements, but their
toil is useless, and without any advantageous result ; and their
gaiety is unsubstantial and hollow.   The phantom of Lord Erick
is supposed to be a spectre of this character.

The story of the Ghostly Barber is told in many countries ;
but the best narrative founded on the passage, is the tale called
Stumme Liebe, among the legends of Musæus.   I think it has
been introduced upon the English stage in some pantomime,
which was one objection to bringing it upon the scene a second
time.

ABBOTSFORD, *April* 1830.

DRAMATIS PERSONÆ.

OSWALD OF DEVORGOIL, *a decayed Scottish Baron*

LEONARD, *a Ranger.*

DURWARD, *a Palmer.*

LANCELOT BLACKTHORN, *a Companion of Leonard, in love with Katleen*

GULLCAMMER, *a conceited Student.*

OWLSPIEGLE *and*
COCKLEDEMOY, } *Maskers, represented by Blackthorn and Flora.*

SPIRIT OF LORD ERICK OF DEVORGOIL.

Peasants, Shepherds, and Vassals of inferior rank.

ELEANOR, *Wife of Oswald, descended of obscure Parentage.*

FLORA, *Daughter of Oswald.*

KATLEEN, *Niece of Eleanor.*

The Doom of Devorgoil.

ACT I.—SCENE I.

*The Scene represents a wild and hilly, but not a mountainous
Country, in a frontier district of Scotland.   The flat scene exhibits the Castle of Devorgoil, decayed, and partly ruinous, situated upon a Lake, and connected with the land by a Drawbridge,
which is lowered.   Time—Sunset.*

FLORA *enters from the Castle, looks timidly around, then
comes forward and speaks.*

HE is not here—those pleasures are not ours
Which placid evening brings to all things else.

SONG.[1]

The sun upon the lake is low,
   The wild birds hush their song,
The hills have evening's deepest glow,
   Yet Leonard tarries long.
Now all whom varied toil and care
   From home and love divide,
In the calm sunset may repair
   Each to the loved one's side.

The noble dame, on turret high,
   Who waits her gallant knight,
Looks to the western beam to spy
   The flash of armour bright.
The village maid, with hand on brow,
   The level ray to shade,
Upon the footpath watches now
   For Colin's darkening plaid.

Now to their mates the wild swans row—
   By day they swam apart;
And to the thicket wanders slow
   The hind beside the hart.
The woodlark at his partner's side,
   Twitters his closing song—
All meet whom day and care divide,
   But Leonard tarries long.

---

[1] The author thought of omitting this song, which was, in fact, abridged
into one in "Quentin Durward," termed County Guy. [See *ante*, vol. i.
p. 382.] It seemed, however, necessary to the sense, that the original stanzas
should be retained here.

[Katleen *has come out of the Castle while* Flora *was
singing, and speaks when the Song is ended.*

Kat. Ah, my dear coz!—if that your mother's niece
May so presume to call your father's daughter—
All these fond things have got some home of comfort
To tempt the rovers back—the lady's bower,
The shepherdess's hut, the wild swan's couch
Among the rushes, even the lark's low nest,
Has that of promise which lures home a lover,—
But we have nought of this.

Flo. How call you, then, this castle of my sire,
The towers of Devorgoil?

Kat. Dungeons for men, and palaces for owls;
Yet no wise owl would change a farmer's barn
For yonder hungry hall—our latest mouse,
Our last of mice, I tell you, has been found
Starv'd in the pantry; and the reverend spider,
Sole living tenant of the Baron's halls,
Who, train'd to abstinence, lived a whole summer
Upon a single fly, he's famish'd too;
The cat is in the kitchen-chimney, seated
Upon our last of fagots, destined soon
To dress our last of suppers, and, poor soul,
Is starved with cold, and mewling mad with hunger.

Flo. D' ye mock our misery, Katleen?

Kat. No, but I am hysteric on the subject,
So I must laugh or cry, and laughing 's lightest.

Flo. Why stay you with us, then, my merry cousin!
From you my sire can ask no filial duty.

Kat. No, thanks to Heaven!
No Noble in wide Scotland, rich or poor,
Can claim an interest in the vulgar blood
That dances in my veins; and I might wed
A forester to-morrow, nothing fearing
The wrath of high-born kindred, and far less
That the dry bones of lead-lapp'd ancestors
Would clatter in their cerements at the tidings.

Flo. My mother, too, would gladly see you placed
Beyond the verge of our unhappiness,[1]
Which, like a witch's circle, blights and taints
Whatever comes within it.

Kat.   Ah! my good aunt!
She is a careful kinswoman, and prudent
In all but marrying a ruin'd baron,
When she could take her choice of honest yeomen;
And now, to balance this ambitious error,
She presses on her daughter's love the suit

---

[1] MS.—"Beyond the circle of our wretchedness."

Of one who hath no touch of nobleness
In manners, birth, or mind, to recommend him,—
Sage Master Gullcrammer, the new-dubb'd preacher.
    Flo. Do not name him, Katleen!
    Kat. Ay, but I must, and with some gratitude.
I said but now, I saw our last of fagots
Destined to dress our last of meals, but said not
That the repast consisted of choice dainties,
Sent to our larder by that liberal suitor,
The kind Melchisedek.
    Flo.   Were famishing the word,
I'd famish ere I tasted them—the fop,
The fool, the low-born, low-bred, pedant coxcomb!
    Kat. There spoke the blood of long-descended sires!
My cottage wisdom ought to echo back,—
O the snug parsonage! the well-paid stipend!
The yew-hedged garden! bee-hives, pigs, and poultry!
But, to speak honestly, the peasant Katleen,
Valuing these good things justly, still would scorn
To wed, for such, the paltry Gullcrammer,
As much as Lady Flora.
    Flo. Mock me not with a title, gentle cousin,
Which poverty has made ridiculous.—   [*Trumpets far off.*
Hark! they have broken up the weapon-shawing;
The vassals are dismiss'd, and marching homeward.
    Kat. Comes your sire back to-night?
    Flo.   He did purpose
To tarry for the banquet. This day only,
Summon'd as a king's tenant, he resumes
The right of rank his birth assigns to him,
And mingles with the proudest.
    Kat.   To return
To his domestic wretchedness to-morrow—
I envy not the privilege. Let us go
To yonder height, and see the marksmen practise:
They shoot their match down in the dale beyond,
Betwixt the Lowland and the Forest district,
By ancient custom, for a tun of wine.
Let us go see which wins.
    Flo.   That were too forward.
    Kat. Why, you may drop the screen before your face,
Which some chance breeze may haply blow aside
Just when a youth of special note takes aim.
It chanced even so that memorable morning,
When, nutting in the woods, we met young Leonard;—
And in good time here comes his sturdy comrade,
The rough Lance Blackthorn.

Enter LANCELOT BLACKTHORN, *a Forester, with the Carcass
of a Deer on his back, and a Gun in his hand.*

BLA.   Save you, damsels!
KAT. Godden, good yeoman.—Come you from the Weaponshaw?
BLA. Not I, indeed; there lies the mark I shot at.
                    [*Lays down the Deer.*
The time has been I had not miss'd the sport,
Although Lord Nithsdale's self had wanted vension;
But this same mate of mine, young Leonard Dacre,
Makes me do what he lists;—he'll win the prize, though!
The Forest district will not lose its honour,
And that is all I care for—(*some shouts are heard.*) Hark! they're
    at it.
I'll go see the issue.
    FLO.   Leave not here
The produce of your hunting.
    BLA.   But I must, though.
This is his lair to-night, for Leonard Dacre   .
Charged me to leave the stag at Devorgoil;
Then show me quickly where to stow the quarry,
And let me to the sports—(*more shots.*) Come, hasten damsels!
    FLO. It is impossible—we dare not take it.
    BLA. There let it lie, then, and I'll wind my bugle,
That all within these tottering walls may know
That here lies venison, whoso likes to lift it.   [*About to blow.*
    KAT. (*to* FLO.) He will alarm your mother; and, besides,
Our Forest proverb teaches, that no question
Should ask where venison comes from.
Your careful mother, with her wonted prudence,
Will hold its presence plead its own apology.—
Come, Blackthorn, I will show you where to stow it.
    [*Exeunt* KATLEEN *and* BLACKTHORN *into the Castle—more shoot-
        ing—then a distant shout—Stragglers, armed in diffcrent
        ways, pass over the stage, as if from the Weaponshaw.*
    FLO. The prize is won; that general shout proclaim'd it.
The marksmen and the vassals are dispersing.
                    [*She draws back.*

FIRST VASSAL (*a peasant.*) Ay, ay,—'tis lost and won,—the
    Forest have it.
'Tis they have all the luck on't.
    SECOND VAS. (*a shepherd.*) Luck, say'st thou, man? 'Tis prac-
    tice, skill, and cunning.
    THIRD VAS. 'Tis no such thing.—I had hit the mark precisely,
But for this cursed flint; and, as I fired,
A swallow cross'd mine eye too—Will you tell me
That that was but a chance, mine honest shepherd?

First Vas. Ay, and last year, when Lancelot Blackthorn won it,
Because my powder happen'd to be damp,
Was there no luck in that?—The worse luck mine.
Sec. Vas. Still I say, 'twas not chance; it might be witchcraft.
First Vas. Faith, not unlikely, neighbours; for these foresters
Do often haunt about this ruin'd castle.
I've seen myself this spark,—Young Leonard Dacre,—
Come stealing like a ghost ere break of day,
And after sunset, too, along this path;
And well you know the haunted towers of Devorgoil
Have no good reputation in the land.
Shep. That have they not.   I've heard my father say,
Ghosts dance as lightly in its moonlight halls,
As ever maiden did at Midsummer
Upon the village-green,
First Vas. Those that frequent such spirit-haunted ruins
Must needs know more than simple Christians do.——
See, Lance this blessed moment leaves the castle,
And comes to triumph o'er us.
                    [Blackthorn *enters from the Castle, and comes*
                              forward while they speak.
Third Vas. A mighty triumph! What is't, after all,
Except the driving of a piece of lead,—
As learned Master Gullcrammer defined it,—
Just through the middle of a painted board?
Black. And if he so define it, by your leave,
Your learned Master Gullcrammer's an ass.
Third Vas. (*angrily.*) He is a preacher, huntsman, under fa-
     vour.
Sec. Vas. No quarrelling, neighbours—you may both be right.

     Enter a Fourth Vassal, *with a gallon stoup of wine.*

Fourth Vas. Why stand you brawling here? Young Leonard
     Dacre
Has set abroach the tun of wine he gain'd,
That all may drink who list.   Blackthorn, I sought you;
Your comrade prays you will bestow this flagon
Where you have left the deer you kill'd this morning.
Black. And that I will ; but first we will take toll
To see if it's worth carriage.   Shepherd, thy horn.
There must be due allowance made for leakage,
And that will come about a draught a-piece.
Skink it about, and, when our throats are liquor'd,
We'll merrily trowl our song of Weaponshaw.
                    [*They drink about out of the* Shepherd's *horn,*
                         and then sing.

SONG.

We love the shrill trumpet, we love the drum's rattle,
They call us to sport, and they call us to battle;
And old Scotland shall laugh at the threats of a stranger,
While our comrades in pastime are comrades in danger.

If there's mirth in our house, 'tis our neighbour that shares it —
If peril approach, 'tis our neighbour that dares it;
And when we lead off to the pipe and the tabor,
The fair hand we press is the hand of a neighbour.

Then close your ranks, comrades — the bands that combine them,
Faith, friendship, and brotherhood, join'd to entwine them;
And we'll laugh at the threats of each insolent stranger,
While our comrades in sport are our comrades in danger.

  BLACK. Well, I must do mine errand. Master flagon [*Shaking it.*
Is too consumptive for another bleeding.
  SHEP. I must to my fold.
  THIRD VAS.   I'll to the butt of wine,
And see if that has given up the ghost yet
  FIRST VAS. Have with you, neighbour.
    [BLACKTHORN *enters the Castle, the rest exeunt severally.* MEL-
      CHISEDEK GULLCRAMMER *watches them off the stage, and
      then enters from the side-scene. His costume is a Geneva
      cloak and band, with a high-crowned hat; the rest of his
      dress in the fashion of James the First's time. He looks
      to the windows of the Castle, then draws back as if to
      escape observation, while he brushes his cloak, drives the
      white threads from his waistcoat with his wetted thumb,
      and dusts his shoes, all with the air of one who would not
      willingly be observed engaged in these offices. He then
      adjusts his collar and band, comes forward and speaks.*
  GULL. Right comely is thy garb, Melchisedek;
As well beseemeth one, whom good Saint Mungo,
The patron of our land and university,
Hath graced with license both to teach and preach —
Who dare opine thou hither plod'st on foot?
Trim sits thy cloak, unruffled is thy band,
And not a speck upon thine outward man
Bewrays the labours of thy weary sole.
      [*Touches his shoe, and smiles complacently.*
Quaint was that jest and pleasant! — Now will I
Approach and hail the dwellers of this fort;
But specially sweet Flora Devorgoil,
Ere her proud sire return. He loves me not,
Mocketh my lineage, flouts at mine advancement —
Sour as the fruit the crab-tree furnishes,

And hard as is the cudgel it supplies;
But Flora — she 's a lily on the lake,
And I must reach her, though I risk a ducking.
　　[As GULLCRAMMER *moves towards the drawbridge,* BAULDIE
　　　　DURWARD *enters, and interposes himself betwixt him and
　　　　the Castle.* GULLCRAMMER *stops and speaks.*
Whom have we here ? — that ancient fortune-teller,
Papist and sorcerer, and sturdy beggar,
Old Bauldie Durward! Would I were well past him!
　　　*[*DURWARD *advances, partly in the dress of a palmer, partly
　　　　in that of an old Scottish mendicant, having coarse blue
　　　　cloak and badge, white beard, &c.*
　DUR. The blessing of the evening on your worship,
And on your taff'ty doublet.　Much I marvel
Your wisdom chooseth such trim garb,[1] when tempests
Are gathering to the bursting.
　　GULLCRAMMER (*looks to his dress, and then to the sky, with some
　　　　apprehension.*) Surely, Bauldie,
Thou dost belie the evening — in the west
The light sinks down as lovely as this band
Drops o'er this mantle — Tush, man! 't will be fair.
　DUR. Ay, but the storm I bode is big with blows,
Horsewhips for hailstones, clubs for thunderbolts ;
And for the wailing of the midnight wind,
The unpitied howling of a cudgell'd coxcomb,
Come, come, I know thou seek'st fair Flora Devorgoil.
　GUL. And if I did, I do the damsel grace.
Her mother thinks so, and she has accepted
At these poor hands gifts of some consequence,
And curious dainties for the evening cheer,
To which I am invited — she respects me.
　DUR. But not so doth her father, haughty Oswald.
Bethink thee, he 's a baron ——
　　GUL.　　　　　　　　　　And a bare one;
Construe me that, old man! — The crofts of Mucklewhame —
Destined for mine so soon as heaven and earth
Have shared my uncle's soul and bones between them —
The crofts of Mucklewhame, old man, which nourish
Three scores of sheep, three cows, with each her follower,
A female palfrey eke — I will be candid,
She is of that meek tribe whom, in derision,
Our wealthy southern neighbours nickname donkeys ——
　DUR. She hath her follower too, — when thou art there.
　GUL. I say to thee, these crofts of Mucklewhame,
In the mere tything of their stock and produce,
Outvie whatever patch of land remains

　　　[1] MS.—"*That you should walk in such trim guise.*'

To this old rugged castle and its owner.
Well, therefore, may Melchisedek Gullcrammer,
Younger of Mucklewhame, for such I write me,
Master of Arts, by grace of good Saint Andrew,
Preacher, in brief expectance of a kirk,
Endow'd with ten score Scottish pounds per annum,
Being eight pounds seventeen eight in sterling coin —
Well then, I say, may this Melchisedek,
Thus highly graced by fortune — and by nature
E'en gifted as thou seest — aspire to woo
The daughter of the beggar'd Devorgoil.

   Dur. Credit an old man's word, kind Master Gullcrammer,
You will not find it so. — Come, Sir, I've known
The hospitality of Mucklewhame;
It reach'd not to profuseness — yet, in gratitude
For the pure water of its living well,
And for the barley loaves of its fair fields,
Wherein chopp'd straw contended with the grain
Which best should satisfy the appetite,
I would not see the hopeful heir of Mucklewhame
Thus fling himself on danger.

   Gul. Danger! what danger? — Know'st thou not, old Oswald
This day attends the muster of the shire,
Where the crown-vassals meet to show their arms,
And their best horse of service? 'Twas good sport
(An if a man had dared but laugh at it)
To see old Oswald with his rusty morion,
And huge two-handed sword, that might have seen
The field of Bannockburn or Chevy-Chase,
Without a squire or vassal, page or groom,
Or e'en a single pikeman at his heels,
Mix with the proudest nobles of the county,
And claim precedence for his tatter'd person
O'er armours double gilt and ostrich-plumage.

   Dur. Ay! 'twas the jest at which fools laugh the loudest,
The downfall of our old nobility —
Which may forerun the ruin of a kingdom.
I've seen an idiot clap his hands, and shout
To see a tower like yon (*points to a part of the Castle*) stoop to
     its base
In headlong ruin; while the wise look'd round,
And fearful sought a distant stance to watch
What fragment of the fabric next should follow;
For when the turrets fall, the walls are tottering.

   Gul. (*after pondering.*) If that means aught, it means thou
     saw'st old Oswald
Expell'd from the assembly.

DUR.   Thy sharp wit
Hath glanced unwittingly right nigh the truth.
Expell'd he was not, but, his claim denied
At some contested point of ceremony.
He left the weaponshaw in high displeasure,
And hither comes — his wonted bitter temper
Scarce sweeten'd by the chances of the day.
'T were much like rashness should you wait his coming,
And thither tends my counsel.
  GUL.   And I'll take it;
Good Bauldie Durward, I will take thy counsel,
And will requite it with this minted farthing,
That bears our sovereign's head in purest copper.
  DUR. Thanks.to thy bounty — Haste thee, good young master:
Oswald, besides the old two-handed sword,
Bears in his hand a staff of potency,
To charm intruders from his castle purlieus.
  GUL. I do abhor all charms, nor will abide
To hear or see, far less to feel their use.
Behold, I have departed.   *[Exit hastily.*

Manet DURWARD.

  DUR. Thus do I play the idle part of one
Who seeks to save the moth from scorching him
In the bright taper's flame — And Flora's beauty [1]
Must, not unlike that taper, waste away,
Gilding the rugged walls that saw it kindled.
This was a shard-born beetle, heavy, drossy, [2]
Though boasting his dull drone and gilded wing.
Here comes a flutterer of another stamp,
Whom the same ray is charming to his ruin.

Enter LEONARD, *dressed as a huntsman; he pauses before the
  Tower, and whistles a note or two at intervals — drawing back,
  as if fearful of observation — yet waiting, as if expecting some
  reply —* DURWARD, *whom he had not observed, moves round, so
  as to front* LEONARD *unexpectedly.*

  LEON. I am too late — it was no easy task
To rid myself from yonder noisy revellers.
Flora! — I fear she 's angry — Flora — Flora! [3]

SONG.

Admire not that I gain'd the prize
From all the village crew ;

---

 [1] MS.—"And Flora's years of beauty."
 [2] MS.—"This was an earth-born beetle, dull, and drossy."
 [3] From the MS., the following song appears to have been a *recent* interpo-
lation.

How could I fail with hand or eyes,
When heart and faith were true?

And when in floods of rosy wine
My comrades drown'd their cares,
I thought but that thy heart was mine,
My own leapt light as theirs.

My brief delay then do not blame,
Nor deem your swain untrue;
My form but linger'd at the game,
My soul was still with you.

She hears not!
DUR. But a friend hath heard—Leonard, I pity thee.
LEON. (*starts, but recovers himself.*) Pity, good father, is
for those in want,
In age, in sorrow, in distress of mind,
Or agony of body. I 'm in health—
Can match my limbs against the stag in chase,
Have means enough to meet my simple wants,
And am so free of soul that I can carol
To woodland and to wild in notes as lively
As are my jolly bugle's.
DUR. Even therefore dost thou need my pity, Leonard.
And therefore I bestow it, praying thee,
Before thou feel'st the need, my mite of pity.
Leonard, thou lovest; and in that little word
There lies enough to claim the sympathy
Of men who wear such hoary locks as mine,
And know what misplaced love is sure to end in.[1]
LEON. Good father, thou art old, and even thy youth,
As thou hast told me, spent in cloister'd cells,
Fits thee but ill to judge the passions
Which are the joy and charm of social life.

The MS. here adds:—

    "*Leonard.* But mine is not misplaced—If I sought beauty,
Resides it not with Flora Devorgoil?
If piety, if sweetness, if discretion,
Patience beneath ill-suited tasks of labour,
And filial tenderness that can beguile
Her moody sire's dark thoughts, as the soft moonshine
Illumes the cloud of night—if I seek these,
Are they not all with Flora? Number me
The list of female virtues one by one,
And I will answer all with Flora Devorgoil.
    "*Durward.* This is the wonted pitch of youthful passion:
And every woman who hath had a lover,
However now deem'd crabbed, cross, and canker'd,
And crooked both in temper and in shape,
Has in her day been thought the purest, wisest,
Gentlest, and best condition'd—and o'er all
Fairest and liveliest of Eve's numerous daughters.
    "*Leonard.* Good father, thou art old," &c.

Press me no farther, then, nor waste those moments
Whose worth thou canst not estimate. [*As turning from him.*
   Dur. *(detains him.)* Stay, young man!
'Tis seldom that a beggar claims a debt;
Yet I bethink me of a gay young stripling,
That owes to these white locks and hoary beard
Something of reverence and of gratitude
More than he wills to pay.
   Leon. Forgive me, father.   Often hast thou told me,
That in the ruin of my father's house   .
You saved the orphan Leonard in his cradle;
And well I know, that to thy care alone—
Care seconded by means beyond thy seeming—
I owe whate'er of nurture I can boast.
   Dur. Then for thy life preserved,
And for the means of knowledge I have furnish'd,
(Which lacking, man is levell'd with the brutes,)
Grant me this boon:—Avoid these fated walls!
A curse is on them, bitter, deep, and heavy,
Of power to split the massiest tower they boast
From pinnacle to dungeon vault.   It rose
Upon the gay horizon of proud Devorgoil,
As unregarded as the fleecy cloud,
The first forerunner of the hurricane,
Scarce seen amid the welkin's shadeless blue.
Dark grew it, and more dark, and still the fortunes
Of this doom'd family have darken'd with it
It hid their sovereign's favour, and obscured
The lustre of their service, gender'd hate
Betwixt them and the mighty of the land;
Till by degrees the waxing tempest rose,
And stripp'd the goodly tree of fruit and flowers,
And buds, and boughs, and branches.   There remains
A rugged trunk, dismember'd and unsightly,
Waiting the bursting of the final bolt
To splinter it to shivers.   Now, go pluck
Its single tendril to enwreath thy brow,
And rest beneath its shade—to share the ruin!
   Leon. This anathema,
Whence should it come!—How merited!—and when!
   Dur. 'Twas in the days
Of Oswald's grandsire,—'mid Galwegian chiefs
The fellest foe, the fiercest champion.
His blood-red pennons scared the Cumbrian coasts,
And wasted towns and manors mark'd his progress.
His galleys stored with treasure, and their decks
Crowded with English captives, who beheld,

With weeping eyes, their native shores retire,
He bore him homeward; but a tempest rose——
    Leon. So far I've heard the tale,
And spare thee the recital,—The grim chief
Marking his vessels labour on the sea,
And loth to lose his treasure, gave command
To plunge his captives in the raging deep.
    Dur. There sunk the lineage of a noble name,
And the wild waves boom'd over sire and son,
Mother and nursling, of the House of Aglionby,[1]
Leaving but one frail tendril.— Hence the fate
That hovers o'er these turrets,—hence the peasant,
Belated, hying homewards, dreads to cast
A glance upon that portal, lest he see
The unshrouded spectres of the murder'd dead;[2]
Or the avenging Angel, with his sword,
Waving destruction; or the grisly phantom
Of that fell Chief, the doer of the deed,
Which still, they say, roams through his empty halls,
And mourns their wasteness and their lonelihood.
    Leon. Such is the dotage
Of superstition, father—ay, and the cant
Of hoodwink'd prejudice. — Not for atonement
Of some foul deed done in the ancient warfare,
When war was butchery, and men were wolves,
Doth Heaven consign the innocent to suffering.
I tell thee, Flora's virtues might atone
For all the massacres her sires have done,
Since first the Pictish race their stained limbs[3]
Array'd in wolf's skin.
    Dur. Leonard, ere yet this beggar's scrip and cloak
Supplied the place of mitre and of crosier,[4]
Which in these alter'd lands must not be worn,
I was superior of a brotherhood
Of holy men,—the Prior of Lanercost.
Nobles then sought my footstool many a league,
There to unload their sins—questions of conscience
Of deepest import were not deem'd too nice
For my decision, youth. But not even then,
With mitre on my brow, and all the voice
Which Rome gives to a father of her church,
Dared I pronounce so boldly on the ways

    MS.— ——" House of Ehrenwald."
  [2] MS.— ——" spectres of the murder'd captives."
  [3] MS.— ——" their painted limbs."
MS —[4] ' Supplied the { place / want } of palmer's cowl and staff.'

Of hidden Providence, as thou, young man,
Whose chiefest knowledge is to track a stag,
Or wind a bugle, hast presumed to do.
   Leon. Nay, I pray forgive me,
Father; thou know'st I meant not to presume ——
   Dur. Can I refuse thee pardon?—Thou art all
That war and change have left to the poor Durward.
Thy father, too, who lost his life and fortune
Defending Lanercost, when its fair aisles
Were spoil'd by sacrilege—I bless'd his banner,
And yet it prosper'd not.   But—all I could—
Thee from the wreck I saved, and for thy sake
Have still dragg'd on my life of pilgrimage
And penitence upon the hated shores
I else had left for ever.   Come with me,
And I will teach thee there is healing in
The wounds which friendship gives.   [*Exeunt.*

SCENE II

*The Scene changes to the Interior of the Castle. An apartment is
discovered, in which there is much appearance of present poverty, mixed with some relics of former grandeur. On the wall
hangs, amongst other things, a suit of ancient armour; by the
table is a covered basket; behind, and concealed by it, the carcass
of a roe-deer. There is a small latticed window, which, appear-
ing to perforate a wall of great thickness, is supposed to look out
towards the drawbridge. It is in the shape of a loop-hole for mus-
ketry; and, as is not unusual in old buildings, is placed so high
up in the wall, that it is only approached by five or six narrow
stone steps.*

*Eleanor, the wife of Oswald of Devorgoil, Flora and Kat-
leen, her Daughter and Niece, are discovered at work. The
former spins, the latter are embroidering. Eleanor quits her
own labour to examine the manner in which Flora is executing
her task, and shakes her head as if dissatisfied.*

   Ele. Fy on it, Flora!—this botch'd work of thine
Shows that thy mind is distant from thy task.
The finest tracery of our old cathedral
Had not a richer, freer, bolder pattern,
Than Flora once could trace. Thy thoughts are wandering.
   Flo. They're with my father.   Broad upon the lake
The evening sun sunk down; huge piles of clouds,
Crimson and sable, rose upon his disk,

And quench'd him ere his setting, like some champion
In his last conflict, losing all his glory.
Sure signals those of storm. And if my father
Be on his homeward road——
　　ELE.　　　　　　　　　But that he will not.
Baron of Devorgoil, this day at least
He banquets with the nobles—who, the next,
Would scarce vouchsafe an alms to save his household
From want or famine.　Thanks to a kind friend,
For one brief space we shall not need their aid.
　　FLO. (*joyfully*.)　What! knew you then his gift?
How silly I that would, yet durst not tell it!
I fear my father will condemn us both,
That easily accepted such a present.
　　KAT. Now, here's the game a bystander sees better
Than those who play it.—My good aunt is pondering
On the good cheer which Gullcrammer has sent us,
And Flora thinks upon the forest venison.　　[*Aside.*
　　ELE. (*to* FLO.) Thy father need not know on 't—'t is a
Comes timely, when frugality,—nay, abstinence,　[boon
Might scarce avail us longer.　I had hoped
Ere now a visit from the youthful donor,
That we might thank his bounty; and perhaps
My Flora thought the same, when Sunday's kerchief
And the best kirtle were sought out, and donn'd
To grace a work-day evening.
　　FLO. Nay, mother, that is judging all too close!
My work-day gown was torn—my kerchief sullied;
And thus—But, think you, will the gallant come?
　　ELE. He will, for with these dainties came a message
From gentle Master Gullcrammer, to intimate——
　　FLO. (*greatly disappointed.*) Gullcrammer?
　　KAT. There burst the bubble—down fell house of cards,
And cousin's like to cry for 't!　　　　　　[*Aside.*
　　ELE. Gullcrammer! ay, Gullcrammer; thou scorn'st not at
'T were something short of wisdom in a maiden,　　[him!
Who, like the poor bat in the Grecian fable,
Hovers betwixt two classes in the world,
And is disclaim'd by both the mouse and bird.
　　KAT.　　　　　　　　　I am the poor mouse,
And may go creep into what hole I list,
And no one heed me—Yet I'll waste a word
Of counsel on my betters.—Kind my aunt,
And you, my gentle cousin, were't not better
We thought of dressing this same gear for supper,
Than quarrelling about the worthless donor?
　　ELE. Peace, minx!

Flo.　　　　　　　Thou hast no feeling, cousin Katleen.

Kat. So ! I have brought them both on my poor shoul-
　　　　ders : ·
So meddling peace-makers are still rewarded :
E'en let them to 't again, and fight it out.

Flo. Mother, were I disclaim'd of every class,
I would not therefore so disclaim myself,
As even a passing thought of scorn to waste
On cloddish Gullcrammer.

Ele. List to me, love, and let adversity
Incline thine ear to wisdom.　Look around thee—
Of the gay youths who boast a noble name,
Which will incline to wed a dowerless damsel?
And of the yeomanry, who, think'st thou, Flora,
Would ask to share the labours of his farm
An high-born beggar?— This young man is modest——

Flo. Silly, good mother; sheepish, if you will it.

Ele. E'en call it what you list—the softer temper,
The fitter to endure the bitter sallies
Of one whose wit is all too sharp for mine.

Flo. Mother, you cannot mean it as you say;
You cannot bid me prize conceited folly?

Ele. Content thee, child—each lot has its own blessings.
This youth, with his plain-dealing honest suit,
Proffers thee quiet, peace, and competence,
Redemption from a home, o'er which fell Fate
Stoops like a falcon.—Oh! if thou couldst choose
(As no such choice is given) 'twixt such a mate
And some proud noble!—Who, in sober judgment,
Would like to navigate the heady river,
Dashing in fury from its parent mountain,
More than the waters of the quiet lake?

Kat. Now can I hold no longer—Lake, good aunt!
Nay, in the name of truth, say mill-pond, horse-pond;
Or if there be a pond more miry,
More sluggish, mean-derived, and base than either,
Be such Gullcrammer's emblem—and his portion!

Flo. I would that he or I were in our grave,
Rather than thus his suit should goad me!—Mother,
Flora of Devorgoil, though low in fortunes,
Is still too high in mind to join her name
With such a base-born churl as Gullcrammer.

Ele. You are trim maidens both!
　　　　(*To* Flora.)　　　　　　Have you forgotten,
Or did you mean to call to *my* remembrance
Thy father chose a wife of peasant blood?

Flo. Will you speak thus to me, or think the stream

Can mock the fountain it derives its source from !
My venerated mother !—in that name
Lies all on earth a child should chiefest honour ;
And with that name to mix reproach or taunt,
Were only short of blasphemy to Heaven.
  ELE. Then listen, Flora, to that mother's counsel,
Or rather profit by that mother's fate.
Your father's fortunes were but bent, not broken,
Until he listen'd to his rash affection.
Means were afforded to redeem his house,
Ample and large—the hand of a rich heiress
Awaited, almost courted, his acceptance ;
He saw my beauty—such it then was call'd,
Or such at least he thought it—the wither'd bush,
Whate'er it now may seem, had blossoms then,—
And he forsook the proud and wealthy heiress,
To wed with me and ruin——
  KAT. (*aside.*)   The more fool,
Say I, apart, the peasant maiden then,
Who might have chose a mate from her own hamlet.
  ELE. Friends fell off,
And to his own resources, his own counsels,
Abandon'd, as they said. the thoughtless prodigal,
Who had exchanged rank, riches, pomp, and honour,
For the mean beauties of a cottage maid.
  FLO. It was done like my father,
Who scorn'd to sell what wealth can never buy—
True love and free affections.   And he loves you !
If you have suffer'd in a weary world,
Your sorrows have been jointly borne, and love
Has made the load sit lighter.
  ELE. Ay, but a misplaced match hath that deep curse in 't,
That can embitter e'en the purest streams
Of true affection.   Thou hast seen me seek,
With the strict caution early habits taught me,
To match our wants and means—hast seen thy father,
With aristocracy's high brow of scorn,
Spurn at economy, the cottage virtue,
As best befitting her whose sires were peasants :
Nor can I, when I see my lineage scorn'd,
Always conceal in what contempt I hold
The fancied claims of rank he clings to fondly.
  FLO. Why will you do so ?—well you know it chafes him.
  ELE. Flora, thy mother is but mortal woman,
Nor can at all times check an eager tongue.   [ter.
  KAT. (*aside.*) That's no new tidings to her niece and daugh-
  ELE. O may'st thou never know the spited feelings

That gender discord in adversity
Betwixt the dearest friends and truest lovers!
In the chill damping gale of poverty,
If Love's lamp go not out, it gleams but palely,
And twinkles in the socket.

FLO. But tenderness can screen it with her veil, [1]
Till it revive again. By gentleness, good mother,
How oft I've seen you soothe my father's mood!

KAT. Now there speak youthful hope and fantasy! [*Aside.*

ELE. That is an easier task in youth than age;
Our temper hardens, and our charms decay,
And both are needed in that art of soothing.

KAT. And there speaks sad experience. [*Aside.*

ELE. Besides, since that our state was utter desperate,
Darker his brow, more dangerous grow his words:
Fain would I snatch thee from the woe and wrath
Which darken'd long my life, and soon must end it.
[*A knocking without;* ELEANOR *shows alarm.*
It was thy father's knock,—haste to the gate.
[*Exeunt* FLORA *and* KATLEEN.
What can have happ'd?—he thought to stay the night.
This gear must not be seen.
[*As she is about to remove the basket, she sees the
body of the roe-deer.*
What have we here? a roe-deer!—as I fear it,
This was the gift of which poor Flora thought.
The young and handsome hunter——But time presses.
[*She removes the basket and the roe into a closet.
As she has done—*

Enter OSWALD *of* DEVORGOIL, FLORA, *and* KATLEEN.

[*He is dressed in a scarlet cloak, which should seem worn
and old—a headpiece, and old-fashioned sword—the
rest of his dress that of a peasant. His countenance
and manner should express the moody and irritable
haughtiness of a proud man involved in calamity, and
who has been exposed to recent insult.*

Ows. (*addressing his wife*)—
The sun hath set—why is the drawbridge lower'd

ELE. The counterpoise has fail'd, and Flora's strength,
Katleen's, and mine united, could not raise it.

Osw. Flora and thou!—a goodly garrison
To hold a castle, which, if fame say true,
Once foil'd the King of Norse and all his rovers.

ELE. It might be so in ancient times, but now——

Osw. A herd of deer might storm proud Devorgoil

---

[1] MS.—"Ay, but the veil of tenderness can screen it."

KAT. (*aside to* FLO.) You, Flora, know full well, one deer
Has enter'd at the breach; and, what is worse,   [already
The escort is not yet march'd off, for Blackthorn
Is still within the castle.

FLO. In heaven's name, rid him out on't, ere my father
Discovers he is here!   Why went he not before?

KAT. Because I staid him on some little business;
I had a plan to scare poor paltry Gullcrammer
Out of his paltry wits.

FLO.   Well, haste ye now
And try to get him off.

KAT.   I will not promise that.
I would not turn an honest hunter's dog,
So well I love the woodcraft, out of shelter
In such a night as this—far less his master:
But I'll do this,—I'll try to hide him for you.

OSW. (*whom his wife has assisted to take off his cloak and
            feathered cap*)—
Ay, take them off, and bring my peasant's bonnet
And peasant's plaid—I'll noble it no further.
Let them erase my name from honour's lists,
And drag my scutcheon at their horses' heels;
I have deserved it all, for I am poor,
And poverty hath neither right of birth,
Nor rank, relation, claim, nor privilege,
To match a new-coin'd viscount, whose good-grandsire,
The lord be with him, was a careful skipper,
And steer'd his paltry skiff 'twixt Leith and Campvere—
Marry, sir, he could buy Geneva cheap,
And knew the coast by moonlight.

FLO. Mean you the Viscount Ellondale, my father?
What strife has been between you?

OSW.   O, a trifle!
Not worth a wise man's thinking twice about;—
Precedence is a toy—a superstition
About a table's end, joint-stool, and trencher.
Something was once thought due to long descent,
And something to Galwegia's oldest baron,—
But let that pass—a dream of the old time.

ELE. It is indeed a dream.

OSW. (*turning upon her rather quickly*)—
Ha! said ye?—let me hear these words more plain.

ELE. Alas! they are but echoes of your own.
Match'd with the real woes that hover o'er us,
What are the idle visions of precedence,
But, as you term them, dreams, and toys, and trifles,
Not worth a wise man's thinking twice upon?

Osw. Ay, 'twas for you I framed that consolation,
The true philosophy of clouted shoe
And linsey-woolsey kirtle.   I know, that minds
Of nobler stamp receive no dearer motive[1]
Than what is link'd with honour.   Ribands, tassels,
Which are but shreds of silk and spangled tinsel —[2]
The right of place, which in itself is momentary —
A word, which is but air — may in themselves,
And to the nobler file, be steep'd so richly
In that elixir, honour, that the lack
Of things so very trivial in themselves
Shall be misfortune.   One shall seek for them[3]
O'er the wild waves — one in the deadly breach
And battle's headlong front — one in the paths
Of midnight study, — and, in gaining these
Emblems of honour, each will hold himself
Repaid for all his labours, deeds, and dangers.
What then should he think, knowing them his own,
Who sees what warriors and what sages toil for,
The formal and establish'd marks of honour.
Usurp'd from him by upstart insolence ?

   Ele. (*who has listened to the last speech with some impa-*
       tience) — This is but empty declamation, Oswald.
The fragments left at yonder full-spread banquet,
Nay, even the poorest crust swept from the table,
Ought to be far more precious to a father,
Whose family lacks food, than the vain boast,
He sate at the board-head.

   Osw. Thou'lt drive me frantic ! — I will tell thee, wo-
    man —
Yet why to thee ?   There is another ear
Which that tale better suits, and he shall hear it.
      [*Looks at his sword, which he has unbuckled, and*
         addresses the rest of the speech to it.
Yes, trusty friend, my father knew thy worth,
And often proved it — often told me of it.
Though thou and I be now held lightly of,
And want the gilded hatchments of the time,
I think we both may prove true metal still.
'Tis thou shalt tell this story, right this wrong:
Rest thou till time is fitting.   [*Hangs up the sword.*
      [*The Women look at each other with anxiety*
        during this speech, which they partly over-
        hear.   They both approach Oswald.

    MS.— ——"Yet, I know, for minds
       Of nobler stamp earth has no dearer motive."
    MS.— ——" tinsell'd spangle."
   [3] MS.— ——" One shall seek these emblems."

ELE. Oswald—my dearest husband!

FLO. 　　　　　　　　　　My dear father!

Osw. Peace, both!—we speak no more of this. I go
To heave the drawbridge up. 　　　　　　　　[*Exit.*

KATLEEN *mounts the steps towards the loop-hole, looks out,*
and speaks.

KAT. The storm is gathering fast; broad, heavy drops
Fall plashing on the bosom of the lake,
And dash its inky surface into circles;
The distant hills are hid in wreaths of darkness.
'T will be a fearful night.

OSWALD *re-enters, and throws himself into a seat.*

ELE. 　　　　　　　　　　More dark and dreadful
Than is our destiny, it cannot be.

Osw. (*to* FLO.) Such is Heaven's will—it is our part to
We 're warranted, my child, from ancient story 　[bear it.
And blessed writ, to say, that song assuages
The gloomy cares that prey upon our reason,
And wake a strife betwixt our better feelings
And the fierce dictates of the headlong passions.
Sing, then, my love; for if a voice have influence
To mediate peace betwixt me and my destiny,
Flora, it must be thine.

FLO. 　　　　　　　　　My best to please you!

SONG.

WHEN the tempest 's at the loudest,
　On its gale the eagle rides;
When the ocean rolls the proudest,
　Through the foam the sea-bird glides—
All the rage of wind and sea
Is subdued by constancy.

Gnawing want and sickness pining,
　All the ills that men endure;
Each their various pangs combining,
　Constancy can find a cure—
Pain, and Fear, and Poverty,
Are subdued by constancy.

Bar me from each wonted pleasure,
　Make me abject, mean, and poor;
Heap on insults without measure,
　Chain me to a dungeon floor—
I 'll be happy, rich, and free,
If endow'd with constancy.

ACT II.—SCENE I.

*A Chamber in a distant part of the Castle. A large Window in
the flat scene, supposed to look on the Lake, which is occasion
ally illuminated by lightning. There is a couch-bed in the room
and an antique cabinet.*

Enter KATLEEN, *introducing* BLACKTHORN.[1]

KAT. This was the destined scene of action, Blackthorn,
And here our properties. But all in vain,
For of Gullcrammer we 'll see nought to-night,
Except the dainties that I told you of.

BLA. O, if he 's left that same hog's face and sausages,
He will try back upon them, never fear it.
The cur will open on the trail of bacon,
Like my old brach-hound.

KAT. And should that hap, we 'll play our comedy,—
Shall we not, Blackthorn? Thou shalt be Owlspiegle——

BLA. And who may that hard-named person be?

KAT. I 've told you nine times over.

BLA. Yes, pretty Katleen, but my eyes were busy
In looking at you all the time you were talking;
And so I lost the tale.

KAT. Then shut your eyes, and let your goodly ears
Do their good office.

BLA.   That were too hard penance.
Tell but thy tale once more, and I will hearken
As if I were thrown out, and listening for
My bloodhound's distant bay.

KAT.   A civil simile!
Then, for the tenth time, and the last,—be told,
Owlspiegle was of old the wicked barber
To Erick, wicked Lord of Devorgoil.

BLA. The chief who drown'd his captives in the Solway?
We all have heard of him.

KAT. A hermit hoar, a venerable man—
So goes the legend—came to wake repentance
In the fierce lord, and tax'd him with his guilt;
But he, heart-harden'd, turn'd into derison
The man of heaven, and, as his dignity
Consisted much in a long reverend beard,
Which reach'd his girdle, Erick caused his barber
This same Owlspiegle, violate its honours
With sacrilegious razor, and clip his hair
After the fashion of a roguish fool.

---

[1] The MS., throughout the First Act reads *Buckthorn.*

BLA. This was reversing of our ancient proverb,
And shaving for the devil's, not for God's sake.
KAT. True, most grave Blackthorn ; and in punishment
Of this foul act of scorn, the barber's ghost
Is said to have no resting after death,
But haunts these halls, and chiefly this same chamber, •
Where the profanity was acted, trimming
And clipping all such guests as sleep within it.
Such is at least the tale our elders tell,
With many others, of this haunted castle.
BLA. And you would have me take this shape of Owlspiegle,
And trim the wise Melchisedek !—I wonnot.
KAT. You will not !
BLA.   No—unless you bear a part.
KAT. What ! can you not alone play such a farce ?
BLA. Not I—I'm dull.   Besides, we foresters
Still hunt our game in couples.   Look you, Katleen,
We danced at Shrovetide—then you were my partner ;
We sung at Christmas—you kept time with me ;
And if we go a mumming in this business,
By heaven, you must be one, or Master Gullcrammer.
Is like to rest unshaven——
KAT.   Why, you fool,
What end can this serve ?
BLA.   Nay, I know not, I.
But if we keep this wont of being partners,
Why, use makes perfect—who knows what may happen ?
KAT. Thou art a foolish patch—But sing our carol,
As I have alter'd it, with some few words
To suit the characters, and I will bear—— [*Gives a paper.*
BLA. Part in the gambol.   I'll go study quickly.
Is there no other ghost, then, haunts the castle,
But this same barber shave-a-penny goblin ?
I thought they glanced in every beam of moonshine,
As frequent as a bat.
KAT. I've heard my aunt's high husband tell of prophecies,
And fates impending o'er the house of Devorgoil ;
Legends first coin'd by ancient superstition,
And render'd current by credulity
And pride of lineage.   Five years have I dwelt,
And ne'er saw anything more mischievous
Than what I am myself.
BLA. And that is quite enough, I warrant you.
But, stay, where shall I find a dress
To play this—what d'ye call him—Owlspiegle ?
KAT. (*takes dresses out of the cabinet*) Why, there are his
     own clothes,

Preserved with other trumpery of the sort,
For we have kept nought but what is good for nought.
        [*She drops a cap as she draws out the clothes.*
            Blackthorn lifts it, and gives it to her.
Nay, keep it for thy pains — it is a coxcomb, —
So call'd in ancient times, in ours a fool's cap, —
For you must know they kept a Fool at Devorgoil
In former days; but now are well contented
To play the fool themselves, to save expenses.
Yet give it me, I 'll find a worthy use for 't.
I 'll take this page's dress, to play the page
Cockledemoy, who waits on ghostly Owlspiegle;
And yet 't is needless, too, for Gullcrammer
Will scarce be here to-night.

    BLA. I tell you that he will — I will uphold
His plighted faith and true allegiance
Unto a sows'd sow's face and sausages,
And such the dainties that you say he sent you,
Against all other likings whatsoever,
Except a certain sneaking of affection,
Which makes some folks I know of play the fool,
To please some other folks.

    KAT. Well, I do hope he 'll come. There 's first a chance
He will be cudgell'd by my noble uncle —
I cry his mercy — by my good aunt's husband,
Who did vow vengeance, knowing nought of him
But by report, and by a limping sonnet
Which he had fashion'd to my cousin's glory,
And forwarded by blind Tom Long the carrier;
So there 's the chance, first of a hearty beating,
Which failing, we 've this after-plot of vengeance.

    BLA. Kind damsel, how considerate and merciful!
But how shall we get off, our parts being play'd?

    KAT. For that we are well fitted :—here 's a trap-door
Sinks with a counterpoise — you shall go that way.
I 'll make my exit yonder — 'neath the window,
A balcony communicates with the tower
That overhangs the lake.

    BLA. 'T were a rare place, this house of Devorgoil,
To play at hide-and-seek-in — shall we try,
One day, my pretty Katleen?

    KAT. Hands off, rude ranger! I 'm no managed hawk
To stoop to lure of yours. — But bear you gallantly;
This Gullcrammer hath vex'd my cousin much, —
I fain would have some vengeance.

    BLA. I 'll bear my part with glee;—he spoke irreverently
Of practice at a mark!

KAT.   That cries for vengeance.
But I must go—I hear my aunt's shrill voice!
My cousin and her father will scream next.
    ELE. (*at a distance.*) Katleen! Katleen!
    BLA.   Hark to old Sweetlips!
Away with you before the full cry open—
But stay, what have you there?
    KAT. (*with a bundle she has taken from the wardrobe*)—
My dress, my page's dress—let it alone.
    BLA. Your tiring-room is not, I hope, far distant;
You're inexperienced in these new habiliments—
I am most ready to assist your toilet.
    KAT. Out, you great ass! was ever such a fool! [*Runs off*

BLA. (sings.)

O, Robin Hood was a bowman good,
  And a bowman good was he,
And he met with a maiden in merry Sherwood,
  All under the greenwood tree.

Now give me a kiss, quoth bold Robin Hood,
  Now give me a kiss, said he,
For there never came maid into merry Sherwood,
  But she paid the forester's fee.

I've coursed this twelvemonth this sly puss, young Katleen,
And she has dodged me, turn'd beneath my nose,
And flung me out a score of yards at once;
If this same gear fadge right, I'll cote and mouth her,
And then! whoop! dead! dead! dead!—She is the metal
To make a woodman's wife of!———   [*Pauses a moment.*
Well—I can find a hare upon her form
With any man in Nithsdale—stalk a deer,
Run Reynard to the earth for all his doubles,
Reclaim a haggard hawk that's wild and wayward,
Can bait a wild-cat,—sure the devil's in't
But I can match a woman—I'll to study.
        [*Sits down on the couch to examine the paper.*

———

SCENE II.

*Scene changes to the inhabited apartment of the Castle, as in the
last Scene of the preceding Act. A fire is kindled, by which
OSWALD sits in an attitude of deep and melancholy thought,
without paying attention to what passes around him. ELEANOR
is busy in covering a table; FLORA goes out and re-enters, as if*

busied in the kitchen. There should be some by-play—the Women whispering together, and watching the state of OSWALD *; then separating, and seeking to avoid his observation, when he casually raises his head and drops it again. This must be left to taste and management. The Women, in the first part of the scene, talk apart, and as if fearful of being overheard ; the by-play of stopping occasionally, and attending to* OSWALD'S *movements, will give liveliness to the Scene.*

ELE. Is all prepared?
FLO.   Ay ; but I doubt the issue
Will give my sire less pleasure than you hope for.
ELE. Tush, maid—I know thy father's humour better.
He was high-bred in gentle luxuries ;
And when our griefs began, I've wept apart,
While lordly cheer and high-fill'd cups of wine
Were blinding him against the woe to come
He has turn'd his back upon a princely banquet ;
We will not spread his board—this night at least,
Since chance hath better furnish'd—with dry bread,
And water from the well.

Enter KATLEEN, *and hears the last speech.*

KAT. (*aside.*) Considerate aunt ! she deems that a good
Were not a thing indifferent even to him   [supper
Who is to hang to-morrow. Since she thinks so,
We must take care the venison has due honour—
So much I owe the sturdy knave, Lance Blackthorn.
FLO. Mother, alas ! when Grief turns reveller,
Despair is cup-bearer. What shall hap to-morrow ?
ELE. I have learn'd carelessness from fruitless care.
Too long I've watch'd to-morrow ; let it come
And cater for itself—Thou hear'st the thunder.
                         [*Low and distant thunder.*
This is a gloomy night—within, alas !
                         [*Looking at her husband.*
Still gloomier and more threatening—Let us use
Whatever means we have to drive it o'er,
And leave to Heaven to-morrow. Trust me, Flora,
'Tis the philosophy of desperate want
To match itself but with the present evil,
And face one grief at once.
Away ! I wish thine aid, and not thy council.
               [*As* FLORA *is about to go off,* GULLCRAMMER'S
                  *voice is heard behind the flat scene, as if
                  from the drawbridge.*
GUL. (*behind.*) Hillo—hillo—hilloa—hoa—hoa !

    [OSWALD *raises himself and listens;* ELEANOR *goes up*
      the steps, and opens the window at the loop-hole :
      GULLCRAMMER'S *voice is then heard more distinctly.*

GUL. Kind Lady Devorgoil — sweet Mistress Flora ! —
The night grows fearful, I have lost my way,
And wander'd till the road turn'd round with me,
And brought me back. For Heaven's sake, give me shelter !
    KAT. (*aside.*) Now, as I live, the voice of Gullcrammer !
Now shall our gambol be play'd off with spirit ;
I 'll swear I am the only one to whom
That screech-owl whoop was e'er acceptable.
    Osw. What bawling knave is this, that takes our dwelling
For some hedge-inn, the haunt of lated drunkards?
    ELE. What shall I say? — Go, Kathleen, speak to him.
    KAT. (*aside.*) The game is in my hands — I will say some
      thing
Will fret the Baron's pride — and then he enters.
(*She speaks from the window*) — Good sir, be patient !
We are poor folks — it is but six Scotch miles
To the next borough town, where your Reverence
May be accommodated to your wants ;
We are poor folks, an 't please your Reverence,
And keep a narrow household — there 's no track
To lead your steps astray——
    GUL. Nor none to lead them right. — You kill me, lady,
If you deny me harbour. To budge from hence,
And in my weary plight, were sudden death,
Interment, funeral-sermon, tombstone, epitaph.
    Osw. Who 's he that is thus clamorous without?
      (*To* ELE.) Thou know'st him ?
    ELE. (*confused.*) I know him ? — No — yes — 't is a worthy
      clergyman,
Benighted on his way; — but think not of him.
    KAT. The morn will rise when that the tempest 's past,
And if he miss the marsh, and can avoid
The crags upon the left, the road is plain.
    Osw. Then this is all your piety ! — to leave
One whom the holy duties of his office
Have summon'd over moor and wilderness,
To pray beside some dying wretch's bed,
Who (erring mortal) still would cleave to life, —
Or wake some stubborn sinner to repentance, —
To leave him, after offices like these,
To choose his way in darkness 'twixt the marsh
And dizzy precipice ?[1]
    ELE.   What can I do?

      [1] MS.—"And headlong dizzy precipice."

Osw. Do what thou canst—the wealthiest do no more;
And if so much, 'tis well. These crumbling walls,
While yet they bear a roof, shall now, as ever,
Give shelter to the wanderer.[1]—Have we food?
He shall partake it—Have we none? the fast
Shall be accounted with the good man's merits
And our misfortunes——
  [*He goes to the loop-hole while he speaks, and places himself*
   there in room of his Wife, who comes down with reluctance.
Gul. (*without.*) Hillo—hoa—hoa!
By my good faith, I cannot plod it farther;
The attempt were death.
  Osw. (*speaks from the window*)—Patience, my friend, I come
   to lower the drawbridge.   [*Descends, and exit.*
  Ele. O that the screaming bittern had his couch
Where he deserves it,[2] in the deepest marsh!
  Kat. I would not give this sport for all the rent
Of Devorgoil, when Devorgoil was richest!
(*To* Ele.) But now you chided me, my dearest aunt,
For wishing him a horse-pond for his portion?
  Ele. Yes, saucy girl; but, an it please you, then
He was not fretting me. If he had sense enough,
And skill to bear him as some casual stranger,—
But he is dull as earth, and every hint
Is lost on him, as hail-shot on the cormorant,
Whose hide is proof except to musket-bullets!
  Flo. (*apart.*) And yet to such a one would my kind
   mother,
Whose chiefest fault is loving me too fondly,
Wed her poor daughter!

Enter Gullcrammer, *his dress damaged by the storm;* Eleanor *runs to meet him, in order to explain to him that she
wished him to behave as a stranger.* Gullcrammer, *mis-
taking her approach for an invitation to familiarity, advances with the air of pedantic conceit belonging to his
character, when* Oswald *enters,—*Eleanor *recovers herself, and assumes an air of distance—*Gullcrammer *is
confounded, and does not know what to make of it.*

  Osw. The counterpoise has clean given way; the bridge
Must e'en remain unraised, and leave us open,
For this night's course at least, to passing visitants.—
What have we here?—is this the reverend man?

---

[1] MS.— ———— "shall give, as ever,
  Their shelter to the { needy"
         { wanderer." }
[2] MS.—"Where it is fittest," &c.

> [*He takes up the candle, and surveys* GULLCRAMMER,
> *who strives to sustain the inspection with confidence,
> while fear obviously contends with conceit and desire
> to show himself to the best advantage.*

GUL. Kind sir—or, good my lord—my band is ruffled,
But yet 't was fresh this morning. This felt shower
Hath somewhat smirch'd my cloak, but you may note
It rates five marks per yard; my doublet
Hath fairly 'scaped —'t is three-piled taffeta.
> [*Opens his cloak, and displays his doublet.*

OSW. A goodly inventory—Art thou a preacher?
GUL. Yea—I laud Heaven and good Saint Mungo for it.
OSW. 'Tis the time's plague, when those that should weed
     follies
Out of the common field, have their own minds
O'errun with foppery—Envoys 'twixt heaven and earth,
Example should with precept join, to show us
How we may scorn the world with all its vanities.

GUL. Nay, the high heavens forefend that I were vain!
When our learn'd Principal such sounding laud
Gave to mine Essay on the hidden qualities
Of the sulphuric mineral, I disclaim'd
All self-exaltment. And (*turning to the women*) when at the
The lovely Saccharissa Kirkencroft,   [dance,
Daughter to Kirkencroft of Kirkencroft,
Graced me with her soft hand, credit me, ladies,
That still I felt myself a mortal man,
Though beauty smiled on me.

OSW. Come, sir, enough of this.
That you 're our guest to-night, thank the rough heavens,
And all our worser fortunes; be conformable
Unto my rules; these are no Saccharissas
To gild with compliments. There 's in your profession,
As the best grain will have its piles of chaff,
A certain whiffler, who hath dared to bait
A noble maiden with love tales and sonnets;
And if I meet him, his Geneva cap
May scarce be proof to save his ass's ears.

KAT. (*aside.*) Umph—I am strongly tempted;
And yet I think I will be generous,
And give his brains a chance to save his bones.
Then there 's more humour in our goblin plot,
Than in a simple drubbing.

ELE. (*apart to* FLO.) What shall we do! If he discover
     him,
He'll fling him out at window.

Flo. My father's hint to keep himself unknown
Is all too broad, I think, to be neglected.
 Ele. But yet the fool, if we produce his bounty,
May claim the merit of presenting it;
And then we're but lost women for accepting
A gift our needs made timely.
 Kat.   Do not produce them.
E'en let the fop go supperless to bed,
And keep his bones whole.
 Osw. (*to his Wife*)—Hast thou aught
To place before him ere he seek repose?
 Ele. Alas! too well you know our needful fare
Is of the narrowest now, and knows no surplus.
 Osw. Shame us not with thy niggard housekeeping:
He is a stranger—were it our last crust,
And he the veriest coxcomb ere wore taffeta,
A pitch he's little short of—he must share it,
Though all should want to-morrow.
 Gul. (*partly overhearing what passes between them*)—
Nay, I am no lover of your sauced dainties—
Plain food and plenty is my motto still.
Your mountain air is bleak, and brings an appetite:
A soused sow's face, now, to my modest thinking,
Has ne'er a fellow.   What think these fair ladies
Of a sow's face and sausages?   (*Makes signs to* Eleanor.)
 Flo. Plague on the vulgar hind, and on his courtesies!
The whole truth will come out!
 Osw. What should they think, but that you're like to lack
Your favourite dishes, sir, unless perchance
You bring such dainties with you.
 Gul. No, not *with* me; not, indeed,
Directly *with* me; but—Aha! fair ladies!
                              (*Makes signs again.*)
 Kat. He'll draw the beating down—Were that the worst,
Heaven's will be done!   (*Aside.*)
 Osw. (*apart.*) What can he mean?—this is the veriest dog-
Still he's a stranger, and the latest act   [whelp—
Of hospitality in this old mansion
Shall not be sullied.
 Gul. Troth, sir, I think, under the ladies' favour,
Without pretending skill in second sight,
Those of my cloth being seldom conjurors——
 Osw. I'll take my Bible-oath that thou art none. (*Aside.*)
 Gul. I do opine, still with the ladies' favour,
That I could guess the nature of our supper:
I do not say in such and such precedence
The dishes will be placed—housewives, as you know,

On such forms have their fancies ; but, I say still,
That a sow's face and sausages——
   Osw.   Peace, sir !
O'er-driven jests (if this be one) are insolent.
   Flo. (*apart, seeing her mother uneasy*)—
The old saw still holds true—a churl's benefits,
Sauced with his lack of feeling, sense, and courtesy,
Savour like injuries.   [*A horn is winded without ; then
                a loud knocking at the gate.*
   Leo. (*without.*) Ope, for the sake of love and charity !
                [Oswald *goes to the loop-hole.*
   Gul. Heaven's mercy ! should there come another strau-
And he half starved with wandering on the wolds,   [ger,
The sow's face boasts no substance, nor the sausages,
To stand our reinforced attack !   I judge, too,
By this starved Baron's language, there's no hope
Of a reserve of victuals.
   Flo. Go to the casement, cousin.
   Kat.   Go yourself,
And bid the gallant, who that bugle winded,
Sleep in the storm-swept waste ; as meet for him
As for Lance Blackthorn.—Come, I 'll not distress you ;
I 'll get admittance for this second suitor,
And we 'll play out this gambol at cross purposes.
But see, your father has prevented me.
   Osw. (*seems to have spoken with those without, and answers*)—
Well, I will ope the door ; one guest already,
Driven by the storm, has claim'd my hospitality,
And you, if you were fiends, were scarce less welcome
To this my mouldering roof, than empty ignorance
And rank conceit.   I hasten to admit you.   [*Exit.*
   Ele. (*to* Flo) The tempest thickens. By that winded bugle,
I guess the guest that next will honour us.—
Little deceiver, that didst mock my troubles,
'T is now thy turn to fear !
   Flo. Mother, if I knew less or more of this
Unthought-of and most perilous visitation,
I would your wishes were fulfill'd on me,
And I were wedded to a thing like yon.
   Gul. (*approaching.*) Come, ladies, now you see the jest is
       threadbare.
And you must own that amse sow's face and sausages——

Re-enter Oswald *with* Leonard, *supporting* Bauldie Durward.
  Oswald *takes a view of them, as formerly of* Gullcrammer,
then speaks—

Osw. (*to* Leo.) By thy green cassock, hunting-spear and
I guess thou art a huntsman ?   [bugle,
    Leo. (*bowing with respect*)—
A ranger of the neighbouring royal forest,
Under the good Lord Nithsdale ; huntsman, therefore,
In time of peace ; and when the land has war,
To my best powers a soldier.
    Osw. Welcome, as either.   I have loved the chase,
And was a soldier once.—This aged man,
What may he be ?
    Dur. (*recovering his breath*) —
Is but a beggar, sir, an humble mendicant,
Who feels it passing strange, that from this roof,
Above all others, he should now crave shelter.
    Osw. Why so ! You're welcome both—only the word
Warrants more courtesy than our present means
Permit us to bestow. A huntsman and a soldier
May be a prince's comrade, much more mine ;
And for a beggar—friend, there little lacks,
Save that blue gown and badge, and clouted pouches,
To make us comrades too ; then welcome both,
And to a beggar's feast. I fear, brown bread,
And water from the spring, will be the best on 't ;
For we had cast to wend abroad this evening,
And left our larder empty.
    Gul.   Yet, if some kindly fairy,
In our behalf, would search its hid recesses,—
(*Apart*) We 'll not go supperless now—we 're three to one.—
Still do I say, that a soused face and sausages——
    Osw. (*looks sternly at him, then at his wife*)—
There 's something under this, but that the present
Is not a time to question.—(*To* Ele.) Wife, my mood
Is at such height of tide, that a turn'd feather
Would make me frantic now, with mirth or fury !
Tempt me no more—but if thou hast the things
This carrion crow so croaks for, bring them forth ;
For, by my father's beard, if I stand caterer,
'T will be a fearful banquet !
    Ele. Your pleasure be obey'd — Come aid me, Flora.
                                        [*Exeunt.*
        (*During the following speeches, the Women place
            dishes on the table.*)
    Osw. (*to* Dur.) How did you lose your path ?
    Dur. E'en when we thought to find it, a wild meteor
Danced in the moss, and led our feet astray.—
I give small credence to the tales of old,
Of Friar's-lantern told, and Will-o'-Wisp,

Else would I say, that some malicious demon
Guided us in a round; for to the moat,
Which we had pass'd two hours since, were we led,
And there the gleam flicker'd and disappear'd,
Even on your drawbridge.   I was so worn down,
So broke with labouring through marsh and moor,
That, wold I nold I, here my young conductor
Would needs implore for entrance; else, believe rfie,
I had not troubled you.

   Osw. And why not, father?—have you e'er heard aught,
Or of my house or me, that wanderers,
Whom or their roving trade or sudden circumstance
Oblige to seek a shelter, should avoid
The House of Devorgoil?

   Dur.   Sir, I am English born—
Native of Cumberland.   Enough is said
Why I should shun those towers, whose lords were hostile
To English blood, and unto Cumberland
Most hostile and most fatal.

   Osw. Ay, father. Once my grandsire plough'd and harrow'd,
And sow'd with salt, the streets of your fair towns:
But what of that?—you have the 'vantage now.

   Dur. True, Lord of Devorgoil, and well believe I,
That not in vain we sought these towers to-night,
So strangely guided, to behold their state.

   Osw. Ay, thou wouldst say, 'twas fit a Cumbrian beggar
Should sit an equal guest in his proud halls,
Whose fathers beggar'd Cumberland—Greybeard, let it be so,
I'll not dispute it with thee.
        (*To* Leo. *who was speaking to* Flora, *but, on being sur-*
           prised, occupied himself with the suit of armour)—
               What makest thou there, young man?

   Leo. I marvell'd at this harness; it is larger
Than arms of modern days.   How richly carved
With gold inlaid on steel—how close the rivets—
How justly fit the joints!   I think the gauntlet
Would swallow twice my hand.
        (*He is about to take down some part of the armour;*
          Oswald *interferes.*)

   Osw.   Do not displace it.
My grandsire, Erick, doubled human strength,
And almost human size—and human knowledge,
And human vice, and human virtue also,
As storm or sunshine chanced to occupy
His mental hemisphere.   After a fatal deed,
He hung his armour on the wall, forbidding
It e'er should be ta'en down.   There is a prophecy,

That of itself 't will fall, upon the night
When, in the fiftieth year from his decease,
Devorgoil's feast is full.   This is the era;
But, as too well you see, no meet occasion
Will do the downfall of the armour justice,
Or grace it with a feast.   There let it bide,
Trying its strength with the old walls it hangs on,
Which shall fall soonest.

 Dur. (*looking at the trophy with a mixture of feeling*)—
Then there stern Erick's harness hangs untouch'd,
Since his last fatal raid on Cumberland!

 Osw. Ay, waste and want, and recklessness—a comrade
Still yoked with waste and want—have stripp'd these walls
Of every other trophy.   Antler'd skulls,
Whose branches vouch'd the tales old vassals told
Of desperate chases—partisans and spears—
Knights' barred helms and shields—the shafts and bows,
Axes and breastplates, of the hardy yeomanry—
The banners of the vanquish'd—signs these arms
Were not assumed in vain, have disappear'd;
Yes, one by one they all have disappear'd;—
And now Lord Erick's harness hangs alone,
'Midst implements of vulgar husbandry
And mean economy; as some old warrior,
Whom want hath made an inmate of an alms-house,
Shows, mid the beggar'd spendthrifts, base mechanics,
And bankrupt pedlars, with whom fate has mix'd him.

 Dur. Or rather like a pirate, whom the prison-house,
Prime leveller next the grave, hath for the first time
Mingled with peaceful captives, low in fortunes,[1]
But fair in innocence.

 Osw. (*looking at* Durward *with surprise*)—
       Friend, thou art bitter!

 Dur. Plain truth, sir, like the vulgar copper coinage,
Despised amongst the gentry, still finds value
And currency with beggars.

 Osw.   Be it so.   .
I will not trench on the immunities
I soon may claim to share.   Thy features, too,
Though weather-beaten, and thy strain of language,
Relish of better days.[2] Come hither, friend,
          [*They speak apart.*
And let me ask thee of thine occupation.
 [Leonard *looks round, and, seeing* Oswald *engaged with*
   Durward, *and* Gullcrammer *with* Eleanor, *approaches*

---

[1] MS.—"Mingled with peaceful men, broken in fortunes."
 [2] MS.—"Both smack of better days," &c.

towards FLORA, *who must give him an opportunity of doing so, with obvious attention on her part to give it the air of chance. The by-play here will rest with the Lady, who must engage the attention of the audience by playing off a little female hypocrisy and simple coquetry.*

LEO. Flora——

FLO. Ay, gallant huntsman, may she deign to question
Why Leonard came not at the appointed hour;
Or why he came at midnight?

LEO. Love has no certain loadstar, gentle Flora,
And oft gives up the helm to wayward pilotage.
To say the sooth—A beggar forced me hence,
And Will-o'-wisp did guide us back again.

FLO. Ay, ay, your beggar was the faded spectre
Of Poverty, that sits upon the threshold
Of these our ruin'd walls. I've been unwise,
Leonard, to let you speak so oft with me;
And you a fool to say what you have said.
E'en let us here break short; and, wise at length,
Hold each our separate way through life's wide ocean.

LEO. Nay, let us rather join our course together,
And share the breeze or tempest, doubling joys,
Relieving sorrows, warding evils off
With mutual effort, or enduring them
With mutual patience.

FLO. This is but flattering counsel—sweet and baneful;
But mine had wholesome bitter in't.

KAT. Ay, ay; but like the sly apothecary,
You'll be the last to take the bitter drug
That you prescribe to others. [*They whisper.* ELEANOR *advances to interrupt them, followed by* GULLCRAMMER.

ELE. What, maid, no household cares? Leave to your elders
The task of filling passing strangers' ears
With the due notes of welcome.

GUL.   Be it thine,
O, Mistress Flora, the more useful talent
Of filling strangers' stomachs with substantials;
That is to say,—for learn'd commentators
Do so expound substantials in some places,—
With a sous'd bacon-face and sausages.

FLO. (*apart.*) Would thou wert sous'd, intolerable pedant,
Base, greedy, perverse, interrupting coxcomb!

KAT. Hush, coz, for we'll be well avenged on him,
And ere this night goes o'er, else woman's wit
Cannot o'ertake her wishes.
                    [*She proceeds to arrange seats.* OSWALD *and*
                        DURWARD *come forward in conversation.*

Osw. I like thine humour well.— So all men beg——

Dur. Yes—I can make it good by proof. Your soldier
Begs for a leaf of laurel, and a line
In the Gazette;—he brandishes his sword
To back his suit, and is a sturdy beggar.—
The courtier begs a riband or a star,
And, like our gentler mumpers, is provided
With false certificates of health and fortune
Lost in the public service.—For your lover,
Who begs a sigh, a smile, a lock of hair,
A buskin-point, he maunds upon the pad,
With the true cant of pure mendicity,
" The smallest trifle to relieve a Christian,
And if it like your ladyship!"—(*In a begging tone.*)

Kat. (*apart.*) This is a cunning knave, and feeds the
        humour
Of my aunt's husband, for I must not say
Mine honour'd uncle. I will try a question.—
Your man of merit though, who serves the commonwealth,
Nor asks for a requital?——(*To* Durward.)

Dur.   Is a dumb beggar,
And lets his actions speak like signs for him,
Challenging double guerdon.—Now, I'll show
How your true beggar has the fair advantage
O'er all the tribes of cloak'd mendicity
I have told over to you.—The soldier's laurel,
The statesman's riband, and the lady's favour,
Once won and gain'd, are not held worth a farthing
By such as longest, loudest, canted for them;
Whereas your charitable halfpenny,[1]
Which is the scope of a true beggar's suit,
Is worth *two* farthings, and, in times of plenty,
Will buy a crust of bread.

Flo. (*interrupting him, and addressing her father*)—
Sir, let me be a beggar with the time,
And pray you come to supper.

Ele. (*to* Oswald, *apart.*) Must *he* sit with us?
                        [*Looking at* Durward.

Osw. Ay, ay, what else—since we are beggars all?
When cloaks are ragged, sure their worth is equal,
Whether at first they were of silk or woollen.

Ele. Thou art scarce consistent.
This day thou didst refuse a princely banquet,
Because a new-made lord was placed above thee;
And now——

Osw. Wife, I have seen, at public executions,

<hr>

1 MS.—" Whereas your genuine copper halfpenny."

A wretch that could not brook the hand of violence
Should push him from the scaffold, pluck up courage,
And, with a desperate sort of cheerfulness,
Take the fell plunge himself —
Welcome then, beggars, to a beggar's feast!
   Gul. (*who has in the meanwhile seated himself*) —
But this is more. — A better countenance,—
Fair fall the hands that sous'd it! — than this hog's,
Or prettier provender than these same sausages,
(By what good friend sent hither, shall be nameless —
Doubtless some youth whom love hath made profuse,)
        (*Smiling significantly at* Eleanor *and* Flora.)
No prince need wish to peck at. Long, I ween,
Since that the nostrils of this house (by metaphor,
I mean the chimneys) smell'd a steam so grateful. —
By your good leave I cannot dally longer. [*Helps himself.*
   Osw. (*places* Durward *above* Gullcrammer.) Meanwhile,
Please it your youthful learning to give place   [sir,
To grey hairs and to wisdom; and, moreover,
If you had tarried for the benediction——
   Gul. (*somewhat abashed.*) I said grace to myself.
   Osw. (*not minding him*) — And waited for the company of
It had been better fashion. Time has been,   [others,
I should have told a guest at Devorgoil,
Bearing himself thus forward, he was saucy.
      [*He seats himself, and helps the company and him-*
        self in dumb-show. There should be a contrast be-
        twixt the precision of his aristocratic civility, and
        the rude underbreeding of Gullcrammer.
   Osw. (*having tasted the dish next him*)—Why, this is veni-
    son, Eleanor!
   Gul. Eh! What! Let's see—(*Pushes across* Oswald *and*
    helps himself.) It may be venison—
I'm sure 'tis not beef, veal, mutton, lamb, or pork,
Eke am I sure, that be it what it will,
It is not half so good as sausages,
 Or as a sow's face sous'd.
   Osw. Eleanor, whence all this?——
   Ele.   Wait till to-morrow,
You shall know all. It was a happy chance
That furnish'd us to meet so many guests — (*Fills wine.*)
Try if your cup be not as richly garnish'd
As is your trencher.[1]
   Kat. (*apart.*) My aunt adheres to the good cautious maxim
Of "Eat your pudding, friend, and hold your tongue."

---

[1] Wooden trenchers should be used, and the quaigh, a Scottish
drinking cup.

Osw. (*tastes the wine.*) It is the grape of Bordeaux.
Such dainties, once familiar to my board,
Have been estranged from 't long.
> [*He again fills his glass, and continues to speak
> as he holds it up.*

Fill round, my friends—here is a treacherous friend, now,
Smiles in your face, yet seeks to steal the jewel,
Which is distinction between man and brute—
I mean our reason;—this he does, and smiles.
But are not all friends treacherous? One shall cross you
Even in your dearest interests—one shall slander you—
This steal your daughter, that defraud your purse;
But this gay flask of Bordeaux will but borrow
Your sense of mortal sorrows for a season,
And leave, instead, a gay delirium.
Methinks my brain, unused to such gay visitants,
The influence feels already!—we will revel!—
Our banquet shall be loud!—it is our last.
Katleen, thy song.

Kat. Not now, my lord—I mean to sing to-night
For this same moderate, grave, and reverend clergyman;
I 'll keep my voice till then.

Ele. Your round refusal shows but cottage breeding.

Kat. Ay, my good aunt, for I was cottage-nurtured,
And taught, I think, to prize my own wild will
Above all sacrifice to compliment.
Here is a huntsman—in his eyes I read it,
He sings the martial song my uncle loves,
What time fierce Claver'se with his Cavaliers,
Abjuring the new change of government,
Forcing his fearless way through timorous friends,
And enemies as timorous, left the capital
To rouse in James's cause the distant Highlands.
Have you ne'er heard the song, my noble uncle?

Osw. Have I not heard, wench?—It was I rode next
        him—
'Tis thirty summers since—rode by his rein;
We marched on through the alarm'd city,
As sweeps the osprey through a flock of gulls,
Who scream and flutter, but dare no resistance
Against the bold sea-empress. They did murmur,
The crowds before us, in their sullen wrath,
And those whom we had pass'd, gathering fresh courage,
Cried havoc in the rear—we minded them
E'en as the brave bark minds the bursting billows,
Which, yielding to her bows, burst on her sides,
And ripple in her wake.—Sing me that strain,   (*To* Leo.)

And thou shalt have a meed I seldom tender,
Because they 're all I have to give — my thanks.
  Leo. Nay, if you 'll bear with what I cannot help,
A voice that 's rough with hollowing to the hounds,
I 'll sing the song even as old Rowland taught me.

SONG.[1]

AIR,—" *The Bonnets of Bonny Dundee.*"

To the Lords of Convention 'twas Claver'se who spoke,
" Ere the King's crown shall fall, there are crowns to be broke :
So let each Cavalier who loves honour and me,
Come follow the bonnet of Bonny Dundee.

Come fill up my cup, come fill up my can,
Come saddle your horses, and call up your men ;
Come open the West Port, and let me gang free,
And it's room for the bonnets of bonny Dundee ! "

· " Dundee, enraged at his enemies, and still more at his friends, resolved
to retire to the Highlands, and to make preparations for civil war, but with
secrecy ; for he had been ordered by James to make no public insurrection
until assistance should be sent him from Ireland.

" Whilst Dundee was in this temper, information was brought him, whether true or false is uncertain, that some of the Covenanters had associated
themselves to assassinate him, in revenge for his former severities against
their party. He flew to the Convention and demanded justice. The Duke
of Hamilton, who wished to get rid of a troublesome adversary, treated his
complaint with neglect ; and in order to sting him in the tenderest part, reflected upon that courage which could be alarmed by imaginary dangers.
Dundee left the house in a rage, mounted his horse, and with a troop of fifty
horsemen who had deserted to him from his regiment in England, gallopped
through the city. Being asked by one of his friends, who stopt him, ' Where
he was going ? ' he waved his hat, and is reported to have answered, ' Where-
ever the spirit of Montrose shall direct me.' In passing under the walls of
the Castle, he stopt, scrambled up the precipice at a place difficult and dangerous, and held a conference with the Duke of Gordon at a postern gate,
the marks of which are still to be seen, though the gate itself is built up.
Hoping, in vain, to infuse the vigour of his own spirit into the Duke, he
pressed him to retire with him into the Highlands, raise his vassals there, who
were numerous, brave, and faithful, and leave the command of the Castle
to Winram, the lieutenant-governor, an officer on whom Dundee could rely.
The Duke concealed his timidity under the excuse of a soldier. ' A soldier,'
said he, ' cannot in honour quit the post that is assigned him.' The novelty
of the sight drew numbers to the foot of the rock upon which the conference was held. These numbers every minute increased, and, in the end,
were mistaken in the city for Dundee's adherents. The Convention was then
sitting : news were carried thither that Dundee was at the gates with an
army, and had prevailed upon the governor of the Castle to fire upon the
town. The Duke of Hamilton, whose intelligence was better, had the presence of mind, by improving the moment of agitation, to overwhelm the one
party, and provoke the other, by their fears. He ordered the doors of the
house to be shut, and the keys to be laid on the table before him. He cried
out, ' That there was danger within as well as without doors; that traitors
must be held in confinement until the present danger was over : but that
the friends of liberty had nothing to fear, for that thousands were ready to
start up in their defence, at the stamp of his foot.' He ordered the drums
to be beat and the trumpets to sound through the city. In an instant, vast
swarms of those who had been brought into town by him and Sir John Dal-

Dundee he is mounted, he rides up the street,
The bells are rung backward, the drums they are beat;
But the Provost, douce man, said, " Just e'en let him be,
The Gude Town is weel quit of that Deil of Dundee."

Come fill up my cup, &c.

As he rode down the sanctified bends of the Bow,
Ilk carline was flyting and shaking her pow;
But the young plants of grace they look'd couthie and slee,
Thinking, luck to thy bonnet, thou Bonny Dundee!

Come fill up my cup, &c.

With sour-featured Whigs the Grassmarket was cramm'd,
As if half the West had set tryst to be hang'd;[1]
There was spite in each look, there was fear in each e'e,
As they watch'd for the bonnets of Bonny Dundee.

Come fill up my cup, &c.

These cowls of Kilmarnock had spits and had spears
And lang-hafted gullies to kill Cavaliers;
But they shrunk to close-heads, and the causeway was free,
At the toss of the bonnet of Bonny Dundee.

Come fill up my cup, &c.

He spurr'd to the foot of the proud Castle rock,
And with the gay Gordon he gallantly spoke,
" Let Mons Meg and her marrows speak twa words or three,
For the love of the bonnet of Bonny Dundee."

Come fill up my cup, &c.

The Gordon demands of him which way he goes—
" Where'er shall direct me the shade of Montrose!
Your Grace in short space shall hear tidings of me,
Or that low lies the bonnet of Bonny Dundee.

Come fill up my cup, &c.

---

rymple from the western counties, and who had been hitherto hid in garrets
and cellars, showed themselves in the streets; not, indeed, in the proper habiliments of war, but in arms, and with looks fierce and sullen, as if they
felt disdain at their former concealment. This unexpected sight increased
the noise and tumult of the town, which grew loudest in the square adjoin-
ing to the house where the members were confined, and appeared still louder
to those who were within, because they were ignorant of the cause from
which the tumult arose, and caught contagion from the anxious looks of
each other. After some hours, the doors were thrown open, and the Whig
members, as they went out, were received with acclamations, and those of
the opposite party with the threats and curses of a *prepared* populace. Terrified by the prospect of future alarms, many of the adherents of James
quitted the Convention, and retired to the country; most of them changed
sides; only a very few of the most resolute continued their attendance."—
Dalrymple's Memoirs, vol. ii. p. 305.

[1] Previous to 1784, the Grassmarket was the common place of execution
in Edinburgh.

" There are hills beyond Pentland, and lands beyond Forth,
If there 's lords in the Lowlands, there 's chiefs in the North ;
There are wild Duniewassals three thousand times three,
Will cry *hoigh!* for the bonnet of Bonny Dundee.

      Come fill up my cup, &c.

" There 's brass on the target of barken'd bull-hide ;
There 's steel in the scabbard that dangles beside ;
The brass shall be burnish'd, the steel shall flash free,
At a toss of the bonnet of Bonny Dundee.

      Come fill up my cup, &c.

" Away to the hills, to the caves, to the rocks !—
Ere I own an usurper, I 'll couch with the fox !—
And tremble, false Whigs, in the midst of your glee,
You have not seen the last of my bonnet and me !"

      Come fill up my cup, &c.

He waved his proud hand, and the trumpets were blown,
The kettle-drums clash'd, and the horsemen rode on,
Till on Ravelston's cliffs and on Clermiston's lee,
Died away the wild war-notes of Bonny Dundee.

      Come fill up my cup, come fill up my can,
      Come saddle the horses and call up the men,
      Come open your gates, and let me gae free,
      For it 's up with the bonnets of Bonny Dundee !

ELE. Kathleen, do thou sing now. Thy uncle 's cheerful :
We must not let his humour ebb again.
KAT. But I 'll do better, aunt, than if I sung,
For Flora can sing blithe ; so can this huntsman,
As he has shown e'en now ; let them duet it.
Osw. Well, huntsman, we must give to freakish maiden
The freedom of her fancy.—Raise the carol,
And Flora, if she can, will join the measure.

SONG.

    When friends are met o'er merry cheer,
    And lovely eyes are laughing near,
    And in the goblet's bosom clear
      The cares of day are drown'd ;
    When puns are made, and bumpers quaff'd,
    And wild Wit shoots his roving shaft,
    And Mirth his jovial laugh has laugh'd,
      Then is our banquet crown'd,
          Ah gay,
    Then is our banquet crown'd.

When glees are sung, and catches troll'd,
And bashfulness grows bright and bold,
And beauty is no longer cold,
   And age no longer dull;
When chimes are brief, and cocks do crow,
To tell us it is time .to go,
Yet how to part we do not know,
   Then is our feast at full,
      Ah gay,
   Then is our feast at full.

Osw. (*rises with the cup in his hand*)—
Devorgoil's feast is full—Drink to the pledge!
   [*A tremendous burst of thunder follows these words of the
     Song; and the Lightning should seem to strike the
     suit of black Armour, which falls with a crash.[1] All
     rise in surprise and fear except* GULLCRAMMER, *who
     tumbles over backwards, and lies still.*
Osw. That sounded like the judgment-peal—the roof
Still trembles with the volley.
  Dur.   Happy those
Who are prepared to meet such fearful summons.—
Leonard, what dost thou there?
  Leo. (*supporting* Flo.)   The duty of a man—
Supporting innocence. Were it the final call,
I were not misemploy'd.
  Osw. The armour of my grandsire hath fall'n down,
And old saws have spoke truth.—(*Musing.*) The fiftieth
   year—
Devorgoil's feast at fullest! What to think of it——
  Leo. (*lifting a scroll which had fallen with the armour*)—
This may inform us.—(*Attempts to read the manuscript,
   shakes his head, and gives it to* Oswald)—
But not to eyes unlearn'd it tells its tidings.
  Osw. Hawks, hounds, and revelling consumed the hours
I should have given to study. (*Looks at the manuscript.*)
These characters I spell not more than thou.
They are not of our day, and, as I think,
Not of our language.—Where's our scholar now,
So forward at the banquet? Is he laggard
Upon a point of learning?
  Leo. Here is the man of letter'd dignity,
E'en in a piteous case. (*Drags* GULLCRAMMER *forward.*)
  Osw. Art waking, craven? Canst thou read this scroll?

---

[1] I should think this may be contrived, by having a transparent zig-zag
in the flat-scene, immediately above the armour, suddenly and very strongly
illuminated.

Or art thou only learn'd in sousing swine's flesh,
And prompt in eating it?
   Gul. Eh—ah!—oh—ho!—Have you no better time
To tax a man with riddles, than the moment
When he scarce knows whether he 's dead or living?
   Osw. Confound the pedant?—Can you read the scroll,
Or can you not, sir?   If you *can*, pronounce
Its meaning speedily.
   Gul.   *Can* I read it, quotha!
When at our learned University,
I gain'd first premium for Hebrew learning,—
Which was a pound of high-dried Scottish snuff,
And half a peck of onions, with a bushel
Of curious oatmeal,—our learned Principal
Did say, " Melchisedek, thou canst do any thing!"
Now comes he with his paltry scroll of parchment,
And, "*Can* you read it?"—After such affront,
The point is, if I *will*.
   Osw.   A point soon solved,
Unless you choose to sleep among the frogs;
For look you, sir, there is the chamber window,—
Beneath it lies the lake.
   Ele. Kind master Gullcrammer, beware my husband:
He brooks no contradiction —'t is his fault,
And in his wrath he 's dangerous.
   Gul. (*looks at the scroll, and mutters as if reading*)—
Hashgaboth hotch-potch—
A simple matter this to make a rout of—
Ten rashersen bacon, mish-mash venison,
Sausagian soused-face—'T is a simple catalogue
Of our small supper —made by the grave sage
Whose prescience knew this night that we should feast
On venison, hash'd sow's face, and sausages,
And hung his steel-coat for a supper bell.
E'en let us to our provender again,
For it is written, we shall finish it,
And bless our stars the lightning left it us.
   Osw. This must be impudence or ignorance!—
The spirit of rough Erick stirs within me,
And I will knock thy brains out if thou palterest!
Expound the scroll to me!
   Gul.   You 're over hasty;
And yet you may be right too—'T is Samaritan,
Now I look closer on 't, and I did take it
For simple Hebrew.
   Dur. 'T is Hebrew to a simpleton,
That we see plainly, friend — Give me the scroll.
   Gul. Alas, good friend! what would you do with it?

DUR. (*takes it from him.*)
My best to read it, sir — The character is Saxon,
Used at no distant date within this district;
And thus the tenor runs — not in Samaritan,
Nor simple Hebrew, but in wholesome English: —
　　" Devorgoil, thy bright moon waneth,
　　And the rust thy harness staineth;
　　Servile guests the banquet soil
　　Of the once proud Devorgoil.
　　But should Black Erick's armour fall,
　　Look for guests shall scare you all!
　　They shall come ere peep of day, —
　　Wake and watch, and hope and pray."
KAT. (*to* FLO.) Here is fine foolery! An old wall shakes
At a loud thunder-clap — down comes a suit
Of ancient armour, when its wasted braces
Were all too rotten to sustain its weight —
A beggar cries out, Miracle! — and your father,
Weighing the importance of his name and lineage,
Must needs believe the dotard![1]
FLO. Mock not, I pray you; this may be too serious.
KAT. And if I live till morning, I will have
The power to tell a better tale of wonder
Wrought on wise Gullcrammer. I'll go prepare me. [*Exit.*
FLO. I have not Katleen's spirit, yet I hate
This Gullcrammer too heartily, to stop
Any disgrace that's hasting towards him.
OSW. (*to whom the Beggar has been again reading the scroll.*)
'Tis a strange prophecy! — The silver moon,
Now waning sorely, is our ancient bearing —
Strange and unfitting guests —
GUL. (*interrupting him.*) Ay, ay, the matter
Is, as you say, all moonshine in the water.
OSW. How mean you, sir? (*threatening.*)
GUL. 　　　　　　　　　To show that I can rhyme
With yonder bluegown. Give me breath and time,
I will maintain, in spite of his pretence,
Mine exposition had the better sense —
It spoke good victuals and increase of cheer;
And his, more guests to eat what we have here —
An increment right needless.
OSW. 　　　　　　　　Get thee gone!
To kennel, hound!
GUL. 　　　　　　The hound will have his bone.
　　　　　(*Takes up the platter of meat, and a flask.*)

1 MS. — " A begging knave cries out, a Miracle!
　　And your good sire, doting on the importance
　　Of his high birth and house, must needs believe him."

Osw. Flora, show him his chamber— take him hence,
Or, by the name I bear, I 'll see his brains!
  Gul. Ladies, good-night!— I spare you, sir, the pains.
                [*Exit, lighted by* Flora *with a lamp.*
  Osw. The owl is fled.— I 'll not to bed to-night;
There is some change impending o'er this house,
For good or ill. I would some holy man
Were here, to counsel us what we should do!
Yon witless thin-faced gull is but a cassock
Stuff'd out with chaff and straw.
  Dur. (*assuming an air of dignity.*) I have been wont,
In other days, to point to erring mortals
The rock which they should anchor on.
        [*He holds up a Cross —the rest take a posture*
          of devotion, and the Scene closes.

ACT III.—SCENE I.

A ruinous Anteroom in the Castle.

Enter Katleen, *fantastically dressed to play the character of
Cockledemoy, with the visor in her hand.*

  Kat. I 've scarce had time to glance at my sweet person,
Yet this much could I see, with half a glance,
My elfish dress becomes me — I 'll not mask me,
Till I have seen Lance Blackthorn. Lance, I say! (*Calls.*)
Blackthorn, make haste!

    Enter Blackthorn, *half dressed as Owlspiegle.*

  Bla. Here am I—Blackthorn in the upper half,
Much at your service; but my nether parts
Are goblinized and Owlspiegled. I had much ado
To get these trankums on. I judge Lord Erick
Kept no good house, and starved his quondam barber.
  Kat. Peace, ass, and hide you—Gullcrammer is coming;
He left the hall before, but then took fright,
And e'en sneak'd back. The Lady Flora lights him—
Trim occupation for her ladyship!
Had you seen Leonard, when she left the hall
On such fine errand!
  Bla. This Gullcrammer shall have a bob extraordinary
For my good comrade's sake.— But tell me, Katleen,
What dress is this of yours?
  Kat. A page's, fool!
  Bla.   I 'm accounted no great scholar,

But 't is a page that I would fain peruse
A little closer. (*Approaches her.*)
    KAT.   Put on your spectacles,
And try if you can read it at this distance,
For you shall come no nearer.
    BLA. But is there nothing, then, save rank imposture,
In all these tales of goblinry at Devorgoil?
    KAT. My aunt's grave lord thinks otherwise, supposing
That his great name so interests the Heavens,
That miracles must needs bespeak its fall.
I would that I were in a lowly cottage
Beneath the greenwood, on its walls no armour
To court the levin-bolt———
    BLA.   And a kind husband, Katleen,
To ward such dangers as must needs come nigh.—
My father's cottage stands so low and lone,
That you would think it solitude itself;
The greenwood shields it from the northern blast,
And, in the woodbine round its latticed casement,
The linnet's sure to build the earliest nest
In all the forest.
    KAT.   Peace, you fool,—they come.
        [FLORA *lights* GULLCRAMMER *across the Stage*
    KAT. (*when they have passed*)—Away with you!
On with your cloak—be ready at the signal.
    BLA. And shall we talk of that same cottage, Katleen,
At better leisure? I have much to say
In favour of my cottage.
    KAT.   If you will be talking,
You know I can't prevent you.
    BLA.   That's enough.
(*Aside.*) I shall have leave, I see, to spell the page
A little closer, when the due time comes.

———

SCENE II.

Scene changes to GULLCRAMMER's *sleeping Apartment. He enters,
ushered in by* FLORA, *who sets on the table a flask, with the lamp.*

    FLO. A flask, in case your Reverence be athirsty;
A light, in case your Reverence be afear'd;—
And so, sweet slumber to your Reverence.
    GUL. Kind Mistress Flora, will you?—eh! eh! eh!
    FLO. Will I what!
    GUL. Tarry a little!
    FLO. (*smiling.*) Kind Master Gullcrammer,
How can you ask me aught so unbecoming!

Gul. Oh, fie, fie, fie!—Believe me, Mistress Flora,
'T is not for that—but being guided through
Such dreary galleries, stairs, and suites of rooms,
To this same cubicle, I 'm somewhat loth
To bid adieu to pleasant company.   [frighten'd.
    Flo. A flattering compliment!—In plain truth, you are
    Gul. What! frighten'd?—I—I—am not timorous.
    Flo. Perhaps you 've heard this is our haunted chamber!
But then it is our best—Your Reverence knows,
That in all tales which turn upon a ghost,
Your traveller belated has the luck
To enjoy the haunted room—it is a rule :—
To some it were a hardship, but to you,
Who are a scholar, and not timorous——
    Gul. I did not say I was not timorous,
I said I was not temerarious.—
I 'll to the hall again.
    Flo.   You 'll do your pleasure,
But you have somehow moved my father's anger,
And you had better meet our playful Owlspiegle—
So is our goblin call'd—than face Lord Oswald.
    Gul. Owlspiegle ?—
It is an uncouth and outlandish name,
And in mine ear sounds fiendish.
    Flo. Hush, hush, hush !   [spirit;
Perhaps he hears us now—(*in an under tone*)—A merry
None of your elves that pinch folks black and blue,
For lack of cleanliness.
    Gul. As for that, Mistress Flora,
My taffeta doublet hath been duly brush'd,
My shirt hebdomadal put on this morning.
    Flo. Why, you need fear no goblins. But this Owlspiegle
Is of another class ;—yet has his frolics ;
Cuts hair, trims beards, and plays amid his antics
The office of a sinful mortal barber.
Such is at least the rumour.
    Gul. He will not cut my clothes, or scar my face,
Or draw my blood?
    Flo.   Enormities like these
Were never charged against him.
    Gul. And, Mistress Flora, would you smile on me,
If, prick'd by the fond hope of your approval,
I should endure this venture?
    Flo.   I do hope
I shall have cause to smile.
    Gul.   Well ! in that hope
I will embrace the achievement for thy sake. (*She is going.*)

Yet, stay, stay, stay!—on second thoughts I will not—
I've thought on it, and will the mortal cudgel
Rather endure than face the ghostly razor!
Your crab-tree's tough but blunt,—your razor's polish'd,
But, as the proverb goes, 't is cruel sharp,
I'll to thy father, and unto his pleasure
Submit these destined shoulders.

   Flo.   But you shall not –
Believe me, sir, you shall not; he is desperate,
And better far be trimm'd by ghost or goblin,
Than by my sire in anger;—there are stores
Of hidden treasure, too, and Heaven knows what,
Buried among these ruins—you shall stay.
(*Apart.*) And if indeed there be such sprite as Owlspiegle,
And, lacking him, that thy fear plague thee not
Worse than a goblin, I have miss'd my purpose,
Which else stands good in either case.—Good-night, sir.
          [Exit, and double-locks the door.

  Gul. Nay, hold ye, hold!—Nay, gentle Mistress Flora,
Wherefore this ceremony?—She has lock'd me in,
And left me to the goblin!—(*Listening.*)—So, so, so!
I hear her light foot trip to such a distance,
That I believe the castle's breadth divides me
From human company. I'm ill at ease—
But if this citadel (*Laying his hand on his stomach*) were
   better victual'd,
It would be better mann'd. (*Sits down and drinks.*)
She has a footstep light, and taper ankle. (*Chuckles.*)
Aha! that ankle! yet, confound it too,
But for those charms Melchisedek had been
Snug in his bed at Mucklewhame—I say,
Confound her footstep, and her instep too,
To use a cobbler's phrase.—There I was quaint.
Now, what to do in this vile circumstance,
To watch or go to bed, I can't determine;
Were I a-bed, the ghost might catch me napping,
And if I watch, my terrors will increase
As ghostly hours approach. I'll to my bed
E'en in my taffeta doublet, shrink my head
Beneath the clothes—leave the lamp burning there,
And trust to fate the issue.   (*Sets it on the table.*)
   *[He lays aside his cloak, and brushes it, as from habit,
    starting at every moment; ties a napkin over his
    head; then shrinks beneath the bed-clothes. He
    starts once or twice, and at length seems to go to
    sleep. A bell tolls* ONE. *He leaps up in his bed.*

  Gul. I had just coax'd myself to sweet forgetfulness,
And that confounded bell—I hate all bells,

Except a dinner-bell — and yet I lie, too, —
I love the bell that soon shall tell the parish
Of Gabblegoose, Melchisedek's incumbent —
And shall the future minister of Gabblegoose,
Whom his parishioners will soon require
To exorcise their ghosts, detect their witches,
Lie shivering in his bed for a pert goblin,
Whom, be he switch'd or cocktail'd, horn'd or poll'd,
A few tight Hebrew words will soon send packing!
Tush! I will rouse the parson up within me,
And bid defiance —— (*A distant noise.*) In the name of
      Heaven,
What sounds are these? — O Lord! this comes of rashness!
    [*Draws his head down under the bed-clothes.*

Duet without, between OWLSPIEGLE *and* COCKLEDEMOY.

OWLS.   Cockledemoy!
        My boy, my boy ——
COCKL.   Here, father, here.
OWLS.   Now the pole-star 's red and burning,
        And the witch's spindle turning,
            Appear, appear!

GUL. (*who has again raised himself, and listened with
      great terror to the Duet*) —
I have heard of the devil's dam before,
But never of his child. Now, Heaven deliver me!
The Papists have the better of us there, —
They have their Latin prayers, cut and dried,
And pat for such occasion. — I can think
On nought but the vernacular.

OWLS.   Cockledemoy!
        My boy, my boy,
            We 'll sport us here —
COCKL.   Our gambols play,
        Like elve and fay;
OWLS.   And domineer,
BOTH. Laugh, frolic, and frisk, till the morning appear.
COCKL.   Lift latch — open clasp —
        Shoot bolt — and burst hasp!

[*The door opens with violence. Enter* BLACKTHORN *as*
  OWLSPIEGLE, *fantastically dressed as a Spanish Bar-
  ber, tall, thin, emaciated, and ghostly;* KATLEEN, *as*
  COCKLEDEMOY, *attends as his page. All their man-
  ners, tones, and motions, are fantastic, as those of
  Goblins. They make two or three times the circuit of*

the Room, without seeming to see GULCRAMMER. *They
then resume their Chaunt, or Recitative.*

OWLS.   Cockledemoy!
                    My boy, my boy,
What wilt thou do that will give thee joy?
Wilt thou ride on the midnight owl?

COCKL.   No; for the weather is stormy and foul.

OWLS.   Cockledemoy!
                    My boy, my boy,
What wilt thou do that can give thee joy?
With a needle for a sword, and a thimble for a hat,
Wilt thou fight a traverse with the castle cat?

COCKL.   Oh no! she has claws, and I like not that.

GUL. I see the devil is a doting father,
And spoils his children — 'tis the surest way
To make cursed imps of them. They see me not —
What will they think on next? It must be own'd,
They have a dainty choice of occupations.

OWLS.   Cockledemoy!
                    My boy, my boy,
What shall we do that can give thee joy?
Shall we go seek for a cuckoo's nest?

COCKL.   That's best, that's best!

BOTH.   About, about,
                    Like an elvish scout,
The cookoo's a gull, and we'll soon find him out.

        [*They search the room with mops and mows. At
        length* COCKLEDEMOY *jumps on the bed.* GULL-
        CRAMMER *raises himself half up, supporting
        himself by his hands.* COCKLEDEMOY *does the
        same, and grins at him, then skips from the
        bed, and runs to* OWLSPIEGLE.

COCKL.   I've found the nest,
                    And in it a guest,
With a sable cloak and a taffeta vest;
He must be wash'd, and trimm'd, and dress'd,
To please the eyes he loves the best.

OWLS.   That's best, that's best.

BOTH.   He must be shaved, and trimm'd, and dress'd
To please the eyes he loves the best.
        [*They arrange shaving things on the table, and
        sing as they prepare them.*

BOTH. Know that all of the humbug, the bite, and the buz,
        Of the make-believe world, becomes forfeit to us.

OWLS. (*sharpening his razor*)—

The sword this is made of was lost in a fray
By a fop, who first bullied and then ran away;
And the strap, from the hide of a lame racer, sold
By Lord Match, to his friend, for some hundreds in gold.

BOTH. For all of the humbug, the bite, and the buz,
Of the make-believe world, becomes forfeit to us.

COCKL. (*placing the napkin*)—
And this cambric napkin, so white and so fair,
At an usurer's funeral I stole from the heir.
      [*Drops something from a vial, as going to make suds*
This dewdrop I caught from one eye of his mother,
Which wept while she ogled the parson with t'other.

BOTH. For all of the humbug, the bite, and the buz,
Of the make-believe world, becomes forfeit to us.

OWLS. (*arranging the lather and the basin*)—
My soap-ball is of the mild alkali made,
Which the soft dedicator employs in his trade;
And it froths with the pith of a promise, that's sworn
By a lover at night, and forgot on the morn.

BOTH. For all of the humbug, the bite, and the buz,
Of the make-believe world, becomes forfeit to us.
      Halloo, halloo,
      The blackcock crew,
Thrice shriek'd hath the owl, thrice croak'd hath the raven,
Here, ho! Master Gullcrammer, rise and be shaven!

      Da capo.

GUL. (*who has been observing them.*)
I'll pluck a spirit up; they're merry goblins,
And will deal mildly. I will soothe their humour;
Besides, my beard lacks trimming.
      [*He rises from his bed, and advances with great
        symptoms of trepidation, but affecting an air
        of composure. The Goblins receive him with
        fantastic ceremony.*
Gentlemen, 'tis your will I should be trimm'd—
E'en do your pleasure. (*They point to a seat—he sits.*)
      Think, howsoe'er,
Of me as one who hates to see his blood;
Therefore I do beseech you, signior,
Be gentle in your craft. I know those barbers,
One would have harrows driven across his visnomy,
Rather than they should touch it with a razor.

OWLSPIEGLE *shaves* GULLCRAMMER, *while* COCKLEDEMOY *sings.*

      Father never started hair,
      Shaved too close, or left too bare—

Father's razor slips as glib
As from courtly tongue a fib.
Whiskers, mustache, he can trim in
Fashion meet to please the women;
Sharp's his blade, perfumed his lather!
Happy those are trimm'd by father!

GUL. That's a good boy.   I love to hear a child
Stand for his father, if he were the devil.
                                    (*He motions to rise.*)
Craving your pardon, sir.—What! sit again!
My hair lacks not your scissors.
                          (OWLSPIEGLE *insists on his sitting.*)
Nay, if you're peremptory, I'll ne'er dispute it,
Nor eat the cow and choke upon the tail—
E'en trim me to your fashion.
                    (OWLSPIEGLE *cuts his hair, and shaves his head,*
                          ridiculously.)

          COCKLEDEMOY (*sings as before.*)
Hair-breadth 'scapes, and hair-breadth snares,
Hair-brain'd follies, ventures, cares,
Part when father clips your hairs.
If there is a hero frantic,
Or a lover too romantic;—
If threescore seeks second spouse,
Or fourteen lists lover's vows,
Bring them here—for a Scotch boddle,
Owlspiegle shall trim their noddle.
          [*They take the napkin from about* GULLCRAMMER'S
              neck.   He makes bows of acknowledgment, which
              they return fantastically, and sing—
Thrice crow'd hath the blackcock, thrice croak'd hath the
          raven,
And Master Melchisedek Gullcrammer's shaven!

GUL. My friends, your are too musical for me;
But though I cannot cope with you in song,
I would, in humble prose, inquire of you,
If that you will permit me to acquit
Even with the barber's pence the barber's service!
                              (*They shake their heads.*)
Or if there is aught else that I can do for you,
Sweet Master Owlspiegle, or your loving child,
The hopeful Cockle'moy!

COCKL. Sir, you have been trimm'd of late,
          Smooth's your chin, and bald your pate;
          Lest cold rheums should work you harm,
          Here's a cap to keep you warm.

Gul. Welcome, as Fortunatus' wishing cap,
For 't was a cap that I was wishing for.
(There I was quaint in spite of mortal terror.)
          (*As he puts on the cap, a pair of ass's ears dis-
          engage themselves.*)
Upon my faith, it is a dainty head-dress,
And might become an alderman !—Thanks, sweet Monsieur,
Thou 'rt a considerate youth.
          [*Both Goblins bow with ceremony to* GULLCRAMMER,
          who returns their salutation. OWLSPIEGLE *de-
          scends by the trap-door.* COCKLEDEMOY *springs
          out at window.*

          SONG (*without.*)
OWLS. Cockledemoy, my hope, my care,
          Where art thou now, O tell me where ?
COCKL.   Up in the sky,
On the bonny dragonfly,
Come, father, come you too—
She has four wings and strength enow,
And her long body has room for two.

Gul. Cockledemoy now is a naughty brat—
Would have the poor old stiff-rump'd devil, his father,
Peril his fiendish neck.   All boys are thoughtless.

          SONG.
OWLS.   Which way didst thou take ?
COCKL.   I have fall'n in the lake—
          Help, father, for Beëlzebub's sake.

Gul. The imp is drown'd—a strange death for a devil !—
O, may all boys take warning, and be civil ;
Respect their loving sires, endure a chiding,
Nor roam by night on dragonflies a-riding !

COCKL. (*sings.*) Now merrily, merrily, row I to shore,
          My bark is a bean-shell, a straw for an oar.
OWLS. (*sings.*)   My life, my joy,
          My Cockledemoy !

Gul. I can bear this no longer—thus children are spoil'd.
(*Strikes into the tune.*)— Master Owlspiegle, hoy !
          He deserves to be whipp'd, little Cockledemoy !
          (*Their vocies are heard, as if dying away.*)
Gul. They 're gone !— Now, am I scared, or am I not ?
I think the very desperate ecstasy
Of fear has given me courage.[1]   This is strange, now !

---

[1] " Cowards, upon necessity, assume
    A fearful bravery ; thinking by this face
    To fasten in men's minds that they have courage."—*Shakspeare*

When they were here, I was not half so frighten'd
As now they 're gone — they were a sort of company.
What a strange thing is use ! — A horn, a claw,
The tip of a fiend's tail, was wont to scare me ;—
Now am I with the devil hand and glove ;
His soap has lather'd, and his razor shaved me ;
I 've joined him in a catch, kept time and tune,
Could dine with him, nor ask for a long spoon ;
And if I keep not better company,
What will become of me when I shall die ?   [*Exit.*

SCENE III.

*A Gothic Hall, waste and ruinous. The moonlight is at times seen
through the shafted windows.*[1] *Enter* KATLEEN *and* BLACKTHORN
—They have thrown off the more ludicrous parts of their disguise.

KAT. This way — this way. Was ever fool so gull'd !
BLA. I play'd the barber better than I thought for.
Well, I 've an occupation in reserve,
When the long-bow and merry musket fail me. —
But, hark ye, pretty Katleen.
KAT.   What should I hearken to !
BLA. Art thou not afraid,
In these wild halls while playing feigned goblins,
That we may meet with real ones ?
KAT.   Not a jot.
My spirit is too light, my heart too bold,
To fear a visit from the other world.
BLA. But is not this the place, the very hall
In which men say that Oswald's grandfather,
The black Lord Erick, walks his penance round ?
Credit me, Katleen, these half-moulder'd columns
Have in their ruin something very fiendish,
And, if you 'll take an honest friend's advice,
The sooner that you change their shatter'd splendour
For the snug cottage that I told you of,
Believe me, it will prove the blither dwelling.
KAT. If I e'er see that cottage, honest Blackthorn,
Believe me, it shall be from other motive
Than fear of Erick's spectre. (*A rustling sound is heard.*)
BLA.   I heard a rustling sound —
Upon my life, there 's something in the hall,
Katleen, besides us two !

[1] I have a notion that this can be managed so as to represent imperfect
or flitting moonlight, upon the plan of the Eidophusikon.

KAT.   A yeoman thou,
A forester, and frighten'd! I am sorry
I gave the fool's-cap to poor Gullerammer,
And let thy head go bare.   (*The same rushing sound is re-
                            peated.*)
BLA. Why, are you mad, or hear you not the sound!
KAT. And if I do, I take small heed of it.
Will you allow a maiden to be bolder
Than you, with beard on chin and sword at girdle?
BLA. Nay, if I had my sword, I would not care;
Though I ne'er heard of master of defence,
So active at his weapon as to brave
The devil, or a ghost—See! see! see yonder!
    [*A Figure is imperfectly seen between two of the pillars.*
KAT. There's something moves, that's certain, and the
                            moonlight,
Chased by the flitting gale, is too imperfect
To show its form; but, in the name of God,
I'll venture on it boldly.
BLA.   Wilt thou so?
Were I alone, now, I were strongly tempted
To trust my heels for safety; but with thee,
Be it fiend or fairy, I'll take risk to meet it.
KAT. It stands full in our path, and we must pass it,
Or tarry here all night.
BLA.   In its vile company?
    [*As they advance towards the Figure, it is more plainly
        distinguished, which might, I think, be contrived by
        raising successive screens of crape.   The Figure is
        wrapped in a long robe, like the mantle of a Her-
        mit, or Palmer.*
PAL. Ho! ye who thread by night these wildering scenes,
In garb of those who long have slept in death,
Fear ye the company of those you imitate?
BLA. This is the devil, Katleen, let us fly! (*Runs off.*)
KAT. I will not fly—why should I? My nerves shake
To look on this strange vision, but my heart
Partakes not the alarm.—If thou dost come in Heaven's
In Heaven's name art thou welcome!   [name,
PAL. I come, by Heaven permitted.   Quit this castle:
There is a fate on't—if for good or evil,
Brief space shall soon determine.   In that fate,
If good, by lineage thou canst nothing claim,
If evil, much may'st suffer.—Leave these precincts.
KAT. Whate'er thou art, be answer'd—Know, I will not
Desert the kinswoman who train'd my youth;
Know, that I will not quit my friend, my Flora;

Know, that I will not leave the aged man
Whose roof has shelter'd me.   This is my resolve—
If evil come, I aid my friends to bear it;
If good, my part shall be to see them prosper,
A portion in their happiness from which
No fiend can bar me.

    PAL.   Maid, before thy courage,
Firm built on innocence, even beings of nature
More powerful far than thine, give place and way;
Take then this key, and wait the event with courage.
        [*He drops the key.—He disappears gradually — the
          moonlight failing at the same time.*

    KAT. (*after a pause.*) Whate'er it was, 'tis gone! My head
          turns round—
The blood that lately fortified my heart
Now eddies in full torrent to my brain,
And makes wild work with reason.   I will haste,
If that my steps can bear me so far safe,
To living company.   What if I meet it
Again in the long aisle, or vaulted passage?
And if I do, the strong support that bore me
Through this appalling interview, again
Shall strengthen and uphold me.
      (*As she steps forward, she stumbles over the key.*)
What's this? The key?—there may be mystery in 't.
I'll to my kinswoman, when this dizzy fit
Will give me leave to choose my way aright.
                   (*She sits down exhausted.*)

   Re-enter BLACKTHORN, *with a drawn sword and torch.*

    BLA. Katleen!—what, Katleen!—What a wretch was I
To leave her!—Katleen!—I am weapon'd now,
And fear nor dog nor devil.—She replies not!
Beast that I was!—nay, worse than beast! The stag,
As timorous as he is, fights for his hind.
What's to be done?—I'll search this cursed castle
From dungeon to the battlements; if I find her not,
I'll fling me from the highest pinnacle—
    KATLEEN (*who has somewhat gathered her spirits in con-
      sequence of his entrance, comes behind and touches him;
      he starts.*)   Brave sir!
I'll spare you that rash leap—You're a bold woodsman!
Surely I hope that from this night henceforward
You'll never kill a hare, since you're akin to them.
O I could laugh—but that my head's so dizzy.
    BLA. Lean on me, Katleen—By my honest word,
I thought you close behind—I was surprised,
Not a jot frightened.

KAT. Thou art a fool to ask me to thy cottage,
And then to show me at what slight expense
Of manhood I might master thee and it.
 BLA. I 'll take the risk of that—This goblin business
Came rather unexpected; the best horse
Will start at sudden sights. Try me again,
And if I prove not true to bonny Katleen,
Hang me in mine own bowstring.   [*Exeunt.*

SCENE IV.

The Scene returns to the Apartment at the beginning of Act Second.
OSWALD *and* DURWARD *are discovered with* ELEANOR, FLORA,
and LEONARD—DURWARD *shuts a Prayer-book, which he seems*
to have been reading.

 DUR. 'Tis true—the difference betwixt the churches,
Which zealots love to dwell on, to the wise.
Of either flock are of far less importance
Than those great truths to which all Christian men
Subscribe with equal reverence.
 OSW. We thank thee, father, for the holy office,
Still best performed when the pastor's tongue
Is echo to his breast: of jarring creeds
It ill beseems a layman's tongue to speak.—
Where have you stow'd yon prater? (*To* FLORA.)
 FLO. Safe in the goblin-chamber.
 ELE.   The goblin-chamber.
Maiden, wert thou frantic?—if his Reverence
Have suffer'd harm by waspish Owlspiegle,
Be sure thou shalt abye it.
 FLO.   Here he comes,
Can answer for himself!

Enter GULCRAMMER, *in the fashion in which* OWLSPIEGLE *had put*
him; having the fool's-cap on his head, and towel about his neck,
&c. His manner through the scene is wild and extravagant, as
if the fright had a little affected his brain.

 DUR. A goodly spectacle!—Is there such a goblin?
(*To* Osw.) Or has sheer terror made him such a figure?
 OSW. There is a sort of wavering tradition
Of a malicious imp who teazed all strangers;
My father wont to call him Owlspiegle.
 GUL. Who talks of Owlspiegle?
He is an honest fellow for a devil.
So is his son, the hopeful Cockle'moy.

(*Sings.*) " My hope, my joy,
    My Cockledemoy!"

Leo. The fool 's bewitch'd—the goblin hath furnish'd him
A cap which well befits his reverend wisdom.

Flo. If I could think he had lost his slender wits,
I should be sorry for the trick they play'd him.

Leo. O fear him not; it were a foul reflection
On any fiend of sense and reputation,
To filch such petty wares as his poor brains.

Dur. What saw'st thou, sir?—what heardst thou?

Gul. What was't I saw and heard?
That which old greybeards,
Who conjure Hebrew into Anglo-Saxon,
To cheat starved barons with, can little guess at.

Flo. If he begin so roundly with my father,
His madness is not like to save his bones.

Gul. Sirs, midnight came, and with it came the goblin.
I had reposed me after some brief study;
But as the soldier, sleeping in the trench,
Keeps sword and musket by him, so I had
My little Hebrew manual prompt for service.

Flo. *Sausagian sous'd-face;* that much of your Hebrew
Even I can bear in memory.

Gul.   We counter'd,
The goblin and myself, even in mid-chamber,
And each stepp'd back a pace, as 'twere to study
The foe he had to deal with!—I bethought me,
Ghosts ne'er have the first word, and so I took it,
And fired a volley of round Greek at him.
He stood his ground, and answer'd in the Syriac;
I flank'd my Greek with Hebrew, and compell'd him—

          (*A noise heard.*)

Osw. Peace, idle prater!—Hark—what sounds are these?
Amid the growling of the storm without,
I hear strange notes of music, and the clash
Of coursers' trampling feet.

Voices (*without.*) We come, dark riders of the night,
       And flit before the dawning light;
       Hill and valley, far aloof,
       Shake to hear our chargers' hoof;
       But not a foot-stamp on the green
       At morn shall show where we have been.

Osw. These must be revellers belated—
Let them pass on; the ruin'd halls of Devorgoil
Open to no such guests.—

    (*Flourish of trumpets at a distance, then nearer.*)

         They sound a summons;
What can they lack at this dead hour of night?
Look out, and see their number, and their bearing.
 Leo. (*goes up to the window*)—
'Tis strange — one single shadowy form alone
Is hovering on the drawbrige — far apart
Flit through the tempest banners, horse, and riders,
In darkness lost, or dimly seen by lightning.—
Hither the figure moves — the bolts revolve—
The gate uncloses to him.
 Ele.   Heaven protect us!

  The Palmer *enters* — Gullcrammer *runs off.*

 Osw. Whence, and what art thou? for what end come
    hither?
 Pal. I come from a far land, where the storm howls not,
And the sun sets not, to pronounce to thee,
Oswald of Devorgoil, thy house's fate.
 Dur. I charge thee, in the name we late have kneel'd
    to ———
 Pal. Abbot of Lanercost, I bid thee peace!
Uninterrupted let me do mine errand:
Baron of Devorgoil, son of the bold, the proud,
The warlike and the mighty, wherefore wear'st thou
The habit of a peasant? Tell me, wherefore
Are thy fair halls thus waste — thy chambers bare?—
Where are the tapestries, where the conquer'd banners,
Trophies, and gilded arms, that deck'd the walls
Of once proud Devorgoil?
   (He advances, and places himself where the Armou~
    hung, so as to be nearly in the centre of the Scene.)
 Dur. Whoe'er thou art — if thou dost know so much,
Needs must thou know ———
 Osw. Peace! I will answer here; to me he spoke —
Mysterious stranger, briefly I reply:
A peasant's dress befits a peasant's fortune;
And 't were vain mockery to array these walls
In trophies, of whose memory nought remains,
Save that the cruelty outvied the valour
Of those who wore them.
 Pal.   Degenerate as thou art,
Know'st thou to whom thou say'st this?
   (He drops his mantle, and is discovered arm(d as
    nearly as may be to the suit which hung on the
    wall; all express terror.)
 Osw. It is himself — the spirit of mine Ancestor!

Eri. Tremble not, son, but hear me !
     (*He strikes the wall; it opens, and discovers the
        Treasure-Chamber.*) There lies piled
The wealth I brought from wasted Cumberland,
Enough to reinstate thy ruin'd fortunes.—
Cast from thine high-born brows that peasant bonnet,
Throw from thy noble grasp-the peasant's staff—
O'er all, withdraw thine hand from that mean mate,
Whom in an hour of reckless desperation
Thy fortunes cast thee on. This do,
And be as great as ere was Devorgoil,
When Devorgoil was richest ![1]

  Dur. Lord Oswald, thou art tempted by a fiend,
Who doth assail thee on thy weakest side,—
Thy pride of lineage, and thy love of grandeur.
Stand fast—resist—contemn his fatal offers !

  Ele. Urge him not, father ; if the sacrifice
Of such a wasted woe-worn wretch as I am,
Can save him from the abyss of misery,
Upon whose verge he 's tottering, let me wander
An unacknowledged outcast from his castle,
Even to the humble cottage I was born in.

  Osw. No, Ellen, no—it is not thus they part,
Whose hearts and souls, disasters borne in common
Have knit together, close as summer saplings
Are twined in union by the eddying tempest.—
Spirit of Erick, while thou bear'st his shape,
I 'll answer with no ruder conjuration
Thy impious counsel, other than with these words,
Depart, and tempt me not !

  Eri. Then Fate will have her course. —Fall, massive
      grate,
Yield them the tempting view of these rich treasures,
But bar them from possession ! (*A portcullis falls before
  the door of the Treasure-Chamber.*) Mortals, hear !
No hand may ope that grate, except the Heir
Of plunder'd Aglionby, whose mighty wealth
Ravish'd in evil hour, lies yonder piled ;
And not his hand prevails without the key
Of Black Lord Erick. Brief space is given
To save proud Devorgoil—So wills high Heaven.
                [*Thunder ; he disappears.*

  Dur. Gaze not so wildly ; you have stood the trial
That his commission bore, and Heaven designs,

      [1] MS.—" And be as rich as ere was Devorgoil,
        When Devorgoil was proudest."

If I may spell his will, to rescue Devorgoil
Even by the Heir of Aglionby—Behold him
In that young forester, unto whose hand
Those bars shall yield the treasures of his house,
Destined to ransom yours.—Advance, young Leonard,
And prove the adventure.

   Leo. (*advances, and attempts the grate.*) It is fast
As is the tower, rock-seated.

   Osw. We will fetch other means, and prove its strength,
Nor starve in poverty, with wealth before us.

   Dur. Think what the vision spoke;
The key—the fated key——

Enter GULLCRAMMER.

   Gul. A key?—I say a quay is what we want,
Thus by the learn'd orthographized—Q, u, a, y.
The lake is overflow'd!—A quay, a boat,
Oars, punt, or sculler, is all one to me!—
We shall be drown'd, good people!!!

Enter KATLEEN *and* BLACKTHORN.

   Kat.   Deliver us!
Haste, save yourselves—the lake is rising fast.[1]

   Bla. 'T has risen my bow's height in the last five minutes,
And still is swelling strangely.

   Gul. (*who has stood astonished upon seeing them*)—
We shall be drown'd without your kind assistance.
Sweet Master Owlspiegle, your dragonfly—
Your straw, your bean-stalk, gentle Cockle'moy!

   Leo. (*looking from the shot-hole.*) 'Tis true, by all that's
               fearful! The proud lake
Peers, like ambitious tyrant, o'er his bounds,
And soon will whelm the castle—even the drawbridge
Is under water now.

   Kat. Let us escape! Why stand you gazing there?

   Dur. Upon the opening of that fatal grate
Depends the fearful spell that now entraps us,
The key of Black Lord Erick—ere we find it,
The castle will be whelm'd beneath the waves,
And we shall perish in it!

   Kat. (*giving the key.*) Here, prove this;
A chance most strange and fearful gave it me.

   Osw. (*puts it into the lock, and attempts to turn it—a loud
          clap of thunder.*)

---

[1] If it could be managed to render the rising of the lake visible, it would
answer well for a *coup-de-théâtre.*

Flo. The lake still rises faster.—Leonard, Leonard,
Canst thou not save us !
   [Leonard *tries the lock—it opens with a violent
    noise, and the Portcullis rises. A loud strain of
    wild music.—There may be a Chorus here.*
   [Oswald *enters the apartment, and brings out a scroll.*
Leo. The lake is ebbing with as wondrous haste
As late it rose—the drawbridge is left dry !
Osw. This may explain the cause —
(Gullcrammer *offers to take it.*) But soft you, sir,
We 'll not disturb your learning for the matter ;
Yet, since you 've borne a part in this strange drama,
You shall not go unguerdon'd. Wise or learn'd,
Modest or gentle, Heaven alone can make thee,
Being so much otherwise ; but from this abundance
Thou shalt have that shall gild thine ignorance,
Exalt thy base descent, make thy presumption
Seem modest confidence, and find thee hundreds
Ready to swear that same fool's-cap of thine
Is reverend as a mitre.
Gul. Thanks, mighty baron, now no more a bare one !—
I will be quaint with him, for all his quips. (*Aside*)
Osw. Nor shall kind Katleen lack
Her portion in our happiness.
Kat. Thanks, my good lord, but Katleen's fate is fix'd—
There is a certain valiant forester,
Too much afear'd of ghosts to sleep anights
In his lone cottage, without one to guard him.—
Leo. If I forget my comrade's faithful friendship,
May I be lost to fortune, hope, and love !
Dur. Peace, all ! and hear the blessing which this scroll
Speaks unto faith, and constancy, and virtue :—

  " No more this castle's troubled guest,
   Dark Erick's spirit hath found rest.
   The storms of angry Fate are past
   For Constancy defies their blast.
   Of Devorgoil the daughter free
   Shall wed the Heir of Aglionby;
   Nor ever more dishonour soil
   The rescued house of Devorgoil !" [1]

 [1] MS.—" The storms of angry fate are past —
   Constancy abides their blast.
   Of Devorgoil the daughter fair
   Shall wed with Dacre's injured heir ;
   The silver moon of Devorgoil."

END OF THE DOOM OF DEVORGOIL.

Auchindrane;

OR,

THE AYRSHIRE TRAGEDY.

Cur aliquid vidi? cur noxia lumina feci
Cur imprudenti cognita culpa mihi est?
Ovidii Tristium, Liber Secundus.

PREFACE.

THERE is not, perhaps, upon record, a tale of horror which gives us a more perfect picture than is afforded by the present, of the violence of our ancestors, or the complicated crimes into which they were hurried, by what their wise, but ill-enforced, laws termed the heathenish and accursed practice of Deadly Feud. The author has tried to extract some dramatic scenes out of it; but he is conscious no exertions of his can increase the horror of that which is in itself so iniquitous. Yet, if we look at modern events, we must not too hastily venture to conclude that our own times have so much the superiority over former days as we might at first be tempted to infer. One great object has indeed been obtained: the power of the laws extends over the country universally, and if criminals at present sometimes escape punishment, this can only be by eluding justice,—not, as of old, by defying it.

But the motives which influence modern ruffians to commit actions at which we pause with wonder and horror, arise, in a great measure, from the thirst of gain. For the hope of lucre, we have seen a wretch seduced to his fate, under the pretext that he was to share in amusement and conviviality; and, for gold, we have seen the meanest of wretches deprived of life, and their miserable remains cheated of the grave.

The loftier, if equally cruel, feelings of pride, ambition, and love of vengeance, were the idols of our forefathers, while the caitiffs of our day bend to Mammon, the meanest of the spirits who fell.[1] The criminals, therefore, of former times, drew their

---

[1] "———— Mammon led them on :
Mammon, the least erected spirit that fell
From Heaven."—*Milton.*

hellish inspiration from a loftier source than is known to modern
villains.   The fever of unsated ambition, the frenzy of ungrati-
fied revenge, the *perfervidum ingenium Scotorum*, stigmatized by
our jurists and our legislators, held life but as passing breath;
and such enormities as now sound like the acts of a madman,
were then the familiar deeds of every offended noble.   With
these observations we proceed to our story.

   John Muir, or Mure, of Auchindrane, the contriver and exe-
cutor of the following cruelties, was a gentleman of an ancient
family and good estate in the west of Scotland; bold, ambitious,
treacherous to the last degree, and utterly unconscientious,— a
Richard the Third in private life, inaccessible alike to pity and
to remorse.   His view was to raise the power, and extend the
grandeur of his own family.   This gentleman had married the
daughter of Sir Thomas Kennedy of Barganie, who was, except-
ing the Earl of Cassilis, the most important person in all Carrick,
the district of Ayrshire which he inhabited, and where the name
of Kennedy held so great a sway as to give rise to the popular
rhyme,—

> " 'Twixt Wigton and the town of Air,
>   Portpatrick and the Cruives of Cree,
> No man need think for to bide there,
>   Unless he court Saint Kennedie."

   Now, Mure of Auchindrane, who had promised himself high
advancement by means of his father-in-law Barganie, saw, with
envy and resentment, that his influence remained second and
inferior to the House of Cassilis, chief of all the Kennedys.   The
Earl was indeed a minor, but his authority was maintained, and
his affairs well managed, by his uncle, Sir Thomas Kennedy of
Cullayne, the brother of the deceased Earl, and tutor and guardian to the present.   This worthy gentleman supported his nephew's dignity and the credit of the house so effectually, that
Barganie's consequence was much thrown into the shade, and
the ambitious Auchindrane, his son-in-law, saw no better remedy
than to remove so formidable a rival as Cullayne by violent
means.

   For this purpose, in the year of God 1597, he came with a
party of followers to the town of Maybole (where Sir Thomas
Kennedy of Cullayne then resided,) and lay in ambush in an
orchard, through which he knew his destined victim was to pass,
in returning homewards from a house where he was engaged to
sup.   Sir Thomas Kennedy came alone, and unattended, when
he was suddenly fired upon by Auchindrane and his accomplices,
who, having missed their aim, drew their swords, and rushed
upon him to slay him.   But the party thus assailed at disadvantage, had the good fortune to hide himself for that time in a
ruinous house, where he lay concealed till the inhabitants of the
place came to his assistance.

Sir Thomas Kennedy prosecuted Mure for this assault, who, finding himself in danger from the law, made a sort of apology and agreement with the Lord of Cullayne, to whose daughter he united his eldest son, in testimony of the closest friendship in future. This agreement was sincere on the part of Kennedy, who, after it had been entered into, showed himself Auchindrane's friend and assistant on all occasions. But it was most false and treacherous on that of Mure, who continued to nourish the purpose of murdering his new friend and ally on the first opportunity.

Auchindrane's first attempt to effect this was by means of the young Gilbert Kennedy of Barganie (for old Barganie, Auchindrane's father-in-law, was dead), whom he persuaded to brave the Earl of Cassilis, as one who usurped an undue influence over the rest of the name. Accordingly, this hot-headed youth, at the instigation of Auchindrane, rode past the gate of the Earl of Cassilis, without waiting on his chief, or sending him any message of civility. This led to mutual defiance, being regarded by the Earl, according to the ideas of the time, as a personal insult. Both parties took the field with their followers, at the head of about 250 men on each side. The action which ensued was shorter and less bloody than might have been expected. Young Barganie, with the rashness of headlong courage, and Auchindrane, fired by deadly enmity to the House of Cassilis, made a precipitate attack on the Earl, whose men were strongly posted, and under cover. They were received by a heavy fire. Barganie was slain. Mure of Auchindrane, severely wounded in the thigh, became unable to sit his horse, and, the leaders thus slain or disabled, their party drew off without continuing the action. It must be particularly observed, that Sir Thomas Kennedy remained neuter in this quarrel, considering his connexion with Auchindrane as too intimate to be broken even by his desire to assist his nephew.

For this temperate and honourable conduct he met a vile reward; for Auchindrane, in resentment of the loss of his relative Barganie, and the downfall of his ambitious hopes, continued his practices against the life of Sir Thomas of Cullayne, though totally innocent of contributing to either. Chance favoured his wicked purpose.

The Knight of Cullayne, finding himself obliged to go to Edinburgh on a particular day, sent a message by a servant to Mure, in which he told him, in the most unsuspecting confidence, the purpose of his journey, and named the road which he proposed to take, inviting Mure to meet him at Duppill, to the west of the town of Ayr, a place appointed, for the purpose of giving him any commissions which he might have for Edinburgh, and assuring his treacherous ally he would attend to any business which he might have in the Scottish metropolis as anxiously as to his own. Sir Thomas Kennedy's message was carried to the town of Maybole, where his messenger, for some trivial reason, had the import committed to writing by a schoolmaster in that town, and despatched it to its destination by means of a poor student, named Dalrymple, instead of carrying it to the house of Auchindrane in person.

This suggested to Mure a diabolical plot. Having thus received tidings of Sir Thomas Kennedy's motions, he conceived the infernal purpose of having the confiding friend who sent the information, waylaid and murdered at the place appointed to meet with him, not only in friendship, but for the purpose of rendering him service. He dismissed the messenger Dalrymple, cautioning the lad to carry back the letter to Maybole, and to say that he had not found him, Auchindrane, in his house. Having taken this precaution, he proceeded to instigate the brother of the slain Gilbert of Barganie, Thomas Kennedy of Drumurghie by name, and Walter Muir of Cloncaird, a kinsman of his own, to take this opportunity of revenging Barganie's death. The fiery young men were easily induced to undertake the crime. They waylaid the unsuspecting Sir Thomas of Cullayne at the place appointed to meet the traitor Auchindrane, and the murderers having in company five or six servants, well mounted and armed, assaulted and cruelly murdered him with many wounds. They then plundered the dead corpse of his purse, containing a thousand merks in gold, cut off the gold buttons which he wore on his coat, and despoiled the body of some valuable rings and jewels.[1]

[1] "No papers which have hitherto been discovered appear to afford so striking a picture of the savage state of barbarism into which that country must have sunk, as the following Bond by the Earl of Cassilis, to his brother and heir-apparent, Hew, Master of Cassilis. The uncle of these young men, Sir Thomas Kennedy of Culzean, Tutor of Cassilis, as the reader will recollect, was murdered, May 11th, 1602, by Auchindrane's accomplices.

"The Master of Cassilis, for many years previous to that event, was in open hostility to his brother. During all that period, however, the Master maintained habits of the closest intimacy with Auchindrane and his dissolute associates, and actually joined him in various hostile enterprises against his brother the Earl. The occurrence of the Laird of Culzean's murder was embraced by their mutual friends, as a fitting opportunity to effect a permanent reconciliation between the brothers; 'bot,' (as 'the Historie of the Kennedies,' p. 59, quaintly informs us,) 'the cuntry thocht that he wald not be eirnest in that cause, for the auld luiff betuix him and Auchindrayne.' The unprincipled Earl, (whose *sobriquet,* and that of some of his ancestors, was *King of Carrick,* to denote the boundless sway which he exercised over his own vassals and the inhabitants of that district,) relying on his brother's necessities, held out the infamous bribe contained in the following bond, to induce his brother, the Master of Cassilis, to murder his former friend, the old Laird of Auchindrane. Though there be honour among thieves, it would seem that there is none among assassins; for the younger brother insisted upon having the price of blood assured to him by a written document, drawn up in the form of a regular bond!

"Judging by the Earl's former and subsequent history, he probably

The revenge due for his uncle's murder was keenly pursued by the Earl of Cassilis. As the murderers fled from trial, they were declared outlaws; which doom, being pronounced by three blasts of a horn, was called " being put to the horn, and declared the king's rebel." Mure of Auchindrane was strongly suspected of having been the instigator of the crime. But he conceived there could be no evidence to prove his guilt if he could keep the boy Dalrymple out of the way, who delivered the letter which made him acquainted with Cullayne's journey, and the place at which he meant to halt. On the contrary, he saw, that if the lad could be produced at the trial, it would afford ground of fatal presumption, since it could be then proved that persons so nearly connected with him as Kennedy and Cloncaird had left his house, and committed the murder at the very spot which Cullayne had fixed for their meeting.

To avoid this imminent danger, Mure brought Dalrymple to his house, and detained him there for several weeks. But the youth tiring of this confinement, Mure sent him to reside with a friend, Montgomery of Skellmorly, who maintained him under a borrowed name, amid the desert regions of the then almost savage island of Arran. Being confident in the absence of this material witness, Auchindrane, instead of flying, like his agents Drumurghie and Cloncaird, presented himself boldly at the bar, demanded a fair trial, and offered his person in combat to the death against any of Lord Cassilis's friends who might impugn his innocence. This audacity was successful, and he was dismissed without trial.

Still, however, Mure did not consider himself safe, so long as Dalrymple was within the realm of Scotland; and the danger grew more pressing when he learned that the lad had become

---

thought that, in *either* event, his purposes would be attained, by ' killing two birds with one stone.' On the other hand, however, it is but doing justice to the Master's acuteness, and the experience acquired under his quondam preceptor, Auchindrane, that we should likewise conjecture that, on his part, he would hold firm possession of the bond, to be used as a checkmate against his brother, should he think fit afterwards to turn his heel upon him, or attempt to betray him into the hands of justice.

" The following is a correct copy of the bond granted by the Earl : — ' We, Johne, Earle of Cassilis, Lord Kennedy, etc., bindis and oblissis ws, that that howsovne our broder, Hew Kennedy of Branstoun, with his complices, taikis the Laird of Auchindraneis lyf, that we sall mak guid and thankfull payment to him and thame, of the sowme of tuelff hundreth merkis, yeirlie, togidder with corne to sex horsis, ay and quhil [1] we ressaw [2] thame in houshald with our self : Beginning the first payment immediatlie efter thair committing of the said deid. Attour,[3] howsovne we ressaw thame in houshald, wo sall pay to the twa serwing gentillmen the feis, yeirlie, as our awin houshald serwandis. And heirto we obliss ws, vpoun our honour. Subscryvit with our hand, at Maybole, the ferd day of September, 1602.
' JOHN ERLE OFF CASSILLIS.' "
Pilcairn's Criminal Trials of Scotland, vol. iii. p. 622.—ED.

1 Aye and untill.   2 Receive.   3 Moreover.

Impatient of the restraint which he sustained in the island of
Arran, and returned to some of his friends in Ayrshire. Mure
no sooner heard of this than he again obtained possession of the
boy's person, and a second time concealed him at Auchindrane,
until he found an opportunity to transport him to the Low
Countries, where he contrived to have him enlisted in Buccleuch's
regiment, trusting, doubtless, that some one of the numerous
chances of war might destroy the poor young man whose life
was so dangerous to him.

But after five or six years' uncertain safety, bought at the
expense of so much violence and cunning, Auchindrane's fears
were exasperated into frenzy, when he found this dangerous
witness, having escaped from all the perils of climate and battle,
had left, or been discharged from, the Legion of Borderers, and
had again accomplished his return to Ayrshire. There is ground
to suspect that Dalrymple knew the nature of the hold which he
possessed over Auchindrane, and was desirous of extorting from
his fears some better provision than he had found either in Arran
or the Netherlands. But if so, it was a fatal experiment to tam-
per with the fears of such a man as Auchindrane, who determined
to rid himself effectually of this unhappy young man.

Mure now lodged him in a house of his own, called Chapeldonan, tenanted by a vassal and connexion of his, called James
Bannatyne. This man he commissioned to meet him at ten
o'clock at night on the sea-sands near Girvan, and bring with
him the unfortunate Dalrymple, the object of his fear and dread.
The victim seems to have come with Bannatyne without the least
suspicion, though such might have been raised by the time and
place appointed for the meeting. When Bannatyne and Dalrymple came to the appointed spot, Auchindrane met them, accompanied by his eldest son, James. Old Auchindrane, having
taken Bannatyne aside, imparted his bloody purpose of ridding
himself of Dalrymple for ever, by murdering him on the spot.
His own life and honour were, he said, endangered by the manner in which this inconvenient witness repeatedly thrust himself
back into Ayrshire, and nothing could secure his safety but taking
the lad's life, in which action he requested James Bannatyne's
assistance. Bannatyne felt some compunction, and remonstrated
against the cruel expedient, saying, it would be better to transport
Dalrymple to Ireland, and take precautions against his return.
While old Auchindrane seemed disposed to listen to this proposal, his son concluded that the time was come for accomplishing
the purpose of their meeting, and, without waiting the termination
of his father's conference with Bannatyne, he rushed suddenly on
Dalrymple, beat him to the ground, and, kneeling down on him,
with his father's assistance accomplished the crime by strangling
the unhappy object of their fear and jealousy. Bannatyne, the

witness, and partly the accomplice, of the murder, assisted them in their attempt to make a hole in the sand, witn a spade which they had brought on purpose, in order to conceal the dead body. But as the tide was coming in, the holes which they made filled with water before they could get the body buried, and the ground seemed to their terrified consciences, to refuse to be accessory to concealing their crime. Despairing of hiding the corpse in the manner they proposed, the murderers carried it out into the sea as deep as they dared wade, and there abandoned it to the billows, trusting that a wind, which was blowing off the shore, would drive these remains of their crime out to sea, where they would never more be heard of. But the sea, as well as the land, seemed unwilling to conceal their cruelty. After floating for some hours, or days, the dead body was, by the wind and tide, again driven on shore, near the very spot where the murder had been committed.

This attracted general attention, and when the corpse was known to be that of the same William Dalrymple whom Auchindrane had so often spirited out of the country, or concealed when he was in it, a strong and general suspicion arose, that this young person had met with foul play from the bold bad man who had shown himself so much interested in his absence. It was always said or supposed, that the dead body had bled at the approach of a grandchild of Mure of Auchindrane, a girl who, from curiosity, had come to look at a sight which others crowded to see. The bleeding of a murdered corpse at the touch of the murderer, was a thing at that time so much believed, that it was admitted as a proof of guilt; but I know no case, save that of Auchindrane, in which the phenomenon was supposed to be extended to the approach of the innocent kindred; nor do I think that the fact itself, though mentioned by ancient lawyers, was ever admitted to proof in the proceedings against Auchindrane.

It is certain, however, that Auchindrane found himself so much the object of suspicion from this new crime, that he resolved to fly from justice, and suffer himself to be declared a rebel and outlaw rather than face a trial. But his conduct in preparing to cover his flight with another motive than the real one, is a curious picture of the men and manners of the times. He knew well that if he were to shun his trial for the murder of Dalrymple, the whole country would consider him as a man guilty of a mean and disgraceful crime in puting to death an obscure lad, against whom he had no personal quarrel. He knew, besides, that his powerful friends, who would have interceded for him had his offence been merely burning a house, or killing a neighbour, would not plead for or stand by him in so pitiful a concern as the slaughter of this wretched wanderer.

Accordingly, Mure sought to provide himself with some ostensible cause for avoiding law, with which the feelings of his kindred and friends might sympathize ; and none occurred to him so natural as an assault upon some friend and adherent of the Earl of Cassilis. Should he kill such a one, it would be indeed an unlawful action, but so far from being infamous, would be accounted the natural consequence of the avowed quarrel between the families. With this purpose, Mure, with the assistance of a relative, of whom he seems always to have had some ready to execute his worst purposes, beset Hugh Kennedy of Garriehorne, a follower of the Earl's, against whom they had especial ill-will, fired their pistols at him, and used other means to put him to death. But Garriehorne, a stout-hearted man, and well armed, defended himself in a very different manner from the unfortunate Knight of Cullayne, and beat off the assailants, wounding young Auchindrane in the right hand, so that he wellnigh lost the use of it.

But though Auchindrane's purpose did not entirely succeed, he availed himself of it to circulate a report, that if he could obtain a pardon for firing upon his feudal enemy with pistols, weapons declared unlawful by act of Parliament, he would willingly stand his trial for the death of Dalrymple, respecting which he protested his total innocence. The King, however, was decidedly of opinion that the Mures, both father and son, were alike guilty of both crimes, and used intercession with the Earl of Abercorn, as a person of power in those western counties, as well as in Ireland, to arrest and transmit them prisoners to Edinburgh. In consequence of the Earl's exertions, old Auchindrane was made prisoner, and lodged in the tolbooth of Edinburgh.

Young Auchindrane no sooner heard that his father was in custody, than he became as apprehensive of Bannatyne (the accomplice in Dalrymple's murder) telling tales, as ever his father had been of Dalrymple. He therefore hastened to him, and prevailed on him to pass over for a while to the neighbouring coast of Ireland, finding him money and means to accomplish the voyage, and engaging in the meantime to take care of his affairs in Scotland. Secure, as they thought, in this precaution, old Auchindrane persisted in his innocence, and his son found security to stand his trial. Both appeared with the same confidence at the day appointed, and braved the public justice, hoping to be put to a formal trial, in which Auchindrane reckoned upon an acquittal for want of the evidence which he had removed. The trial was, however, postponed, and Mure the elder was dismissed, under high security to return when called for.

But King James, being convinced of the guilt of the accused, ordered young Auchindrane, instead of being sent to trial, to be examined under the force of torture, in order to compel him to tell whatever he knew of the things charged against him. He was accordingly severely tortured ; but the result only served to show that such examinations are as useless as they are cruel. A man of weak resolution, or of a nervous habit, would probably have assented to any confession, however false, rather than have endured the extremity of fear and pain to which Mure was subjected. But young Auchindrane, a strong and determined ruffian, endured the torture with the utmost firmness, and by the constant audacity with which, in spite of the intolerable pain, he continued to assert his innocence, he spread so favourable an opinion of his case, that the detaining him in prison, instead of bringing him to open trial, was censured as severe and oppressive. James, however, remained firmly persuaded of his guilt, and by an exertion of authority quite inconsistent with our present laws, commanded young Auchindrane to be still detained in close custody till further light could be thrown on these dark proceedings. He was detained accordingly by the King's express personal command, and against the opinion even of his privy councillors. This exertion of authority was much murmured against.

In the meanwhile, old Auchindrane, being, as we have seen, at liberty on pledges, skulked about in the west, feeling how little security he had gained by Dalrymple's murder, and that he had placed himself by that crime in the power of Bannatyne, whose evidence concerning the death of Dalrymple could not be less fatal than what Dalrymple might have told concerning Auchindrane's accession to the conspiracy against Sir Thomas Kennedy of Cullayne. But though the event had shown the error of his wicked policy, Auchindrane could think of no better mode in this case than that which had failed in relation to Dalrymple. When any man's life became inconsistent with his own safety, no idea seems to have occurred to this inveterate ruffian, save to murder the person by whom he might himself be in any way endangered. He therefore attempted the life of James Bannatyne by more agents than one. Nay, he had nearly ripened a plan, by which one Pennycuke was to be employed to slay Bannatyne, while, after the deed was done, it was devised that Mure of Auchnull, a connexion of Bannatyne, should be instigated to slay Pennycuke; and thus close up this train of murders by one, which, flowing in the ordinary course of deadly feud, should have nothing in it so particular as to attract much attention.

But the justice of Heaven would bear this complicated train of iniquity no longer. Bannatyne, knowing with what sort of men he had to deal, kept on his guard, and, by his caution, disconcerted more than one attempt to take his life, while another miscarried by the remorse of Pennycuke, the agent whom Mure employed. At length Bannatyne, tiring of this state of insecurity, and in despair of escaping such repeated plots, and also feeling remorse for the crime to which he had been accessory, resolved rather to submit himself to the severity of the law, than

remain the object of the principal criminal's practices. He sur-
rendered himself to the Earl of Abercorn, and was transported
to Edinburgh, where he confessed before the King and council all
the particulars of the murder of Dalrymple, and the attempt to
hide his body by committing it to the sea.

When Bannatyne was confronted with the two Mures before
the Privy Council, they denied with vehemence every part of the
evidence he had given, and affirmed that the witness had been
bribed to destroy them by a false tale. Bannatyne's behaviour
seemed sincere and simple, that of Auchindrane more resolute
and crafty. The wretched accomplice fell upon his knees, invoking God to witness that all the land in Scotland could not have
bribed him to bring a false accusation against a master whom he
had served, loved, and followed in so many dangers, and calling
upon Auchindrane to honour God by confessing the crime he had
committed. Mure the elder, on the other hand, boldly replied,
that he hoped God would not so far forsake him as to permit him
to confess a crime of which he was innocent, and exhorted Bannatyne in his turn to confess the practices by which he had been
induced to devise such falsehoods against him.

The two Mures, father and son, were therefore put upon their
solemn trial, along with Bannatyne, in 1611, and, after a great
deal of evidence had been brought in support of Bannatyne's confession, all three were found guilty.[1] The elder Auchindrane was
convicted of counselling and directing the murder of Sir Thomas
Kennedy of Cullayne, and also of the actual murder of the lad
Dalrymple. Bannatyne and the younger Mure were found guilty
of the latter crime, and all three were sentenced to be beheaded.
Bannatyne, however, the accomplice, received the King's pardon,
in consequence of his voluntary surrender and confession. The
two Mures were both executed. The younger was affected by the
remonstrances of the clergy who attended him, and he confessed
the guilt of which he was accused. The father, also, was at length
brought to avow the fact, but in other respects died as impenitent

[1] " Efter the pronunceing and declairing of the quhilk determination and
delyuerance of the saidis persones of Assyse, ' The Justice, in respect thairof,
be the mouth of Alexander Kennydie, dempster of Court, docernit and ad-
iudget the saidis Johune Mure of Auchindrane elder, James Mure of Auchindrane younger, his eldest sone and appeirand air, and James Bannatyne,
callit of Chapel-Donane, and ilk ane of thame, to be tane to the mercat
croce of the burcht of Edinburgh, and thair, upon ane scaffold, their heidis
to be strukin frome thair bodeyis: And all' thair landis, heritages, takis,
steidingis, rowmes, possessiones, teyndis, coirnes, cattell, insicht pleniasing,
guidis, geir, tytillis, proffeitis, commoditeis, and richtis quhatsumeuir, di-
rectlie or indirectlie pertening to thame, or ony of thame, at the committing
of the saidis tressonabill Murthouris, or sensyne; or to the quilkis they, or
ony of thame, had richt, claim, or actioun, to be forfalt, escheit, and in-
brocht to our soueraine lordis vse; as culpable and conviot of the saidis
tressonabill crymes.'

"Quhilk was pronuncet for Donne."

Pitcairn's Criminal Trials, vol. iii. p. 156.—Ed.

as he had lived;—and so ended this dark and extraordinary tragedy.

The Lord Advocate of the day, Sir Thomas Hamilton, afterwards successively Earl of Melrose and of Haddington, seems to have busied himself much in drawing up a statement of this foul transaction, for the purpose of vindicating to the people of Scotland the severe course of justice observed by King James VI. He assumes the task in a high tone of prerogative law, and, on the whole, seems at a loss whether to attribute to Providence, or to his most sacred Majesty, the greatest share in bringing to light these mysterious villanies, but rather inclines to the latter opinion. There is, I believe, no printed copy of the intended tract, which seems never to have been published; but the curious will be enabled to judge of it, as it appears in the next *fasciculus* of Mr. Robert Pitcairn's very interesting publications from the Scottish Criminal Record.[1]

The family of Auchindrane did not become extinct on the death of the two homicides. The last descendant existed in the eighteenth century, a poor and distressed man. The following anecdote shows that he had a strong feeling of his situation.

There was in front of the old-castle a huge ash-tree, called the Dule-tree (*mourning-tree*) of Auchindrane, probably because it was the place where the Baron executed the criminals who fell under his jurisdiction. It is described as having been the finest tree of the neighbourhood. This last representative of the family of Auchindrane had the misfortune to be arrested for payment of a small debt; and, unable to discharge it, was preparing to accompany the messenger (bailiff) to the jail of Ayr. The servant of the law had compassion for his prisoner, and offered to accept of this remarkable tree as of value adequate to the discharge of the debt, "What!" said the debtor—"sell the Dule-tree of Auchindrane! I will sooner die in the worst dungeon of your prison." In this luckless character the line of Auchindrane ended. The family, blackened with the crimes of its predecessors, became extinct, and the estate passed into other hands.

[1] See an article in the Quarterly Review, February 1831, on Mr. Pitcairn's valuable collection, where Sir Walter Scott particularly dwells on the original documents connected with the story of Auchindrane; and where Mr. Pitcairn's important services to the history of his profession, and of Scotland, are justly characterised. (1833.)—Ed.

" Sir Walter's reviewal of the early parts of Mr. Pitcairn's Ancient Criminal Trials had, of course, much gratified the editor, who sent him, on his arrival in Edinburgh, the proof-sheets of the number then in hand, and directed his attention particularly to its details on the extraordinary case of Mure of Auchindrane, A. D. 1611. Scott was so much interested with these documents, that he resolved to found a dramatic sketch on their terrible story; and the result was a composition far superior to any of his previous

attempts of that nature. Indeed there are several passages in his ' Ayrshire
Tragedy'—especially that where the murdered corpse floats upright in the
wake of the assassin's bark—(an incident suggested by a lamentable chapter in Lord Nelson's history)—which may bear comparison with anything
but Shakspeare. Yet I doubt whether the prose narrative of the preface be
not, on the whole, more dramatic than the versified scenes. It contains, by
the way, some very striking allusions to the recent atrocities of Gill's Hill
and the West Port."—LOCKHART, vol. ix. p. 334.

DRAMATIS PERSONÆ.

JOHN MURE OF AUCHINDRANE, *an Ayrshire Baron.* He has been a follower
of the Regent, Earl of Morton, during the Civil Wars, and hides an oppressive, ferocious, and unscrupulous disposition, under some pretences to
strictness of life and doctrine, which, however, never influence his conduct. He is in danger from the law, owing to his having been formerly
active in the assassination of the Earl of Cassilis.

PHILIP MURE, *his Son,* a wild, debauched profligate, professing and prac-
tising a contempt for his Father's hypocrisy, while he is as fierce and
licentious as Auchindrane himself.

GIFFORD, *their Relation,* a Courtier.

QUENTIN BLANE, *a Youth,* educated for a Clergyman, but sent by AUCHIN-
DRANE to serve in a Band of Auxiliaries in the Wars of the Netherlands,
and lately employed as Clerk or Comptroller to the Regiment—disbanded,
however, and on his return to his native Country. He is of a mild, gentle, and rather feeble character, liable to be influenced by any person of
stronger mind who will take the trouble to direct him. He is somewhat
of a nervous temperament, varying from sadness to gaiety, according to
the impulse of the moment; an amiable hypochondriac.

HILDEBRAND, *a stout old Englishman,* who, by feats of courage, has raised
himself to the rank of Sergeant-Major, (then of greater consequence than
at present.) He, too, has been disbanded, but cannot bring himself to believe that he has lost his command over his Regiment.

ABRAHAM,   } *Privates dismissed from the same Regiment in which* QUENTIN
WILLIAMS, } *and* HILDEBRAND *had served.* These are mutinous, and
JENKIN,   } are much disposed to remember former quarrels with their
And Others, } late Officers.

NEIL MACLELLAN, *Keeper of Auchindrane Forest and Game.*

EARL OF DUNBAR, *commanding an Army as Lieutenant of James I, for execution of Justice on Offenders.*

Guards, Attendants, &c. &c.

MARION, *Wife of* NEIL MACLELLAN.
ISABEL, *their Daughter,* a Girl of six years old.
Other Children and Peasant Women.

Auchindrane;

OR,

THE AYRSHIRE TRAGEDY

ACT I.—SCENE I.

*A rocky Bay on the Coast of Carrick, in Ayrshire, not far from
the Point of Turnberry. The sea comes in upon a bold rocky
Shore. The remains of a small half-ruined Tower are seen on
the right hand, overhanging the sea. There is a Vessel at a
distance in the offing. A Boat at the bottom of the Stage lands
eight or ten persons, dressed like disbanded, and in one or two
cases like disabled Soldiers. They come straggling forward
with their knapsachs and bundles. HILDEBRAND, the Sergeant
belonging to the party, a stout elderly man, stands by the boat,
as if superintending the disembarkation. QUENTIN remains apart.*

ABRAHAM. Farewell the flats of Holland, and right welcome
The cliffs of Scotland! Fare thee well, black beer
And Schiedam gin! and welcome twopenny,
Oatcakes, and usquebaugh!
    WILLIAMS (*who wants an arm.*) Farewell the gallant field,
        and " Forward, pikemen!"
For the bridge-end, the suburb, and the lane—
And, " Bless your honour, noble gentleman,
Remember a poor soldier!"
    ABR. My tongue shall never need to smooth itself
To such poor sounds, while it can boldly say,
" Stand and deliver!"
    WIL. Hush! the sergeant hears you.
    ABR. And let him hear: he makes a bustle yonder,
And dreams of his authority, forgetting
We are disbanded men, o'er whom his halberd
Has not such influence as the beadle's baton.
We are no soldiers now, but every one
The lord of his own person.
    WIL. A wretched lordship—and our freedom such
As that of the old cart-horse, when the owner
Turns him upon the common. I for one
Will still continue to repect the sergeant,
And the comptroller, too,—while the cash lasts.

ABR. I scorn them both. I am too stout a Scotsman
To bear a Southron's rule an instant longer
Than discipline obliges ; and for Quentin,
Quentin the quillman, Quentin the comptroller,
We have no regiment now ; or, if we had,
Quentin's no longer clerk to it.
    WIL. For shame ! for shame !—What, shall old com-
        rades jar thus,
And on the verge of parting, and for ever?—
Nay, keep thy temper, Abraham, though a bad one.—
Good Master Quentin, let thy song last night
Give us once more our welcome to old Scotland.
    ABR. Ay, they sing light whose task is telling money,
When dollars clink for chorus.
    QUE. I've done with counting silver,[1] honest Abraham,
As thou, I fear, with pouching thy small share on 't.
But lend your voices, lads, and I will sing
As blithely yet as if a town were won ;
As if upon a field of battle gain'd,
Our banners waved victorious.—(*He sings, and the rest
bear chorus.*)

SONG.

Hither we come,
Once slaves to the drum,
But no longer we list to its rattle ·
Adieu to the wars,
With their slashes and scars,
The march, and the storm, and the battle.

There are some of us maim'd,
And some that are lamed,
And some of old aches are complaining ;
But we 'll take up the tools, ·
Which we flung by like fools,
'Gainst Don Spaniard to go a-campaigning.

Dick Hathorn doth vow
To return to the plough,
Jack Steele to his anvil and hammer ;
The weaver shall find room
At the wight-wapping loom,
And your clerk shall teach writing and grammar.

    ABR. And this is all that thou canst do, gay Quentin!
To swagger o'er a herd of parish brats,
Cut cheese or dibble onions with thy poniard,
And turn the sheath into a ferula!

    [1] MS.—"I've done with counting dollars," &c.

Que. I am the prodigal in holy writ;
I cannot work — to beg I am ashamed.
Besides, good mates, I care not who may know it,
I 'm e'en as fairly tired of this same fighting,
As the poor cur that 's worried in the shambles
By all the mastiff dogs of all the butchers;
Wherefore, farewell sword, poniard, petronel,
And welcome poverty and peaceful labour.
　Abr. Clerk Quentin, if of fighting thou art tired,
By my good word, thou 'rt quickly satisfied,
For thou 'st seen but little on 't.
　Wil. Thou dost belie him — I have seen him fight
Bravely enough for one in his condition.
　Abr. What, he! that counter-casting, smock-faced boy!
What was he but the colonel's scribbling drudge,
With men of straw to stuff the regiment roll;
With cipherings unjust to cheat his comrades,
And cloak false musters for our noble captain!
He bid farewell to sword and petronel!
He should have said, farewell my pen and standish.
These, with the rosin used to hide erasures,
Were the best friends he left in camp behind him.
　Que. The sword you scoff at is not far, but scorns
The threats of an unmanner'd mutineer.
　Ser. (*interposes.*) We'll have no brawling — Shall it e'er
That being comrades six long years together,　　[be said,
While gulping down the frowsy fogs of Holland,
We tilted at each other's throats so soon
As the first draught of native air refresh'd them!
No! by Saint Dunstan, I forbid the combat.
You all, methinks, do know this trusty halberd;
For I opine, that every back amongst you
Hath felt the weight of the tough ashen staff,
Endlong or overthwart. Who is it wishes
A remembrancer now! (*Raises his halberd.*)
　Abr.　　　　　　　Comrades, have you ears
To hear the old man bully! — eyes to see
His staff rear'd o'er your heads, as o'er the hounds
The huntsman cracks his whip!
　Wil. Well said! — stout Abraham has the right on 't. —
I tell thee, sergeant, we do reverence thee,
And pardon the rash humours thou hast caught,
Like wiser men, from thy authority.
'T is ended, howsoe'er, and we'll not suffer
A word of sergeantry, or halberd-staff,
Nor the most petty threat of discipline.
If thou wilt lay aside thy pride of office,

And drop thy wont of swaggering and commanding,
Thou art our comrade still for good or evil.
Else take thy course apart, or with the clerk there—
A sergeant thou, and he being all thy regiment.

  SER. Is 't come to this, false knaves? And think you not,
That if you bear a name o'er other soldiers,
It was because you follow'd to the charge
One that had zeal and skill enough to lead you
Where fame was won by danger?

  WIL. We grant thy skill in leading, noble sergeant;
Witness some empty boots and sleeves amongst us,
Which else had still been tenanted with limbs
In the full quantity; and for the arguments
With which you used to back our resolution,
Our shoulders do record them.   At a word,
Will you conform, or·must we part our company?

  SER. Conform to you? Base dogs! I would not lead you
A bolt-flight farther to be made a general.
Mean mutineers! when you swill'd off the dregs
Of my poor sea-stores, it was, "Noble Sergeant!—
Heaven bless old Hildebrand!—we 'll follow him,
At least, until we safely see him lodged
Within the merry bounds of his own England!"

  WIL. Ay, truly, sir; but, mark, the ale was mighty,
And the Geneva potent.   Such stout liquor
Makes violent protestations.   Skink it round,
If you have any left, to the same tune,
And we may find a chorus for it still.

  ABR. We lose our time.—Tell us at once, old man,
If thou wilt march with us, or stay with Quentin?

  SER. Out, mutineers! Dishonour dog your heels!

  ABR. Wilful will have his way. Adieu, stout Hildebrand!
          [*The Soldiers go off laughing, and taking leave,
             with mockery, of the* SERGEANT *and* QUENTIN,
             who remain on the Stage.

  SER. (*after a pause.*) Fly you not with the rest?—fail you
Yon goodly fellowship and fair example?   [to follow
Come, take your wild-goose flight.   I know you Scots,
Like your own sea-fowl, seek your course together.

  QUE. Faith, a poor heron I, who wing my flight
In loneliness, or with a single partner;
And right it is that I should seek for solitude,
Bringing but evil luck on them I herd with.

  SER. Thou 'rt thankless.   Had we landed on the coast,
Where our course bore us, thou wert far from home;
But the fierce wind that drove us round the island,
Barring each port and inlet that we aim'd at,

Hath wafted thee to harbour; for I judge
This is thy native land we disembark on.
   Que. True, worthy friend. Each rock, each stream I
        look on,
Each bosky wood, and every frowning tower,
Awakens some young dream of infancy.
Yet such is my hard hap, I might more safely
Have look'd on Indian cliffs, or Afric's desert,
Than on my native shores. I 'm like a babe,
Doom'd to draw poison from my nurse's bosom.
   Ser. Thou dream'st, young man. Unreal terrors haunt,
As I have noted, giddy brains like thine—
Flighty, poetic, and imaginative—
To whom a minstrel whim gives idle rapture,
And, when it fades, fantastic misery.
   Que. But mine is not fantastic. I can tell thee,
Since I have known thee still my faithful friend,
In part at least the dangerous plight I stand in.
   Ser. And I will hear thee willingly, the rather
That I would let these vagabonds march on,
Nor join their troop again. Besides, good sooth,
I 'm wearied with the toil of yesterday,
And revel of last night.—And I may aid thee;
Yes, I may aid thee, comrade, and perchance
Thou may'st advantage me.
   Que. May it prove well for both!—But note, my friend,
I can but intimate my mystic story.
Some of it lies so secret,—even the winds
That whistle round us must not know the whole —
An oath!—an oath!——
   Ser. That must be kept, of course.
I ask but that which thou may'st freely tell.
   Que. I was an orphan boy, and first saw light
Not far from where we stand—my lineage low,
But honest in its poverty. A lord,
The master of the soil for many a mile,
Dreaded and powerful, took a kindly charge
For my advance in letters, and the qualities
Of the poor orphan lad drew some applause.
The knight was proud of me, and, in his halls,
I had such kind of welcome as the great
Give to the humble, whom they love to point to
As objects not unworthy their protection,
Whose progress is some honour to their patron —
A cure was spoken of, which I might serve,
My manners, doctrine, and acquirements fitting.
   Ser. Hitherto thy luck

Was of the best, good friend. Few lords had cared
If thou couldst read thy grammar or thy psalter:
Thou hadst been valued couldst thou scour a harness,
And dress a steed distinctly.

 Que.   My old master
Held different doctrine, at least it seem'd so—
But he was mix'd in many a deadly feud—
And here my tale grows mystic. I became,
Unwitting and unwilling, the depositary
Of a dread secret, and the knowledge on 't
Has wreck'd my peace for ever. It became
My patron's will, that I, as one who knew
More than I should, must leave the realm of Scotland,
And live or die within a distant land. [1]

 Ser. Ah! thou hast done a fault in some wild raid,
As you wild Scotsmen call them.

 Que.   Comrade, nay;
Mine was a peaceful part, and happ'd by chance.
I must not tell you more. Enough, my presence
Brought danger to my benefactor's house.
Tower after tower conceal'd me, willing still
To hide my ill-omen'd face with owls and ravens, [2]
And let my patron's safety be the purchase
Of my severe and desolate captivity.
So thought I, when dark Arran, with its walls
Of native rock, enclosed me. There I lurk'd,
A peaceful stranger amid armed clans,
Without a friend to love or to defend me,
Where all beside were link'd by close alliances.
At length I made my option to take service
In that same legion of auxiliaries
In which we lately served the Belgian.
Our leader, stout Montgomery, hath been kind
Through full six years of warfare, and assign'd me
More peaceful tasks than the rough front of war,
For which my education little suited me.

 Ser. Ay, therein was Montgomery kind indeed;

[1] MS.—"*Quentin.* My short tale
  Grows mystic now. Among the deadly feuds
  Which curse our country, something once it chanced
  That I, unwilling and unwitting, witness'd;
  And it became my benefactor's will,
  That I should breathe the air of other climes."

[2] The MS. here adds:

  "And then wild Arran, with its darksome { clefts / walls
  Of naked rock received me; till at last
  I yielded to take service in the legion
  Which lately has discharged us. Stout Montgomery,
  Our colonel, hath been kind through five years' warfare."

Nay, kinder than you think, my simple Quentin.
The letters which you brought to the Montgomery,
Pointed to thrust thee on some desperate service,
Which should most like'y end thee.

　　Que. Bore I such letters?—Surely, comrade, no.
Full deeply was the writer bound to aid me.
Perchance he only meant to prove my mettle;
And it was but a trick of my bad fortune
That gave his letters ill interpretation.

　　Ser. Ay, but thy better angel wrought for good,
Whatever ill thy evil fate designed thee.
Montgomery pitied thee, and changed thy service
In the rough field for labour in the tent,
More fit for thy green years and peaceful habits.

　　Que. Even there his well-meant kindness injured me.
My comrades hated, undervalued me,
And whatsoe'er of service I could do them,
They guerdon'd with ingratitude and envy—
Such my strange doom, that if I serve a man
At deepest risk, he is my foe for ever!

　　Ser. Hast thou worse fate than others if it were so?
Worse even than me, thy friend, thine officer,
Whom yon ungrateful slaves have pitch'd ashore,
As wild waves heap the sea-weed on the beach,
And left him here, as if he had the pest
Or leprosy, and death were in his company?

　　Que. They think at least you have the worst of plagues,
The worst of leprosies,—they think you poor.

　　Ser. They think like lying villains then;—I'm rich,
And they too might have felt it. I've a thought—
But stay—what plans your wisdom for yourself?

　　Que. My thoughts are wellnigh desperate. But I purpose
Return to my stern patron—there to tell him
That wars, and winds, and waves, have cross'd his pleasure,
And cast me on the shore from whence he banish'd me.
Then let him do his will, and destine for me
A dungeon or a grave.

　　Ser. Now, by the rood, thou art a simple fool!
I can do better for thee. Mark me, Quentin.
I took my license from the noble regiment,
Partly that I was worn with age and warfare,
Partly that an estate of yeomanry,
Of no great purchase, but enough to live on,
Has call'd me owner since a kinsman's death.
It lies in merry Yorkshire, where the wealth
Of fold and furrow, proper to Old England,
Stretches by streams which walk no sluggish pace,

But dance as light as yours.   Now, good friend Quentin,
This copyhold can keep two quiet inmates,
And I am childless.   Wilt thou be my son?

    QUE. Nay, you can only jest, my worthy friend!
What claim have I to be a burden to you?

    SER. The claim of him that wants, and is in danger,
On him that has, and can afford protection:
Thou wouldst not fear a foeman in my cottage,
Where a stout mastiff slumber'd on the hearth,
And this good halberd hung above the chimney?
But come—I have it—thou shalt earn thy bread
Duly, and honourably, and usefully.
Our village schoolmaster hath left the parish,
Forsook the ancient school-house with its yew-trees,
That lurk'd beside a church two centuries older,—
So long devotion took the lead of knowledge;
And since his little flock are shepherdless,
'Tis thou shalt be promoted in his room;
And rather than thou wantest scholars, man,
Myself will enter pupil.   Better late,
Our proverb says, than never to do well.
And look you, on the holydays I'd tell,
To all the wondering boors and gaping children,
Strange tales of what the regiment did in Flanders,
And thou shouldst say Amen, and be my warrant
That I speak truth to them.

    QUE. Would I might take thy offer!   But, alas!
Thou art the hermit who compell'd a pilgrim,
In name of heaven and heavenly charity,
To share his roof and meal, but found too late
That he had drawn a curse on him and his,
By sheltering a wretch foredoom'd of heaven!

    SER. Thou talk'st in riddles to me.
    QUE.   If I do,
'Tis that I am a riddle to myself.
Thou know'st I am by nature born a friend
To glee and merriment; can make wild verses;
The jest or laugh has never stopp'd with me,
When once 'twas set a rolling.

    SER.   I have known thee
A blithe companion still, and wonder now
Thou shouldst become thus crest-fallen.

    QUE. Does the lark sing her descant when the falcon
Scales the blue vault with bolder wing than hers,
And meditates a stoop?   The mirth thou'st noted
Was all deception, fraud—Hated enough
For other causes, I did veil my feelings

Beneath the mask of mirth,—laugh'd, sung, and caroll'd,
To gain some interest in my comrades' bosoms,
Although mine own was bursting.
    SER.   Thou 'rt a hypocrite
Of a new order.
    QUE. But harmless as the innoxious snake,
Which bears the adder's form, lurks in his haunts,
Yet neither hath his fang-teeth nor his poison.
Look you, kind Hildebrand, I would seem merry,
Lest other men should, tiring of my sadness,
Expel me from them, as the hunted wether
Is driven from the flock.
    SER. Faith, thou hast borne it bravely out.
Had I been ask'd to name the merriest fellow
Of all our muster-roll—that man wert thou.
    QUE. See'st thou, my friend, yon brook dance down the
And sing blithe carols over broken rock   [valley,
And tiny waterfall, kissing each shrub
And each gay flower it nurses in its passage,—
Where, thinkst thou, is its source, the bonny brook?—
It flows from forth a cavern, black and gloomy,
Sullen and sunless, like this heart of mine,
Which others see in a false glare of gaiety,
Which I have laid before you in its sadness.
    SER. If such wild fancies dog thee, wherefore leave
The trade where thou wert safe 'midst others' dangers,
And venture to thy native land, where fate
Lies on the watch for thee?   Had old Montgomery
Been with the regiment, thou hadst had no congé.
    QUE. No, 'tis most likely—But I had a hope,
A poor vain hope, that I might live obscurely
In some far corner of my native Scotland,
Which, of all others, splinter'd into districts,
Differing in manners, families, even language,
Seem'd a safe refuge for the humble wretch
Whose highest hope was to remain unheard of.
But fate has baffled me—the winds and waves,
With force resistless, have impell'd me hither—
Have driven me to the clime most dang'rous to me;
And I obey the call, like the hurt deer,
Which seeks instinctively his native lair,
Though his heart tells him it is but to die there.
    SER. 'Tis false, by Heaven, young man! This same de-
Though showing resignation in its banner,   [spair,
Is but a kind of covert cowardice.
Wise men have said, that though our stars incline,
They cannot force us—Wisdom is the pilot,

And if he cannot cross, he may evade them.
You lend an ear to idle auguries,
The fruits of our last revels—still most sad
Under the gloom that follows boisterous mirth,
As earth looks blackest after brilliant sunshine.
 Que. No, by my honest word. I joined the revel,
And aided it with laugh, and song, and shout,
But my heart revell'd not; and, when the mirth
Was at the loudest, on yon galliot's prow
I stood unmark'd, and gazed upon the land,
My native land—each cape and cliff I knew.
" Behold me now," I said, " your destined victim!"
So greets the sentenced criminal the headsman,
Who slow approaches with his lifted axe.
" Hither I come," I said, " ye kindred hills,
Whose darksome outline in a distant land
Haunted my slumbers; here I stand, thou ocean,
Whose hoarse voice, murmuring in my dreams, required
See me now here, ye winds, whose plaintive wail, [me;
On yonder distant shores, appear'd to call me—
Summon'd, behold me." And the winds and waves,
And the deep echoes of the distant mountain,
Made answer—" Come, and die!"
 Ser. Fantastic all! Poor boy, thou art distracted
With the vain terrors of some feudal tyrant,
Whose frown hath been from infancy thy bugbear.
Why seek his presence?
 Que.   Wherefore does the moth
Fly to the scorching taper?—why the bird,
Dazzled by lights at midnight, seek the net?—
Why does the prey, which feels the fascination
Of the snake's glaring eye, drop in his jaws?
 Ser. Such wild examples but refute themselves.
Let bird, let moth, let the coil'd adder's prey,
Resist the fascination and be safe.
Thou goest not near this Baron—if thou goest,
I will go with thee. Known in many a field,
Which he in a whole life of petty feud
Has never dream'd of, I will teach the knight
To rule him in this matter—be thy warrant,
That far from him, and from his petty lordship,
You shall henceforth tread English land, and never
Thy presence shall alarm his conscience more.
 Que. 'T were desperate risk for both. I will far rather
Hastily guide thee through this dangerous province,
And seek thy school, thy yew-trees, and thy churchyard;—
The last, perchance, will be the first I find.
 Ser. I would rather face him,

Like a bold Englishman that knows his right,
And will stand by his friend.   And yet 't is folly—
Fancies like these are not to be resisted;
'T is better to escape them.   Many a presage,
Too rashly braved, becomes its own accomplishment.
Then let us go—But whither? My old head
As little knows where it shall lie to-night,
As yonder mutineers that left their officer,
As reckless of his quarters as these billows,
That leave the withered sea-weed on the beach,
And care not where they pile it.

    Que. Think not for that, good friend. We are in Scotland,
And if it is not varied from its wont,
Each cot, that sends a curl of smoke to heaven,
Will yield a stranger quarters for the night,
Simply because he needs them.

    Ser. But are there none within an easy walk
Give lodgings here for hire? for I have left
Some of the Don's piastres, (though I kept
The secret from yon gulls,) and I had rather
Pay the fair reckoning I can well afford,
And my host takes with pleasure, than I 'd cumber
Some poor man's roof with me and all my wants,
And tax his charity beyond discretion.

    Que. Some six miles hence there is a town and hostelry.
But you are wayworn, and it is most likely
Our comrades must have fill'd it.

    Ser.   Out upon them!—
Were there a friendly mastiff who would lend me
Half of his supper, half of his poor kennel,
I would help Honesty to pick his bones,
And share his straw, far rather than I 'd sup
On jolly fare with these base varlets!

    Que. We 'll manage better; for our Scottish dogs,
Thou stout and trusty, are but ill-instructed[1]
In hospitable rights.—Here is a maiden,
A little maid, will tell us of the country,
And sorely it is changed since I left it,
If we should fail to find a harbourage.

Enter Isabel MacLellan, *a girl of about six years old, bearing
a milk-pail on her head; she stops on seeing the* Sergeant *and*
Quentin.

    Que. There's something in her look that doth remind me—
But 't is not wonder I find recollections
In all that here I look on.—Pretty maid——
    Ser. You 're slow, and hesitate. I will be spokesman.—

   [1] MS.—"Gallant and grim, may be but ill-instructed."

Good even, my pretty maiden—canst thou tell us,
Is there a Christian house would render strangers,
For love or guerdon, a night's meal and lodging?
   Isa. Full surely, sir; we dwell in yon old house
Upon the cliff—they call it Chapeldonan.
(Points to the building.)
Our house is large enough, and if our supper
Chance to be scant, you shall have half of mine,
For, as I think, sir, you have been a soldier.
Up yonder lies our house; I'll trip before,
And tell my mother she has guests a-coming;
The path is something steep, but you shall see
I'll be there first.   I must chain up the dogs, too;
Nimrod and Bloodylass are cross to strangers,
But gentle when you know them.
    [Exit, and is seen partially ascending to the Castle.
   Ser.   You have spoke
Your country folk aright, both for the dogs
And for the people. We had luck to light
On one too young for cunning and for selfishness.—
He's in a reverie—a deep one sure,
Since the gibe on his country wakes him not.—
Bestir thee, Quentin!
   Que.   'T was a wondrous likeness!
   Ser. Likeness! of whom? I'll warrant thee of one
Whom thou hast loved and lost.   Such fantasies
Live long in brains like thine, which fashion visions
Of woe and death when they are cross'd in love,
As most men are or have been.
   Que. Thy guess has touch'd me, though it is but slight
'Mongst other woes: I knew in former days,
A maid that view'd me with some glance of favour;
But my fate carried me to other shores,
And she has since been wedded.   I did think on't
But as a bubble burst, a rainbow vanish'd;
It adds no deeper shade to the dark gloom
Which chills the springs of hope and life within me.
Our guide hath got a trick of voice and feature
Like to the maid I spoke of—that is all.
   Ser. She bounds before us like a gamesome doe,
Or rather as the rock-bred eaglet soars
Up to her nest, as if she rose by will
Without an effort. Now a Netherlander,
One of our Frogland friends, viewing the scene,
Would take his oath that tower, and rock, and maiden,
Were forms too light and lofty to be real,
And only some delusion of the fancy,
Such as men dream at sunset.   I myself

Have kept the level ground so many years,
I have wellnigh forgot the art to climb,
Unless assisted by thy younger arm.
    [*They go off as if to ascend to the Tower, the*
      SERGEANT *leaning upon* QUENTIN.

SCENE II.

Scene changes to the Front of the Old Tower. ISABEL *comes forward
with her Mother,—* MARION *speaking as they advance.*

MAR. I blame thee not, my child, for bidding wanderers
Come share our food and shelter, if thy father
Were here to welcome them ; but, Isabel,
He waits upon his lord at Auchindrane,
And comes not home to-night.
  ISA.   What then, my mother ?
The travellers do not ask to see my father ;
Food, shelter, rest, is all the poor men want,
And we can give them these without my father.
  MAR. Thou canst not understand, nor I explain,
Why a lone female asks not visitants
What time her husband's absent.—(*Apart.*) My poor child,
And if thou 'rt wedded to a jealous husband,
Thou 'lt know too soon the cause.
  ISA. (*partly overhearing what her mother says*)—
Ay, but I know already—Jealousy
Is, when my father chides, and you sit weeping.
  MAR. Out, little spy ! thy father never chides ;
Or, if he does, 'tis when his wife deserves it.—
But to our strangers ; they are old men, Isabel,
That seek this shelter ? are they not ?
  ISA.   One is old —
Old as this tower of ours, and worn like that,
Bearing deep marks of battles long since fought.
  MAR. Some remnant of the·wars ; he 's welcome, surely,
Bringing no quality along with him
Which can alarm suspicion.—Well, the other ?
  ISA. A young man, gentle-voiced and gentle-eyed,
Who looks and speaks like one the world has frown'd on ;
But smiles when you smile, seeming that he feels
Joy in your joy, though he himself is sad.
Brown hair, and downcast looks.
  MAR. (*alarmed.*) 'Tis but an idle thought — it cannot be !
(*Listens.*) I hear his accents — It is all too true—
My terrors were prophetic !—— I 'll compose myself.
And then accost him firmly. Thus it must be.

    [She retires hastily into the Tower. — The voices of
       the SERGEANT *and* QUENTIN *are heard ascend*
       ing behind the Scenes.

QUE. One effort more — we stand upon the level.
I 've seen thee work thee up glacis and cavalier
Steeper than this ascent, when cannon, culverine,
Musket, and hackbut, shower'd their shot upon thee,
And form'd, with ceaseless blaze, a fiery garland
Round the defences of the post you storm'd.
       [They come on the stage, and at the same time
        MARION *re-enters from the Tower.*

SER. Truly thou speak'st.   I am the tardier,
That I, in climbing hither, miss the fire,
Which wont to tell me there was death in loitering. —
Here stands, methinks, our hostess.
       [He goes forward to address MARION. QUENTIN,
        struck on seeing her, keeps back.

SER. Kind Dame, yon little lass hath brought you stran-
Willing to be a trouble, not a charge to you,   [gers,
We are disbanded soldiers, but have means
Ample enough to pay our journey homeward.

MAR. We keep no house of general entertainment,
But know our duty, sir, to locks like yours,
Whiten'd and thinn'd by many a long campaign.
Ill chances that my husband should be absent —
(*Apart.*) — Courage alone can make me struggle through
For in your comrade, though he hath forgot me,   [it —
I spy a friend whom I have known in school-days,
And whom I think MacLellan well remembers. —
(*She goes up to* QUENTIN.) You see a woman's memory
Is faithfuller than yours; for Quentin Blane
Hath not a greeting left for Marion Harkness.

QUE. (*with effort.*) I seek, indeed, my native land, good
     Marion,
But seek it like a stranger. — All is changed,
And thou thyself —

MAR.   You left a giddy maiden,
And find, on your return, a wife and mother.
Thine old acquaintance, Quentin, is my mate —
Stout Niel MacLellan, ranger to our lord,
The Knight of Auchindrane.   He 's absent now,
But will rejoice to see his former comrade,
If, as I trust, you tarry his return.
(*Apart.*) Heaven grant he understand my words by con-
He must remember Niel and he were rivals;   [traries!
He must remember Niel and he were foes;
He must remember Niel is warm of temper,
And think, instead of welcome, I would blithely

Bid him, God speed you.   But he is as simple
And void of guile as ever.
   QUE. Marion, I gladly rest within your cottage,
And gladly wait return of Niel MacLellan,
To clasp his hand. and wish him happiness.
Some rising feelings might perhaps prevent this—
But 'tis a peevish part to grudge our friends
Their share of fortune because we have miss'd it:
I can wish others joy and happiness,
Though I must ne'er partake them.
   MAR. But if it grieve you——
   QUE. No! do not fear.   The brightest gleams of hope
That shine on me are such as are reflected
From those which shine on others.—[*The* SERGEANT *and*
        QUENTIN *enter the Tower with the little Girl*
   MAR. (*comes forward, and speaks in agitation*)—
Even so! the simple youth has miss'd my meaning!
I shame to make it plainer, or to say,
In one brief word, Pass on—Heaven guide the bark,
For we are on the breakers!   [*Exit into the Tower*

ACT II.—SCENE I.

A Withdrawing Apartment in the Castle of Auchindrane. Servants place a Table, with a Flask of Wine and Drinking-Cups.

Enter MURE *of* AUCHINDRANE, *with* ALBERT GIFFORD, *his Relation and Visitor. They place themselves by the Table after some complimentary ceremony. At some distance is heard the noise of revelling.*

   AUCH. We're better placed for confidential talk,
Then in the hall fill'd with disbanded soldiers,
And fools and fiddlers gather'd on the highway,—
The worthy guests whom Philip crowds my hall with,
And with them spends his evening.
   GIF. But think you not, my friend, that your son Philip
Should be participant of these our councils,
Being so deeply mingled in the danger—
Your house's only heir—your only son!
   AUCH. Kind cousin Gifford, if thou lack'st good counsel
At race, at cockpit, or at gambling table,
Or any freak by which men cheat themselves
As well of life as of the means to live,
Call for assistance upon Philip Mure;
But in all serious parley spare invoking him.

Gif. You speak too lightly of my cousin Philip;
All name him brave in arms.
        Auch.   A second Bevis;
But I, my youth bred up in graver fashions,
Mourn o'er the mode of life in which he spends,
Or rather dissipates, his time and substance.
No vagabond escapes his search—The soldier
Spurn'd from the service, henceforth to be ruffian
Upon his own account, is Philip's comrade;
The fiddler, whose crack'd crowd has still three strings on't;
The balladeer, whose voice has still two notes left;
Whate'er is roguish, and whate'er is vile,
Are welcome to the board of Auchindrane,
And Philip will return them shout for shout,
And pledge for jovial pledge, and song for song,
Until the shamefaced sun peep at our windows,
And ask, " What have we here?"
        Gif. You take such revel deeply;—we are Scotsmen,
Far known for rustic hospitality,
That mind not birth or titles in our guests:
The harper has his seat beside our hearth,
The wanderer must find comfort at our board,
His name unask'd, his pedigree unknown;
So did our ancestors, and so must we.
        Auch. All this is freely granted, worthy kinsman;
And prithee do not think me churl enough
To count how many sit beneath my salt.
I've wealth enough to fill my father's hall
Each day at noon, and feed the guests who crowd it,
I am near mate with those whom men call Lord,
Though a rude western knight.   But mark me, cousin.
Although I feed wayfaring vagabonds,
I make them not my comrades.   Such as I,
Who have advanced the fortunes of my line,
And swell'd a baron's turret to a palace,
Have oft the curse awaiting on our thrift,
To see, while yet we live, the things which must be
At our decease—the downfall of our family,
The loss of land and lordship, name and knighthood,
The wreck of the fair fabric we have built,
By a degenerate heir.   Philip has that
Of inborn meanness in him, that he loves not
The company of betters nor of equals;
Never at ease, unless he bears the bell,
And crows the loudest in the company.
He's mesh'd, too, in the snares of every female
Who deigns to cast a passing glance on him—
Licentious, disrespectful, rash, and profligate.

GIF. Come, my good coz, think we too have been young,
And I will swear that in your father's lifetime
You have yourself been trapp'd by toys like these.
    AUCH. A fool I may have been—but not a madman ;
I never play'd the rake among my followers,
Pursuing this man's sister, that man's wife ;
And therefore never saw I man of mine,
When summon'd to obey my hest, grow restive,
Talk of his honour, of his peace destroy'd,
And, while obeying, mutter threats of vengeance.
But now the humour of an idle youth,
Disgusting trusted followers, sworn dependents,
Plays football with his honour and my safety.
    GIF. I 'm sorry to find discord in your house,
For I had hoped, while bringing you cold news,
To find you arm'd in union 'gainst the danger.
    AUCH. What can man speak that I would shrink to hear,
And where the danger I would deign to shun? (*He rises.*)
What should appal a man inured to perils,
Like the bold climber on the crags of Ailsa?
Winds whistle past him, billows rage below,
The sea-fowl sweep around, with shriek and clang,
One single slip, one unadvised pace,
One qualm of giddiness—and peace be with him !
But he whose grasp is sure, whose step is firm,
Whose brain is constant—he makes one proud rock
The means to scale another, till he stand
Triumphant on the peak.
    GIF.   And so I trust
Thou wilt surmount the danger now approaching,
Which scarcely can I frame my tongue to tell you,
Though I rode here on purpose.
    AUCH. Cousin, I think thy heart was never coward,
And strange it seems thy tongue should take such semblance.
I 've heard of many a loud-mouth'd, noisy braggart,
Whose hand gave feeble sanction to his tongue ;
But thou art one whose heart can think bold things,
Whose hand can act them—but who shrinks to speak them '
    GIF. And if I speak them not, 'tis that I shame
To tell thee of the calumnies that load thee.
Things loudly spoken at the city Cross—
Things closely whisper'd in our Sovereign's ear—
Things which the plumed lord and flat-capp'd citizen
Do circulate amid their different ranks—
Things false, no doubt ; but, falsehoods while I deem them,
Still honouring thee, I shun the odious topic.
    AUCH. Shun it not, cousin ; 'tis a friend's best office

To bring the news we hear unwillingly.
The sentinel, who tells the foe's approach,
And wakes the sleeping camp, does but his duty:
Be thou as bold in telling me of danger,
As I shall be in facing danger told of.

 Gif. I need not bid thee recollect the death-feud
That raged so long betwixt thy house and Cassilis;
I need not bid thee recollect the league,
When royal James himself stood mediator
Between thee and Earl Gilbert.

  Auch. Call you these news?—You might as well have
      told me
That old King Coil is dead, and graved at Kylesfeld.
I'll help thee out—King James commanded us
Henceforth to live in peace, made us clasp hands too.
O, sir, when such an union hath been made,
In heart and hand conjoining mortal foes,
Under a monarch's royal mediation,
The league is not forgotten.　And with this
What is there to be told?　The King commanded—
" Be friends."　No doubt we were so—Who dares doubt
 Gif. You speak but half the tale.　　　　　　　　　[it?

 Auch. By good Saint Trimon, but I'll tell the whole!
There is no terror in the tale for me—[1]
Go speak of ghosts to children!—This Earl Gilbert
(God sain him) loved Heaven's peace as well as I did,
And we were wondrous friends whene'er we met
At church or market, or in burrows town.
Midst this, our good Lord Gilbert, Earl of Cassilis,
Takes purpose he would journey forth to Edinburgh.
The King was doling gifts of abbey-lands,
Good things that thrifty house was wont to fish for.
Our mighty Earl forsakes his sea-wash'd castle,
Passes our borders some four miles from hence;
And, holding it unwholesome to be fasters
Long after sunrise, lo! the Earl and train
Dismount, to rest their nags and eat their breakfast.
The morning rose, the small birds caroll'd sweetly—
The corks were drawn, the pasty brooks incision—
His lordship jests, his train are choked with laughter;
When,—wondrous change of cheer, and most unlook'd for,
Strange epilogue to bottle and to baked meat!—
Flash'd from the greenwood half a score of carabines;
And the good Earl of Cassilis, in his breakfast,
Had nooning, dinner, supper, all at once,
Even in the morning that he closed his journey;

  " There is no terror, Cassius, in your threats."—*Shakspeare.*

And the grim sexton, for his chamberlain,
Made him the bed which rests the head for ever.
  GIF. Told with much spirit, cousin—some there are
Would add, and in a tone resembling triumph.
And would that with these long establish'd facts
My tale began and ended! I must tell you,
That evil-deeming censures of the events,
Both at the time and now, throw blame on thee—
Time, place, and circumstance, they say, proclaim thee,
Alike, the author of that morning's ambush.
  AUCH. Ay, 'tis an old belief in Carrick here,
Where natives do not always die in bed,
That if a Kennedy shall not attain
Methuselah's last span, a Mure has slain him:
Such is the general creed of all their clan.
Thank Heaven, that they're bound to prove the charge
They are so prompt in making. They have clamour'd
Enough of this before, to show their malice.
But what said these coward pickthanks when I came
Before the King, before the Justicers,
Rebutting all their calumnies, and daring them
To show that I knew aught of Cassilis' journey—
Which way he meant to travel—where to halt—
Without which knowledge I possess'd no means
To dress an ambush for him? Did I not
Defy the assembled clan of Kennedys,
To show, by proof direct or inferential,
Wherefore they slander'd me with this foul charge!
My gauntlet rung before them in the court,
And I did dare the best of them to lift it,
And prove such charge a true one—Did I not?
  GIF. I saw your gauntlet lie before the Kennedys,
Who look'd on it as men do on an adder,
Longing to crush, and yet afraid to grasp it.
Not an eye sparkled—not a foot advanced—
No arm was stretch'd to lift the fatal symbol.
  AUCH. Then, wherefore do the hildings murmur now!
Wish they to see again, how one bold Mure
Can baffle and defy their assembled valour?
  GIF. No; but they speak of evidence suppress'd.
  AUCH. Suppress'd!—what evidence?—by whom sup-
What Will-o'-Wisp—what idiot of a witness,   [press'd?
Is he to whom they trace an empty voice,
But cannot show his person?
  GIF.   They pretend,
With the King's leave, to bring it to a trial;
Averring that a lad, named Quentin Blane,

Brought thee a letter from the murder'd Earl,
With friendly greetings, telling of his journey,
The hour which he set forth, the place he halted at,—
Affording thee the means to form the ambush,
Of which your hatred made the application.

AUCH. A prudent Earl, indeed, if such his practice,
When dealing with a recent enemy!
And what should he propose by such strange confidence
In one who sought it not?

GIF. His purposes were kindly, say the Kennedys—
Desiring you would meet him where he halted,
Offering to undertake whate'er commissions
You listed trust him with, for court or city:
And, thus apprised of Cassilis' purposed journey,
And of his halting-place, you placed the ambush,
Prepared the homicides——

AUCH. They're free to say their pleasure. They are men
Of the new court—and I am but a fragment
Of stout old Morton's faction. It is reason
That such as I be rooted from the earth,
That they may have full room to spread their branches.
No doubt, 't is easy to find strolling vagrants
To prove whate'er they prompt. This Quentin Blanc—
Did you not call him so?—why comes he now?
And wherefore not before? This must be answered —
(*Abruptly*)—Where is he now?

GIF.   Abroad—they say—kidnapp'd,
By you kidnapp'd, that he might die in Flanders.
But orders have been sent for his discharge,
And his transmission hither.

AUCH. (*assuming an air of composure*)—
When they produce such witness, cousin Gifford,
We'll be prepared to meet it. In the meanwhile,
The King doth ill to throw his royal sceptre
In the accuser's scale, ere he can know
How justice shall incline it.

GIF.   Our sage prince
Resents, it may be, less the death of Cassilis,
Than he is angry that the feud should burn,
After his royal voice had said, " Be quench'd :"
Thus urging prosecution less for slaughter,
Than that, being done against the King's command,
Treason is mix'd with homicide.

AUCH.   Ha! ha! most true, my cousin.
Why, well consider'd, 'tis a crime so great
To slay one's enemy, the King forbidding it,
Like parricide, it should be held impossible.

'Tis just as if a wretch retain'd the evil,
When the King's touch had bid the sores be heal'd ;
And such a crime merits the stake at least.
What ! can there be within a Scottish bosom
A feud so deadly, that it kept its ground
When the King said, Be friends ! It is not credible.
Were I King James, I never would believe it :
I 'd rather think the story all a dream,
And that there was no friendship, feud, nor journey,
No halt, no ambush, and no Earl of Cassilis,
Than dream anointed Majesty has wrong !—
    GIF. Speak within door, coz.
    AUCH.   O, true.—(*Aside*)—I shall betray myself
Even to this half-bred fool.—I must have room,
Room for an instant, or I suffocate.—
Cousin, I prithee call our Philip hither—
Forgive me ; 'twere more meet I summon'd him
Myself ; but then the sight of yonder revel .
Would chafe my blood, and I have need of coolness.
    GIF. I understand thee—I will bring him straight. [*Exit*
    AUCH. And if thou dost, he 's lost his ancient trick
To fathom, as he wont, his five-pint flaggons.—
This space is mine—O for the power to fill it,
Instead of senseless rage and empty curses,
With the dark spell which witches learn from fiends,
That smites the object of their hate afar,
Nor leaves a token of its mystic action,
Stealing the soul from out the unscathed body,
As lightning melts the blade, nor harms the scabbard !
—'Tis vain to wish for it—Each curse of mine
Falls to the ground as harmless as the arrows
Which children shoot at stars ! The time for thought,
If thought could aught avail me, melts away,
Like to a snowball in a schoolboy's hand,
That melts the faster the more close he grasps it !—-
If I had time, this Scottish Solomon,
Whom some call son of David the Musician,[1]
Might find it perilous work to march to Carrick.
There 's many a feud still slumbering in its ashes,
Whose embers are yet red. Nobles we have,
Stout as old Graysteel, and as hot as Bothwell ;
Here too are castles look from crags as high
On seas as wide as Logan's. So the King —
Pshaw ! He is here again —

---

[1] The calumnious tale which ascribed the birth of James VI. to
an intrigue of Queen Mary with Rizzio.—ED.

Enter GIFFORD.

GIF.   I heard you name
The King, my kinsman ; know, he comes not hither.
    AUCH. (*affecting indifference.*) Nay, then we need not
                broach our barrels, cousin,
Nor purchase us new jerkins.—Comes not Philip?
    GIF. Yes, sir. He tarries but to drink a service
To his good friends at parting.
    AUCH. Friends for the beadle or the sheriff-officer.
Well, let it pass. Who comes, and how attended,
Since James designs not westward?
    GIF. O you shall have, instead, his fiery functionary,
George Home that was, but now Dunbar's great Earl ;
He leads a royal host, and comes to show you
How he distributes justice on the Border,
Where judge and hangman oft reverse their office,
And the noose does its work before the sentence.
But I have said my tidings best and worst.
None but yourself can know what course the time
And peril may demand. To lift your banner,
If I might be a judge, were desperate game :
Ireland and Galloway offer you convenience
For flight, if flight be thought the better remedy ;
To face the court requires the conciousness
And confidence of innocence. You alone
Can judge if you possess these attributes. (*A noise behind
                the scenes.*)
    AUCH. Philip, I think, has broken up his revels ;
His ragged regiment are dispersing them,
Well liquor'd, doubtless. They're disbanded soldiers,
Or some such vagabonds.—Here comes the gallant.

Enter PHILIP. *He has a buff-coat and head-piece, wears a sword
    and dagger, with pistols at his girdle. He appears to be affected
    by liquor, but to be by no means intoxicated.*

    AUCH. You scarce have been made known to one another,
Although you sate together at the board.—
Son Philip, know and prize our cousin Gifford,
    PHI. (*tastes the wine on the table*)—
If you had prized him, sir, you had been loth
To have welcomed him in bastard Alicant
I'll make amends, by pledging his good journey
In glorious Burgundy.—The stirrup-cup, ho!
And bring my cousin's horses to the court.
    AUCH. (*draws him aside*)—
The stirrup-cup! He doth not ride to-night—
Shame on such churlish conduct to a kinsman !

PHI. (*aside to his father.*) I 've news of pressing import.
Send the fool off.—Stay, I will start him for you.
(*To* GIF.) Yes, my kind cousin, Burgundy is better,
On a night-ride, to those who thread our moors,
And we may deal it freely to our friends,
For we came freely by it.   Yonder ocean
Rolls many a purple cask upon our shore,
Rough with embossed shells and shagged sea-weed,
When the good skipper and his careful crew
Have had their latest earthly draught of brine,
And gone to quench, or to endure their thirst,
Where nectar 's plenty, or even water 's scarce,
And filter'd to the parched crew by dropsfull.
   AUCH. Thou 'rt mad, son Philip ! Gifford 's no intruder,
That we should rid him hence by such wild rants :
My kinsman hither rode at his own danger,
To tell us that Dunbar is hasting to us,
With a strong force, and with the King's commission,
To enforce against our house a hateful charge,
With every measure of extremity.
   PHI. And is this all that our good cousin tells us !
I can say more, thanks to the ragged regiment,
With whose good company you have upbraided me,
On whose authority, I tell thee, cousin,
Dunbar is here already.
   GIF.   Already ?
   PHI. Yes, gentle coz.   And you, my sire, be hasty
In what you think to do.
   AUCH. I think thou darest not jest on such a subject.
Where hadst thou these fell tidings ?
   PHI. Where you, too, might have heard them, noble
            father,
Save that your ears, nail'd to our kinsman's lips,
Would list no coarser accents.   O, my soldiers,
My merry crew of vagabonds, for ever !
Scum of the Netherlands, and wash'd ashore
Upon this coast like unregarded sea-weed,
They had not been two hours on Scottish land,
When, lo ! they met a military friend,
An ancient fourier, known to them of old,
Who, warm'd by certain stoups of searching wine,
Inform'd his old companions that Dunbar
Left Glasgow yesterday, comes here to-morrow ;
Himself, he said, was sent a spy before,
To view what preparations we were making.
   AUCH. (*to* GIF.) If this be sooth, good kinsman, thou
            must claim

To take a part with us for life and death,
Or speed from hence, and leave us to our fortune.
  Gif. In such dilemma,
Believe me, friend, I'd choose upon the instant—
But I lack harness, and a steed to charge on,
For mine is overtired, and, save my page,
There's not a man to back me. But I'll hie
To Kyle, and raise my vassals to your aid.
  Phi. 'T will be when the rats,
That on these tidings fly this house of ours,
Come back to pay their rents.—(*Apart.*)
  Auch.   Courage, cousin!—
Thou goest not hence ill mounted for thy need:
Full forty coursers feed in my wide stalls—
The best of them is yours to speed your journey.
  Phi. Stand not on ceremony, good our cousin,
When safety signs, to shorten courtesy.
  Gif. (*to* Auch.) Farewell, then, cousin, for my tarrying
          here
Were ruin to myself, small aid to you;
Yet loving well your name and family,
I'd fain—
  Phi. Be gone?—that is our object, too—
Kinsman, adieu.
                  [*Exit* Gifford. Philip *calls after him.*
                  You yeoman of the stable,
Give Master Gifford there my fleetest steed,
Yon cut-tail'd roan that trembles at a spear.—
             (*Trampling of the horse heard going off.*)
Hark! he departs. How swift the dastard rides,
To shun the neighbourhood of jeopardy!
  (*He lays aside the appearance of levity which he has
    hitherto worn, and says very seriously*)—
                And, now, my father—
  Auch. And now, my son—thou'st ta'en a perilous game
Into thine hands, rejecting elder counsel,—
How dost thou mean to play it?
  Phi. Sir, good gamesters play not
Till they review the cards which fate has dealt them,
Computing thus the chances of the game;
And wofully they seem to weigh against us.
  Auch. Exile's a passing ill, and may be borne;
And when Dunbar and all his myrmidons
Are eastward turn'd, we'll seize our own again.
  Phi. Would that were all the risk we had to stand to!
But more and worse,—a doom of treason, forfeiture,
Death to ourselves, dishonour to our house,

Is what the stern Justiciary menaces;
And, fatally for us, he hath the means
To make his threatenings good.
    Auch. It cannot be. I tell thee, there's no force
In Scottish law to raze a house like mine,
Coeval with the time the Lords of Galloway
Submitted them unto the Scottish sceptre,
Renouncing rights of Tanistry and Brehon.
Some dreams they have of evidence—some suspicion;
But old Montgomery knows my purpose well,
And long before their mandate reach the camp
To crave the presence of this mighty witness,
He will be fitted with an answer to it.
    Phi. Father, what we call great, is often ruin'd
By means so ludicrously disproportion'd,
They make me think upon the gunner's linstock,
Which, yielding forth a light about the size
And semblance of the glowworm, yet applied
To powder, blew a palace into atoms,
Sent a young King—a young Queen's mate at least—
Into the air, as high as e'er flew night-hawk,
And made such wild work in the realm of Scotland,
As they can tell who heard,—and you were one
Who saw, perhaps, the night-flight which began it.
    Auch. If thou hast nought to speak but drunken folly,
I cannot listen longer.
    Phi. I will speak brief and sudden.—There is one
Whose tongue to us has the same perilous force
Which Bothwell's powder had to Kirk of Field;
One whose least tones, and those but peasant accents,
Could rend the roof off our fathers' castle,
Level its tallest turret with its base;
And he that doth possess this wondrous power
Sleeps this same night not five miles distant from us.
    Auch. (*who had looked on* Philip *with much appearance*
          of astonishment and doubt, exclaims)—
Then thou art mad indeed! Ha! ha! I'm glad on't.
I'd purchase an escape from what I dread,
Even by the frenzy of my only son!
    Phi. I thank you, but agree not to the bargain.
You rest on what yon civet cat has said:
Yon silken doublet, stuff'd with rotten straw,
Told you but half the truth, and knew no more.
But my good vagrants had a perfect tale:
They told me, little judging the importance,
That Quentin Blane had been discharged with them.
They told me, that a quarrel happ'd at landing,

And that the youngster and an ancient sergeant
Had left their company, and taken refuge
In Chapeldonan, where our ranger dwells;[1]
They saw him scale the cliff on which it stands,
Ere they were out of sight; the old man with him.
And therefore laugh no more at me as mad;
But laugh, if thou hast list for merriment,
To think he stands on the same land with us,
Whose absence thou wouldst deem were cheaply purchased
With thy soul's ransom and thy body's danger.

    AUCH. 'Tis then a fatal truth! Thou art no yelper
To open rashly on so wild a scent;
Thou 'rt the young bloodhound, which careers and springs
Frolics and fawns, as if the friend of man,
But seizes on his victim like a tiger.

    PHI. No matter what I am—I 'm as you bred me;
So let that pass till there be time to mend me,
And let us speak like men, and to the purpose.
This object of our fear and of our dread,
Since such our pride must own him, sleeps to-night
Within our power:—to-morrow in Dunbar's,
And we are then his victims.[2]

    AUCH. He is in *ours* to-night.[3]

    PHI. He is.   I 'll answer that MacLellan's trusty.

    AUCH. Yet he replied to you to-day full rudely.

    PHI. Yes! the poor knave has got a handsome wife,
And is gone mad with jealousy

    AUCH. Fool!—when we need the utmost faith, allegiance,
Obedience. and attachment in our vassals,
Thy wild intrigues pour gall into their hearts,
And turn their love to hatred!

    PHI. Most reverend sire, you talk of ancient morals,
Preach'd on by Knox, and practised by Glencairn;[4]

---

[1] MS.—"In the old tower where Niel MacLellan dwells,
    And therefore laugh no more," &c.

[2] MS.—"And we are then in his power."

[3] MS.—"He 's in *our* power to-night."

[4] Alexander, fifth Earl of Glencairn, for distinction called "The Good Earl," was among the first of the peers of Scotland who concurred in the Reformation, in aid of which he acted a conspicuous part, in the employment both of his sword and pen. In a remonstrance with the Queen Regent, he told her, that "if she violated the engagements which she had come under to her subjects, they would consider themselves as absolved from their allegiance to her." He was author of a satirical poem against the Roman Catholics, entitled "The Hermit of Allareit," (Loretto.)—See *Sibbald's Chronicle of Scottish Poetry.*—He assisted the Reformers with his sword, when they took arms at Perth, in 1559; had a principal command in the army embodied against Queen Mary, in June 1567, and demolished the altar, broke the images, tore down the pictures, &c., in the Chapel-royal of Holyroodhouse, after the Queen was conducted to Lochleven. He died in 1574.—ED.

Respectable, indeed, but somewhat musty
In these our modern nostrils. In our days,
If a young baron chance to leave his vassal
The sole possessor of a handsome wife,
'T is sign he loves his follower ; and if not,
He loves his follower's wife, which often proves
The surer bond of patronage. Take either case—
Favour flows in of course, and vassals rise.

   AUCH. Philip, this is infamous,
And, what is worse, impolitic. Take example :
Break not God's laws or man's for each temptation
That youth and blood suggest. I am a man—
A weak and erring man ;—full well thou know'st
That I may hardly term myself a pattern
Even to my son ;—yet thus far will I say,
I never swerved from my integrity,
Save at the voice of strong necessity,
Or such o'erpowering view of high advantage
As wise men liken to necessity,
In strength and force compulsive. No one saw me
Exchange my reputation for my pleasure,
Or do the Devil's work without his wages.
I practised prudence, and paid tax to virtue,
By following her behests, save where strong reason
Compell'd a deviation. Then, if preachers
At times look'd sour, or elders shook their heads,
They could not term my walk irregular ;
For I stood up still for the worthy cause,
A pillar, though a flaw'd one, of the altar,
Kept a strict walk, and led three hundred horse.

   PHI. Ah, these three hundred horse in such rough times
Were better commendation to a party
Than all your efforts at hypocrisy,
Betray'd so oft by avarice and ambition,
And dragg'd to open shame. But, righteous father,
When sire and son unite in mutual crime,
And join their efforts to the same enormity,
It is no time to measure other's faults,
Or fix the amount of each. Most moral father,
Think if it be a moment now to weigh
The vices of the Heir of Auchindrane,
Or 'take precaution that the ancient house
Shall have another heir than the sly courtier
That 's gaping for the forfeiture.

   AUCH. We 'll disappoint him, Philip,—
We 'll disappoint him yet. It is a folly,
A wilful cheat, to cast our eyes behind.

When time, and the fast flitting opportunity,
Call loudly—nay, compel us to look forward:
Why are we not already at MacLellan's,
Since there the victim sleeps?
 Phi.   Nay, soft, I pray thee.
I had not made your piety my confessor,
Nor enter'd in debate on these sage councils,
Which you're more like to give than I to profit by,
Could I have used the time more usefully;
But first an interval must pass between
The fate of Quentin and the little artifice
That shall detach him from his comrade,
The stout old soldier that I told you of.
 Auch. How work a point so difficult—so dangerous?
 Phi. 'Tis cared for. Mark, my father, the convenience
Arising from mean company. My agents
Are at my hand, like a good workman's tools,
And if I mean a mischief, ten to one
That they anticipate the deed and guilt.
Well knowing this, when first the vagrant's tattle
Gave me the hint that Quentin was so near us,
Instant I sent MacLellan, with strong charges
To stop him for the night, and bring me word,
Like an accomplish'd spy, how all things stood,
Lulling the enemy into security.
 Auch. There was a prudent general!
 Phi. MacLellan went and came within the hour.
The jealous bee, which buzzes in his nightcap,
Had humm'd to him, this fellow, Quentin Blanc,
Had been in schoolboy days an humble lover
Of his own pretty wife—
 Auch.   Most fortunate!
The knave will be more prompt to serve our purpose.
 Phi. No doubt on 't. 'Mid the tidings he brought back,
Was one of some importance. The old man
Is flush of dollars; this I caused him tell
Among his comrades, who became as eager
To have him in their company, as e'er
They had been wild to part with him. And in brief space,
A letter's framed by an old hand amongst them,
Familiar with such feats. It bore the name
And character of old Montgomery,
Whom he might well suppose at no great distance,
Commanding his old Sergeant Hildebrand,
By all the ties of late authority,
Conjuring him by ancient soldiership,
To hasten to his mansion instantly,

On business of high import, with a charge
To come alone——
   AUCH. Well, he sets out, I doubt it not: what follows?
   PHI. I am not curious into other's practices,—
So far I'm an economist in guilt,
As you, my sire, advise. But on the road
To old Montgomery's he meets his comrades;
They nourish grudge against him and his dollars,
And things may hap, which counsel, learn'd in law,
Call Robbery and Murder. Should he live,
He has seen nought that we would hide from him.
   AUCH. Who carries the forged letter to the veteran?
   PHI. Why, Niel MacLellan, who, return'd again
To his own tower, as if to pass the night there.
They pass'd on him, or tried to pass, a story,
As if they wish'd the sergeant's company,
Without the young comptroller's — that is, Quentin's,
And he became an agent of their plot,
That he might better carry on our own.
   AUCH. There's life in it — yes, there is life in 't;
And we will have a mounted party ready
To scour the moors in quest of the banditti
That kill'd the poor old man — they shall die instantly.
Dunbar shall see us use sharp justice here,
As well as he in Teviotdale. You are sure
You gave no hint nor impulse to their purpose?
   PHI. It needed not. The whole pack oped at once
Upon the scent of dollars. — But time comes
When I must seek the tower, and act with Niel
What farther's to be done.
   AUCH. Alone with him thou goest not. He bears grudge —
Thou art my only son, and on a night   .
When such wild passions are so free abroad,
When such wild deeds are doing, 'tis but natural.
I guarantee thy safety. — I 'll ride with thee.
   PHI. E'en as you will, my lord. But — pardon me —
If you will come, let us not have a word
Of conscience, and of pity, and forgiveness;
Fine words to-morrow, out of place to-night.
Take counsel, then — leave all this work to me;
Call up your household, make fit preparation,
In love and peace, to welcome this Earl Justiciar,
As one that 's free of guilt. Go, deck the castle
As for an honour'd guest. Hallow the chapel
(If they have power to hallow it) with thy prayers.
Let me ride forth alone, and ere the sun
Comes o'er the eastern hill, thou shalt accost him:

" Now do thy worst, thou oft-returning spy,
Here 's nought thou canst discover."
 Auch. Yet goest thou not alone with that MacLellan !
He deems thou bearest will to injure him,
And seek'st occasion suiting to such will.
Philip, thou art irreverent, fierce, ill-nurtured,
Stain'd with low vices, which disgust a father ;
Yet ridest thou not alone with yonder man,—
Come weal, come woe, myself will go with thee.
     [Exit, and calls to horse behind the scene.
 Phi. (*alone.*) Now would I give my fleetest horse to know
What sudden thought roused this paternal care,
And if 'tis on his own account or mine :
'Tis true, he hath the deepest share in all
That 's likely now to hap, or which has happen'd.
Yet strong through Nature's universal reign,
The link which binds the parent to the offspring :
The she-wolf knows it, and the tigress owns it.
So that dark man, who, shunning what is vicious,
Ne'er turn'd aside from an atrocity,
Hath still some care left for his hapless offspring.
Therefore 'tis meet, though wayward, light, and stubborn,
That I should do for him all that a son
Can do for sire—and his dark wisdom join'd
To influence my bold courses, 'twill be hard
To break our mutual purpose.—Horses there !　*[Exit.*

ACT III.—SCENE I.

*It is Moonlight.　The Scene is the Beach beneath the Tower which
was exhibited in the first scene,—the Vessel is gone from her
anchorage.　*Auchindrane *and* Philip, *as if dismounted from
their horses, come forward cautiously.*

 Phi. The nags are safely stow'd. Their noise might scare
Let them be safe, and ready when we need them. [him ;
The business is but short.　We 'll call MacLellan,
To wake him, and in quiet bring him forth,
If he be so disposed, for here are waters
Enough to drown, and sand enough to cover him.
But if he hesitate, or fear to meet us,
By heaven I 'll deal on him in Chapeldonan
With my own hand !—
 Auch. Too furious boy ! alarm or noise undoes us :
Our practice must be silent as 't is sudden.
Bethink thee that conviction of this slaughter

Confirms the very worst of accusations
Our foes can bring against us.   Wherefore should we
Who by our birth and fortune mate with nobles,
And are allied with them, take this lad's life,—
His peasant life,—unless to quash his evidence,
Taking such pains to rid him from the world,
Who would, if spared, have fix'd a crime upon us

 Phi. Well, I do own me one of those wise folks,
Who think that when a deed of fate is plann'd,
The execution cannot be too rapid.
But do we still keep purpose ? Is 't determined
He sails for Ireland — and without a wherry ?
Salt water is his passport — is it not so ?

 Auch. I would it could be otherwise !
Might he not go there while in life and limb,
And breathe his span out in another air ?
Many seek Ulster never to return —
Why might this wretched youth not harbour there ?

 Phi. With all my heart.   It is small honour to me
To be the agent in a work like this.—
Yet this poor caitiff, having thrust himself
Into the secrets of a noble house,
And twined himself so closely with our safety,
That we must perish, or that he must die,
I 'll hesitate as little on the action,
As I would do to slay the animal
Whose flesh supplies my dinner.   'Tis as harmless,
That deer or steer, as is this Quentin Blane,
And not more necessary is its death
To our accommodation — so we slay it
Without a moment's pause or hesitation.

 Auch. 'Tis not, my son, the feeling called remorse,
That now lies tugging at this heart of mine,
Engendering thoughts that stop the lifted hand.
Have I not heard John Knox pour forth his thunders
Against the oppressor and the man of blood,
In accents of a minister of vengeance ?
Were not his fiery eyeballs turn'd on me,
As if he said expressly, " Thou 'rt the man ? "
Yet did my solid purpose, as I listen'd,
Remain unshaken as that massive rock.

 Phi. Well, then, I 'll understand 't is not remorse,—
As 't is a foible little known to thee,—
That interrupts thy purpose.   What, then, is it ?
Is 't scorn, or is 't compassion ?   One thing's certain,—
Either the feeling must have free indulgence,
Or fully be subjected to your reason—

There is no room for these same treach'rous courses,
Which men call moderate measures.
We must confide in Quentin, or must slay him.
   Auch. In Ireland he might live afar from us.
   Phi. Among Queen Mary's faithful partisans,
Your ancient enemies, the haughty Hamiltons,
The stern MacDonnells, and resentful Græmes—
With these around him, and with Cassilis' death
Exasperating them against you, think, my father,
What chance of Quentin's silence.
   Auch. Too true—too true.   He is a silly youth, too,
Who had not wit to shift for his own living—
A bashful lover, whom his rivals laugh'd at—
Of pliant temper, which companions play'd on—
A moonlight waker, and a noontide dreamer—
A torturer of phrases into sonnets,
Whom all might lead that chose to praise his rhymes.
   Phi. I marvel that your memory has room
To hold so much on such a worthless subject.
   Auch. Base in himself, and yet so strangely link'd
With me and with my fortunes, that I've studied
To read him through and through, as I would read
Some paltry rhyme of vulgar prophecy,
Said to contain the fortunes of my house;
And let me speak him truly—He is grateful,
Kind, tractable, obedient—a child
Might lead him by a thread—He shall not die!
   Phi. Indeed!—then have we had our midnight ride
To wondrous little purpose.
   Auch.   By the blue heaven,
Thou shalt not murder him, cold selfish sensualist!
Yon pure vault speaks it—yonder summer moon,
With its ten million sparklers, cries, Forbear!
The deep earth sighs it forth—Thou shalt not murder!
Thou shalt not mar the image of thy maker!
Thou shalt not from thy brother take the life,
The gracious gift which God alone can give!
   Phi. Here is a worthy guerdon now, for stuffing
His memory with old saws and holy sayings!
They come upon him in the very crisis,
And when his resolution should be firmest,
They shake it like a palsy.—Let it be,
He'll end at last by yielding to temptation,
Consenting to the thing which must be done,
With more remorse the more he hesitates.—
   (To his Father, who has stood fixed after his last speech)—
Well, sir, 'tis fitting you resolve at last,

How the young clerk should be disposed upon ;
Unless you would ride home to Auchindrane,
And bid them rear the Maiden in the court-yard,
That when Dunbar comes, he have nought to do
But bid us kiss the cushion and the headsman.

AUCH. It is too true—There is no safety for us,
Consistent with the unhappy wretch's life !
In Ireland he is sure to find my enemies.
Arran I've proved—the Netherlands I've tried,
But wilds and wars return him on my hands.

PHI. Yet fear not, father, we'll make surer work ;
The land has caves, the sea has whirlpools,
Where that which they suck in returns no more.

AUCH. I will know nought of it, hard-hearted boy !

PHI. Hard-hearted ! Why—my heart is soft as yours ;
But then they must not feel remorse at once—
We can't afford such wasteful tenderness :
I can mouth forth remorse as well as you.
Be executioner, and I'll be chaplain,
And say as mild and moving things as you can ;
But one of us must keep his steely temper.

AUCH. Do thou the deed—I cannot look on it.

PHI. So be it.   Walk with me—MacLellan brings him.
The boat lies moor'd within that reach of rock,
And 'twill require our greatest strength combined
To launch it from the beach.   Meantime, MacLellan
Brings our man hither.—See the twinkling light
That glances in the tower.

AUCH. Let us withdraw—for should he spy us suddenly,
He may suspect us, and alarm the family.

PHI. Fear not—MacLellan has his trust and confidence,
Bought with a few sweet words and welcomes home.

AUCH. But think you that the Ranger may be trusted?

PHI. I'll answer for him.—Let's go float the shallop.

    [*They go off, and as they leave the Stage,* MACLELLAN
       is seen descending from the Tower with QUENTIN.
       *The former bears a dark lantern.   They come upon
       the Stage.*

MAC. (*showing the light*)—
So—bravely done—that's the last ledge of rocks,
And we are on the sands.—I have broke your slumbers
Somewhat untimely.

QUE.   Do not think so, friend.
These six years past I have been used to stir
When the réveillé rung ; and that, believe me,
Chooses the hours for rousing me at random,
And, having given its summons, yields no license

To indulge a second slumber.   Nay more, I'll tell thee,
That, like a pleased child, I was e'en too happy
For sound repose.
  Mac.   The greater fool were you.
Men should enjoy the moments given to slumber;
For who can tell how soon may be the waking,
Or where we shall have leave to sleep again?
  Que. The God of Slumber comes not at command.
Last night the blood danced merry through my veins:
Instead of finding this our land of Carrick
The dreary waste my fears had apprehended,
I saw thy wife, MacLellan, and thy daughter,
And had a brother's welcome;—saw thee, too,
Renew'd my early friendship with you both,
And felt once more that I had friends and country.
So keen the joy that tingled through my system,
Join'd with the searching powers of yonder wine,
That I am glad to leave my feverish lair,
Although my hostess smooth'd my couch herself,
To cool my brow upon this moonlight beach,
Gaze on the moonlight dancing on the waves.
Such scenes are wont to soothe me into melancholy;
But such the hurry of my spirits now,
That every thing I look on makes me laugh.
  Mac. I've seen but few so gamesome, Master Quentin,
Being roused from sleep so suddenly as you were.
  Que. Why, there's the jest on 't. Your old castle's haunted
In vain the host—in vain the lovely hostess,
In kind addition to all means of rest,
Add their best wishes for our sound repose,
When some hobgoblin brings a pressing message:
Montgomery presently must see his sergeant,
And up gets Hildebrand, and off he trudges.
I can't but laugh to think upon the grin
With which he doff'd the kerchief he had twisted
Around his brows, and put his morion on—
Ha! ha! ha! ha!
  Mac.   I'm glad to see you merry, Quentin.
  Que. Why, faith, my spirits are but transitory,
And you may live with me a month or more,
And never see me smile.   Then some such trifle
As yonder little maid of yours would laugh at,
Will serve me for a theme of merriment—
Even now, I scarce can keep my gravity;
We were so snugly settled in our quarters,
With full intent to let the sun be high
Ere we should leave our beds—and first the one

And then the other's summon'd briefly forth,
To the old tune, " Black Bandsmen, up and march !"
　　Mac. Well, you shall sleep anon — rely upon it —
And make up time misspent.　Meantime, methinks,
You are so merry on your broken slumbers,
You ask'd not why I call'd you.
　　Que.　　　　　　　　　　　I can guess,
You lack my aid to search the weir for seals,
You lack my company to stalk a deer.
Think you I have forgot your silvan tasks,
Which oft you have permitted me to share,
Till days that we were rivals?
　　Mac.　　　　　　　　　You have memory
Of that too? —
　　Que.　　　　　Like the memory of a dream,
Delusion far too exquisite to last.
　　Mac. You guess not then for what I call you forth !
It was to meet a friend —
Que　　　　　　　　What friend? Thyself excepted,
The good old man who's gone to see Montgomery,
And one to whom I once gave dearer title,
I know not in wide Scotland man or woman
Whom I could name a friend.
　　Mac.　　　　　　　　　　　Thou art mistaken.
There is a Baron, and a powerful one ——
　　Que. There flies my fit of mirth.　You have a grave
And alter'd man before you.
　　Mac. Compose yourself, there is no cause for fear, —
He will and must speak with you.
　　Que. Spare me the meeting, Niel, — I cannot see him
Say, I 'm just landed on my native earth ;
Say, that I will not cumber it a day ;
Say, that my wretched thread of poor existence
Shall be drawn out in solitude and exile,
Where never memory of so mean a thing
Again shall cross his path — but do not ask me
To seek or speak again with that dark man !
　　Mac. Your fears are now as foolish as your mirth —
What should the powerful Knight of Auchindrane
In common have with such a man as thou?
　　Que. No matter what — Enough, I will not see him.
　　Mac. He is thy master, and he claims obedience.
　　Que. My master? Ay, my task-master — Ever since
I could write man, his hand hath been upon me ;
No step I 've made but cumber'd with his chain,
And I am weary on 't — I will not see him.
　　Mac. You must and shall — there is no remedy.
　　Que. Take heed that you compel me not to find one,

I've seen the wars since we had strife together;
To put my late experience to the test
Were something dangerous—Ha! I am betray'd!
    [*While the latter part of this dialogue is passing,* Auchin
        drane *and* Philip *enter on the Stage from behind,*
        and suddenly present themselves.
    Auch. What says the runagate?
    Que. (*laying aside all appearance of resistance*)—
Nothing.   You are my fate;
And in a shape more fearfully resistless,
My evil angel could not stand before me.
    Auch. And so you scruple, slave, at my command,
To meet me when I deign to ask thy presence?
    Que. No, sir; I had forgot—I am your bond-slave;
But sure a passing thought of independence,
For which I've seen whole nations doing battle,
Was not, in one who has so long enjoyed it,
A crime beyond forgiveness.
    Auch.   We shall see:
Thou wert my vassal, born upon my land,
Bred by my bounty—It concern'd me highly,
Thou know'st it did—and yet, against my charge,
Again I find thy worthlessness in Scotland.
    Que. Alas! the wealthy and the powerful know not
How very dear to those who have least share in't,
Is that sweet word of country! The poor exile
Feels, in each action of the varied day,
His doom of banishment. The very air
Cools not his brow as in his native land;
The scene is strange, the food is loathly to him;
The language—nay, the music jars his ear.[1]
Why should I, guiltless of the slightest crime,
Suffer a punishment which, sparing life,
Deprives that life of all which men hold dear?
    Auch. Hear ye the serf I bred, begin to reckon
Upon his rights and pleasure! Who am I—
Thou abject, who am I, whose will thou thwartest?
    Phi. Well spoke, my pious sire. There goes remorse!
Let once thy precious pride take fire, and then,
MacLellan, you and I may have small trouble.
    Que. Your words are deadly, and your power resistless;
I'm in your hands—but, surely, less than life
May give you the security you seek,
Without commission of a mortal crime.
    Auch. Who is't would deign to think upon thy life?
I but require of thee to speed to Ireland,
Where thou may'st sojourn for some little space,

    [1] MS.—" The strains of foreign music jar his ear."

Having due means of living dealt to thee,
And, when it suits the changes of the times,
Permission to return.
   QUE.   Noble my lord,
I am too weak to combat with your pleasure;
Yet, O, for mercy's sake, and for the sake
Of that dear land which is our common mother
Let me not part in darkness from my country!
Pass but an hour or two, and every cape,
Headland, and bay, shall gleam with new-born light,
And I'll take boat as gaily as the bird
That soars to meet the morning.
Grant me but this—to show no darker thoughts
Are on your heart than those your speech expresses!
   PHI. A modest favour, friend, is this you ask!
Are we to pace the beach like watermen,
Waiting your worship's pleasure to take boat?
No, by my faith! you go upon the instant.
The boat lies ready, and the ship receives you
Near to the Point of Turnberry.—Come, we wait you;
Bestir you!
   QUE.   I obey.—Then farewell, Scotland!
And Heaven forgive my sins, and grant that mercy,
Which mortal man deserves not!
   AUCH. (*speaks aside to his Son*)—What signal
Shall let me know 'tis done?
   PHI.   When the light is quench'd,
Your fears for Quentin Blane are at an end.—
(*To* QUE.) Come, comrade, come, we must begin our voyage.
   QUE. But when—O when to end it!
          [*He goes off reluctantly with* PHILIP *and* MACLELLAN.
            AUCHINDRANE *stands looking after them. The Moon*
            becomes overclouded, and the Stage dark. AUCHIN-
            DRANE, *who has gazed fixedly and eagerly after those*
            who have left the stage, becomes animated, and speaks.
   AUCH. It is no fallacy!—The night is dark,
The moon has sunk before the deepening clouds;
I cannot on the murky beach distinguish
The shallop from the rocks which lie beside it;
I cannot see tall Philip's floating plume,
Nor trace the sullen brow of Niel MacLellan;
Yet still that caitiff's visage is before me,
With chattering teeth, mazed look, and bristling hair,
As he stood here this moment!—Have I changed
My human eyes for those of some night prowler,
The wolf's, the tiger-cat's, or the hoarse bird's
That spies its prey at midnight? I can see him—
Yes, I can see him, seeing no one else,—

And well it is I do so.   In his absence,
Strange thoughts of pity mingled with my purpose,
And moved remorse within me — But they vanish'd
Whene'er he stood a living man before me;
Then my antipathy awaked within me,
Seeing its object close within my reach,
Till I could scarce forbear him.[1] — How they linger!
The boat's not yet to sea! — I ask myself,
What has the poor wretch done to wake my hatred —
Docile, obedient, and in sufferance patient? —
As well demand what evil has the hare
Done to the hound that courses her in sport.
Instinct infallible supplies the reason —
And that must plead my cause. — The vision's gone!
Their boat now walks the waves; a single gleam,
Now seen, now lost, is all that marks her course;
That soon shall vanish too — then all is over! —
Would it were o'er, for in this moment lies
The agony of ages![2] — Now, 'tis gone —
And all is acted! — No — she breasts again
The opposing wave, and bears the tiny sparkle
Upon her crest — (*A faint cry heard as from seaward.*)
                          Ah! there was fatal evidence,
All's over now, indeed! — The light is quench'd —
And Quentin, source of all my fear, exists not. —
The morning tide shall sweep his corpse to sea,
And hide all memory of this stern night's work.

> [*He walks in a slow and deeply meditative manner
> towards the side of the Stage, and suddenly meets
> MARION, the wife of MACLELLAN, who has de-
> scended from the Castle.*

Now, how to meet Dunbar — Heaven guard my senses!
Stand! who goes there? — Do spirits walk the earth
Ere yet they've left the body!
    MAR.   Is it you,
My Lord, on this wild beach at such an hour?
    AUCH. It is MacLellan's wife, in search of him,
Or of her lover — of the murderer,
Or of the murder'd man. — Go to, Dame Marion;
Men have their hunting-gear to give an eye to,
Their snares and trackings for their game.   But women
Should shun the night air.   A young wife also,
Still more a handsome one, should keep her pillow

---

[1] MS.— ——— "my antipathy,
Strong source of inward hate, arose within me,
Feeling its object was within my reach,
And scarcely could forbear."

[2] ——— "In that moment, o'er his soul
Winters of memory seem'd to roll." — *Byron — The Giaour.*

Till the sun gives example for her wakening.
Come, dame, go back — back to your bed again.
  Mar. Hear me, my lord! there have been sights and sounds
That terrified my child and me — Groans, screams,
As if of dying seamen, came from ocean —
A corpse-light danced upon the crested waves
For several minutes' space, then sunk at once.
When we retired to rest, we had two guests,
Besides my husband Niel — I'll tell your lordship
Who the men were ——
  Auch.   Pshaw, woman, can you think
That I have any interest in your gossips?
Please your own husband, and that you may please him,
Get thee to bed, and shut up doors, good dame.
Were I MacLellan, I should scarce be satisfied
To find thee wandering here in mist and moonlight,
When silence should be in thy habitation,
And sleep upon thy pillow.
  Mar.   Good my lord,
This is a holyday. — By an ancient custom
Our children seek the shore at break of day,
And gather shells, and dance, and play, and sport them
In honour of the Ocean.   Old men say
The custom is derived from heathen times.   Our Isabel
Is mistress of the feast, and you may think
She is awake already, and impatient
To be the first shall stand upon the beach,
And bid the sun good-morrow.
  Auch.   Ay, indeed?
Linger such dregs of heathendom among you?
And hath Knox preach'd, and Wishart died, in vain?
Take notice, I forbid these sinful practices,
And will not have my followers mingle in them.
  Mar. If such your honour's pleasure, I must go
And lock the door on Isabel; she is wilful,
And voice of mine will have small force to keep her
From the amusement she so long has dream'd of.
But I must tell your honour, the old people,
That were survivors of the former race,
Prophesied evil if this day should pass
Without due homage to the mighty Ocean.
  Auch. Folly and Papistry — Perhaps the Ocean
Hath had his morning sacrifice already;
Or can you think the dreadful element,
Whose frown is death, whose roar the dirge of navies,
Will miss the idle pageant you prepare?
I've business for you, too — the dawn advances —
I'd have thee lock thy little child in safety,

And get to Auchindrane before the sun rise;
Tell them to get a royal banquet ready,
As if a king were coming there to feast him.
   MAR. I will obey your pleasure. But my husband ——
   AUCH. I wait him on the beach, and bring him in
To share the banquet.
   MAR.   But he has a friend,
Whom it would ill become him to intrude
Upon your hospitality.
   AUCH. Fear not; his friend shall be made welcome
Should he return with Niel.   [too,
   MAR. He must—he will return—he has no option.
   AUCH. (*apart.*) Thus rashly do we deem of others' des-
He has indeed no option—but he comes not.   [tiny—
Begone on thy commission—I go this way
To meet thy husband.

> [MARION *goes to her Tower, and after entering it, is
> seen to come out, lock the door, and leave the stage,
> as if to execute* AUCHINDRANE'S *commission. He,
> apparently going off in a different direction, has
> watched her from the side of the stage, and on her
> departure speaks.*

   AUCH. Fare thee well, fond woman,
Most dangerous of spies—thou prying, prating,
Spying, and telling woman! I've cut short
Thy dangerous testimony— Hated word!
What other evidence have we cut short,
And by what fated means, this dreary morning!—
Bright lances here and helmets?— I must shift
To join the others.   [*Exit.*

Enter from the other side the SERGEANT, *accompanied with an
Officer and two Pikemen.*

   SER. 'Twas in good time you came; a minute later
The knaves had ta'en my dollars and my life.
   OFF. You fought most stoutly. Two of them were down
Ere we came to your aid.
   SER.   Gramercy, halberd!
And well it happens, since your leader seeks
This Quentin Blane, that you have fall'n on me;
None else can surely tell you where he hides,
Being in some fear, and bent to quit this province.
   OFF. 'Twill do our Earl good service. He has sent
Despatches into Holland for this Quentin.
   SER. I left him two hours since in yonder tower,
Under the guard of one who smoothly spoke,
Although he look'd but roughly— I will chide him
For bidding me go forth with yonder traitor.

Off. Assure yourself 'twas a concerted stratagem.
Montgomery's been at Holyrood for months,
And can have sent no letter—'twas a plan
On you and on your dollars, and a base one,
To which this Ranger was most likely privy;
Such men as he hang on our fiercer barons,
The ready agents of their lawless will;
Boys of the belt, who aid their master's pleasures,
And in his moods ne'er scruple his injunctions.
But haste, for now we must unkennel Quentin;
1 've strictest charge concerning him.
    Ser. Go up, then, to the tower.
You've younger limbs than mine: there shall you find him
Lounging and snoring, like a lazy cur
Before a stable door; it is his practice.
        [*The* Officer *goes up to the Tower, and after knock-
            ing without receiving an answer, turns the key
            which* Marion *had left in the lock, and enters;*
            Isabel, *dressed as if for her dance, runs out and
            descends to the Stage; the* Officer *follows.*
    Off. There's no one in the house, this little maid
Excepted——
    Isa.   And for me, I'm there no longer,
And will not be again for three hours good:
I 'm gone to join my playmates on the sands.
    Off. (*detaining her.*) You shall, when you have told to
            me distinctly
Where are the guests who slept up there last night.
    Isa. Why, there is the old man, he stands beside you,
The merry old man with the glistening hair;
He left the tower at midnight, for my father
Brought him a letter.
    Ser.   In ill hour I left you,
I wish to Heaven that I had stay'd with you!
There is a nameless horror that comes o'er me.—
Speak pretty maiden, tell us what chanced next,
And thou shalt have thy freedom.
    Isa. After you went last night, my father
Grew moody, and refused to doff his clothes,
Or go to bed, as sometimes he will do
When there is aught to chafe him. Until past midnight,
He wander'd to and fro, then call'd the stranger,
The gay young man, that sung such merry songs,
Yet ever look'd most sadly whilst he sung them;
And forth they went together.
    Off.   And you've seen
Or heard nought of them since?

Isa. Seen surely nothing, and I cannot think
That they have lot or share in what I heard.
I heard my mother praying, for the corpse-lights
Were dancing on the waves ; and at one o'clock,
Just as the Abbey steeple toll'd the knell,
There was a heavy plunge upon the waters,
And some one cried aloud for mercy !—mercy !
It was the water-spirit, sure, which promised
Mercy to boat and fisherman, if we
Perform'd to-day's rites duly.   Let me go—
I am to lead the ring.

  Off. (*to* Ser.) Detain her not. She cannot tell us more ;
To give her liberty is the sure way
To lure her parents homeward.—Strahan, take two men,
And should the father or the mother come,
Arrest them both, or either. Auchindrane
May come upon the beach ; arrest him also,
But do not state a cause. I'll back again,
And take directions from my Lord Dunbar.
Keep you upon the beach, and have an eye
To all that passes there.   [*Exeunt separately.*

SCENE II.

Scene changes to a remote and rocky part of the Seabeach.

Enter Auchindrane, *meeting* Philip.

  Auch. The devil's brought his legions to this beach,
That wont to be so lonely ; morions, lances,
Show in the morning beam as thick as glowworms
At summer midnight.

  Phi.   I'm right glad to see them,
Be they whoe'er they may, so they are mortal ;
For I've contended with a lifeless foe,
And I have lost the battle. I would give
A thousand crowns to hear a mortal steel
Ring on a mortal harness.

  Auch. How now! art mad? or hast thou done the turn—
The turn we came for, and must live or die by?

  Phi. 'Tis done, if man can do it ; but I doubt
If this unhappy wretch have Heaven's permission
To die by mortal hands.

  Auch. Where is he?—where's MacLellan?

  Phi.   In the deep—
Both in the deep, and what's immortal of them
Gone to the judgment-seat, where we must meet them.

AUCH. MacLellan dead, and Quentin too?—So be it
To all that menace ill to Auchindrane,
Or have the power to injure!—Thy words
Are full of comfort, but thine eye and look
Have in this pallid gloom a ghastliness,
Which contradicts the tidings of thy tongue.[1]

PHI. Hear me, old man—There *is* a heaven above us,
As you have heard old Knox and Wishart preach,
Though little to your boot.   The dreaded witness
Is slain, and silent.   But his misused body
Comes right ashore, as if to cry for vengeance;
It rides the waters like a living thing,[2]
Erect, as if he trode the waves which bear him.

AUCH. Thou speakest frenzy, when sense is most required.

PHIL. Hear me yet more!—I say I did the deed
With all the coolness of a practised hunter
When dealing with a stag.   I struck him overboard,
And with MacLellan's aid I held his head
Under the waters, while the Ranger tied
The weights we had provided to his feet.
We cast him loose when life and body parted,
And bid him speed for Ireland.   But even then,
As in defiance of the words we spoke,
The body rose upright behind our stern,
One half in ocean, and one half in air,
And tided after as in chase of us.[3]

[1] ——— "This man's brow, like to a title leaf,
Foretels the nature of a tragic volume.
Thou tremblest; and the whiteness in thy cheek
Is apter than thy tongue to tell thy errand."
                                        2d King Henry IV.

[2] ——— "Walks the waters like a thing of life."
                                        Byron—The Corsair.

[3] This passage was probably suggested by a striking one in Southey's *Life of Nelson*, touching the corpse of the Neapolitan Prince Caraccioli, executed on board the Foudroyant, then the great British Admiral's flag-ship, in the bay of Naples in 1799.   The circumstances of Caraccioli's trial and death form, it is almost needless to observe, the most unpleasant chapter in Lord Nelson's history:—

"The body," says Southey, "was carried out to a considerable distance and sunk in the bay, with three double-headed shot, weighing two hundred and fifty pounds, tied to its legs.   Between two or three weeks afterwards, when the King (of Naples) was on board the Foudroyant, a Neapolitan fisherman came to the ship, and solemnly declared, that Caraccioli had risen from the bottom of the sea, and was coming as fast as he could to Naples, swimming half out of the water.   Such an account was listened to like a tale of idle credulity.   The day being fair, Nelson, to please the King, stood out to sea; but the ship had not proceeded far before a body was distinctly seen, upright in the water, and approaching them.   It was recognised to be indeed the corpse of Caraccioli, which had risen and floated, while the great weights attached to the legs kept the body in a position like that of a living man.   A fact so extraordinary astonished the King, and perhaps excited some feelings of superstitious fear, akin to regret.   He gave permission for the body to be taken on shore, and receive Christian burial."—*Life of Nelson*, chap. vi.—ED.

Auch. It was enchantment!—Did you strike at it?

Phi. Once and again.   But blows avail'd no more
Than on a wreath of smoke, where they may break
The column for a moment, which unites
And is entire again.   Thus the dead body
Sunk down before my oar, but rose unharm'd,
And dogg'd us closer still, as in defiance.

Auch. 'T was Hell's own work!——

Phi.   MacLellan then grew restive
And, desperate in his fear, blasphemed aloud,
Cursing us both as authors of his ruin.
Myself was well nigh frantic while pursued
By this dread shape, upon whose ghastly features
The changeful moonbeam spread a grisly light;
And, baited thus, I took the nearest way[1]
To ensure his silence, and to quell his noise;
I used my dagger, and I flung him overboard,
And half expected his dead carcass also
Would join the chase—but he sunk down at once.

Auch. He had enough of mortal sin about him,
To sink an argosy.

Phi. But now resolve you what defence to make,
If Quentin's body shall be recognised;
For 't is ashore already; and he bears
Marks of my handiwork— so does MacLellan.

Auch. The concourse thickens still—Away, away!
We must avoid the multitude.   [*They rush out.*

SCENE III.

*Scene changes to another part of the Beach.   Children are seen
dancing, and Villagers looking on.   Isabel seems to take the
management of the Dance.*

Vil. Wom. How well she queens it, the brave little maiden!

Vil. Ay, they all queen it from their very cradle,
These willing slaves of haughty Auchindrane.
But now I hear the old man's reign is ended;—
'T is well—he has been tyrant long enough.

Second Vil. Finlay, speak low—you interrupt the sports.

Third Vil. Look out to sea—There's something coming
          yonder,
Bound for the beach, will scare us from our mirth.

Fourth Vil. Pshaw! it is but a sea-gull on the wing,
Between the wave and sky.

Third Vil.   Thou art a fool,
Standing on solid land—'t is a dead body.

    [1] MS.—"And, baited by my slave, I used my dagger."

Second Vil. And if it be, he bears him like a live one,
Not prone and weltering like a drowned corpse,
But bolt erect, as if he trode the waters,
And used them as his path.
    Fourth Vil.   It is a merman,
And nothing of this earth, alive or dead.
        (*By degrees all the Dancers break off from their sport,
           and stand gazing to seaward, while an object, imper-
           fectly seen, drifts towards the Beach, and at length
           arrives among the rocks which border the tide.*)
    Third Vil. Perhaps it is some wretch who needs assistance;
Jasper, make in and see.
    Second Vil.   Not I, my friend;
E'en take the risk yourself, you'd put on others.
        (Hildebrand *has entered, and heard the two last words.*)
    Ser. What, are you men?
Fear ye to look on what you must be one day?
I, who have seen a thousand dead and dying
Within a flight-shot square, will teach you how in war
We look upon the corpse when life has left it.
        (*He goes to the back scene, and seems attempting to turn
           the body, which has come ashore with its face down-
           wards.*)
Will none of you come aid to turn the body?
    Isa. You're cowards all.—I'll help thee, good old man.
        (*She goes to aid the* Sergeant *with the body, and pre-
           sently gives a cry, and faints.* Hildebrand *comes
           forward. All crowd round him; he speaks with an
           expression of horror.*)
    Ser. 'Tis Quentin Blane! Poor youth, his gloomy bodings
Have been the prologue to an act of darkness;
His feet are manacled, his bosom stabb'd,
And he is foully murder'd. The proud Knight
And his dark Ranger must have done this deed,
For which no common ruffian could have motive.
    A Pea. Caution were best, old man—Thou art a stranger,
The Knight is great and powerful.
    Ser.   Let it be so.
Call'd on by Heaven to stand forth an avenger,
I will not blench for fear of mortal man.
Have I not seen that when that innocent
Had placed her hands upon the murder'd body,
His gaping wounds,[1] that erst were soak'd with brine,
Burst forth with blood as ruddy as the cloud
Which now the sun doth rise on!
    Pea.   What of that?

---

[1] MS.—"His unblooded wounds," &c.

SER. Nothing that can affect the innocent child,
But murder's guilt attaching to her father,
Since the blood musters in the victim's veins
At the approach of what holds lease from him
Of all that parents can transmit to children.
And here comes one to whom I 'll vouch the circumstance.

The EARL OF DUNBAR *enters with Soldiers and others,
having* AUCHINDRANE *and* PHILIP *prisoners.*

DUN. Fetter the young ruffian and his trait'rous father !
                    (*They are made secure.*)
AUCH. 'T was a lord spoke it—I have known a knight,
Sir George of Home, who had not dared to say so.
DUN. 'Tis Heaven, not I, decides upon your guilt.
A harmless youth is traced within your power,
Sleeps in your Ranger's house—his friend at midnight
Is spirited away.   Then lights are seen,
And groans are heard, and corpses come ashore
Mangled with daggers, while (*to* PHI.) your dagger wears
The sanguine livery of recent slaughter :
Here, too, the body of a murder'd victim,
(Whom none but you had interest to remove,)
Bleeds on a child's approach, because the daughter
Of one the abettor of the wicked deed ;—
All this, and other proofs corroborative,
Call on us briefly to pronounce the doom
We have in charge to utter.
AUCH. If my house perish, Heaven's will be done !
I wish not to survive it ; but, O Philip,
Would one could pay the ransom for us both !
PHI. Father, 'tis fitter that we both should die,
Leaving no heir behind.—The piety
Of a bless'd saint, the morals of an anchorite,
Could not atone thy dark hypocrisy,
Or the wild profligacy I have practised.
Ruin'd our house, and shatter'd be our towers,
And with them end the curse our sins have merited !

"The poet, in his play of Auchindrane, displayed real tragic power, and
soothed all those who cried out before for a more direct story, and less of the
retrospective.   Several of the scenes are conceived and executed with all the
powers of the best parts of ' Waverley.'   The verse, too, is more rough, natural, and nervous, than that of ' Halidon Hill ;' but, noble as the effort was,
it was eclipsed so much by his splendid romances, that the public still com-
plained that he had not done his best, and that his genius was not dramatic."
—*Allan Cunningham.—Athenæum, 14th Dec. 1833.*

END OF AUCHINDRANE.

The House of Aspen.

A TRAGEDY.

ADVERTISEMENT.

THIS attempt at dramatic composition was executed nearly thirty years since, when the magnificent works of Goethe and Schiller were for the first time made known to the British public, and received, as many now alive must remember, with universal enthusiasm. What we admire we usually attempt to imitate; and the author, not trusting to his own efforts, borrowed the substance of the story and a part of the diction from a dramatic romance called "Der Heilige Vehmé" (the Secret Tribunal,) which fills the sixth volume of the "Sagen der Vorzeit" (Tales of Antiquity,) by Beit Weber. The Drama must be termed rather a rifacimento of the original than a translation, since the whole is compressed, and the incidents and dialogue occasionally much varied. The imitator is ignorant of the real name of his ingenious contemporary, and has been informed that of Beit Weber is fictitious.[1]

The late Mr. John Kemble at one time had some desire to bring out the play at Drury-Lane, then adorned by himself and his matchless sister, who were to have supported the characters of the unhappy son and mother: but great objections appeared to this proposal. There was danger that the main spring of the story, — the binding engagements formed by members of the secret tribunal,—might not be sufficiently felt by an English audience, to whom the nature of that singularly mysterious institution was unknown from early association. There was also, according to Mr. Kemble's experienced opinion, too much blood, too much of the dire catastrophe of Tom Thumb, when all die on the stage. It was besides esteemed perilous to place the fifth act and the parade and show of the secret conclave, at the mercy of underlings and scene-shifters, who, by a ridiculous motion, gesture, or accent, might turn what should be grave into farce.

---

[1] George Wachter, who published various works under the pseudonym of *Veit Weber*, was born in 1763, and died in 1837.— ED.

The author, or rather the translator, willingly acquiesced in this reasoning, and never afterwards made any attempt to gain the honour of the buskin. The German taste also, caricatured by a number of imitators, who, incapable of copying the sublimity of the great masters of the school, supplied its place by extravagance and bombast, fell into disrepute, and received a *coup de grace* from the joint efforts of the late lamented Mr. Canning and Mr. Frere. The effect of their singularly happy piece of ridicule called " The Rovers," a mock play which appeared in the Anti-Jacobin, was, that the German school, with its beauties and its defects, passed completely out of fashion, and the following scenes were consigned to neglect and obscurity. Very lately, however, the writer chanced to look them over with feelings very different from those of the adventurous period of his literary life during which they had been written, and yet with such as perhaps a reformed libertine might regard the illegitimate production of an early amour. There is something to be ashamed of, certainly; but, after all, paternal vanity whispers that the child has a resemblance to the father.

To this it need only be added, that there are in existence so many manuscript copies of the following play, that if it should not find its way to the public sooner, it is certain to do so when the author can no more have any opportunity of correcting the press, and consequently at greater disadvantage than at present. Being of too small a size or consequence for a separate publication, the piece is sent as a contribution to the Keepsake, where its demerits may be hidden amid the beauties of more valuable articles. [1]

ABBOTSFORD, 1*st April* 1829.

[1] See *Life of Scott*, vol. ii. pp. 18, 20, 72; iii. 2; ix. 218.

DRAMATIS PERSONÆ.

MEN.

RUDIGER, *Baron of Aspen, an old German Warrior.*

GEORGE OF ASPEN,
HENRY OF ASPEN, } *Sons to Rudiger.*

RODERICK, *Count of Maltingen, Chief of a department of the Invisible Tribunal, and the hereditary enemy of the family of Aspen.*

WILLIAM, *Baron of Wolfstein, Ally of Count Roderic.*

BERTRAM OF EBERSDORF, *Brother to the former Husband of the Baroness of Aspen, disguised as a Minstrel.*

DUKE OF BAVARIA.

WICKERD,
REYNOLD, } *Followers of the House of Aspen.*

CONRAD, *Page of Honour to Henry of Aspen.*

MARTIN, *Squire to George of Aspen.*

HUGO, *Squire to Count Roderic.*

PETER, *an ancient Domestic of Rudiger.*

FATHER LUDOVIC, *Chaplain to Rudiger.*

WOMEN.

ISABELLA, *formerly married to Arnolf of Ebersdorf, now Wife of Rudiger.*

GERTRUDE, *Isabella's Niece, betrothed to Henry.*

Soldiers, Judges of the Invisible Tribunal, &c. &c.

Scene. — The Castle of Ebersdorf in Bavaria, the Ruins of Griefenhaus, and the adjacent Country.

The House of Aspen.

———

ACT I.—SCENE I.

An ancient Gothic Chamber in the Castle of Ebersdorf. Spears, crossbows, and arms, with the horns of buffaloes and of deer, are hung round the wall. An antique buffet with beakers and stone bottles.

RUDIGER, *Baron of Aspen, and his Lady,* ISABELLA, *are discovered sitting at a large oaken table.*

RUD. A plague upon that roan horse !—had he not stumbled with me at the ford after our last skirmish, I had been now with my sons. And yonder the boys are, hardly three miles off, battling with Count Roderic, and their father must lie here like a worm-eaten manuscript in a convent library ! Out upon it ! Out upon it ! Is it not hard that a warrior, who has travelled so many leagues to display the cross on the walls of Zion, should be now unable to lift a spear before his own castle gate !

ISA. Dear husband, your anxiety retards your recovery.

RUD. May be so ; but not less than your silence and melancholy. Here have I sate this month and more, since that cursed fall ! Neither hunting, nor feasting, nor lance-breaking for me ! And my sons—George enters cold and reserved, as if he had the weight of the empire on his shoulders, utters by syllables a cold " How is it with you ?" and shuts himself up for days in his solitary chamber ;— Henry, my cheerful Henry—

ISA. Surely, he at least—

RUD. Even he forsakes me, and skips up the tower staircase like lightning to join your fair ward, Gertrude, on the battlements. I cannot blame him ; for, by my knightly faith, were I in his place, I think even these bruised bones would hardly keep me from her side. Still, however, here I must sit alone.

ISA. Not alone, dear husband. Heaven knows what I would do to soften your confinement.

RUD. Tell me not of that, lady. When I first knew thee, Isabella the fair maid of Arnheim was the joy of her companions, and breathed life wherever she came. Thy father married thee to Arnolf of Ebersdorf — not much with thy will, 'tis true — (*she hides her face.*) Nay — forgive me, Isabella — but that is over — he died, and the ties between us, which thy marriage had broken, were renewed — but the sunshine of my Isabella's light heart returned no more.

Isa. (*weeping.*) Beloved Rudiger, you search my very soul! Why will you recall past times — days of spring that can never return? Do I not love thee more than ever wife loved husband?

Rud. (*stretches out his arms — she embraces him.*) And therefore art thou ever my beloved Isabella. But still, is it not true? — has not thy cheerfulness vanished since thou hast become Lady of Aspen? — Dost thou repent of thy love to Rudiger?

Isa. Alas! no! never! never!

Rud. Then why dost thou herd with monks and priests, and leave thy old knight alone, when, for the first time in his stormy life, he has rested for weeks within the walls of his castle? Hast thou committed a crime from which Rudiger's love cannot absolve thee?

Isa. O many! many!

Rud. Then be this kiss thy penance. And tell me, Isabella, hast thou not founded a convent, and endowed it with the best of thy late husband's lands? Ay, and with a vineyard which I could have prized as well as the sleek monks. Dost thou not daily distribute alms to twenty pilgrims? Dost thou not cause ten masses to be sung each night for the repose of thy late husband's soul?

Isa. It will not know repose.

Rud. Well, well — God's peace be with Arnolf of Ebersdorf! The mention of him makes thee ever sad, though so many years have passed since his death.

Isa. But at present, dear husband, have I not the most just cause for anxiety? — are not Henry and George, our beloved sons, at this very moment, perhaps, engaged in doubtful contest with our hereditary foe, Count Roderic of Maltingen?

Rud. Now, there lies the difference: you sorrow that they are in danger, — I that I cannot share it with them. — Hark! I hear horses' feet on the drawbridge. Go to the window, Isabella.

Isa. (*at the window.*) It is Wickerd, your squire.

Rud. Then shall we have tidings of George and Henry. (*Enter* Wickerd.) How now, Wickerd? Have you come to blows yet?

Wic. Not yet, noble sir.

Rud. Not yet? — Shame on the boys' dallying! — what wait they for?

Wic. The foe is strongly posted, sir knight, upon the Wolfshill, near the ruins of Griefenhaus; therefore your noble son, George of Aspen, greets you well, and requests twenty more men-at-arms, and, after they have joined him, he hopes, with the aid of St. Theodore, to send you news of victory.

Rud. (*attempts to rise hastily.*) Saddle my black barb! — I will head them myself. (*Sits down.*) A murrain on that stumbling roan! I had forgot my dislocated bones. — Call Reynold, Wickerd, and bid him take all whom he can spare from defence of the castle—(WICKERD *is going.*)—and ho, Wickerd! carry with you my black barb, and bid George charge upon him. (*Exit* WICKERD.) Now see, Isabella, if I disregard the boy's safety; I send him the best horse ever knight bestrode. When we lay before Ascalon, indeed, I had a bright bay Persian—Thou dost not heed me.

ISA. Forgive me, dear husband! Are not our sons in danger? Will not our sins be visited upon them? Is not their present situation——

RUD. Situation? I know it well—as fair a field for open fight as I ever hunted over. See here—(*makes lines on the table*)—here is the ancient castle of Griefenhaus in ruins, here the Wolfs-hill; and here the marsh on the right.

ISA. The marsh of Griefenhaus!

RUD. Yes; by that the boys must pass.

ISA. Pass there!—(*Apart.*) Avenging Heaven! thy hand is upon us! [*Exit hastily.*

RUD. Whither now?—whither now?—She is gone. Thus it goes. Peter! Peter! (*Enter* PETER.) Help me to the gallery, that I may see them on horseback. [*Exit, leaning on* PETER.

SCENE II.

The Inner Court of the Castle of Ebersdorf; a Quadrangle, surrounded with Gothic buildings; Troopers, followers of RUDIGER, *pass and repass in haste, as if preparing for an excursion.*

WICKERD *comes forward.*

WIC. What, ho! Reynold! Reynold!—By our Lady, the spirit of the Seven Sleepers is upon him—So ho! not mounted yet? Reynold!

Enter REYNOLD.

REY. Here! here! A devil choke thy bawling! think'st thou old Reynold is not as ready for a skirmish as thou?

WIC. Nay, nay—I did but jest; but, by my sooth, it were a shame should our youngsters have yoked with Count Roderic before we greybeards come.

REY. Heaven forefend! Our troopers are but saddling their horses; five minutes more, and we are in our stirrups, and then let Count Roderic sit fast.

WIC. A plague on him! he has ever lain hard on the skirts of our noble master.

REY. Especially since he was refused the hand of our lady's niece, the pretty Lady Gertrude.

WIC. Ay, marry! would nothing less serve the fox of Maltingen than the lovely lamb of our young Baron Henry? By my

sooth, Reynold, when I look upon these two lovers, they make
me full twenty years younger; and when I meet the man that
would divide them — I say nothing — but let him look to it.

REY. And how fare our young lords?

WIC. Each well in his humour. — Baron George stern and
cold, according to his wont, and his brother as cheerful as ever.

REY. Well — Baron Henry for me.

WIC. Yet George saved thy life.

REY. True — with as much indifference as if he had been
snatching a chestnut out of the fire. Now Baron Henry wept
for my danger and my wounds. Therefore George shall ever
command my life, but Henry my love.

WIC. Nay, Baron George shows his gloomy spirit even by the
choice of a favourite.

REY. Ay — Martin, formerly the squire of Arnolf of Ebersdorf,
his mother's first husband. I marvel he could not have fitted
himself with an attendant from among the faithful followers of
his worthy father, whom Arnolf and his adherents used to hate
as the Devil hates holy water. But Martin is a good soldier,
and has stood toughly by George in many a hard brunt.

WIC. The knave is sturdy enough, but so sulky withal — I have
seen, brother Reynold, that when Martin showed his moody visage
at the banquet, our noble mistress has dropped the wine she was
raising to her lips, and exchanged her smiles for a ghastly frown,
as if sorrow went by sympathy, as kissing goes by favour.

REY. His appearance reminds her of her first husband, and
thou hast well seen *that* makes her ever sad.

WIC. Dost thou marvel at that? She was married to Arnolf
by a species of force, and they say that before his death he
compelled her to swear never to espouse Rudiger. The priests
will not absolve her for the breach of that vow, and therefore
she is troubled in mind. For, d'ye mark me, Reynold ——

(Bugle sounds.)

REY. A truce to your preaching! — To horse! and a blessing
on our arms!

WIC. St. George grant it!   [*Exeunt.*

SCENE III.

*The Gallery of the Castle, terminating in a large Balcony com-
manding a distant prospect.— Voices, bugle-horns, kettle-drums,
trampling of horses, &c. are heard without.*

RUDIGER, *leaning on* PETER, *looks from the balcony.*
GERTRUDE *and* ISABELLA *are near him.*

RUD. There they go at length — look, Isabella! look, my pretty
Gertrude — these are the iron-handed warriors who shall tell

Roderick what it will cost him to force thee from my protection. (*Flourish without,* RUDIGER *stretches his arms from the balcony.*) Go, my children, and God's blessing with you !— Look at my black barb, Gertrude. That horse shall let daylight in through a phalanx, were it twenty pikes deep. Shame on it that I cannot mount him ! Seest thou how fierce old Reynold looks !

GER. I can hardly know my friends in their armour. (*The bugles and kettle-drums are heard as at a greater distance.*)

RUD. Now I could tell every one of their names, even at this distance ; ay, and were they covered, as I have seen them, with dust and blood. He on the dapple-grey is Wickerd — a hardy fellow, but somewhat given to prating. That is young Conrad who gallops so fast, page to thy Henry, my girl. — (*Bugles, &c. at a greater distance still.*)

GER. Heaven guard them ! Alas ! the voice of war, that calls the blood into your cheeks, chills and freezes mine.

RUD. Say not so — it is glorious, my girl, glorious ! See how their armour glistens as they wind round yon hill ! how their spears glimmer amid the long train of dust ! Hark! you can still hear the faint notes of their trumpets—(*Bugles very faint.*)—And Rudiger, old Rudiger with the iron arm, as the crusaders used to call me, must remain behind with the priests and the women. Well ! well !—(*Sings*)—

> " It was a knight to battle rode,
> And as his war-horse he bestrode."

Fill me a bowl of wine, Gertrude ; and do thou, Peter, call the minstrel who came hither last night —(*Sings*)—

> " Off rode the horseman, dash, sa, sa !
> And stroked his whiskers, tra, la, la!" —

(PETER *goes out.* — RUDIGER *sits down, and* GERTRUDE *helps him with wine.*) Thanks, my love. It tastes ever best from thy hand. Isabella, here is glory and victory to our boys! — (*Drinks.*) — Wilt thou not pledge me?

ISA. To their safety ! — and God grant it! — (*Drinks.*)

Enter BERTRAM *as a Minstrel, with a Boy bearing his harp.—*
Also PETER.

RUD. Thy name, minstrel?

BER. Minhold, so please you.

RUD. Art thou a German?

BER. Yes, noble sir; and of this province.

RUD. Sing me a song of battle.—(BERTRAM *sings to the harp.*)

RUD. Thanks, minstrel : well sung, and lustily. What say'st thou, Isabella ?

ISA. I marked him not.

RUD. Nay, in sooth, you are too anxious. Cheer up !—And

thou, too, my lovely Gertrude! In a few hours thy Henry shall return, and twine his laurels into a garland for thy hair. He fights for thee, and he must conquer.

GER. Alas! must blood be spilled for a silly maiden!

RUD. Surely: for what should knights break lances, but for honour and ladies' love — ha, minstrel?

BER. So please you — also to punish crimes.

RUD. Out upon it!—wouldst have us executioners, minstrel! Such work would disgrace our blades. We leave malefactors to the Secret Tribunal.

ISA. Merciful God! Thou hast spoken a word, Rudiger, of dreadful import.

GER. They say that, unknown and invisible themselves, these awful judges are ever present with the guilty; that the past and the present misdeeds, the secrets of the confessional — nay, the very thoughts of the heart, are before them; that their doom is as sure as that of fate, the means and executioners unknown.

RUD. They say true — the secrets of that association, and the names of those who compose it, are as inscrutable as the grave: we only know that it has taken deep root, and spread its branches wide.   I sit down each day in my hall, nor know I how many of these secret judges may surround me, all bound by the most solemn vow to avenge guilt.   Once, and but once, a knight, at the earnest request and inquiries of the emperor, hinted that he belonged to the society: the next morning he was found slain in a forest : the poniard was left in the wound, and bore this label— " Thus do the Invisible Judges punish treachery."

GER. Gracious! aunt, you grow pale.

ISA. A slight indisposition only.

RUD. And what of it all ? We know our hearts are open to our Creator: shall we fear any earthly inspection? Come to the battlements ; there we shall soonest descry the return of our warriors.   [*Exit* RUDIGER, *with* GERTRUDE *and* PETER.

ISA. Minstrel, send the chaplain hither. —(*Exit* BERTRAM.) Gracious Heaven ! the guileless innocence of my niece, the manly honesty of my upright-hearted Rudiger, become daily tortures to me.   While he was engaged in active and stormy exploits, fear for his safety, joy when he returned to his castle, enabled me to disguise my inward anguish from others. But from myself— Judges of blood, that lie concealed in noontide as in midnight, who boast to avenge the hidden guilt, and to penetrate the recesses of the human breast, how blind is your penetration, how vain your dagger and your cord, compared to the conscience of the sinner !

Enter FATHER LUDOVIC.

LUD. Peace be with you, lady !

ISA. It is not with me : it is thy office to bring it.

Lud. And the cause is the absence of the young knights?

Isa. Their absence and their danger.

Lud. Daughter, thy hand has been stretched out in bounty to the sick and to the needy;—thou hast not denied a shelter to the weary, nor a tear to the afflicted. Trust in their prayers, and in those of the holy convent thou hast founded; peradventure they will bring back thy children to thy bosom.

Isa. Thy brethren cannot pray for me or mine. Their vow binds them to pray night and day for another — to supplicate, without ceasing, the Eternal Mercy for the soul of one who — Oh, only Heaven knows how much he needs their prayer!

Lud. Unbounded is the mercy of Heaven. The soul of thy former husband ——

Isa. I charge thee, priest, mention not the word.—(*Apart.*) Wretch that I am, the meanest menial in my train has power to goad me to madness!

Lud. Hearken to me, daughter; thy crime against Arnolf of Ebersdorf cannot bear in the eye of Heaven so deep a dye of guilt.

Isa. Repeat that once more—say once again that it cannot— cannot bear so deep a dye. Prove to me that ages of the bitterest penance, that tears of the dearest blood, can erase such guilt;— Prove but *that* to me, and I will build thee an abbey which shall put to shame the fairest fane in Christendom.

Lud. Nay, nay, daughter, your conscience is over tender. Sup- posing that, under dread of the stern Arnolf, you swore never to marry your present husband, still the exacting such an oath was unlawful, and the breach of it venial.

Isa. (*resuming her composure.*) Be it so, good father; I yield to thy better reasons. And now tell me, has thy pious care achieved the task I entrusted to thee?

Lud. Of superintending the erection of thy new hospital for pilgrims? I have, noble lady: and last night the minstrel now in the castle lodged there.

Isa. Wherefore came he then to the castle?

Lud. Reynold brought the commands of the Baron.

Isa. Whence comes he, and what is his tale? When he sung before Rudiger, I thought that long before I had heard such tones—seen such a face.

Lud. It is possible you might have seen him, lady, for he boasts to have been known to Arnolf of Ebersdorf, and to have lived formerly in this castle. He enquires much after *Martin*, Arnolf's squire.

Isa. Go, Ludov'c—go q ick, good father, seek him out, give him this purse, and bid him leave the castle, and speed him on his way.

Lud. May I ask why, noble lady?

Isa. Thou art inquisitive, priest: I honour the servants of God, but I foster not the prying spirit of a monk. Begone!

Lud. But the Baron, lady, will expect a reason why I dismiss his guest?

Isa. True, true—(*recollecting herself;*)—pardon my warmth, good father,—I was thinking of the cuckoo that grows too big for the nest of the sparrow, and strangles its foster-mother. Do no such birds roost in convent-walls?

Lud. Lady, I understand you not.

Isa. Well, then, say to the Baron, that I have dismissed long ago all the attendants of the man of whom thou hast spoken, and that I wish to have none of them beneath my roof.

Lud. (*inquisitively.*) Except Martin?

Isa. (*sharply.*) Except Martin—who saved the life of my son George. Do as I command thee.   [*Exit.*

Manet Ludovic.

Lud. Ever the same—stern and peremptory to others as rigorous to herself; haughty even to me, to whom, in another mood, she has knelt for absolution, and whose knees she has bathed in tears. I cannot fathom her. The unnatural zeal with which she performs her dreadful penances cannot be religion, for shrewdly I guess she believes not in their blessed efficacy. Well for her that she is the foundress of our convent, otherwise we might not have erred in denouncing her as a heretic! [*Exit.*

———

ACT II.—SCENE I.

A Woodland Prospect.— Through a long avenue, half grown up by brambles, are discerned in the back-ground the Ruins of the ancient Castle of Griefenhaus.— The distant noise of battle is heard during this scene.

Enter George of Aspen, *armed with a battle-axe in his hand, as from horseback. He supports* Martin, *and brings him forward.*

Geo. Lay thee down here, old friend. The enemy's horsemen will hardly take their way among these brambles, through which I have dragged thee.

Mar. Oh, do not leave me! leave me not an instant! My moments are now but few, and I would profit by them.

Geo. Martin, you forget yourself and me—I must back to the field.

Mar. (*attempts to rise.*) Then drag me back thither also; I cannot die but in your presence—I dare not be alone. Stay, to give peace to my parting soul.

Geo. I am no priest, Martin. (*Going.*)

Mar. (*raising himself with great pain.*) Baron George of Aspen, I saved thy life in battle: for that good deed, hear me but one moment.

Geo. I hear thee, my poor friend. (*Returning.*)

Mar. But come close—very close. See'st thou, sir knight—this wound I bore for thee—and this—and this—dost thou not remember?

Geo. I do.

Mar. I have served thee since thou wast a child—served thee faithfully—was never from thy side.

Geo. Thou hast.

Mar. And now I die in thy service.

Geo. Thou may'st recover.

Mar. I cannot. By my long service—by my scars—by this mortal gash, and by the death that I am to die—Oh, do not hate me for what I am now to unfold!

Geo. Be assured I can never hate thee.

Mar. Ah! thou little knowest——Swear to me thou wilt speak a word of comfort to my parting soul!

Geo. (*takes his hand.*) I swear I will. (*Alarm and shouting.*) But be brief—thou knowest my haste.

Mar. Hear me, then. I was the squire, the beloved and favourite attendant, of Arnolf of Ebersdorf. Arnolf was savage as the mountain bear. He loved the Lady Isabel, but she requited not his passion. She loved thy father; but her sire, old Arnheim, was the friend of Arnolf, and she was forced to marry him. By midnight, in the chapel of Ebersdorf, the ill omened rites were performed;—her resistance, her screams were in vain. These arms detained her at the altar till the nuptial benediction was pronounced. Canst thou forgive me?

Geo. I do forgive thee. Thy obedience to thy savage master has been obliterated by a long train of services to his widow.

Mar. Services!—ay, bloody services! for they commenced—do not quit my hand—they commenced with the murder of my master. (George *quits his hand, and stands aghast in speechless horror.*) Trample on me! pursue me with your dagger! I aided your mother to poison her first husband!—I thank Heaven, it is said.

Geo. My mother? Sacred Heaven! Martin, thou ravest—the fever of thy wound has distracted thee.

Mar. No! I am not mad! would to God I were!—Try me! Yonder is the Wolfshill—yonder the old castle of Griefenhaus—and yonder is the hemlock marsh (*in a whisper*) where I gathered the deadly plant that drugged Arnold's cup of death. (George *traverses the stage in the utmost agitation, and sometimes stands over* Martin *with his hands clasped together.*) Oh, had you seen him when the potion took effect!—had you heard his ravings, and seen the contortions of his ghastly visage!—He died furious and impenitent, as he lived; and went—where I am shortly to go. You do not speak?

GEO. (*with exertion.*) Miserable wretch! how can I?
MAR. Can you not forgive me?
GEO. May God pardon thee!—I cannot!
MAR. I saved thy life——
GEO. For that, take my curse! (*He snatches up his battle-axe, and rushes out to the side from which the noise is heard.*)
MAR. Hear me! yet more—more horror! (*Attempts to rise, and falls heavily. A loud alarm.*)

Enter WICKERD, *hastily*

WIC. In the name of God, Martin, lend me thy brand!
MAR. Take it.
WIC. Where is it?
MAR. (*looks wildly at him.*) In the chapel at Ebersdorf, or buried in the hemlock marsh.
WIC. The old grumbler is crazy with his wounds. Martin, if thou hast a spark of reason in thee, give me thy sword. The day goes sore against us.
MAR. There it lies. Bury it in the heart of thy master George; thou wilt do him a good office—the office of a faithful servant.

Enter CONRAD.

CON. Away, Wickerd! to horse, and pursue! Baron George has turned the day; he fights more like a fiend than a man: he has unhorsed Roderic, and slain six of his troopers—they are in headlong flight—the hemlock marsh is red with their gore! (MARTIN *gives a deep groan, and faints.*) Away! away! (*They hurry off, as to the pursuit.*)

Enter RODERIC OF MALTINGEN, *without his helmet, his arms disordered and broken, holding the truncheon of a spear in his hand; with him,* BARON WOLFSTEIN.

ROD. A curse on fortune, and a double curse upon George of Aspen! Never, never will I forgive him my disgrace—overthrown like a rotten trunk before a whirlwind!
WOLF. Be comforted, Count Roderic; it is well we have escaped being prisoners. See how the troopers of Aspen pour along the plain, like the billows of the Rhine! It is good we are shrouded by the thicket.
ROD. Why took he not my life, when he robbed me of my honour and of my love? Why did his spear not pierce my heart, when mine shivered on his arms like a frail bulrush? (*Throws down the broken spear.*) Bear witness, heaven and earth, I outlive this disgrace only to avenge!
WOLF. Be comforted;—the knights of Aspen have not gained a bloodless victory. And see, there lies one of George's followers —(*seeing* MARTIN.)

Rod. His squire Martin. If he be not dead, we will secure him: he is the depositary of the secrets of his master. Arouse thee, trusty follower of the house of Aspen!

Mar. (*reviving.*) Leave me not! leave me not, Baron George! my eyes are darkened with agony! I have not yet told all.

Wolf. The old man takes you for his master.

Rod. What wouldst thou tell?

Mar. Oh, I would tell all the temptations by which I was urged to the murder of Ebersdorf!

Rod. Murder!—this is worth marking. Proceed.

Mar. I loved a maiden, daughter of Arnolf's steward; my master seduced her—she became an outcast, and died in misery: I vowed vengeance—and I did avenge her.

Rod. Hadst thou accomplices?

Mar. None but thy mother.

Rod. The Lady Isabella!

Mar. Ay. She hated her husband: he knew her love to Rudiger, and when she heard that thy father was returned from Palestine, her life was endangered by the transports of his jealousy. Thus prepared for evil, the fiend tempted us, and we fell.

Rod. (*breaks into a transport.*) Fortune! thou hast repaid me all! Love and vengeance are my own!—Wolfstein, recall our followers! quick, sound thy bugle. (Wolfstein *sounds.*)

Mar. (*stares wildly round.*) That was no note of Aspen—Count Roderic of Maltingen—Heaven! what have I said!

Rod. What thou canst not recall.

Mar. Then is my fate decreed!—'Tis as it should be! in this very place was the poison gather'd—'t is retribution!

Enter three or four Soldiers of Roderic.

Rod. Secure this wounded trooper; bind his wounds, and guard him well: carry him to the ruins of Griefenhaus, and conceal him till the troopers of Aspen have retired from the pursuit;—look to him, as you love your lives.

Mar. (*led off by soldiers.*) Ministers of vengeance! my hour is come! [*Exeunt.*

Rod. Hope, joy, and triumph, once again are ye mine! Welcome to my heart, long-absent visitants! One lucky chance has thrown dominion into the scale of the house of Maltingen, and Aspen kicks the beam.

Wolf. I foresee, indeed, dishonour to the family of Aspen, should this wounded squire make good his tale.

Rod. And how thinkest thou this disgrace will fall on them?

Wolf. Surely, by the public punishment of Lady Isabella.

Rod. And is that all?

Wolf. What more?

Rod. Shortsighted that thou art, is not George of Aspen, as

well as thou, a member of the holy and invisible circle, over which I preside?

WOLF. Speak lower, for God's sake!—these are things not to be mentioned before the sun.

ROD. True: but stands he not bound by the most solemn oath religion can devise, to discover to the tribunal whatever conceal-ed iniquity shall come to his knowledge, be the perpetrator whom he may—ay, were that perpetrator his own father—or mother; and can you doubt that he has heard Martin's confession?

WOLF. True: but, blessed Virgin! do you think he will accuse his own mother before the invisible judges?

ROD. If not, he becomes forsworn, and, by our law, must die. Either way my vengeance is complete—perjured or parricide, I care not; but, as the one or the other shall I crush the haughty George of Aspen.

WOLF. Thy vengeance strikes deep.

ROD. Deep as the wounds I have borne from this proud family. Rudiger slew my father in battle—George has twice baffled and dishonoured my arms, and Henry has stolen the heart of my be-loved. But no longer can Gertrude now remain under the care of the murderous dam of this brood of wolves; far less can she wed the smooth-cheeked boy, when this scene of villany shall be disclosed. (*Bugle.*)

WOLF. Hark! they sound a retreat: let us go deeper into the wood.

ROD. The victors approach! I shall dash their triumph!—Issue the private summons for convoking the members this very evening; I will direct the other measures.

WOLF. What place?

ROD. The old chapel in the ruins of Griefenhaus, as usual.

[Exuent.

SCENE II.

Enter GEORGE OF ASPEN, *as from the pursuit.*

GEO. (*comes slowly forward.*) How many wretches have sunk under my arm this day, to whom life was sweet, though the wretched bondsmen of Count Roderic! And I—I who sought death beneath every lifted battle-axe, and offered my breast to every arrow—I am cursed with victory and safety. Here I left the wretch —— Martin!—Martin!—what, ho! Martin!—— Mother of God! he is gone! Should he repeat the dreadful tale to any other——Martin!—He answers not. Perhaps he has crept into the thicket, and died there—were it so, the horrible secret is only mine.

Enter HENRY OF ASPEN, *with* WICKERD, REYNOLD, *and followers.*

HEN. Joy to thee, brother! though, by St. Francis, I would not gain another field at the price of seeing thee fight with such reckless desperation. Thy safety is little less than miraculous.

REY. By'r Lady, when Baron George struck, I think he must have forgot that his foes were God's creatures. Such furious doings I never saw, and I have been a trooper these forty-two years come St. Barnaby——

GEO. Peace! Saw any of you Martin?

WIC. Noble sir, I left him here not long since.

GEO. Alive or dead?

WIC. Alive, noble sir, but sorely wounded. I think he must be prisoner, for he could not have budged else from hence.

GEO. Heedless slave! why didst thou leave him?

HEN. Dear brother, Wickerd acted for the best: he came to our assistance and the aid of his companions.

GEO. I tell thee, Henry, Martin's safety was of more importance than the lives of any ten that stand here.

WIC. (*muttering.*) Here's much to do about an old crazy trencher-shifter.

GEO. What mutterest thou?

WIC. Only, sir knight, that Martin seemed out of his senses when I left him, and has perhaps wandered into the marsh, and perished there.

GEO. How—out of his senses? Did he speak to thee?— (*apprehensively.*)

WIC. Yes, noble sir.

GEO. Dear Henry, step for an instant to yon tree—thou wilt see from thence if the foe rally upon the Wolfshill. (HENRY *retires.*) And do you (*to the soldiers*) stand back. (*He brings* WICKERD *forward.*)

GEO. (*with marked apprehension.*) What did Martin say to thee, Wickerd?—tell me, on thy allegiance.

WIC. Mere ravings, sir knight—offered me his sword to kill you.

GEO. Said he aught of killing any one else?

WIC. No: the pain of his wound seemed to have brought on a fever.

GEO. (*clasps his hands together.*) I breathe again!—I spy comfort! Why could I not see as well as this fellow, that the wounded wretch may have been distracted? Let me at least think so till proof shall show the truth (*aside.*)—Wickerd, think not on what I said—the heat of the battle had chafed my blood. Thou hast wished for the Nether farm at Ebersdorf—it shall be thine.

WIC. Thanks, my noble lord.

Re-enter HENRY.

HEN. No—they do not rally—they have had enough of it;—but Wickerd and Conrad shall remain, with twenty troopers and a score of crossbowmen, and scour the woods towards Griefenhaus, to prevent the fugitives from making head. We will, with the rest, to Ebersdorf. What say you, brother?

GEO. Well ordered. Wickerd, look thou search everywhere for Martin: bring him to me dead or alive; leave not a nook of the wood unsought.

WIC. I warrant you, noble sir, I shall find him, could he clew himself up like a dormouse.

HEN. I think he must be prisoner.

GEO. Heaven forfend! Take a trumpet, Eustace (*to an attendant;*) ride to the castle of Maltingen, and demand a parley. If Martin is prisoner, offer any ransom: offer ten — twenty — all our prisoners in exchange.

EUS. It shall be done, sir knight.

HEN. Ere we go, sound trumpets—strike up the song of victory.

SONG.

Joy to the victors! the sons of old Aspen!
 Joy to the race of the battle and scar!
Glory's proud garland triumphantly grasping;
 Generous in peace, and victorious in war.
   Honour acquiring,
   Valour inspiring,
Bursting, resistless, through foemen they go:
   War-axes wielding,
   Broken ranks yielding,
Till from the battle proud Roderic retiring,
Yields in wild rout the fair palm to his foe.

Joy to each warrior, true follower of Aspen!
 Joy to the heroes that gain'd the bold day!
Health to our wounded, in agony gasping;
 Peace to our brethren that fell in the fray!
   Boldly this morning,
   Roderic's power scorning,
Well for their chieftain their blades did they wield:
   Joy blest them dying,
   As Maltingen flying,
Low laid his banners, our conquest adorning,
Their death-clouded eyeballs descried on the field!

Now to our home, the proud mansion of Aspen,
 Bend we, gay victors, triumphant away;
There each fond damsel, her gallant youth clasping,
 Shall wipe from his forehead the stains of the fray.

Listening the prancing
Of horses advancing;
E'en now on the turrets our maidens appear.
Love our hearts warming,
Songs the night charming,
Round goes the grape in the goblet gay dancing;
Love, wine, and song, our blithe evening shall cheer!

Hen. Now spread our banners, and to Ebersdorf in triumph! We carry relief to the anxious, joy to the heart of the aged, brother George. (*Going off.*)

Geo. Or treble misery and death. (*Apart, and following slowly.*)

The music sounds, and the followers of Aspen begin to file across the Stage. The curtain falls.

ACT III.—SCENE I.

Castle of Ebersdorf.

Rudiger, Isabella, *and* Gertrude.

Rud. I prithee, dear wife, be merry. It must be over by this time, and happily, otherwise the bad news had reached us.

Isa. Should we not, then, have heard the tidings of the good?

Rud. Oh! these fly slower by half. Besides, I warrant all of them engaged in the pursuit. Oh! not a page would leave the skirts of the fugitives till they were fairly beaten into their holds; but had the boys lost the day, the stragglers had made for the castle. Go to the window, Gertrude: seest thou anything?

Ger. I think I see a horseman.

Isa. A single rider? then I fear me much.

Ger. It is only Father Ludovic.

Rud. A plague on thee! didst thou take a fat friar on a mule for a trooper of the house of Aspen?

Ger. But yonder is a great cloud of dust.

Rud. (*eagerly.*) Indeed!

Ger. It is only the wine sledges going to my aunt's convent.

Rud. The devil confound the wine sledges, and the mules and the monks! Come from the window, and torment me no longer, thou seer of strange sights.

Ger. Dear uncle, what can I do to amuse you? Shall I tell you what I dreamed this morning?

Rud. Nonsense!—but say on; anything is better than silence.

Ger. I thought I was in the chapel, and they were burying my aunt Isabella alive. And who, do you think, aunt, were the gravediggers who shovelled in the earth upon you? Even Baron George and old Martin.

Isa. (*appears shocked.*) Heaven! what an idea!

Ger. Do but think of my terror—and Minhold the minstrel played all the while to drown your screams.

Rud. And old Father Ludovic danced a saraband, with the steeple of the new convent upon his thick skull by way of mitre. A truce to this nonsense. Give us a song, my love, and leave thy dreams and visions.

Ger. What shall I sing to you?

Rud. Sing to me of war.

Ger. I cannot sing of battle; but I will sing you the Lament of Eleanor of Toro, when her lover was slain in the wars.

Isa. Oh, no laments, Gertrude.

Rud. Then sing a song of mirth.

Isa. Dear husband, is this a time for mirth?

Rud. Is it neither a time to sing of mirth nor of sorrow? Isabella would rather hear Father Ludovic chant the "De profundis."

Ger. Dear uncle, be not angry. At present, I can only sing the lay of poor Eleanor. It comes to my heart at this moment as if the sorrowful mourner had been my own sister.

SONG.[1]

Sweet shone the sun on the fair lake of Toro,
  Weak were the whispers that waved the dark wood,
As a fair maiden, bewilder'd in sorrow,
  Sigh'd to the breezes, and wept to the flood.—
"Saints from the mansion of bliss lowly bending,
  Virgin, that hear'st the poor suppliant's cry,
Grant my petition, in anguish ascending,
  My Frederick restore, or let Eleanor die."

Distant and faint were the sounds of the battle;
  With the breezes they rise, with the breezes they fail,
Till the shout, and the groan, and the conflict's dread rattle,
  And the chase's wild clamour came loading the gale.
Breathless she gazed through the woodland so dreary,
  Slowly approaching, a warrior was seen;
Life's ebbing tide mark'd his footsteps so weary,
  Cleft was his helmet, and woe was his mien.

"Save thee, fair maid, for our armies are flying;
  Save thee, fair maid, for thy guardian is low;
Cold on yon heath thy bold Frederick is lying,
  Fast through the woodland approaches the foe."

(*The voice of* Gertrude *sinks by degrees, till she
bursts into tears.*)

Rud. How now, Gertrude?

Ger. Alas! may not the fate of poor Eleanor at this moment be mine?

[1] Compare with "The Maid of Toro," *ante*, vol. ii. p. 324.

Rud. Never, my girl, never!—(*Military music is heard.*) Hark! hark! to the sounds that tell thee so.—(*All rise and run to the window.*)

Rud. Joy! joy! they come, and come victorious.—(*The chorus of the war-song is heard without.*) Welcome! welcome! once more have my old eyes seen the banners of the house of Maltingen trampled in the dust.—Isabella, broach our oldest casks: wine is sweet after war.

Enter Henry, *followed by* Reynold *and Troopers.*

Rud. Joy to thee, my boy! let me press thee to this old heart!

Isa. Bless thee, my son!—(*embraces him*)—Oh! how many hours of bitterness are compensated by this embrace! Bless thee, my Henry!—Where hast thou left thy brother?

Hen. Hard at hand: by this he is crossing the drawbridge. Hast thou no greetings for me, Gertrude? (*Goes to her.*)

Ger. I joy not in battles.

Rud. But she had tears for thy danger.

Hen. Thanks, my gentle Gertrude. See, I have brought back thy scarf from no inglorious field.

Ger. It is bloody!—(*shocked.*)

Rud. Dost start at that, my girl? Were it his own blood, as it is that of his foes, thou shouldst glory in it.—Go, Reynold, make good cheer with thy fellows.   [*Exit* Reynold *and Soldiers.*

Enter George *pensively,*

Geo. (*goes straight to* Rudiger.) Father, thy blessing!

Rud. Thou hast it, boy.

Isa. (*rushes to embrace him—he avoids her.*) How! art thou wounded?

Geo. No.

Rud. Thou lookest deadly pale.

Geo. It is nothing.

Isa. Heaven's blessing on my gallant George.

Geo. (*aside.*) Dares she bestow a blessing? Oh, Martin's tale was frenzy!

Isa. Smile upon us for once, my son!—darken not thy brow on this day of gladness! Few are our moments of joy—should not my sons share in them?

Geo. (*aside.*) She has moments of joy—it *was* frenzy then!

Isa. Gertrude, my love, assist me to disarm the knight. (*She loosens and takes off his casque.*)

Ger. There is one, two, three hacks, and none has pierced the steel.

Rud. Let me see—let me see. A trusty casque!

Ger. Else hadst thou gone.

Isa. I will reward the armourer with its weight in gold.

GEO. (*aside.*) She *must* be innocent.

GER. And.Henry's shield is hacked, too! Let me show it to you, uncle.—(*She carries* HENRY'S *to* RUDIGER.)

RUD. Do, my love; and come hither, Henry,—thou shalt tell me how the day went.—(HENRY *and* GERTRUDE *converse apart with* RUDIGER; GEORGE *comes forward;* ISABELLA *comes to him.*)

ISA. Surely, George, some evil has befallen thee. Grave thou art ever, but so dreadfully gloomy—

GEO. *Evil*, indeed.—(*Aside.*) Now for the trial.

ISA. Has your loss been great?

GEO. No!—Yes!—(*Apart.*) I cannot do it.

ISA. Perhaps some friend lost?

GEO. It must be.—*Martin is dead.*—(*He regards her with apprehension, but steadily, as he pronounces these words.*

ISA. (*starts, then shows a ghastly expression of joy.*) Dead!

GEO. (*almost overcome by his feelings.*) Guilty! Guilty! (*apart.*)

ISA. (*without observing his emotion.*) Didst thou say dead?

GEO. Did I—no—I only said mortally wounded.

ISA. Wounded? only wounded? Where is he? Let me fly to him.—(*Going.*)

GEO. (*sternly.*) Hold, lady!—Speak not so loud!—Thou canst not see him!—He is a prisoner.

ISA. A prisoner, and wounded? Fly to his deliverance! Offer wealth, lands, castles—all our possessions, for his ransom. Never shall I know peace till these walls, or till the grave secure him.

GEO. (*apart.*) Guilty! Guilty!

Enter PETER.

PET. Hugo, squire to the Count of Maltingen, has arrived with a message.

RUD. I will receive him in the hall.

[*Exit, leaning on* GERTRUDE *and* HENRY.

ISA. Go, George—see after Martin.

GEO. (*firmly.*) No—I have a task to perform; and though the earth should open and devour me alive, I will accomplish it. But first—but first—Nature, take thy tribute.—(*He falls on his mother's neck, and weeps bitterly.*)

ISA. George! my son! for Heaven's sake, what dreadful frenzy!

GEO. (*walks two turns across the stage, and composes himself.*) Listen, mother!—I knew a knight in Hungary, gallant in battle, hospitable and generous in peace. The king gave him his friendship, and the administration of a province; that province was infested by thieves and murderers. You mark me?—

ISA. Most heedfully.

GEO. The knight was sworn—bound by an oath the most dreadful that can be taken by man—to deal among offenders, even-handed, stern and impartial justice. Was it not a dreadful vow?

Isa. (*with an affectation of composure.*) Solemn, doubtless, as the oath of every magistrate.

Geo. And inviolable?

Isa. Surely — inviolable.

Geo. Well — it happened, that when he rode out against the banditti, he made a prisoner. And who, think you, that prisoner was?

Isa. I know not (*with increasing terror.*)

Geo. (*trembling, but proceeding rapidly.*) His own twin-brother, who sucked the same breasts with him, and lay in the bosom of the same mother; his brother whom he loved as his own soul — What should that knight have done unto his brother?

Isa. (*almost speechless.*) Alas! what did he do?

Geo. He did (*turning his head from her, and with clasped hands)* what I can never do: — he did his duty.

Isa. My son! my son! — Mercy! Mercy! (*Clings to him.*)

Geo. Is it then true?

Isa. What?

Geo. What Martin said? (Isabella *hides her face.*) It is true!

Isa. (*looks up with an air of dignity.*) Hear, Framer of the laws of nature! the mother is judged by the child. — (*Turns towards him*) — Yes, it is true — true that, fearful of my own life, I secured it by the murder of my tyrant. Mistaken coward! I little knew on what terrors I ran, to avoid one moment's agony. — Thou hast the secret!

Geo. Knowest thou to whom thou hast told it?

Isa. To my son.

Geo. No! No! to an executioner!

Isa. Be it so — go, proclaim my crime, and forget not my punishment. Forget not that the murderess of her husband has dragged out years of hidden remorse, to be brought at last to the scaffold by her own cherished son! Thou art silent.

Geo. The language of Nature is no more! How shall I learn another?

Isa. Look upon me, George! Should the executioner be abashed before the criminal — look upon me, my son — from my soul do I forgive thee!

Geo. Forgive me what?

Isa. What thou dost meditate — Be vengeance heavy, but let it be secret — add not the death of a father to that of the sinner! Oh! Rudiger! Rudiger! innocent cause of all my guilt and all my woe, how wilt thou tear thy silver locks when thou shalt hear her guilt whom thou hast so often clasped to thy bosom — hear her infamy proclaimed by the son of thy fondest hopes — (*weeps.*)

Geo. (*struggling for breath.*) Nature will have utterance. — Mother, dearest mother, I will save you or perish! (*throws himself into her arms.*) Thus fall my vows.

Isa. Man thyself! I ask not safety from thee. Never shall it be said, that Isabella of Aspen turned her son from the path of duty, though his footsteps must pass over her mangled corpse. Man thyself!

Geo. No! no! The ties of Nature were knit by God himself. Cursed be the stoic pride that would rend them asunder, and call it virtue!

Isa. My son! My son!—How shall I behold thee hereafter? (*Three knocks are heard upon the door of the apartment.*)

Geo. Hark! One—two—three. Roderic, thou art speedy!
(*Apart.*)

Isa. (*opens the door.*) A parchment stuck to the door with a poniard! (*Opens it.*) Heaven and earth!—a summons from the Invisible Judges!—(*Drops the parchment.*)

Geo. (*reads with emotion*)—" Isabella of Aspen, accused of murder by poison, we conjure thee, by the cord and by the steel, to appear this night before the avengers of blood, who judge in secret and avenge in secret, like the Deity. As thou art innocent or guilty, so be thy deliverance."—Martin, Martin, thou hast played false!

Isa. Alas! whither shall I fly?

Geo. Thou canst not fly!—instant death would follow the attempt—a hundred thousand arms would be raised against thy life—every morsel thou didst taste, every drop which thou didst drink, the very breeze of heaven that fanned thee, would come loaded with destruction! One chance of safety is open:—obey the summons.

Isa. And perish? Yet why should I still fear death? Be it so.

Geo. No—I have sworn to save you. I will not do the work by halves. Does any one save Martin know of the dreadful deed?

Isa. None.

Geo. Then go—assert your innocence, and leave the rest to me.

Isa. Wretch that I am! How can I support the task you would impose?

Geo. Think on my father. Live for him: he will need all the comfort thou canst bestow. Let the thought that his destruction is involved in thine, carry thee through the dreadful trial.

Isa. Be it so. For Rudiger I have lived—for him I will continue to bear the burden of existence: but the instant that my guilt comes to his knowledge shall be the last of my life. Ere I would bear from him one glance of hatred or of scorn, this dagger should drink my blood. (*Puts the poniard into her bosom.*)

Geo. Fear not—he can never know. No evidence shall appear against you.

Isa. How shall I obey the summons, and where find the terrible judgment-seat?

Geo. Leave that to the judges. Resolve but to obey, and a conductor will be found. Go to the chapel, there pray for your sins and for mine. (*He leads her out and returns.*) — Sins, indeed! I break a dreadful vow, but I save the life of a parent; and the penance I will do for my perjury shall appal even the judges of blood.

Enter REYNOLD.

REY. Sir Knight, the messenger of Count Roderick desires to speak with you.

GEO. Admit him.

Enter HUGO.

HUG. Count Roderic of Maltingen greets you. He says he will this night hear the bat flutter and the owlet scream; and he bids me ask if thou also wilt listen to the music.

GEO. I understand him. I will be there.

HUG. And the count says to you, that he will not ransom your wounded squire, though you would down-weigh his best horse with gold. But you may send him a confessor, for the count says he will need one.

GEO. Is he so near death?

HUG. Not as it seems to me: he is weak through loss of blood; but since his wound was dressed, he can both stand and walk. . Our count has a notable balsam, which has recruited him much.

GEO. Enough — I will send a priest. — (*Exit* HUGO.) — I fathom his plot. He would add another witness to the tale of Martin's guilt. But no priest shall approach him. Reynold, thinkest thou not we could send one of the troopers, disguised as a monk, to aid Martin in making his escape?

REY. Noble sir, the followers of your house are so well known to those of Maltingen, that I fear it is impossible.

GEO. knowest thou of no stranger who might be employed? His reward shall exceed even his hopes.

REY. So please you — I think the minstrel could well execute such a commission: he is shrewd and cunning, and can write and read like a priest.

GEO. Call him — (*Exit* REYNOLD.) — If this fails, I must employ open force. Were Martin removed, no tongue can assert the bloody truth.

Enter MINSTREL.

GEO. Come hither, Minhold. Hast thou courage to undertake a dangerous enterprise?

BER. My life, sir Knight, has been one scene of danger and of dread. I have forgotten how to fear.

GEO. Thy speech is above thy seeming. Who art thou?

BER. An unfortunate knight, obliged to shroud myself under this disguise.

GEO. What is the cause of thy misfortunes?

BER. I slew, at a tournament, a prince, and was laid under the ban of the empire.

GEO. I have interest with the emperor. Swear to perform what task I shall impose on thee, and I will procure the recall of the ban.

BER. I swear.

GEO. Then take the disguise of a monk, and go with the follower of Count Roderick, as if to confess my wounded squire Martin. Give him thy dress, and remain in prison in his stead. Thy captivity shall be short, and I pledge my knightly word I will labour to execute my promise, when thou shalt have leisure to unfold thy history.

BER. I will do as you direct. Is the life of your squire in danger.

GEO. It is, unless thou canst accomplish his release.

BER. I will essay it.   [*Exit.*

GEO. Such are the mean expedients to which George of Aspen must now resort. No longer can I debate with Roderick in the field. The depraved, the perjured knight must contend with him only in the arts of dissimulation and treachery. Oh, mother! mother! the most bitter consequence of thy crime has been the birth of thy first-born! But I must warn my brother of the impending storm. Poor Henry, how little can thy gay temper anticipate evil! What, ho there! (*Enter an Attendant.*) Where is Baron Henry?

ATT. Noble sir, he rode forth, after a slight refreshment, to visit the party in the field.

GEO. Saddle my steed; I will follow him.

ATT. So please you, your noble father has twice demanded your presence at the banquet.

GEO. It matters not — say that I have ridden forth to the Wolfshill. Where is thy lady?

ATT. In the chapel, sir knight.

GEO. 'Tis well — saddle my bay-horse — (*apart*) — for the last time.   [*Exit.*

ACT IV.—SCENE I.

The wood of Griefenhaus, with the ruins of the Castle. A nearer view of the Castle than in Act Second, but still at some distance.

Enter RODERIC, WOLFSTEIN, *and Soldiers, as from a reconnoitring party.*

WOLF. They mean to improve their success, and will push their advantage far. We must retreat betimes, Count Roderic.

Rod. We are safe here for the present. They make no immediate motion of advance. I fancy neither George nor Henry are with their party in the wood.

Enter Hugo.

Hug. Noble sir, how shall I tell what has happened?

Rod. What?

Hug. Martin has escaped.

Rod. Villain, thy life shall pay it! (*Strikes at* Hugo — *is held by* Wolfstein.)

Wolf. Hold, hold, Count Roderic! Hugo may be blameless.

Rod. Reckless slave! how came he to escape?

Hug. Under the disguise of a monk's habit, whom by your orders we brought to confess him.

Rod. Has he been long gone?

Hug. An hour and more since he passed our sentinels, disguised as the chaplain of Aspen: but he walked so slowly and feebly, I think he cannot yet have reached the posts of the enemy.

Rod. Where is the treacherous priest?

Hug. He waits his doom not far from hence.

Rod. Drag him hither. — (*Exit* Hugo.) — The miscreant that snatched the morsel of vengeance from the lion of Maltingen, shall expire under torture.

Re-enter Hugo, *with* Bertram *and Attendants.*

Rod. Villain! what tempted thee, under the garb of a minister of religion, to steal a criminal from the hand of justice?

Ber. I am no villain, Count Roderic; and I only aided the escape of one wounded wretch whom thou didst mean to kill basely.

Rod. Liar and slave! thou hast assisted a murderer, upon whom justice had sacred claims.

Ber. I warn thee again, Count, that I am neither liar nor slave. Shortly I hope to tell thee I am once more thy equal.

Rod. Thou! Thou!——

Ber. Yes!—the name of Bertram of Ebersdorf was once not unknown to thee.

Rod. (*astonished.*) Thou Bertram! the brother of Arnold of Ebersdorf, first husband of the Baroness Isabella of Aspen?

Ber. The same.

Rod. Who, in a quarrel at a tournament, many years since, slew a blood-relation of the emperor, and was laid under the ban?

Ber. The same.

Rod. And who has now, in the disguise of a priest, aided the escape of Martin, squire to George of Aspen?

Ber. The same—the same.

Rod. Then, by the holy cross of Cologne, thou hast set at liberty the murderer of thy brother Arnolf!

BER. How! What! I understand thee not!

ROD. Miserable plotter!—Martin, by his own confession, as Wolfstein heard, avowed having aided Isabella in the murder of her husband. I had laid such a plan of vengeance as should have made all Germany shudder. And thou hast counteracted it—thou, the brother of the murdered Arnolf!

BER. Can this be so, Wolfstein?

WOLF. I heard Martin confess the murder.

BER. Then am I indeed unfortunate!

ROD. What, in the name of evil, brought thee here?

BER. I am the last of my race. When I was outlawed, as thou knowest, the lands of Ebersdorf, my rightful inheritance, were declared forfeited, and the Emperor bestowed them upon Rudiger when he married Isabella. I attempted to defend my domain, but Rudiger—Hell thank him for it—enforced the ban against me at the head of his vassals, and I was constrained to fly. Since then I have warred against the Saracens in Spain and Palestine.

ROD. But why didst thou return to a land where death attends thy being discovered?

BER. Impatience urged me to see once more the land of my nativity, and the towers of Ebersdorf. I came there yesterday, under the name of the minstrel Minhold.

ROD. And what prevailed on thee to undertake to deliver Martin?

BER. George, though I told not my name, engaged to procure the recall of the ban: besides, he told me Martin's life was in danger, and I accounted the old villain to be the last remaining follower of our house. But, as God shall judge me, the tale of horror thou hast mentioned I could not have even suspected. Report ran, that my brother died of the plague.

WOLF. Raised for the purpose, doubtless, of preventing attendance upon his sick-bed, and an inspection of his body.

BER. My vengeance shall be dreadful as its cause! The usurpers of my inheritance, the robbers of my honour, the murderers of my brother, shall be cut off, root and branch!

ROD. Thou art, then, welcome here; especially if thou art still a true brother to our invisible order.

BER. I am.

ROD. There is a meeting this night on the business of thy brother's death. Some are now come. I must despatch them in pursuit of Martin.

Enter HUGO.

HUG. The foes advance, sir knight.

ROD. Back! back to the ruins! Come with us, Bertram; on the road thou shalt hear the dreadful history.   [*Exeunt.*

From the opposite side enter GEORGE, HENRY, WICKERD,
CONRAD, *and Soldiers.*

GEO. No news of Martin yet?

WIC. None, sir knight.

GEO. Nor of the minstrel?

WIC. None.

GEO. Then he has betrayed me, or is prisoner — misery either
way.   Begone, and search the wood, Wickerd.

        [Exeunt WICKERD *and followers.*

HEN. Still this dreadful gloom on thy brow, brother?

GEO. Ay! what else?

HEN. Once thou thoughtest me worthy of thy friendship.

GEO. Henry, thou art young—

HEN. Shall I therefore betray thy confidence?

GEO. No! but thou art gentle and well-natured. Thy mind
cannot even support the burden which mine must bear, far less
wilt thou approve the means I shall use to throw it off.

HEN. Try me.

GEO. I may not.

HEN. Then thou dost no longer love me.

GEO. I love thee,— and because I love thee, I will not involve
thee in my distress.

HEN. I will bear it with thee.

GEO. Shouldst thou share it, it would be doubled to me!

HEN. Fear not,—I will find a remedy.

GEO. It would cost thee peace of mind, here and hereafter.

HEN. I take the risk.

GEO. It may not be, Henry. Thou wouldst become the con-
fidant of crimes past—the accomplice of others to come.

HEN. Shall I guess?

GEO. I charge thee, no!

HEN. I must. Thou art one of the secret judges.

GEO. Unhappy boy! what hast thou said?

HEN. Is it not so?

GEO. Dost thou know what the discovery has cost thee?

HEN. I care not.

GEO. He who discovers any part of our mystery must himself
become one of our number.

HEN. How so?

GEO. If he does not consent, his secrecy will be speedily en-
sured by his death. To that we are sworn—take thy choice!

HEN. Well, are you not banded in secret to punish those offenders whom the sword of justice cannot reach, or who are
shielded from its stroke by the buckler of power?

GEO. Such is indeed the purpose of our fraternity; but the end
is pursued through paths dark, intricate, and slippery with blood;

who is he that shall tread them with safety? Accursed be the hour in which I entered the labyrinth, and doubly accursed that in which thou too must lose the cheerful sunshine of a soul without a mystery!

HEN. Yet for thy sake will I be a member.

GEO. Henry, thou didst rise this morning a free man; no one could say to thee, " Why dost thou so?" Thou layest thee down to-night the veriest slave that ever tugged at an oar—the slave of men whose actions will appear to thee savage and incomprehensible, and whom thou must aid against the world, upon peril of thy throat.

HEN. Be it so. I will share your lot.

GEO. Alas, Henry! Heaven forbid! But since thou hast by a hasty word fettered thyself, I will avail myself of thy bondage. Mount thy fleetest steed, and hie thee this very night to the Duke of Bavaria. He is chief and paramount of our chapter. Show him this signet and this letter; tell him that matters will be this night discussed concerning the house of Aspen. Bid him speed him to the assembly, for he well knows the president is our deadly foe. He will admit thee a member of our holy body.

HEN. Who is the foe whom you dread?

GEO. Young man, the first duty thou must learn is implicit and blind obedience.

HEN. Well! I shall soon return and see thee again.

GEO. Return, indeed, thou wilt: but for the rest—well! that matters not.

HEN. I go: thou wilt set a watch here?

GEO. I will. (HENRY *going.*) Return my dear Henry!—let me embrace thee!—Shouldst thou not see me again——

HEN. Heaven! what mean you?

GEO. Nothing. The life of mortals is precarious; and, should we not meet again, take my blessing and this embrace—and this—(*embraces him warmly.*) And now haste to the duke. (*Exit* HENRY.) Poor youth, thou little knowest what thou hast undertaken. But if Martin has escaped, and if the duke arrives, they will not dare to proceed without proof.

Re-enter WICKERD *and followers.*

WIC. We have made a follower of Maltingen prisoner, Baron George, who reports that Martin has escaped.

GEO. Joy! joy! such joy as I can now feel! Set him free for the good news—and, Wickerd, keep a good watch in this spot all night. Send out scouts to find Martin, lest he should not be able to reach Ebersdorf.

WIC. I shall, noble sir.—(*The kettle-drums and trumpets flourish as for setting the watch: the scene closes.*

SCENE II.

The Chapel at Ebersdorf, an ancient Gothic building.

ISABELLA *is discovered rising from before the altar, on which burn two tapers.*

ISA. I cannot pray. Terror and guilt have stifled devotion. The heart must be at ease—the hands must be pure when they are lifted to Heaven. Midnight is the hour of summons: it is now near. How can I pray, when I go resolved to deny a crime which every drop of my blood could not wash away! And my son! Oh! he will fall the victim of my crime!—Arnolf! Arnolf! thou art dreadfully avenged! (*Tap at the door.*) The footstep of my dreadful guide. (*Tap again.*) My courage is no more. (*Enter* GERTRUDE *by the door.*) Gertrude! is it only thou? (*embraces her.*)

GER. Dear aunt, leave this awful place; it chills my very blood. My uncle sent me to call you to the hall.

ISA. Who is in the hall?

GER. Only Reynold and the family, with whom my uncle is making merry.

ISA. Sawest thou no strange faces?

GER. No—none but friends.

ISA. Art thou sure of that? Is George there?

GER. No, nor Henry; both have ridden out. I think they might have staid one day at least. But come, aunt, I hate this place; it reminds me of my dream. See, yonder was the spot where methought they were burying you alive, below yon monument (*pointing.*)

ISA. (*starting.*) The monument of my first husband! Leave me, leave me, Gertrude. I follow in a moment. (*Exit* GERTRUDE.) Ay, there he lies! forgetful alike of his crimes and injuries!— insensible, as if this chapel had never rung with my shrieks, or the castle resounded to his parting groans! When shall I sleep so soundly? (*As she gazes on the monument, a figure muffled in black appears from behind it.*)— Merciful God! is it a vision, such as has haunted my couch! (*it approaches: she goes on with mingled terror and resolution.*) Ghastly phantom! art thou the restless spirit of one who died in agony, or art thou the mysterious being that must guide me to the presence of the avengers of blood? (*Figure bends its head and beckons.*)—To-morrow! To-morrow! I cannot follow thee now! (*Figure shows a dagger from beneath its cloak.*) Compulsion! I understand thee: I will follow. (*She follows the figure a little way; he turns and wraps a black veil round her head, and takes her hand: then both exeunt behind the monument.*)

SCENE III.

The Wood of Griefenhaus.—A watch-fire, round which sit WICK-
ERD, CONRAD, *and others, in their watch-cloaks.*

WIC. The night is bitter cold.

CON. Ay, but thou hast lined thy doublet well with old Rhenish.

WIC. True; and I'll give you warrant for it.—(*Sings*)—

(RHEIN-WEIN LIED.)

What makes the troopers' frozen courage muster?
　　The grapes of juice divine.
Upon the Rhine, upon the Rhine they cluster:
　　Oh, blessed be the Rhine!

Let fringe and furs, and many a rabbit skin, sirs,
　　Bedeck your Saracen;
He'll freeze without what warms our hearts within, sirs,
　　When the night-frost crusts the fen.

But on the Rhine, but on the Rhine they cluster,
　　The grapes of juice divine,
That make our troopers' frozen courage muster:
　　Oh, blessed be the Rhine!

CON. Well sung, Wickerd!—thou wert ever a jovial soul.

Enter a Trooper or two more.

WIC. Hast thou made the rounds, Frank?

FRANK. Yes, up to the hemlock marsh. It is a stormy night.
The moon shone on the Wolfshill, and on the dead bodies with
which to-day's work has covered it. We heard the spirit of the
house of Maltingen wailing over the slaughter of its adherents:
I durst go no farther.

WIC. Hen-hearted rascal! The spirit of some old raven, who
was picking their bones.

CON. Nay, Wickerd, the churchmen say there are such things.

FRANK. Ay, and Father Ludovic told us last sermon, how the
devil twisted the neck of ten farmers at Kletterbach, who refused
to pay Peter's pence.

WIC. Yes, some church devil, no doubt.

FRANK. Nay, old Reynold says, that in passing, by midnight,
near the old chapel at our castle, he saw it all lighted up, and
heard a chorus of voices sing the funeral service.

ANOTHER SOLDIER. Father Ludovic heard the same.

WIC. Hear me, ye hare-livered boys! Can you look death in
the face in battle, and dread such nursery bugbears? Old Reynold saw his vision in the strength of the grape. As for the
chaplain, far be it from me to name the spirit which visits him;

but I know what I know, when I found him confessing Bertrand's pretty Agnes in the chestnut grove.

Con. But, Wickerd, though I have often heard of strange tales which I could not credit, yet there is one in our family so well attested, that I almost believe it. Shall I tell it you?

All Soldiers. Do! do tell it, gentle Conrad!

Wic. And I will take t'other sup of Rhenish to fence against the horrors of the tale.

Con. It is about my own uncle and godfather, Albert of Horsheim.

Wic. I have seen him — he was a gallant warrior.

Con. Well! He was long absent in the Bohemian wars. In an expedition he was benighted, and came to a lone house on the edge of a forest: he and his followers knocked repeatedly for entrance in vain. They forced the door, but found no inhabitants.

Frank. And they made good their quarters?

Con. They did: and Albert retired to rest in an upper chamber. Opposite to the bed on which he threw himself was a large mirror. At midnight he was awaked by deep groans: he cast his eyes upon the mirror, and saw——

Frank. Sacred Heaven! Heard you nothing?

Wic. Ay, the wind among the withered leaves. Go on, Conrad. Your uncle was a wise man.

Con. That's more than grey hairs can make other folks.

Wic. Ha! stripling, art thou so malapert? Though thou art Lord Henry's page, I shall teach thee who commands this party.

All Soldiers. Peace, peace, good Wickerd: let Conrad proceed.

Con. Where was I?

Frank. About the mirror

Con. True. My uncle beheld in the mirror the reflection of a human face, distorted and covered with blood. A voice pronounced articulately, "It is yet time." As the words were spoken, my uncle discerned in the ghastly visage the features of his own father.

Soldier. Hush! By St. Francis, I heard a groan. (*They start up all but* Wickerd.)

Wic. The croaking of a frog, who has caught cold in this bitter night, and sings rather more hoarsely than usual.

Frank. Wickerd, thou art surely no Christian. (*They sit down, and close round the fire.*)

Con. Well — my uncle called up his attendants, and they searched every nook of the chamber, but found nothing. So they covered the mirror with a cloth, and Albert was left alone: but hardly had he closed his eyes, when the same voice proclaimed, "It is now too late;" the covering was drawn aside, and he saw the figure ——

Frank. Merciful Virgin! It comes. (*All rise.*)
Wic. Where? what?
Con. See yon figure coming from the thicket!

Enter Martin, *in the monk's dress, much disordered; his face
is very pale, and his steps slow.*

Wic. (*levelling his pike.*) Man or devil, which thou wilt, thou
shalt feel cold iron, if thou budgest a foot nearer. (Martin
stops.) Who art thou?—what dost thou seek?
Mar. To warm myself at your fire. It is deadly cold.
Wic. See there, ye cravens, your apparition is a poor be-
nighted monk: sit down, father. (*They place* Martin *by the fire.*)
By heaven! it is Martin—our Martin!—Martin, how fares it
with thee? We have sought thee this whole night.
Mar. So have many others (*vacantly.*)
Con. Yes, thy master.
Mar. Did you see him too?
Con. Whom? Baron George?
Mar. No; my first master, Arnolf of Ebersdorf.
Wic. He raves.
Mar. He passed me but now in the wood, mounted upon his
old black steed; its nostrils breathed smoke and flame; neither
tree nor rock-stopped him. He said, " Martin, thou wilt retnrn
this night to my service!"
Wic. Wrap thy cloak around him, Francis; he is distracted
with cold and pain. Dost thou not recollect me, old friend?
Mar. Yes, you are the butler at Ebersdorf: you have the
charge of the large gilded cup, embossed with the figures of the
twelve apostles. It was the favourite goblet of my old master.
Con. By our Lady, Martin, thou must be distracted indeed,
to think our master would intrust Wickerd with the care of the
cellar.
Mar. I know a face so like the apostate Judas on that cup—
I have seen the likeness when I gazed on a mirror.
Wic. Try to go to sleep, dear Martin; it will relieve thy brain.
(*Footsteps are heard in the wood.*) To your arms! (*They take
their arms.*)

Enter two Members *of the Invisible Tribunal, muffled
in their cloaks.*

Con. Stand! Who are ye?
1st Mem. Travellers benighted in the wood.
Wic. Are ye friends to Aspen or Maltingen?
1st Mem. We enter not into their quarrel: we are friends to
the right.
Wic. Then are ye friends to us, and welcome to pass the
night by our fire.

2d MEM. Thanks. (*They approach the fire, and regard* MAR-TIN *very earnestly.*)

CON. Hear ye any news abroad?

2d MEM. None; but that oppression and villany are rife and rank as ever.

WIC. The old complaint.

1st MEM. No! never did former age equal this in wickedness; and yet, as if the daily commission of enormities were not enough to blot the sun, every hour discovers crimes which have lain concealed for years.

CON. Pity the Holy Tribunal should slumber in its office.

2d MEM. Young man, it slumbers not. When criminals are ripe for its vengeance, it falls like the bolt of Heaven.

MAR. (*attempting to rise.*) Let me be gone.

CON. (*detaining him.*) Whither now, Martin?

MAR. To mass.

1st MEM. Even now, we heard a tale of a villain, who, ungrateful as the frozen adder, stung the bosom that had warmed him into life.

MAR. Conrad, bear me off—I would be away from these men.

CON. Be at ease, and strive to sleep.

MAR. Too well I know I shall never sleep again.

2d MEM. The wretch of whom we speak became, from revenge and lust of gain, the murderer of the master whose bread he did eat.

WIC. Out upon the monster!

1st MEM. For nearly thirty years was he permitted to cumber the ground. The miscreant thought his crime was concealed; but the earth which groaned under his footsteps—the winds which passed over his unhallowed head—the stream which he polluted by his lips—the fire at which he warmed his blood-stained hands—every element bore witness to his guilt.

MAR. Conrad, good youth—lead me from hence, and I will show thee where, thirty years since, I deposited a mighty bribe. (*Rises.*)

CON. Be patient, good Martin.

WIC. And where was the miscreant seized?—(*The two* MEM-BERS *suddenly lay hands on* MARTIN, *and draw their daggers; the* Soldiers *spring to their arms.*)

1st MEM. On this very spot.

WIC. Traitors, unloose your hold!

1st MEM. In the name of the Invisible Judges, I charge ye, impede us not in our duty.—(*All sink their weapons, and stand motionless.*)

MAR. Help! help!

1st MEM. Help him with your prayers!

    [*He is dragged off. The scene shuts.*

ACT V.—SCENE 1.

The subterranean Chapel of the Castle of Griefenhaus. It seems deserted, and in decay. There are four entrances, each defended by an iron portal. At each door stands a Warder clothed in black, and masked, armed with a naked sword. During the whole scene they remain motionless on their posts. In the centre of the chapel is the ruinous Altar, half sunk in the ground, on which lie a large book, a dagger, and a coil of ropes, beside two lighted tapers. Antique stone benches of different heights around the chapel. In the back scene is seen a dilapidated entrance into the Sacristy, which is quite dark.
Various Members of the Invisible Tribunal enter by the four different doors of the chapel. Each whispers something as he passes the Warder, which is answered by an inclination of the head. The costume of the Members is a long black robe, capable of muffling the face: some wear it in this manner; others have their faces uncovered, unless on the entrance of a stranger: they place themselves in profound silence upon the stone benches.

Enter Count Roderic, *dressed in a scarlet cloak of the same form with those of the other Members. He takes his place on the most elevated bench.*

Rod. Warders, secure the doors! (*The doors are barred with great care.*) Herald, do thy duty!—(*Members all rise—Herald stands by the altar.*)

Her. Members of the Invisible Tribunal, who judge in secret, and avenge in secret, like the Deity, are your hearts free from malice, and your hands from blood-guiltiness?—(*All the Members incline their heads.*)

Rod. God pardon our sins of ignorance, and preserve us from those of presumption.—(*Again the Members solemnly incline their heads.*)

Her. To the east, and to the west, and to the north, and to the south, I raise my voice; wherever there is treason, wherever there is blood-guiltiness, wherever there is sacrilege, sorcery, robbery, or perjury, there let this curse alight, and pierce the marrow and the bone. Raise then your voices, and say with me, Woe! woe, unto offenders!

All. Woe! woe!— (*Members sit down.*)

Her. He who knoweth of an unpunished crime, let him stand forth as bound by his oath when his hand was laid upon the dagger and upon the cord, and call to the assembly for vengeance!

Mem. (*rises, his face covered.*) Vengeance! vengeance! vengeance!

Rod. Upon whom dost thou invoke vengeance?

Accuser. Upon a brother of this order, who is forsworn and perjured to its laws.

Rod. Relate his crime.

Accu. This perjured brother was sworn, upon the steel and upon the cord, to denounce malefactors to the judgment-seat, from the four quarters of heaven, though it were the spouse of his heart, or the son whom he loved as the apple of his eye: yet did he conceal the guilt of one who was dear unto him; he folded up the crime from the knowledge of the tribunal; he removed the evidence of guilt, and withdrew the criminal from justice. What does his perjury deserve?

Rod. Accuser, come before the altar; lay thy hand upon the dagger and the cord, and swear to the truth of thy accusation.

Accu. (*his hand on the altar.*) I swear!

Rod. Wilt thou take upon thyself the penalty of perjury, should it be found false?

Accu. I will.

Rod. Brethren, what is your sentence?—(*The Members confer a moment in whispers—a silence.*)

Eldest Mem. Our voice is, that the perjured brother merits death.

Rod. Accuser, thou hast heard the voice of the assembly; name the criminal.

Accu. George, Baron of Aspen.—(*A murmur in the assembly.*)

A Mem. (*suddenly rising.*) I am ready, according to our holy laws, to swear, by the steel and the cord, that George of Aspen merits not this accusation, and that it is a foul calumny.

Accu. Rash man! gagest thou an oath so lightly?

Mem. I gage it not lightly. I proffer it in the cause of innocence and virtue.

Accu. What if George of Aspen should not himself deny the charge?

Mem. Then would I never trust man again.

Accu. Hear him, then bear witness against himself — (*throws back his mantle.*)

Rod. Baron George of Aspen!

Geo. The same—prepared to do penance for the crime of which he stands self-accused.

Rod. Still, canst thou disclose the name of the criminal whom thou hast rescued from justice, on that condition alone, thy brethren may save thy life.

Geo. Thinkest thou I would betray, for the safety of my life, a secret I have preserved at the breach of my word?—No! I have weighed the value of my obligation—I will not discharge it — but most willingly will I pay the penalty!

Rod. Retire, George of Aspen, till the assembly pronounce judgment

Geo. Welcome be your sentence!—I am weary of your yoke of iron. A light beams on my soul. Woe to those who seek justice in the dark haunts of mystery and of cruelty! She dwells in the broad blaze of the sun, and mercy is ever by her side. Woe to those who would advance the general weal by trampling upon the social affections! they aspire to be more than men— they shall become worse than tigers. I go: better for me your altars should be stained with my blood, than my soul blackened with your crimes.   [*Exit* George *by the ruinous door in the back scene, into the sacristy.*

Rod. Brethren, sworn upon the steel and upon the cord, to judge and to avenge in secret, without favour and without pity, what is your judgment upon George of Aspen, self-accused of perjury, and resistance to the laws of our fraternity?—(*Long and earnest murmurs in the assembly.*)

Rod. Speak your doom.

Eldest Mem. George of Aspen has declared himself perjured; —the penalty of perjury is death!

Rod. Father of the secret judges—Eldest among those who avenge in secret—take to thee the steel and the cord:—let the guilty no longer cumber the land.

Eldest Mem. I am fourscore and eight years old. My eyes are dim, and my hand is feeble; soon shall I be called before the throne of my Creator;—How shall I stand there, stained with the blood of such a man?

Rod. How wilt thou stand before that throne, loaded with the guilt of a broken oath? The blood of the criminal be upon us and ours!

Eldest Mem. So be it, in the name of God!—(*He takes the dagger from the altar, goes slowly towards the back scene, and reluctantly enters the sacristy.*)

Eldest Judge (*from behind the scene.*) Dost thou forgive me?
Geo. (*behind.*) I do!—(*He is heard to fall heavily.*)

Re-enter the old Judge from the Sacristy. He lays on the Altar the bloody dagger.

Rod. Hast thou done thy duty?
Eldest Mem. I have. (*He faints.*)
Rod. He swoons—Remove him. (*He is assisted off the stage. During this, four members enter the sacristy, and bring out a bier covered with a pall, which they place on the steps of the altar. A deep silence.*)

Rod. Judges of evil, dooming in secret, and avenging in se- cret, like the Deity, God keep your thoughts from evil, and your hands from guilt!

Ber. I raise my voice in this assembly, and cry, Vengeance! vengeance! vengeance!

Rod. Enough has this night been done.—(*He rises and brings* Bertram *forward*.) Think what thou doest—George has fallen —it were murder to slay both mother and son.

Ber. George of Aspen was thy victim—a sacrifice to thy hatred and envy. I claim mine, sacred to justice and to my murdered brother. Resume thy place!—thou canst not stop the rock thou hast put in motion.

Rod. (*resumes his seat*.) Upon whom callest thou for vengeance?

Ber. Upon Isabella of Aspen.

Rod. She has been summoned.

Herald. Isabella of Aspen, accused of murder by poison, I charge thee to appear, and stand upon thy defence.—(*Three knocks are heard at one of the doors; it is opened by the warder*.)

Enter Isabella, *the veil still wrapped around her head, led by her conductor. All the Members muffle their faces.*

Rod. Uncover her eyes.—(*The veil is removed.* Isabella *looks wildly round*.)

Rod. Knowest thou, lady, where thou art?

Isa. I guess.

Rod. Say thy guess.

Isa. Before the Avengers of blood.

Rod. Knowest thou why thou art called to their presence?

Isa. No.

Rod. Speak, accuser.

Ber. I impeach thee, Isabella of Aspen, before this awful assembly, of having murdered, privily and by poison, Arnolf of Ebersdorf, thy first husband.

Rod. Canst thou swear to the accusation?

Ber. (*his hand on the altar*.) I lay my hand on the steel and the cord, and swear.

Rod. Isabella of Aspen, thou hast heard thy accusation—What canst thou answer?

Isa. That the oath of an accuser is no proof of guilt!

Rod. Hast thou more to say?

Isa. I have.

Rod. Speak on.

Isa. Judges invisible to the sun, and seen only by the stars of midnight! I stand before you, accused of an enormous, daring, and premeditated crime. I was married to Arnolf when I was only eighteen years old. Arnolf was wary and jealous—ever suspecting me without a cause, unless it was because he had injured me. How then should I plan and perpetrate such a deed? The lamb turns not against the wolf, though a prisoner in his den.

Rod. Have you finished?

Isa. A moment. Years after years have elapsed without a whisper of this foul suspicion. Arnolf left a brother: though common fame had been silent, natural affection would have been heard against me—why spoke he not my accusation? Or has my conduct justified this horrible charge? No, awful judges! I may answer, I have founded cloisters, I have endowed hospitals. The goods that Heaven bestowed on me I have not held back from the needy. I appeal to you, judges of evil, can these proofs of innocence be down-weighed by the assertion of an unknown and disguised, perchance a malignant accuser?

BER. No longer will I wear that disguise—(*throws back his mantle.*) Dost thou know me now?

ISA. Yes; I know thee for a wandering minstrel, relieved by the charity of my husband.

BER. No, traitress! know me for Bertram of Ebersdorf, brother to him thou didst murder. Call her accomplice, Martin. Ha! turnest thou pale?

ISA. May I have some water?—(*Apart.*) Sacred Heaven! his vindictive look is so like—— (*Water is brought.*)

A MEM. Martin died in the hands of our brethren.

ROD. Dost thou know the accuser, lady?

ISA. *(reassuming fortitude.)* Let not the sinking of nature under this dreadful trial be imputed to the consciousness of guilt. I do know the accuser—know him to be outlawed for homicide, and under the ban of the empire: his testimony cannot be received.

ELDEST JUDGE. She says truly.

BER. (*to* RODERIC.) Then I call upon thee and William a Wolfstein to bear witness to what you know.

ROD. Wolfstein is not in the assembly, and my place prevents me from being a witness.

BER. Then I will call another: meanwhile let the accused be removed.

ROD. Retire, lady.—(ISABELLA *is led to the sacristy.*)

ISA. (*in going off.*) The ground is slippery—Heavens! it is floated with blood!　　　　　　　　[*Exit into the sacristy.*

ROD. (*apart to* BERTRAM.) Whom dost thou mean to call?—(BERTRAM *whispers.*)

ROD. This goes beyond me. (*After a moment's thought*)—But be it so. Maltingen shall behold Aspen humbled in the dust. (*Aloud*)—Brethren, the accuser calls for a witness who remains without: admit him.—(*All muffle their faces.*)

Enter RUDIGER, *his eyes bound or covered, leaning upon two Members; they place a stool for him, and unbind his eyes.*

ROD. Knowest thou where thou art, and before whom?

RUD. I know not, and I care not. Two strangers summoned me from my castle to assist, they said, at a great act of justice. I ascended the litter they brought, and I am here

ROD. It regards the punishment of perjury and the discovery of murder. Art thou willing to assist us?

Rud. Most willingly, as is my duty.

Rod. What if the crime regard thy friend?

Rud. I will hold him no longer so.

Rod. What if thine own blood?

Rud. I would let it out with my poniard.

Rod. Then canst thou not blame us for this deed of justice. Remove the pall.—(*The pall is lifted, beneath which is discovered the body of* George, *pale and bloody.* Rudiger *staggers towards it.*)

Rud. My George! my George!—not slain manly in battle, but murdered by legal assassins! Much, much may I mourn thee, my beloved boy!—But not now—not now: never will I shed a tear for thy death till I have cleared thy fame.— Hear me, ye midnight murderers! he was innocent (*raising his voice*)—upright as the truth itself. Let the man who dares gainsay me lift that gage. If the Almighty does not strengthen these frail limbs, to make good a father's quarrel, I have a son left, who will vindicate the honour of Aspen, or lay his bloody body beside his brother's.

Rod. Rash and insensate! hear first the cause—hear the dishonour of thy house.

Isa. (*from the sacristy.*) Never shall he hear it till the author is no more!—(Rudiger *attempts to rush towards the sacristy, but is prevented.* Isabella *enters wounded, and throws herself on* George's *body.*)

Isa. Murdered for me!—for me! my dear, dear son!

Rud. (*still held.*) Cowardly villains, let me loose! Maltingen, this is thy doing! Thy face thou wouldst disguise, thy deeds thou canst not! I defy thee to instant and mortal combat!

Isa. (*looking up.*) No! no!—endanger not thy life! Myself! myself! I could not bear thou shouldst know——Oh!—(*Dies.*)

Rud. Oh! let me go—let me but try to stop her blood, and I will forgive all.

Rod. Drag him off and detain him. The voice of lamentation must not disturb the stern deliberation of justice.

Rud. Bloodhound of Maltingen! well beseems thee thy base revenge! The marks of my son's lance are still on thy craven crest! Vengeance on the band of ye!—(Rudiger *is dragged off to the sacristy.*)

Rod. Brethren, we stand discovered! What is to be done to him who shall descry our mystery?

Eldest Judge. He must become a brother of our order, or die!

Rod. This man will never join us! He cannot put his hand into ours, which are stained with the blood of his wife and son: he must therefore die! (*Murmurs in the assembly.*) Brethren! I wonder not at your reluctance; but the man is powerful, has friends and allies to buckler his cause. It is over with us, and with our order, unless the laws are obeyed. (*Fainter murmurs.*

Besides, have we not sworn a deadly oath to execute these statutes! (*A dead silence.*)—Take to thee the steel and the cord (*to
the eldest Judge.*)

ELDEST JUDGE. He has done no evil—he was the companion
of my battle—I will not!

ROD. (*to another.*) Do thou—and succeed to the rank of him
who has disobeyed. Remember your oath!—(*Member takes the
dagger, and goes irresolutely forward; looks into the sacristy, and
comes back.*)

MEM. He has fainted—fainted in anguish for his wife and his
son; the bloody ground is strewed with his white hairs, torn by
those hands that have fought for Christendom. I will not be
your butcher.—(*Throws down the dagger.*)

BER. Irresolute and perjured! the robber of my inheritance,
the author of my exile, shall die!

ROD. Thanks, Bertram! Execute the doom—secure the safety
of the holy tribunal!—(BERTRAM *seizes the dagger, and is about
to rush into the sacristy, when three loud knocks are heard at the
door.*)

ALL. Hold! Hold!

The Duke of BAVARIA, *attended by many Members of theInvisible
Tribunal, enters, dressed in a scarlet mantle trimmed with er-
mine, and wearing a ducal crown.—He carries a rod in his
hand.—All rise.—A murmur among the Members, who whisper
to each other, " The Duke," " The Chief," &c.*

ROD. The Duke of Bavaria! I am lost!

DUKE. (*sees the bodies.*) I am too late—the victims have fallen.

HEN. (*who enters with the Duke.*) Gracious Heaven! O George!

RUD. (*from the sacristy.*) Henry—it is thy voice—save me!
(HENRY *rushes into the sacristy.*)

DUKE. Roderic of Maltingen, descend from the seat which
thou hast dishonoured!—(RODERIC *leaves his place, which the
Duke occupies.*)—Thou standest accused of having perverted the
laws of our order; for that, being a mortal enemy to the House
of Aspen, thou hast abused thy sacred authority to pander to thy
private revenge; and to this Wolfstein has been witness.

ROD. Chief among our circles, I have but acted according to
our laws.

DUKE. Thou hast indeed observed the letter of our statutes,
and woe am I that they do warrant this night's bloody work!
I cannot do unto thee as I would, but what I can I will. Thou
hast not indeed transgressed our law, but thou hast wrested and
abused it: kneel down, therefore, and place thy hands betwixt
mine. (RODERIC *kneels as directed.*) I degrade thee from thy
sacred office (*spreads his hands, as pushing* RODERIC *from him.*)
If after two days thou darest to pollute Bavarian ground by thy

footsteps, be it at the peril of the steel and the cord (RODERIC *rises.*)   I dissolve this meeting (*all rise.*)   Judges and condemners of others, God teach you knowledge of yourselves! (*All bend their heads — the Duke breaks his rod, and comes forward.*)

ROD. Lord Duke, thou hast charged me with treachery. Thou art my liege lord; but who else dares maintain the accusation, lies in his throat.

HEN. (*rushing from the sacristy.*) Villain! I accept thy challenge!

ROD. Vain boy! my lance shall chastise thee in the lists — there lies my gage.

DUKE. Henry, on thy allegiance, touch it not!—(*To* RODERIC)—Lists shalt thou never more enter—lance shalt thou never more wield. (*Draws his sword.*)   With this sword wast thou dubbed a knight; with this sword I dishonour thee — I, thy Prince — (*strikes him slightly with the flat of the sword*) — I take from thee the degree of knight, the dignity of chivalry.   Thou art no longer a free German noble; thou art honourless and rightless; the funeral obsequies shall be performed for thee as for one dead to knightly honour and to fair fame; thy spurs shall be hacked from thy heels; thy arms baffled and reversed by the common executioner.   Go, fraudful and dishonoured, hide thy shame in a foreign land! (RODERIC *shows a dumb expression of rage.*)—Lay hands on Bertram of Ebersdorf!—as I live, he shall pay the forfeiture of his outlawry!   Henry, aid us to remove thy father from this charnel-house.   Never shall he know the dreadful secret.   Be it mine to soothe his sorrows, and to restore the honour of the House of Aspen.

(*The Curtain slowly falls.*)

END OF THE HOUSE OF ASPEN.

END OF THE SIXTH AND LAST VOLUME.